The yellowbacks... classics of popular fiction

The yellowjackets or yellowbacks were a great series of bestselling adventure and crime thrillers that had its origins in the mid to late 19th century following on from the 'penny dreadfuls'. They virtually began the mass market revolution of the early 20th century with a clear standard format and imprint/series livery (what would today be called branding). Hodder & Stoughton published the yellowjackets in two main series with series run dates of: 1923-1939 and later 1949-1957.

As the tagline ('where thrillers really began') on the back cover implies, the imprint and series focused on thrillers that were the bestsellers of their time. This current reissue or retro revival if you will, brings back many of these masterpieces, now classics in their own way and extends it further by including key titles from that period that were either great crime or thriller or even general commercial fiction (including sub-genres of noir, horror, gothic, romance, westerns, etc.) influences of their time. There are some perennial favourites and many rarities either lost or not easily available being revived in the current series. Writers and characters ranged from adventure heroes like Bulldog Drummond, Allan Quatermain, Richard Hannay or the Saint through thriller grandmasters Edgar Wallace and E. Phillips Oppenheim, crime and mystery maestros like Patricia Wentworth, GK Chesterton, Agatha Christie and the Detection club, to western and swashbucklers like Zane Grey, Max Brand, Captain Blood and even romance or general fiction classics like Hermina Black, Denise Robins, Marie Corelli or Stella Morton. These were books that had storytelling at their heart and always entertained.

The yellowbacks had both hardback (with varying design elements) and paperback (which built the series look) versions with the latter still carrying the imprint 'yellowjacket'. The current reissues pay tribute to both and use an amalgam of elements from both editions while retaining the complete yellow (or 'mustard-plaster') livery with the author's name in blue beveled type with a 'simulated emboss' effect and a white outer 'outline', and the book title in black. These reissues retain the distinctive size of the original mass market paperback and follow the three main category variations—the thrillers (crime, westerns, mystery, adventure) had blue lettering for the author's name, while Romance and softer general fiction had red; and other categories like humour had green.

For more detail and a full list of titles visit https://www.hachetteindia.com/home/yellowbacks

THE COMPLETE MAX CARRADOS

VOLUME 2

THE COMPLETE MAX CARRADOS

Ernest Bramah Smith was born in Manchester, England in 1868. At 16, he dropped out of Manchester Grammar School, with a poor academic record and went into farming, first as a farm pupil and then in his own right. It was while farming that Bramah began to contribute local vignettes to the Birmingham News. He eventually obtained a position as secretary to Jerome K. Jerome and rose to become editor of one of Jerome's magazines. Bramah attained success with his creation of Kai Lung, a wandering Chinese storyteller. In 1914, Bramah created Max Carrados, a blind detective (arguably amongst the first if not actually the first), and wrote many stories that established him as a staple in detective fiction.

THE COMPLETE Max Carrados

Ernest Bramah

VOLUME 2

The Bunch of Violets (from 'A Specimen Case')

Max Carrados Mysteries

The Bravo of London

HODDER AND STOUGHTON YELLOW JACKET

hachette

The Complete Max Carrados
The Specimen Case was published in 1924 by Hodder & Stoughton in the UK.
Max Carrados Mysteries, published in 1927 by Hodder & Stoughton in the UK.
The final book, *The Bravo of London*, was published in 1934 by Cassell & Co. in the UK.

1

The texts in these editions in most cases have been reprinted as is, with minimal editorial changes and by and large no bowdlerizing for political correctness; though in some editions, a few words and phrases considered archaic, or those considered offensive now, along with archaic punctuation may have been modified in places to make the text more accessible to today's readers. The narratives, language, beliefs, social mores and/or cultural depictions, in these volumes are a reflection of their times and must be viewed as such. They may also contain certain cultural, racial and gender prejudices and stereotypes that may be outdated or clearly wrong then and wrong today; but their removal would be tantamount to claiming these prejudices never existed. The Publisher does not endorse or support those depictions or stereotypes; and these books have been made available for a discerning audience that will read it for entertainment value and a chronicle/record of popular fiction of past times.

Cover design by Priya Singh adapted from the original classic yellowjacket by Hodder & Stoughton.

Cover illustration by Ishan Trivedi.

Series note: Some of the books in the series (unless otherwise credited) may have cover or inside illustrations from the original yellowbacks or early editions, and while full restoration has been attempted, some images may be grainy or faded due to the condition of the original material. The end notes or bonus material or blurb details may have been sourced from the public domain or free use publications such as Wikipedia and attribution is hereby made also allowing similar free use reproduction from here. Sources requiring further specific attribution may write in and further detailing and/or corrections shall be made in subsequent printings/editions.

Reprint specifications may be subject to change including but not limited to finishes, paper, colour sections.

ISBN: 978-81-960269-9-8

Hachette Book Publishing India Pvt. Ltd.
4th & 5th Floors, Corporate Centre,
Plot No. 94, Sector 44, Gurugram - 122 003, India

Typeset in Electra LT STD 10/12.5 pt by Manipal Technologies Limited, Manipal

Printed and bound in India by Manipal Technologies Limited, Manipal

FSC www.fsc.org MIX Paper from responsible sources FSC™ C043100

CONTENTS

1. The Bunch of Violets (from 'A Specimen Case') 1
2. Max Carrados Mysteries 31
3. The Bravo of London 285

THE BUNCH OF VIOLETS
(from 'A Specimen Case')

The Specimen Case was a collection of 21 stories by Bramah that included one Max Carrados story that is now featured here.

AN EPISODE IN THE WAR-TIME ACTIVITIES OF MAX CARRADOS

When Mr J. Beringer Hulse, in the course of one of his periodical calls at the War Office, had been introduced to Max Carrados he attached no particular significance to the meeting. His own business there lay with Mr Flinders, one of the quite inconspicuous departmental powers so lavishly produced by a few years of intensive warfare: business that was more confidential than exacting at that stage and hitherto carried on a deux. The presence on this occasion of a third, this quiet, suave, personable stranger, was not out of line with Mr Hulse's open-minded generalities on British methods: "A little singular, perhaps, but not remarkable.' would have been the extent of his private comment. He favoured Max with a hard, entirely friendly, American stare, said, "Vurry pleased to make your acquaintance, Mr Carrados," as they shook hands, and went on with his own affair.

Of course Hulse was not to know that Carrados had been brought in especially to genialise with him. Most of the blind man's activities during that period came within the "Q-class" order. No one ever heard of them, very often they would have seemed quite meaningless under description, and generally they were things that he alone could do—or do as effectively at all events. In the obsolete phraseology of the day, they were his "bit."

"There's this man Hulse," Flinders had proceeded, when it came to the business on which Carrados had been asked to call at Whitehall. "Needless to say, he's no fool or Jonathan wouldn't have sent him on the ticket he carries. If anything, he's too keen—wants to see everything, do anything and go everywhere. In the meanwhile he's kicking up his heels here in London with endless time on his hands and the Lord only knows who mayn't have a go at him."

"You mean for information—or does he carry papers?" asked Carrados.

"Well, at present, information chiefly. He necessarily knows a lot of things that would be priceless to the Huns, and a clever man or woman might find it profitable to nurse him."

"Still, he must be on his guard if, as you say, he is. No one imagines that London in 1917 is a snakeless Eden or expects that German agents today are elderly professors who say, 'How vos you?' and 'Ja, ja!' "

"My dear fellow," said Flinders sapiently, "every American who came to London before the war was on his guard against a pleasant-spoken gentleman who would accost him with, 'Say, stranger, does this happen to be your wallet lying around here on the sidewalk?' and yet an unending procession of astute, long-headed citizens met him, exactly as described, year after year, and handed over their five hundred or five thousand pounds on a tale that would have made a common or Michaelmas goose blush to be caught listening to."

"It's a curious fact," admitted Carrados thoughtfully. "And this Hulse?"

"Oh, he's quite an agreeable chap, you'll find. He may know a trifle more than you and be a little wider awake and see further through a brick wall and so on,but he won't hurt your feelings about it. Well, will you do it for us?"

"Certainly," replied Carrados. "What is it, by the way?"

Flinders laughed his apologies and explained more precisely.

"Hulse has been over here a month now, and it may be another month before the details come through which he will take on to Paris. Then he will certainly have documents of very special importance that he must carry about with him. Well, in the meanwhile, of course, he is entertained and may pal up with anyone or get himself into Lord knows what. We can't keep him here under lock and key or expect him to make a report of every fellow he has a drink with or every girl he meets."

"Quite so," nodded the blind man.

"Actually, we have been asked to take precautions. It isn't quite a case for the C.I.D.—not at this stage, that is to say. So if I introduce him to you and you fix up an evening for him or something of the sort and find out where his tastes lie, and—and, in fact, keep a general shepherding eye upon him-" He broke off abruptly, and Carrados divined that he had reddened furiously and was kicking himself in spirit. The blind man raised a deprecating hand.

"Why should you think that so neat a compliment would pain me, Flinders?" he asked quietly. "Now if you had questioned the genuineness of some of my favourite tetradrachms I might have had reason to be annoyed. As it is, yes, I will gladly keep a general shepherding ear on J. Beringer as long as may be needful."

"That's curious," said Flinders, looking up quickly. "I didn't think that I had mentioned his front name."

"I don't think that you have," agreed Carrados.

"Then how- Had you heard of him before?"

"You don't give an amateur conjurer much chance," replied the other whimsically. "When you brought me to this chair I found a table by me, and happening to rest a hand on it my fingers had head' a line of writing before I realised it—just as your glance might as unconsciously do," and he held up an envelope addressed to Hulse.

"That is about the limit," exclaimed Flinders with some emphasis. "Do you know, Carrados, if I hadn't always led a very blameless life I should be afraid to have you around the place."

Thus it came about that the introduction was made and in due course the two callers left together.

"You'll see Mr Carrados down, won't you?" Flinders had asked, and, slightly puzzled but not disposed to question English ways, Hulse had assented. In the passage Carrados laid a light hand on his companion's arm. Through some subtle perception he read Hulse's mild surprise.

"By the way, I don't think that Flinders mentioned my infirmity," he remarked. "This part of the building is new to me and I happen to be quite blind."

"You astonish me," declared Hulse, and he had to be assured that the statement was literally exact. "You don't seem to miss much by it, Mr Carrados. Ever happen to hear of Laura Bridgman?"

"Oh, yes," replied Carrados. "She was one of your star cases. But Laura Bridgman's attainments really were wonderful. She was also deaf and dumb, if you remember."

"That is so," assented Hulse. "My people come from New Hampshire not far from Laura's home, and my mother had some of her needlework framed as though it was a picture. That's how I come to know of her, I reckon."

They had reached the street meanwhile and Carrados heard the door of his waiting car opened to receive him.

"I'm going on to my club now to lunch," he remarked with his hand still on his companion's arm. "Of course we only have a wartime menu, but if you would keep me company you would be acting the Good Samaritan," and Beringer Hulse, who was out to see as much as possible of England, France and Berlin within the time—perhaps, also, not uninfluenced by the appearance of the rather sumptuous vehicle—did not refuse.

"Vurry kind of you to put it in that way, Mr Carrados," he said, in his slightly business-like, easy style. "Why, certainly I will."

During the following weeks Carrados continued to make himself very useful to the visitor, and Hulse did not find his stay in London any less agreeably varied thereby. He had a few other friends—acquaintances rather—he had occasion now and then to mention, but they, one might infer, were either not quite so expansive in their range of hospitality or so pressing for his company. The only one for whom he had ever to excuse himself was a Mr Dar- ragh, who appeared to have a house in Densham Gardens (he was a little shrewdly curious as to what might be inferred of the status of a man who lived in Densham Gardens), and, well, yes, there was Darragh's sister, Violet. Carrados began to take a private interest in the Darragh household, but there was little to be learned beyond the fact that the house was let furnished to the occupant from month to month. Even during the complexities of war that fact alone could not be regarded as particularly incriminating.

There came an evening when Hulse, having an appointment to dine with Carrados and to escort him to a theatre afterwards, presented himself in a mixed state of elation and remorse. His number had come through at last, he explained, and he was to leave for Paris in the morning. Carrados had been most awfully, most frightfully—Hulse became quite touchingly incoherent in his anxiety to impress upon the blind man the fullness of the gratitude he felt, but, all the same, he had come to ask whether he might cry off for the evening. There was no need to inquire the cause. Carrados raised an accusing finger and pointed to the little bunch of violets with which the impressionable young man had adorned his button-hole.

"Why, yes, to some extent," admitted Hulse, with a facile return to his ingenuous, easy way. "I happened to see Miss Darragh down town this afternoon. There's a man they know whom I've been crazy to meet for weeks, a Jap who has the whole ju-jitsu business at his finger- ends. Best ju-jitsuist out of Japan, Darragh says. Mighty useful thing, ju-jitsu, nowadays, Carrados."

"At any time, indeed," conceded Carrados. "And he will be there tonight?"

"Certain. They've tried to fix it up for me half-a- dozen times before, but this Kuromi could never fit it in. Of course this will be the only chance."

"True," agreed the blind man, rather absent-mindedly. "Your last night here."

"I don't say that in any case I should not have liked to see Violet—Miss Darragh—again before I went, but I wouldn't have gone back on an arranged thing for that," continued Hulse virtuously. "Now this ju-jitsu I look on more in the light of business."

"Rather a rough-and-tumble business one would think," suggested Carrados. "Nothing likely to drop out of your pockets in the process and get lost?"

Hulse's face displayed a rather more superior smile than he would have permitted himself had his friend been liable to see it and be snubbed thereby.

"I know what you mean, of course," he replied, getting up and going to the blind man's chair, "but don't you worry about me, Father William. Just put your hand to my breast pocket."

"Sewn up," commented Carrados, touching the indicated spot on his guest's jacket.

"Sewn up: that's it; and since I've had any important papers on me it always has been sewn up, no matter how often I change. No fear of anything dropping out now—or being lifted out, eh? No, sir; if what I carry there chanced to vanish, I guess no excuses would be taken and J. B. H. would automatically drop down to the very bottom of the class. As it is, if it's missing I shall be missing too, so that won't trouble me."

"What time do you want to get there?"

"Darragh's? Well, I left that open. Of course I couldn't promise until I had seen you. Anyway, not until after dinner, I said."

"That makes it quite simple, then," declared Carrados. "Stay and have dinner here, and afterwards we will go on to Darragh's together instead of going to the theatre."

"That's most terribly kind of you," replied Hulse. "But won't it be rather a pity—the tickets, I mean, and so forth?"

"There are no tickets as it happens," said Carrados. "I left that over until tonight. And I have always wanted to meet a ju-jitsu champion. Quite providential, isn't it?"

It was nearly nine o'clock, and seated in the drawing- room of his furnished house in Densham Gardens, affecting to read an evening paper, Mr Darragh was plainly ill at ease. The strokes of the hour, sounded by the little gilt clock on the mantelpiece, seemed to mark the limit of his patience. A muttered word escaped him and he looked up with a frown.

"It was nine that Hulse was to be here by, wasn't it, Violet?" he asked.

Miss Darragh, who had been regarding him for some time in furtive anxiety, almost jumped at the simple question.

"Oh, yes, Hugh—about nine, that is. Of course he had to-"

"Yes, yes," interrupted Darragh irritably; "we've heard all that. And Sims," he continued, more for the satisfaction of voicing his annoyance than to engage in conversation, "swore by everything that we should have that coat by eight at the very latest. My God! what rotten tools one has to depend on!"

"Perhaps-" began Violet timidly, and stopped at his deepening scowl.

"Yes?" said Darragh, with a deadly smoothness in his voice. "Yes, Violet; pray continue. You were about to say-"

"It was really nothing, Hugh," she pleaded. "Nothing at all."

"Oh, yes, Violet, I am sure that you have some helpful little suggestion to make," he went on in the same silky, deliberate way. Even when he was silent his unspoken thoughts seemed to be lashing her with bitterness, and she turned painfully away to pick up the paper he had flung aside. "The situation, Kato," resumed Darragh, addressing himself to the third occupant of the room, "is bluntly this: If Sims isn't here with that coat before young Hulse arrives, all our carefully-thought-out plan, a month's patient work, and about the last both of our cash and credit, simply go to the devil! and Violet wants to say that perhaps Mr Sims forgot to wind his watch last night or poor Mrs Sims's cough is worse... Proceed, Violet; don't be diffident."

The man addressed as "Kato" knocked a piece off the chessboard he was studying and stooped to pick it up again before he replied. Then he looked from one to the other with a face singularly devoid of expression.

"Perhaps. Who says?" he replied in his quaintly- ordered phrases. "If it is to be, my friend, it will be."

"Besides, Hugh," put in Violet, with a faint dash of spirit, "it isn't really quite so touch-and-go as that. If Sims comes before Hulse has left, Kato can easily slip out and change coats then."

Darragh was already on his restless way towards the door. Apparently he did not think it worth while to reply to either of the speakers, but his expression, especially when his eyes turned to Violet, was one of active contempt. As the door closed after him, Kato sprang to his feet and his impassive look gave place to one almost of menace. His hands clenched unconsciously and with slow footsteps he seemed to be drawn on in pursuit. A little laugh, mirthless and bitter, from the couch, where Violet had seated herself, recalled him.

"Is it true, Katie," she asked idly, "that you are really the greatest ju-jitsuist outside Japan?"

"Polite other people say so," replied the Japanese, his voice at once gentle and deprecating.

"And yet you cannot keep down even your little temper! "

Kato thought this over for a moment; then he crossed to the couch and stood regarding the girl with his usual impenetrable gravity.

"On contrary, I can keep down my temper very well," he said seriously. "I can keep it so admirably that I, whose ancestors were Samurai and very high nobles, have been able to become thief and swindler and"—his moving hand seemed to beat the air for a phrase—"and low- down dog and still to live. What does anything it matter that is connected with me alone? But there are three things that do matter—three that I do not allow myself to be insulted and still to live: my emperor, my country, and—you. And so," concluded Kato Kuromi, in a somewhat lighter vein, "now and then, as you say, my temper gets the better of me slightly."

"Poor Katie," said Violet, by no means disconcerted at this delicate avowal. "I really think that I am sorrier for you than I am for Hugh, or even for myself. But it's no good becoming romantic at this time of day, my dear man." The lines of her still quite young and attractive face hardened in keeping with her thoughts. "I suppose I've had my chance. We're all of a pattern and I'm as crooked as any of you now."

"No, no," protested Kato loyally; "not you of yourself. It is we bad fellows round you. Darragh ought never to have brought you into these things, and then to despise you for your troubles—that is why my temper now and then ju-jitsues me. This time it is the worst of all—the young man Hulse, for whose benefit you pass yourself as the sister of your husband. How any mortal man possessing you-"

"Another cigarette, Katie, please," interrupted Violet, for the monotonous voice had become slightly more penetrating than was prudent. "That's all in the way of business, my friend. We aren't a firm of family solicitors. Jack Hulse had to be fascinated and I—well, if there is any hitch I don't think that it can be called my fault," and she demonstrated for his benefit the bewitching smile that had so effectually enslaved the ardent Beringer.

"Fascinated!" retorted Kato, fixing on the word jealously, and refusing to be pacified by the bribery of the smile. "Yes, so infatuated has become this very susceptible young man that you lead him about like pet lamb at the end of blue ribbon. Business? Perhaps. But how have you been able to do this, Violet? And you husband—Darragh—to him simply business, very good business—and he forces you to do this full of shame thing and mocks at you for reward."

"Kato, Kato-" urged Violet, breaking through his scornful laughter.

"I am what your people call yellow man," continued Kato relentlessly, "and you are the one white woman of my dreams—dreams that I would not lift finger to spoil by trying to make real. But if I should have been Darragh not ten thousand times the ten thousand pounds that Hulse carries would tempt me to lend you to another man's arms."

"Oh, Katie, how horrid you can be!"

"Horrid for me to say, but 'business' for you to do! How have you discovered so much, Violet—what Hulse carries, where he carries it, the size and shape the packet makes, even the way he so securely keeps it? 'Business' eh? Your husband cares not so long as we succeed. But I, Kato Kuromi, care." He went nearer so that his mere attitude was menacing as he stood over her, and his usually smooth voice changed to a tone she had never heard there before. "How have you learned all this? How, unless you and Hulse-"

"'Sssh!" she exclaimed in sharp dismay as her ear caught a sound beyond.

"—oh yes," continued Kato easily, his voice instantly as soft and unconcerned as ever, "it will be there, you mean. The views in the valley of Kedu are considered very fine and the river itself-"

It was Darragh whom Violet had heard approaching, and he entered the room in a much better temper than he had left it. At the door he paused a moment to encourage someone forward—a seedy, diffident man of more than middle age, who carried a brown-paper parcel.

"Come on, Sim; hurry up, man!" urged Darragh impatiently, but without the sting of contempt that had poisoned his speech before. "And, oh, Phillips"—looking back and dropping his voice—"when Mr Hulse arrives show him into the morning-room at first. Not up here, you understand? Now, Sims."

After a rather helpless look round for something suitable on which to lay his parcel, the woebegone-looking individual was attempting to untie it on an upraised knee.

"Yes, sir," he replied, endeavouring to impart a modicum of briskness into his manner. "I'm sorry to be a bit late, sir; I was delayed."

"Oh, well, never mind that now," said Darragh magnanimously. "Thing quite all right?"

"Mrs Sims isn't worse?" asked Violet kindly.

Mr Sims managed to get his back to the group before he ventured to reply.

"No, miss," he said huskily; "she's better now. She's dead: died an hour ago. That's why I wasn't quite able to get here by eight."

From each of his hearers this tragedy drew a characteristic response. Violet gave a little moan of sympathy and turned away. Kato regarded Sims, and continued to regard him, with the tranquil incuriosity of the unpitying East. Darragh—Darragh alone spoke, and his tone was almost genial.

"Devilish lucky that you were able to get here by now in the circumstances, Sims," he said.

"Well, sir," replied Sims practically, "you see, I shall need the money just as much now—though not quite for the same purpose as I had planned." He took the garment from the paper and shook it out before displaying it for Darragh's approval. "I think you will find that quite satisfactory, sir."

"Exactly the same as the one your people made for Mr Hulse a week ago?" asked Darragh, glancing at the jacket and then passing it on to Violet for her verdict.

"To a stitch, sir. A friend of mine up at the shop got the measurements and the cloth is a length from the same piece."

"But the cut, Sims," persisted his patron keenly; "the cut is the most important thing about it. It makes all the difference in the world."

"Yes, sir," acquiesced Sims dispassionately; "you can rely on that. I used to be a first-class cutter myself before I took to drink. I am yet, when I'm steady. And I machined both coats myself."

"That should do then," said Darragh complacently. "Now you were to have-"

"Ten guineas and the cost of the cloth you promised, sir. Of course it's a very big price, and I won't deny that I've been a bit uneasy about it from time to time when I-"

"That's all right." Darragh had no wish to keep Mr Sims in evidence a minute longer than was necessary.

"I shouldn't like to be doing anything wrong, sir," persisted the poor creature; "and when you stipulated that it wasn't to be mentioned-"

"Well, well, man; it's a bet, didn't I tell you? I stand to win a clear hundred if I can fool Hulse over this coat. That's the long and short of it."

"I'm sure I hope it is, sir. I've never been in trouble for anything yet, and it would break my wife's 'art—" He stopped suddenly and his weak face changed to a recollection of his loss; then without another word he turned and made shakily for the door.

"See him safely away, Katty, and pay him down below," said Darragh. "I'll settle with you later," and the Japanese, with a careless "All right-o," followed.

"Now, Violet, slip into it," continued her husband briskly. "We don't want to keep Hulse waiting when he comes." From a drawer in a cabinet near at hand he took a paper packet, prepared in readiness, and passed it to her. "You have the right cotton?"

"Yes, Hugh," said Violet, opening a little work-basket. She had already satisfied herself that the coat was a replica of the one the young American wrould wear, and she now transferred the dummy package to the corresponding pocket and with a few deft stitches secured it in the same way as she had already learned that the real contents were safeguarded. "And, Hugh-"

"Well, well?" responded Darragh, with a return of his old impatience.

"I don't wish to know all your plans, Hugh," continued Violet meekly, "but I do want to warn you. You are running a most tremendous risk with Kato."

"Oh, Kato!"

"It is really serious, Hugh. You don't believe in patriotism, I know, but Kato happens to. When he learns that it isn't ten thousand pounds at all, but confidential war plans, that this scoop consists of, something terrible may happen."

"It might, Violet. Therefore I haven't told him, and I am so arranging things that he will never know. Cheer up, my girl, there will be no tragedy. All the same, thanks for the hint. It shows a proper regard for your husband's welfare."

"Oh, Hugh, Hugh," murmured Violet, "if only you were more often-"

Whatever might have been the result—if indeed there was yet hope in an appeal to another and a better nature that he might once have possessed—it came too late. The words were interrupted by the sudden reappearance of Kato, his business with Sims completed. He opened and closed the door quietly but very quickly, and at a glance both the Darraghs saw that something unforeseen had happened.

"Here's pretty go," reported the Japanese. "Hulse just come and brought someone with him!"

For a moment all the conspirators stood aghast at the unexpected complication. Hugh Darragh was the first to speak.

"Damnation!" he exclaimed, with a terrible look in his wife's direction; "that may upset everything. What ghastly muddle have you made now?"

"I—I don't know," pleaded Violet weakly. "I never dreamt of such a thing. Are you sure?"

"Slow man," amplified Kato with a nod. "Fellow who walk-" He made a few steps with studied deliberation.

"Blind! It's Max Carrados," exclaimed Violet, in a flash of enlightenment. "They have been great friends lately and Jack has often spoken of him. He's most awfully clever in his way, but stone blind. Hugh, Kato, don't you see? It's rather unfortunate his being here, but it can't really make any difference."

"True, if he is quite blind," admitted Kato.

"I'll look into it," said Darragh briskly. "Coat's all ready for you, Kato."

"I think no, yet," soliloquised the Japanese, critically examining it. "Keep door, 'alf-a-mo', Violet, if please." His own contribution to the coat's appearance was simple but practical—a gentle tension here and there, a general rumple, a dust on the floor and a final shake. "One week wear," he announced gravely as he changed into it and hid his own away.

"Take your time, Mr Carrados," Darragh's voice was heard insisting on the stairs outside, and the next moment he stood just inside the room, and before Hulse had quite guided Carrados into view, drew Violet's attention to the necessity of removing the button-hole that the Americans still wore by a significant movement to the lapel of his own coat. It required no great finesse on the girl's part to effect the transfer of the little bunch of flowers to her own person within five minutes of the guests' arrival.

"A new friend to see you, Violet—Mr Carrados," announced Darragh most graciously. "Mr Carrados, my sister."

"Not to see you exactly, Miss Darragh," qualified Carrados. "But none the less to know you as well as if I did, I hope."

"I wanted you to meet Max before I went, Miss Darragh," explained Hulse; "so I took the liberty of bringing him round."

"You really are going then?" she asked.

"Yes. There seems no doubt about it this time. Twelve hours from now I hope to be in Paris. I should say," amended the ingenuous young man, "I dread to be in Paris, for it may mean a long absence. That's where I rely on Carrados to become what is called a 'connecting file' between us—to cheer my solitude by letting me know when he has met you, or heard of you, or, well, anything in fact."

"Take care, Mr Hulse," she said. "Gallantry by proxy is a dangerous game."

"That's just it," retorted Hulse. "Max is the only man I shouldn't be jealous of—because he can't see you!"

While these amiable exchanges were being carried on between the two young people, with Max Carrados standing benignly by, Darragh found an opportunity to lower his voice for Kato's benefit.

"It's all right about him," he declared. "We carry on."

"As we arranged?" asked Kato.

"Yes; exactly. Come across now." He raised his voice as he led Kato towards the other group. "I don't think that either of you has met Mr Kuromi yet—Mr Hulse, Mr Carrados."

"I have been pining to meet you for weeks, sir," responded Hulse with enthusiasm. "Mr Darragh tells me what a wonderful master of ju-jitsu you are."

"Oh, well; little knack, you know," replied Kato modestly. "You are interested?"

"Yes, indeed. I regard it as a most useful accomplishment at any time and particularly now. I only wish I'd taken it up when I had the leisure."

"Let me find you an easy-chair, Mr Carrados," said Violet attentively.

"I am sure that you won't be interested in so strenuous a subject as jujitsu."

"Oh, yes, I am, though," protested the blind man. "I am interested in everything."

"But surely-"

"I can't actually see the ju-jitsuing, you would say? Quite true, but do you know, Miss Darragh, that makes a great deal less difference than you might imagine. I have my sense of touch, my sense of taste, my hearing— even my unromantic nose—and you would hardly believe how they have rallied to my assistance since sight went. For instance-"

They had reached the chair to which Miss Darragh had piloted him. To guide him into it she had taken both his hands, but now Carrados had gently disengaged himself and was lightly holding her left hand between both of his.

"For instance, Hulse and I were speaking of you the other day—forgive our impertinence—and he happened to mention that you disliked rings of any sort and had never worn one. His eyes, you see, and perhaps a careless remark on your part. Now I know that until quite recently you continually wore a ring upon this finger."

Silence had fallen upon the other men as they followed Carrados's exposition. Into the moment of embarrassment that succeeded this definite pronouncement Mr Hulse threw a cheerful note.

"Oh ho, Max, you've come a cropper this time," he exclaimed. "Miss Darragh has never worn a ring. Have you?"

"N-o," replied Violet, a little uncertain of her ground, as the blind man continued to smile benevolently upon her.

"A smooth and rather broad one," he continued persuasively. "Possibly a wedding ring?"

"Wait a minute, Violet, wait a minute," interposed Darragh, endeavouring to look judicially wise with head bent to one side. He was doubtful if Violet could carry the point without incurring some suspicion, and he decided to give her a lead out of it. "Didn't I see you wearing some sort of plain ring a little time ago? You have forgotten, but I really believe Mr Carrados may be right. Think again."

"Of course!" responded Violet readily; "how stupid of me! It was my mother's wedding ring. I found it in an old desk and wore it to keep it safe. That was really how I found out that I could not bear the feel of one and I soon gave it up."

"What did I say?" claimed Darragh genially. "I thought that we should be right."

"This is really much interesting," said Kato. "I very greatly like your system, Mr Carrados."

"Oh, it's scarcely a system," deprecated Max good-naturedly; "it's almost second nature with me now. I don't have to consider, say, 'Where is the window?' if I want it. I know with certainty that the window lies over here." He had not yet taken the chair provided, and suiting the action to the word he now took a few steps towards the wall where the windows were. "Am I not right?" And to assure himself he stretched out a hand and encountered the heavy curtains.

"Yes, yes," admitted Violet hurriedly, "but, oh, please do be careful, Mr Carrados. They are most awfully particular about the light here since the last raid. We go in fear and trembling lest a glimmer should escape."

Carrados smiled and nodded and withdrew from the dangerous area. He faced the room again.

"Then there is the electric light—heat at a certain height of course."

"True," assented Kato, "but why electric light?"

"Because no other is noiseless and entirely without smell; think—gas, oil, candles, all betray their composition yards away. Then"—indicating the fireplace—"I suppose you can only smell soot in damp weather? The mantelpiece"—touching it—"inlaid marble. The wall- paper"—brushing his hand over its surface—"arrangement of pansies on a criss-cross background"; lifting one finger to his lips—"colour scheme largely green and gold."

Possibly Mr Hulse thought that his friend had demonstrated his qualities quite enough. Possibly—at any rate he now created a diversion:

"Engraving of Mrs Siddons as the Tragic Muse, suspended two feet seven inches from the ceiling on a brassheaded nail supplied by a one-legged ironmonger whose Aunt Jane-"

All contributed a sufficiently appreciative laugh—

Carrados's not the least hearty—except Kato, whose Asiatic dignity was proof against the form of jesting.

"You see what contempt familiarity breeds, Miss Darragh," remarked the blind man. "I look to you, Mr Kuromi, to avenge me by putting Hulse in a variety of undignified attitudes on the floor."

"Oh, I shan't mind that if at the same time you put me up to a trick or two," said Hulse, turning to the Japanese.

"You wish?"

"Indeed I do. I've seen the use of it. It's good; it's scientific. When I was crossing, one of the passengers held up a bully twice his weight in the neatest way possible. It looked quite simple, something like this, if I may?" Kato nodded his grave assent and submitted himself to Mr Hulse's vigorous grasp. " 'Now,' said the man I'm speaking of, 'struggle and your right arm's broken.' But I expect you know the grip?"

"Oh, yes," replied Kato, veiling his private amusement, "and therefore foolish to struggle. Expert does not struggle; gives way." He appeared to do so, to be falling helplessly in fact, but the assailant found himself compelled to follow, and the next moment he was lying on his back with Kato politely extending a hand to assist him up again.

"I must remember that," said Hulse thoughtfully. "Let me see, it goes—do you mind putting me wise on that again, Mr Kuromi? The motion picture just one iota slower this time, please."

For the next ten or twenty minutes the demonstration went on in admirable good humour, and could Max Car- rados have seen he would certainly have witnessed his revenge. At the end of the lesson both men were warm and dusty—so dusty that Miss Darragh felt called upon to apologise laughingly for the condition of the rug. But if clothes were dusty, hands were positively dirty—there was no other word for it.

"No, really, the poor mat can't be so awful as that," declared the girl. "Wherever have you been, Mr Kuromi? and, oh, Mr Hulse you are just as bad."

"I do not know," declared Kato, regarding his grimy fingers seriously. "Nowhere of myself. Yes, I think it must be your London atmosphere among the rug after all."

"At all events you can't- Oh, Hugh, take them to the bathroom, will you? And I'll try to entertain Mr Carrados meanwhile—only he will entertain me instead, I know."

It was well and simply done throughout—nothing forced, and the sequence of development quite natural. Indeed, it was not until Hulse saw Kuromi take off his coat in the bathroom that he even thought of what he carried. "Well, Carrados," he afterwards pleaded to his friend, "now could I wash my hands before those fellows like a guy who isn't used to washing? It isn't natural. It isn't human." So for those few minutes the two coats hung side by side, and Darragh kindly brushed them. When Hulse put on his own again his hand instinctively felt for the hidden packet; his fingers reassured themselves among the familiar objects of his pockets, and his mind was perfectly at ease.

"You old scoundrel, Max," he said, when he returned to the drawing room. "You told Kuromi to wipe the floor with me and, by crumbs, he did! Have a cigarette all the same."

Miss Darragh laughed pleasantly and took the opportunity to move away to learn from her accomplices if all had gone well. Carrados was on the point of passing over the proffered olive branch when he changed his mind. He leaned forward and with slow chose a cigarette from the American's case. Exactly when the first subtle monition of treachery reached him —by what sense it was conveyed—Hulse never learned, for there were experiences among the finer perceptions that the blind man did not willingly discuss. Not by voice or outward manner in that arresting moment did he betray an inkling of his suspicion, yet by some responsive telephony Hulse at once, though scarcely conscious of it then, grew uneasy and alert.

"Thanks; I'll take a light from yours," remarked Carrados, ignoring the lit match, and he rose to avail himself. His back was towards the others, who still had a word of instruction to exchange. With cool precision he handled the cloth on Hulse's outstretched arm, critically touched the pocket he was already familiar with, and then deliberately drew the lapel to his face.

"You wore some violets?" he said beneath his breath.

"Yes," replied Hulse, "but I—Miss Darragh-" "But there never have been any here! By heavens, Hulse, we're in it! You had your coat off just now?"

"Yes, for a minute-"

"Quietly. Keep your cigarette going. You'll have to leave this to me. Back me up—discreetly—whatever I do."

"Can't we challenge it and insist-"

"Not in this world. They have at least one other man downstairs—in Cairo, a Turk by the way, before I was blind, of course. Not up to Mr Kuromi, I expect-"

"Cool again?" asked Miss Darragh sociably It was her approach that had sent Carrados off into irrelevan- cies. "Was the experience up to anticipation?"

"Yes, I think I may say it was," admitted Hulse guardedly. "There is certainly a lot to learn here. I expect you've seen it all before?"

"Oh, no. It is a great honour to get Mr Kuromi to 'show it off,' as he quaintly calls it."

"Yes, I should say so," replied the disillusioned young man with deadly simplicity. "I quite feel that."

"J. B. H. is getting strung up," thought Carrados. "He may say something unfortunate presently." So he deftly insinuated himself into the conversation and for a few minutes the commonplaces of the topic were rigidly maintained.

"Care for a hand at auction?" suggested Darragh, joining the group. He had no desire to keep his guests a minute longer than he need, but at the same time it was his line to behave quite naturally until they left. "Oh, but I forgot—Mr Carrados-"

"I am well content to sit and listen," Carrados assured him. "Consider how often I have to do that without the entertainment of a game to listen to! And you are four without me."

"It really hardly seems-" began Violet.

"I'm sure Max will feel it if he thinks that he is depriving us," put in Hulse loyally, so with some more polite protestation it was arranged and the game began, Carrados remaining where he was. In the circumstances a very high standard of bridge could not be looked for; the calling was a little wild; the play more than a little loose; the laughter rather shrill or rather flat; the conversation between the hands forced and spasmodic. All were playing for time in their several interpretations of it; the blind man alone was thinking beyond the immediate moment.

Presently there was a more genuine burst of laughter than any hitherto. Kato had revoked, and, confronted with it, had made a naive excuse. Carrados rose with the intention of going nearer when a distressing thing occurred. Half-way across the room he seemed to slip, plunged forward helplessly, and came to the floor, involved in a light table as he fell. All the players were on their feet in an instant. Darragh assisted his guest to rise; Violet took an arm; Kato looked about the floor curiously, and Hulse—Hulse stared hard at Max and wondered what the thunder this portended.

"Clumsy, clumsy," murmured Carrados beneath his breath. "Forgive me, Miss Darragh."

"Oh, Mr Carrados!" she exclaimed in genuine distress. "Aren't you really hurt?"

"Not a bit of it," he declared lightly. "Or at all events," he amended, bearing rather more heavily upon her support as he took a step, "nothing to speak of."

"Here is pencil," said Kuromi, picking one up from the polished floor."You must have slipped on this."

"Stepping on a pencil is like that," contributed Hulse wisely. "It acts as a kind of roller-skate."

"Please don't interrupt the game any more," pleaded the victim. "At the most, at the very worst, it is only— oh!—a negligible strain."

"I don't know that any strain, especially of the ankle, is negligible, Mr Carrados," said Darragh with cunning foresight. "I think it perhaps ought to be seen to."

"A compress when I get back will be all .that is required," maintained Carrados. "I should hate to break up the evening."

"Don't consider that for a moment," urged the host hospitably. "If you really think that it would be wiser in the end-"

"Well, perhaps-" assented the other, weakening in his resolution.

"Shall I 'phone up a taxi?" asked Violet.

"Thank you, if you would be so kind—or, no; perhaps my own car would be rather easier in the circumstances. My man will be about, so that it will take very little longer."

"I'll get through for you," volunteered Darragh. "What's your number?"

The telephone was in a corner of the room. The connection was soon obtained and Darragh turned to his guest for the message.

"I'd better speak," said Carrados—he had limped across on Hulse's arm—taking over the receiver. "Excellent fellow, but he'd probably conclude that I'd been killed... That you, Parkinson? Yes, at 155 Densham Gardens. I'm held up here by a slight accident... No, no, nothing serious, but I might have some difficulty in getting back without assistance. Tell Harris I shall need him after all, as soon as he can get here—the car that's handiest. That's—oh, and, Parkinson, bring along a couple of substantial walking-sticks with you. Any time now. That's all... Yes... yes." He put up the receiver with a thrill of satisfaction that he had got his message safely through. "Held up" —a phrase at once harmless and significant—was the arranged shift-key into code. It was easy for a blind man to receive some hurt that held him up. Once or twice Carrados's investigations had got him into tight places but in one way or another he had invariably got out again.

"How far is your place away?" someone asked, and out of the reply a time-marking conversation on the subject of getting about London's darkened streets and locomotion in general arose. Under cover of this Kato drew Darragh aside to the deserted card-table.

"Not your pencil, Darragh?" he said quietly, displaying the one he had picked up.

"No; why?"

"I not altogether like this, is why," replied the Japanese. "I think it Carrados own pencil. That man have too many ways of doing things, Darragh. It was mistake to let him 'phone."

"Oh, nonsense; you heard what he said. Don't get jumpy, man. The thing has gone like clockwork."

"So far, yes. But I think I better go now and come back in one hour or so, safer for all much."

Darragh, for very good reasons, had the strongest objections to allowing his accomplice an opportunity of examining the spoil alone. "Look here, Katty," he said with decision, "I must have you in case there does come a scrimmage. I'll tell Phillips to fasten the front door well, and then we can see that it's all right before anyone comes in. If it is, there's no need for you to run away; if there's the least doubt we can knock these two out and have plenty of time to clear by the back way we've got." Without giving Kato any chance of raising further objection he turned to his guests again.

"I think I remember your tastes, Hulse," he said suavely. "I hope that you have no objection to Scotch whisky, Mr Carrados? We still have a few bottles left. Or perhaps you prefer champagne?"

Carrados, had very little intention of drinking anything in that house, nor did he think that with ordinary procrastination it would be necessary.

"You are very kind," he replied tentatively. "Should you permit the invalid either, Miss Darragh?"

"Oh, yes, in moderation," she smiled. "I think I hear your car," she added, and stepping to the window ventured to peep out.

It was true. Mr Darragh had run it a shade too fine for once. For a moment he hesitated which course to take—to see who was arriving or to convey a warning to his henchman down below. He had turned towards the door when Violet's startled voice recalled him to the window.

"Hugh!" she called sharply. "Here, Hugh;" and as he reached her, in a breathless whisper, "There are men inside the car—two more at least."

Darragh had to decide very quickly this time. His choice was not without its element of fineness. "Go down and see about it, Katty," he said, looking Kato straight in the eyes. "And tell Phillips about the whisky."

"Door locked," said the Japanese tersely. "Key other side."

"The key was on this side," exclaimed Darragh fiercely. "Hulse-"

"Hell!" retorted Beringer expressively. "That jacket doesn't go out of the room without me this journey."

Darragh had him covered before he had finished speaking.

"Quick," he rapped out. "I'll give you up to three, and if the key isn't out then, by God, I'll plug you, Hulse! One, two-"

The little "ping!" that followed was not the automatic speaking, but the release of the electric light switch as Carrados, unmarked among this climax, pressed it up. In the absolute blackness that followed Darragh spun round to face the direction of this new opponent.

"Shoot by all means, Mr Darragh, if you are used to firing in the dark," said Carrados's imperturbable voice. "But in any case remember that I am. As I am a dead shot by sound, perhaps everyone had better remain exactly where he—or she, I regret to have to add, Miss Darragh—now is."

"You dog!" spat out Darragh.

"I should not even talk," advised the blind man. "I am listening for my friends and I might easily mistake your motive among the hum of conversation."

He had not long to wait. In all innocence Phillips had opened the door to Parkinson, and immeasurably to his surprise two formidable-looking men of official type had followed in from somewhere. By a sort of instinct—or possibly a momentary ray of light had been their guide— they came direct to the locked door.

"Parkinson," called Carrados.

"Yes, sir," replied that model attendant.

"We are all in here; Mr Hulse and myself, and three —I am afraid that I can make no exception—three unfriendlies. At the moment the electric light is out of action, the key of the locked door has been mislaid, and firearms are being promiscuously flourished in the dark. That is the position. Now if you have the key, Hulse-"

"I have," replied Hulse grimly, "but for a fact I dropped it down my neck out of harm's way and where the plague it's got to-"

As it happened the key was not required. The heavier of the officers outside, believing in the element of surprise, stood upon one foot and shot the other forward with the force and action of an engine piston-rod. The shattered door swung inward and the three men rushed into the room.

Darragh had made up his mind, and as the door crashed he raised his hand to fire into the thick. But at that moment the light flashed on again and almost instantly was gone. Before his dazzled eyes and startled mind could adjust themselves to this he was borne down. When he rose again his hands were manacled.

"So," he breathed laboriously, bending a vindictive eye upon his outwitter. "When next we meet it will be my turn, I think."

"We shall never meet again," replied Carrados impassively. "There is no other turn for you, Darragh."

"But where the blazes has Kuromi got to?" demanded Hulse with sharp concern. "He can't have quit?"

One of the policemen walked to a table in the farthest corner of the room, looked down beyond it, and silently raised a beckoning hand. They joined him there.

"Rum way these foreigners have of doing things," remarked the other disapprovingly. "Now who the Hanover would ever think of a job like that?"

"I suppose," mused the blind man, as he waited for the official arrangements to go through, "that presently I shall have to live up to Hulse's overwhelming bewonderment. And yet if I pointed out to him that the button-hole of the coat he is now wearing still has a stitch in it to keep it in shape and could not by any possibility... Well, well, perhaps better not. It is a mistake for the conjurer to explain."

Preston Beach, 1917

MAX CARRADOS MYSTERIES

CONTENTS

1. The Secret of Headlam Height 35
2. The Mystery of the Vanished Petition Crown 73
3. The Holloway Flat Tragedy 102
4. The Curious Circumstances of the Two Left Shoes 138
5. The Ingenious Mind of Mr Rigby Lacksome 169
6. The Crime at the House in Culver Street 198
7. The Strange Case of Cyril Bycourt 229
8. The Missing Witness Sensation 255

1

THE SECRET OF HEADLAM HEIGHT

Parkinson, the unquenchable stickler for decorum, paused after receiving the general instructions for the day just long enough to create a sense of hesitation. Mr Carrados, merely concerned with an after-breakfast cigarette, divined the position with his usual unerring instinct.

"Yes, Parkinson," he remarked encouragingly; "is there anything going on?"

A clumsily-folded newspaper enabled the punctilious attendant to salve his conscience as he returned slowly to the table. He shook out the printed sheets into a more orderly arrangement by way of covering the irregularity.

"I understand, sir," he replied in the perfectly controlled respectful voice that accorded with his deliberate actions "I understand that this morning's foreign intelligence is of a disquieting nature."

The blind man's hand went unfalteringly to an open copy of *The Times* lying by him and there a single deft finger touched off the headlines with easy certainty.

"'On the Brink of War.' 'Threatened German Mobilization'," he read aloud. "'The Duty of Great Britain.' Yes, I don't think that 'disquieting' over-states the position."

"No, sir. So I gathered from what I had already heard. That is why I thought it better to speak to you about a trifling incident that has come under my notice, sir."

"Quite right," assented Mr Carrados. "Well?"

"It was at the Museum here, sir—a very instructive establishment in Market Square. I had gone there in order to settle a small matter in dispute between Herbert and myself affecting the distinction between shrimps and prawns. I had always been under the impression that prawns were unusually well-grown shrimps, but I find that I was mistaken. I was directed to the cases of preserved fish by a gentleman with a cut across his cheek. Subsequently I learned from the hall-keeper, to whom I spoke about the weather, that the gentleman was the assistant curator and was called Vangoor, being a native of Holland."

"Vangoor," mused Mr Carrados. "I have never heard the name before."

"No, sir. When I saw the gentleman last we were at Kiel, and he was then a Lieutenant von Groot. I thought perhaps I had better mention it, sir."

Carrados's half-smiling expression did not change in its placid tone and he continued to smoke with leisurely enjoyment. His mind turned back to the details of the Kiel visit of a few years previously as one might turn to a well-kept diary.

"The man you mean called on me once with a complimentary message from the Admiralty department there. I was not in the hotel at the time and he left his card with a few words of explanation in perfect English. We never met and I cannot suppose that he has ever seen me."

"No, sir," acquiesced Parkinson. "You sent me the next day to the Dockyard with a reply. That is the only time I have ever seen the gentleman before today."

"Have you any reason to think that he may have remembered you again?"

"I formed a contrary opinion, sir. On the other occasion, although it was necessary for us to hold some slight conversation together, Lieutenant von Groot did not seem to be aware of my presence, if I may so define it, sir. I received the impression that the gentleman imagined he was talking to someone taller than I am, sir; and I doubt if he really saw me at all."

"You are sure of him, though?"

"I was then making a study of detailed observation under your instruction, sir, and I have no misgiving on the point."

"Very well. It was quite right of you to tell me of this; it may be really important. We are only five miles from a vital naval port, we must remember. Don't say anything to anyone else and I will consider it meanwhile."

"Thank you, sir," replied Parkinson, modestly elated.

In the past, whenever the subject of the English Secret Service came up it was patriotically assumed on all hands that nothing much was to be expected from that quarter, and we were bidden to lift our admiring eyes to German and other continental models. As a matter of history, when the test came the despised organization proved itself signally efficient. In a small way there was evidence of this that same July day, for within a couple of hours of sending a curiously-worded telegram to an official whose name never appeared in any official list Mr Carrados received an equally mysterious reply from which, after a process of disintegration, he extracted the following information:

Ref. Fff. C/M.107.

GROOT, Karl von. Born Friedeberg (Prussia) about 1880. Mother English. Educated Heidelberg and (?) Kiel. Entered navy. Torpedo-lieutenant (staff) 1907. Resigned in doubtful circumstances 1910. Drawn into espionage system under Bluthmel in connexion with resignation. Expelled Holland 1912. Visited Russia 1913. Recognized

> in Cork, June, 1913. Speaks German, French, Dutch, Russian, English (excellent). Blonde, tall, grey eyes, diagonal sword-cut left cheek. Description ends. Please report anything known further.

Carrados read the decoded message twice, and then thoughtfully crushing the thin paper into a loose ball he dropped it upon an ash-tray and applied a match.

"A telegram form, Parkinson."

With his uncanny prescience the blind man selected a pencil from the rack before him, adjusted the paper to a more convenient angle and, not deviating the fraction of an inch beyond the indicated space, wrote his brief reply:

Ref. Fff. C/M.107.
Information received. Regret have nothing further to report. M.C.

"We will investigate Mr Vangoor for ourselves a little first," he remarked, passing across the slip. "London will have its hands pretty full for the next few days and we are on the spot."

"Very well, sir," replied Parkinson with the same trustful equanimity with which he would have received an order to close a window. "Shall I dispatch this now, sir?"

"Yes—from the head office: head offices are generally too busy to be inquisitive. Read it over first in case of an inquiry... Yes, quite right. Something of a feather if we can circumvent a German spy off our own bats, eh, Parkinson?"

"Yes, sir."

"At all events we will open the innings without delay."

"I quite appreciate the necessity of expedition, sir," replied Parkinson, with his devastating air of profound wisdom.

It is doubtful if anyone had yet plumbed the exact limits of the worthy fellow's real capacity. There were moments when he looked more sagacious than any mortal man has any hope of ever being, and there were times when his comment on affairs seemed to reveal a greater depth of mental vacuity than was humanly credible. Carrados found him wholly satisfactory, and Parkinson on his side had ignored a score of hints of betterment.

"Pack a couple of bags with necessaries," was the instruction he received on his return from the post office. "Von Groot may likely enough remember my name, and I can't very well change it while staying at a public hotel. We will keep on our rooms here and go into apartments at the other end of the town for a time. There my name will be Munroe and yours can be—say Paxton. I will tell the office here all that is necessary."

"Very good, sir," assented Parkinson. "I did not think the woodcock toast sent up for your breakfast entirely satisfactory, sir."

In years to come generations now unborn will doubtless speculate how people lived in those early days of August, 1914. The simple truth, of course, is that to the vast majority external life went on almost precisely as before. It is as exacting for the moving machine to stop as for the quiescent one to start, and "Business as usual" was one of the earliest clichés coined. The details of the situation that most impressed the citizen of 1914 are not the details to which the inquirer of 2014 will give a second thought. Individually, it was doubtless very intriguing to have to obtain change for a five-pound note by purchasing postal orders to that amount and immediately cashing them singly again...

Mr Carrados found the Castlemouth Museum open as usual when his leisurely footsteps turned that way on the following morning, and, as usual, the day being fine, deserted. Before they had—Parkinson describing as they went—made the circuit of the first room they were approached by a sociable official—the curator it soon appeared—drawn from his den by the welcome sight of two authentic visitors.

"There are a certain number of specimens that we have to store away for want of space," he remarked hopefully. "If there is any particular subject that you are interested in I should be very pleased—"

This suited Mr Carrados's purpose well enough, but before committing himself he not unnaturally preferred to know what the curator's particular subject was. An enthusiast is always vulnerable through his enthusiasm and no man becomes curator of an obscure museum in order to amass a fortune.

"I understand," he replied tentatively, "that you are rather strong here in—" An impatient gesture with the expressive fingers conveyed the speaker's loss. "Dear me—"

"Palaeontology?" suggested the curator. "My predecessor was a great collector and our series of local fossils is unsurpassed. If you—"

"Ah," replied Mr Carrados; "very instructive no doubt." His alert ear recognized the absence of the enthusiast's note. "But somehow there always seems to me about fossils a—"

"Yes, yes," supplied the curator readily; "I know. No human touch. I feel just the same myself about them. Now flints! There's romance, if you like."

"That is the real thing, isn't it?" exclaimed Mr Carrados with unqualified conviction. "There's more interest to my mind in a neolithic scraper than in a whole show-case-full of ammonites and belemnites."

The curator's eyes sparkled; it was not often that he came across another. "Brings you face to face with the primeval, doesn't it?" he said. "I once picked up a spearhead, beautifully finished except the very last chippings of the point. Not broken off, you understand—just incomplete. Why? Well, one might risk a dozen likely guesses. But there it was, just as it had dropped from the fingers of my prehistoric forefather ten thousand years before—no other hand had touched it between his and mine."

"I should very much like to see what you have here," remarked the affable visitor. "Or, rather, in my case, for I am practically blind, I should ask to be allowed to handle." There were occasions when Mr Carrados found it prudent to qualify his affliction, for more than once astonished strangers had finally concluded that he must be wholly shamming. In his character as an American tourist of leisure—a Mr Daniel Munroe of Connecticut, as he duly introduced himself—the last thing he desired was that ex-Lieutenant von Groot or any of that gentleman's associates should suspect him of playing a part.

For the next half-hour Mr Lidmarsh—his name marked the progress of their acquaintanceship—threw open cabinets and show-cases in his hospitable desire to entertain the passing stranger. Carrados knew quite enough of flint implements—as indeed he seemed to know enough of any subject beneath the sun—to be able to talk on level terms with an expert, and he was quite equal to meeting a reference to Evans or to Nadaillac with another.

"I'm afraid that's all," said the official at length, "—all that's worth showing you, at any rate. We are so handicapped for means, you see—the old story with this sort of institution. Practically everything we have has been given us at one time or another—it has to be, for there is simply no fund to apply to purchasing."

"Surprising," declared Carrados. "One would have thought—"

"We arrange lectures in the winter and try to arouse interest in that way, but the response is small—distressingly small. A great pity. Theatres, cinemas, dancing halls, all crowded—anything for excitement. If we get nine adults we call it a good meeting—free, of course, and Mrs Lidmarsh has tried providing coffee. Now in Holland, my assistant tells me—"

It was the first mention of the absent Karl, for Carrados was too patient and wily a tracker to risk the obliquest reference to his man until he knew the ground he stood on. He listened to a commonplace on the unsophisticated pleasures of the Dutch.

"But surely you have more help for a place like this than a single assistant, Mr Lidmarsh? Why, in the States—"

"It has to be done; it's as much as our endowment and the ha'penny rate will run to," replied the curator, accepting his visitor's surprise in the sense—as, indeed, it was intended—of a delicate compliment to his own industry. "Vangoor, myself, and Byles, the caretaker, carry everything upon our shoulders. I count myself very fortunate in having a helper who makes light of work as Mr Vangoor does. Englishmen, unfortunately, seem mostly concerned in seeing that they don't put in half an hour more than they're paid for, Mr Munroe. At least that's my experience. Then he just happens to be keen on the subjects that I'm most interested in."

"That's always nice," admitted Mr Carrados, unblushingly.

"Well, it all helps to give an added interest, doesn't it? Not that any department of the work here is neglected or cold-shouldered, I hope—no, I am sure it isn't. For instance, neither of us really cares for natural history, but we recognize that others will think differently, so natural history in all its branches receives due attention. As a seaside town, of course, we give prominence to marine zoology, and our local fishermen and sailors are encouraged to bring in any curious or unusual specimen that they may light upon."

"Do they much?" inquired the visitor.

"I am afraid not. Lack of public spirit and the suspicion that something is being got out of them for nothing, I suppose. Why, I have even found Vangoor rewarding them out of his own slender pocket to encourage them to come."

"Fine," was Mr Carrados's simple comment.

"Yes—when you consider that the poor fellow is none too well paid at the best and that he sends a little every week to his old people away in Holland—all that he can save, in fact—and he lives in a tiny, out-of-the-way old cottage quite by himself so as to do it as cheaply as possible."

"Vangoor," considered the blind man thoughtfully; "Vangoor—there was a fellow of that name I used to meet at times up to six months ago. Now I wonder—"

"In America, you mean?"

"Yes. We have a good sprinkling of Dutch of the old stock, you know. Now what was my man's front name—"

"Then it couldn't have been this one, for he has been here just a year now. I wish he was about so that I could introduce him to you, but he won't be back yet."

"Well, as to that, I've been thinking," remarked Mr Carrados. "I've had a real interesting time here, and in return I'd like to show you a few good things in the flint line that I've picked up on my tour. Could you come around to dinner tomorrow—Sunday?"

"That's very kind indeed." Mr Lidmarsh was a little surprised at the attention, but not unflattered. "Sure it won't be—"

"Not a shred," declared the new acquaintance. "Bring Vangoor along as well, of course."

"I'll certainly give him your invitation," promised the curator; "but what his arrangements are, naturally I cannot say."

"Seven o'clock tomorrow then," confirmed Mr Carrados, referring to the fingers of his own rather noticeable watch as he spoke. "'Abbotsford', in your Prospect Avenue here, is the place. So long."

At the slightest of gestures Parkinson broke off his profound meditation among Egyptian mummy-cloth and took his master in charge. Together they passed down the flight of stairs and reached the entrance hall again.

"Let them know at the house that I expect two guests to dinner tomorrow," said Mr Carrados as they crossed the hall. "Mr Lidmarsh will be coming, and very likely Mr Vangoor as well."

"I don't think you'll find the last-named gentleman will favour you, Mr Carrados," said a discreetly lowered and slightly husky voice quite close to them. "Not much I don't."

Parkinson started at the untimely recognition, but Carrados merely stopped.

"Ah, William," he said, without turning, "and pray why not?"

Mr William Byles, caretaker, doorkeeper, and general factotum of the Castlemouth Museum, disclosed himself from behind an antique coffer smiling broadly.

"So you knew me, sir, after all?" he remarked, with easy familiarity. "I thought to surprise you, but it's the other way about, it seems."

"Your voice has much the same rich quality as when you looked after my cellar, a dozen years ago, William," replied Mr Carrados. "Making due allowance for a slight—erosion. One expects that with the strong sea air."

"I wondered what you was up to, sir, when I hear you pitch it to the governor you were Mr Munroe from America. Made me laugh. Now that you're inviting Mr Dutch Vangoor to dinner I can give a straightish guess. You needn't trouble, sir. I'm keeping an observant eye on that identical piece of goods myself."

"Come to the door and point out the way somewhere," directed Mr Carrados, moving on from the dangerous vicinity of the stairs. "What do you know about Vangoor?"

"Not as much yet as I'd like to," admitted Mr Byles, "but I can put two and two together, Mr Carrados, as well as most."

"Yes," mused the blind man reminiscently, "I always had an idea that you were good at that, William. So you don't exactly love him?"

"'Ate isn't the word for it," replied the caretaker frankly. "Too much of the bleeding Crown Prince about Jan Van for my vocabulary. Ready to lick his superior's boots three times a day if requisite, but he's done the double dirty on me more than once. And I don't forget it neither."

"But why do you think he won't come tomorrow?"

"Well, if it's going to be war in a day or two, as most people say, depend on it, sir, Jan Van knows already and it stands to reason that he's busy now. And so shall I be busy, and when he least expects it too."

"Then I can safely leave him in your hands, William," said Mr Carrados pleasantly. "By the way, how do you like it here?" and he indicated the somnolent institution they were leaving.

"Like?" repeated Mr Byles, swallowing with difficulty. "Like it! Me that's been butler in superior West End families the best part of my life to finish up as 'general' in what's nothing more or less than a sort of mouldy peep-show? Oh, Mr Carrados!"

The blind man laughed and a substantial coin found its billet in the caretaker's never-reluctant palm.

"Not 'Mr Carrados' here, William, remember. Please preserve my alias or you'll be doing Mr Vangoor a kindness. And whatever you are at, don't let him guess you're on his track."

Mr Byles's only reply was to place a knowing forefinger against an undeniably tell-tale nose and to close one eye significantly—a form of communication that was presumably lost on the one for whom it was intended though it shocked Parkinson not a little. But the tone and spirit of the whole incident had been a source of pain to that excellent servitor all through.

Another member of Mr Carrados's household—though in point of miles a distant one—was also adversely affected by his employer's visit to the Castlemouth Museum. Less than an hour after Mr Byles's parting gesture a telegram addressed "Secretary" was delivered at "The Turrets" and threw Annesley Greatorex, who was contemplating a bright week-end, into a mild revolt.

"My hat, Auntie! Just listen to this," exclaimed Mr Greatorex, addressing the lady whose benevolent rule as Mr Carrados's housekeeper had led to the mercurial youth conferring this degree of honorary relationship upon her. "Here you have M.C."s latest:

> 'Borrow few dozen flint implements any period but interesting and dispatch fully insured post or rail to reach me first tomorrow. Try Vicars, Bousset, Leicester (Oxford Street), Graham, etc. Wire advice; then stand by.

"Stand by! That means ta-ta to mirth and melody by moonlit streams, until our lord returns, forsooth."

"And not a bad thing either, Mr Greatorex," declared the lady, without pausing in her work. "If there's going to be a war any minute and that German family in Canterbury Road who've got an airship hidden away in their coachhouse fly out and start dropping bombs about, you're much better here safe in bed than gallivanting up and down the open river."

"Then what about Mr Carrados right on the coast and near a naval harbour?"

"I'm no troubling about Mr Carrados," replied the housekeeper decisively. "If the Germans come they'll come by night. So long as it's in the dark Mr Carrados won't be the first one to need the ambulance, ma lad."

Carrados duly received his few dozen flints and smiled as he handled them and removed the labels. Promptly on the stroke of seven the curator arrived, but he came alone; whatever the true cause might be, William Byles was right.

"I'm sorry about Vangoor," apologized Mr Lidmarsh as they greeted. "He quite intended to come and then at the last found that he had an appointment. I'm sorry, because I should like you to have met him, and he isn't having the pleasantest of times just now."

"Oh! How is that?"

"Foolish prejudice, of course. People are excited and regard every neutral as an enemy in esse or in posse. And the irony of it is that Vangoor hears positively that Holland will be in on our side within a month."

They fell to talking of the war-cloud, as everybody did that day. It was known from the special issues that Germany had formally declared war on Russia, and had launched an ultimatum against France; that here and there fighting had actually begun. The extent of our own implication was not yet disclosed, but few doubted that the die was irrevocably cast.

"Will it make any difference to you up at the Museum?" inquired the host. Enlisting had suddenly become a current topic.

"I don't see how it can," replied Mr Lidmarsh, with regret expressed very largely in his tone. "At my age—I've turned thirty-nine, though you mightn't think it—I'm afraid there would be no earthly chance of being accepted even if the war lasted a year."

"A year," repeated the blind man thoughtfully.

"Well, of course, that's an absurdly outside limit. Mrs Lidmarsh comes of a military family, and she has it privately from an aunt, whose daughter is engaged to the nephew of a staff officer, that the Russian commander-in-chief has sent a map of Germany to Lord Kitchener with the words 'Christmas Day' written across Berlin. Naturally everyone at the War Office can guess what that means!"

Carrados nodded politically. Every second person whom he had met that day had a string leading direct to Whitehall.

"Vangoor would go like a shot if they'd raise a Foreign Legion. But of course—then there's only old Byles—so I'm afraid that we shall have to carry on as usual. And, after all, I don't know that it isn't the most patriotic thing to do. People will want distraction more than ever—not hectic gaiety: No one would dream of that, but simple, rational amusement. Soldiers on leave will need entertainment and somewhere to pass their time. A museum—"

Mr Carrados got out his flints and the curator brightened up, but something was plainly on his mind. He hemmed and hawed his intention to confide half a dozen times before the plunge was taken.

There's one thing I should like to tell you about, Mr Munroe, although in a sense I'm—well, I won't say bound to secrecy, but confidentially placed."

"Of course anything that you might say—" encouraged his auditor, discreetly occupied with the cigars.

"Yes, yes; I'm sure of that. And you have been so extremely kind and—er—reciprocal and would, I know, be deeply interested in the find that—well, I feel that if you went away without my saying anything and you afterwards—perhaps when you are back in America—read of what we had been doing, you would think that in the circumstances I had not been quite—eh? Certainly, I know that I should in your place."

"A find," commented Mr Carrados, with no very great hope in that direction—"a find is always exciting, isn't it?"

"Well, perhaps I spoke prematurely in the fullest sense—though something we undoubtedly shall find—Did you ever hear of the golden coffin of Epiovanus?"

"I'm afraid," admitted the other, "that I never even heard of Epiovanus himself. Stay though—doesn't Roger of Wimborne mention something of the sort in his *Chronicle*?"

"The tradition of an early British chief or king being buried in a gold coffin seems to have been curiously persistent, and that would go to give it a certain degree of credibility. Personally, I take it *cum grano*, I am quite prepared for a gold-mounted coffin or a coffin containing certain priceless gold adornments or treasure of gold coin. I question if the richest tribe could at that time disclose sufficient gold to fashion a solid case of the size required."

"There was fairly extensive gold coinage at that period, and then the metal practically disappears from the mints for the next thousand years," suggested Carrados.

"It having gone into the manufacture of royal coffins? I should like to think so, for we believe that we are in fact on the track of something of the kind."

"You are?" exclaimed the sympathetic listener. "That would be great—real unique, I suppose. But I don't quite take it home, you know." Actually he was only bridging conversation out of politeness to a guest. All the treasure of the Indies was of less interest than Vangoor's moves just then.

"Perhaps it sounds too good to be true, but Vangoor is thoroughly convinced, and he is exceptionally well up on the subject and has a veritable craze for digging."

"Go on," said Carrados mechnically. For one concentrated moment he even forget his American citizenship in the blinding inspiration that cleft without warning, shapeless but at the same time essentially complete, into his mind. "I'm tremendously intrigued."

"Nothing is known of Epiovanus beyond the existence of a unique copper coin reading EPIOV. REX. But among the country-people back in the valleys here—the peasants and labourers in whose names you can trace a Saxon ancestry—you will often get a shamefaced admission that they have 'heard tell' from their grandfathers of a golden coffin containing the bones of a great chief. But where? That was the difficulty, Mr Munroe. But, to cut short a long story—nearly two thousand years long, in fact—I may say that we have at last linked up the golden coffin legend with Epiovanus, Epiovanus with this part of the land, and now, finally, Vangoor has established that the solitary mound on Headlam Height is undoubtedly an early British sepulchural barrow of very unusual size and importance."

"Headlam Height?"

"It is a small, rugged promontory a mile or two along the coast here. The barrow is almost on the edge of the land, for the cliff has been falling away for ages—indeed, in another fifty years or less the tumulus would have gone over and whatever it contains been dumped into the sea."

"And you have opened it?"

"We have made a start. There was considerable difficulty in fixing up a reasonable arrangement at first. You would think it a simple and harmless enough undertaking, but there was the lord of the manor to be approached, the landlord to be got round, and the farmer—well, he had to be bought over, and I am sorry to say that Vangoor in his scientific zeal has in the end promised him the greater part of his own share."

"Of the golden coffin?" remarked Mr Carrados. "A very weighty argument."

"Well, of course, we should hope to retain the best things for the Museum, but there would have to be some pecuniary adjustment. If it turns out at all as we anticipate, the find would create a stir beyond anything of the kind before—at least, it would have done if it hadn't been for this wretched war."

"It opens dazzling possibilities," admitted the blind man. "Have you found anything yet?"

"Nothing important but plenty of encouraging trifles—burnt bones and other remains of a funeral feast, fragments of pottery, and so on. We have only been at work a fortnight, and partly from motives of economy, but more because of the extreme care that must be taken, Vangoor has done nearly all the work himself."

"Driving a tunnel from the shore side?" suggested Mr Carrados.

"Why, yes," admitted the curator, looking rather surprised, "but surely you haven't heard it spoken of?"

"Not at all," Carrados hastened to assure him. "Merely an interested guess."

"I hoped it wasn't getting about generally or we shall have all sorts of prying busybodies up there. As it is, we have railed off the part and placarded it 'Dangerous'—which it really is. But it struck me as curious you saying that, because at first we thought of making a sectional cutting right down. Then it was only after trials that Vangoor found the seaward side the safest to tunnel in."

When Carrados decided that there was nothing more of value to be learned—a few aimless remarks elicited this—the conversation imperceptibly slid off to other and less personal themes. The wary investigator had no wish to stir the suggestion that he was curious about Vangoor, and, indeed, the impression that Mr Lidmarsh took away with him was that his host's real hobby in life was the promulgation of phonetic reform.

But what had before been merely a general precautionary suspicion on the blind man's part had now fined down to a very definite conviction, and from whichever side he approached the problem the road led to Headlam Height His first impulse was to investigate that secluded spot at once, but a moment's reflection suggested that the chance of encountering Vangoor there was too substantial to be risked at that stage of the quest. Mr Byles's rather burlesque intervention now began to wear another and a more important face. Was it possible that the disgruntled caretaker knew anything definite of what was going on at Headlam Height?

"This is your affair, Parkinson, and you ought to know all that I do," said Mr Carrados five minutes later, as he retold Lidmarsh's disclosure. "On the one hand we have a harmless Dutch scientist, wholly taken up with investigating a lonely burial mound; on the other a dangerous German spy, constructing to some hostile end a retreat that directly overlooks the Channel while it is itself cunningly hidden from every point of land. What do you think about it?"

"I apprehend that we ought to be prepared for the latter eventuality, sir," replied Parkinson sagely.

"I quite agree with you," assented his master, with all the air of receiving a valuable suggestion. "We will stroll round by the Market Square, as any casual visitors might before turning in. If we encounter Mr Byles it may lead to something further. If not, another time will do."

They made their leisurely perambulation, but nothing came of it. Not only did they fail to encounter Mr Byles but the small curtained upper windows that inevitably suggested his modest suite of rooms displayed no light. The two outstanding hypotheses had to be dismissed, for William had never been an early sleeper in the past, while the public-houses had now been closed some time. Plainly there was nothing left but to retrace their steps.

"Tomorrow morning we will come again," arranged Mr Carrados. "Fortunately the Museum will be open as usual, so that William cannot very well elude us. Afterwards... I expect it will be Headlam Height."

"Tomorrow" was the last day of peace—Monday, the 3rd of August, and thereby a bank holiday. "Five Nations at War", "Invasion of France", and "British Naval Reserves Mobilized", ran the burden of the morning papers. It was no longer a question of peace trembling in the balance: it was merely the detail of when it would kick the beam.

But "Business as usual" was now held to be the thing; and Castlemouth's business being largely that of providing amusement for its visitors, there was very little indication of stress or crisis on its joyous sands or along its glittering front that day. At the railway station perhaps the outward trains were crowded and the inward ones were light, while in every chatting group a single word prevailed, but so far Castlemouth was resolved to take war peacefully.

"I believe, sir," reported Parkinson, as they crossed the Market Square—"I believe that the place is closed."

"The Museum, you mean?"

"Yes, sir. The outer doors are certainly shut."

"Curious. I made a point of asking about today. Mr Lidmarsh was explicit."

"There is Mr Lidmarsh, sir. He has just come up. He is fastening a paper to the door."

Carrados's heart gave a thud, but his pace did not alter, and the curator, looking up, judged the meeting accidental.

"Oh, Mr Munroe," he exclaimed, "this is a shocking business. Have you heard?"

"Not a solitary word," replied the blind man. "What is it?"

"Poor Byles. He was found dead on the shore this morning."

"Where?" dropped from Mr Carrados's lips. A good deal might depend on that.

"Just below Headlam Height, I understand. '*De mortuis*', and all that, you know, but the man certainly had himself largely to blame, I fear. He wasn't supposed to know anything about our work up there, but he had evidently got wind of something. He was a curious, secretive old fellow, and, as I read it, he went up there in the dark last night, and, prying about, he either slid on the slippery grass or did not see the edge. And late at night Byles was sometimes just a little—you understand? However, we have closed the Museum today as a mark of respect. But of course if you want to go in—"

"Thank you," replied Mr Carrados, "but I guess not. I was thinking... Where have they put him?"

"In the mortuary close by. He's fearfully knocked about. He had a couple of rooms up there"—indicating the windows Parkinson had observed the night before—"but he has no wife or people; and in any case the mortuary is the proper place. There'll have to be an inquest, of course; I've sent Vangoor to make inquiries now."

"I was thinking"—he had undoubtedly been thinking, but he had not yet had time to review every possibility—"this Byles did me a service as we left the Museum on Saturday—saved me perhaps from what might have been a nasty fall—and a few friendly words passed afterwards. And now... Dear me; how sad! Well, I'm not up in the customs of your sarcophagi, but if a trifling bouquet—Why, I've a notion that I'd like to."

This impressed Mr Lidmarsh with the sentimentality of masculine America—an attribute he had frequently heard it credited with.

"Why, of course," he replied, "there could be no difficulty about that if you wish it. But did you mean—right now?" The last two words were in the nature of a spontaneous tribute to the visitor's nationality.

"Sure. You see, I might have moved on tomorrow or the day after. There seems to be a flower store open that we passed just back—"

Even as he purchased the sheaf of lilies to lay on William Byles's shroud, Carrados was not altogether free from an illusion of sharing a rather exquisite joke with that mordant individual. How would William have regarded the touching act on the part of his old employer? By whatever means it reached his insight the blind man's mind immediately envisioned the flashlight of a tight-closed humid eye and a nose and finger placed in close conjunction. But, in truth, Carrados had felt the necessity of investigating further, and no other excuse occurred to him at once. He could hardly affect that he wished to see the doorkeeper once more... The sudden intuition that Parkinson was tentatively regarding a wreath of white moss-roses hastened their departure.

"One curious feature is the time this must have happened," remarked Mr Lidmarsh as they walked on. "He was found by the merest chance early this morning—almost as soon as it was light, in fact—and his clothing was not wet. That shows that he could not have fallen down before midnight at any rate. Now, whatever possessed the man to be there at that hour when nothing could be seen? He had the whole of Sunday on his hands if he wished to look about."

"Singular, isn't it?" assented Carrados. "No one saw him up there, I take it?"

"Oh, no—at least we have heard of no one. Who would be likely to be there? Even Vangoor doesn't dig on Sunday—he wouldn't think it right."

The mortuary proved to be quite near—a corner of the market hall in fact. Mr Lidmarsh procured the key from the police station, with no more formality than a neighbourly greeting on either side, and Carrados was free to perform his thoughtful office.

The body lay, outlined beneath a single covering, on one of the two stone benches that the place contained. On the other were arranged the dead man's clothes, with the few trumpery belongings that his pockets had yielded set out beside them.

"They told me that his watch, purse, and keys were taken for safety to the station," remarked their guide, as Carrados's understanding hands moved lightly to and fro. "The rest is of no consequence."

"String, pipe, tobacco-box, matches, small folding measure, odd cuff-link, silver mariner's compass, handkerchief," checked off the leisurely fingers. "How stereotyped we he-things are: my own pockets would show almost the same collection—in a liberal sense, of course."

"It is rather odd about the book," volunteered the curator, pointing to a worn volume of pocket size. It was lying a little apart, and apparently the gesture was for Carrados's eyes to follow—and strangely enough they did seem to follow, for he picked up the book unfalteringly. "It was still tightly held in Byles's hand when he was found. Now, why should the man be holding a book in his hand—one that would obviously go into his pocket—on a dark night? If there was any mystery about the case I suppose this ought to be one of the clues that those wonderful detectives we read about, but never meet in real life, would unravel the secret by."

Mr Carrados laughed appreciatively as he turned the pages of the book.

"*Stories from the Studios of Paris*," he read aloud. "At all events this throws some light on the literary calibre of our departed friend... The only thing that would seem to be missing from the average pocket is a pen-knife."

"Pen-knife?" repeated Mr Lidmarsh looking about. "To be sure he had a knife generally; I've seen it often enough. Well, I don't suppose it matters—a shilling at the outside."

Everything had been seen—everything except the chief "exhibit" lying beneath the merciful coverlet. The curator understood that his new friend relied chiefly on a highly-trained sense of touch—he had marvelled more than once during this short intercourse at what it told—but he was hardly prepared to see Mr Carrados raise the sheet and begin to pass his hand over the—his own eyes perforce went elsewhere—over the dreadful thing which the day before had been William Byles's face.

"I think," said the blind man, turning away suddenly, "that this is rather too much—" His left hand came into contact with his attendant's sleeve and Parkinson felt himself detained by a robust grasp. "Is there anywhere, Mr Lidmarsh, where ... a glass of water?"

"Yes, yes." Almost with a feeling of self-reproach that he had allowed the mishap, Mr Lidmarsh was off to the nearest house. He ought to have warned...

"The book, Parkinson," said Carrados in his usual easy tone, and before Parkinson (who would carry his own blend of simplicity and shrewdness to the grave) quite knew what was happening, *Stories from the Studios of Paris* had disappeared into his master's coat pocket.

"I don't think that there is anything more to detain us here," remarked the strategist dispassionately. "We may as well await our friend outside." He closed the door, locked it, and took out the key in readiness. When Mr Lidmarsh returned with the water he found Carrados seated on a market truck.

"I am glad you came away from the ghastly place," he declared. "I ought to have thought of that." Still accusing himself of some remission, he insisted on accompanying the two half-way through the town and hoped that they might meet again.

As they stood there, exchanging these amiable formalities, an acquaintance of the curator's passed along on the other side of the road and could not forbear to give the news.

"The Germans have invaded Belgium," he called across. "They've just got it at the post office. I bet that means we're in the soup!"

* * * * *

"What happened, Parkinson, is as clear as day," explained Mr Carrados. "The important thing now is to decide what to do ourselves."

They were seated in the private sitting-room at "Abbotsford," a table between them and on the table, with Mr Carrados's eerie fingers never long away from it, the copy of *Stories from the Studios of Paris*.

"We know from Byles's own lips that he only had a general suspicion of Vangoor's business here. Doubtless last night he watched the secluded cottage, and when Jan crept out about midnight he followed him to Headlam Height. Or, of course, he may have gone there earlier and waited. Evidently he did not know what he was going to see or he would have gone better prepared. As it was he had no pencil and he had no proper paper... We are overdue at Headlam Height, Parkinson."

"Yes, sir," acquiesced the model confederate.

"Obviously there is some ground from which Vangoor's signals can be seen, carefully as he has planned his burrow. Byles saw something, and recognizing the importance of what he saw he tried to take it down. These cuts and pricks made with a pocket-knife (which we shall doubtless find up there) on the covers of this book represent quite intelligently a rendering of morse. What that meant he did not know; what this means we do not know, but Byles has done his bit and passed on the responsibility to us."

"I think I appreciate the obligation, sir. Mr Vangoor should not be allowed to remain at large."

"That is the difficulty. We can have a spy snapped up and possibly hanged for murder, or, what would be simpler, he might slip on Headlam Height—in the same way that William Byles did. But we must not lose sight of the fact that the man has been signalling out to sea. That definitely suggests a submarine—a submarine lying off Pentland Harbour, full of battleships. What has he signalled, and, if we give him rope, *what will he signal next*?" The blind man came to his feet and strode to the window, where before him lay the broad waters of the Channel still carrying their wealth of shipping—the panorama he would never see again. Seldom before had Parkinson known his master so visibly concerned as he stood there in the hot sunlight, moodily beating his palm with the thin edge of the book. "Here in my hand are the very words he flashed—the key to every other message he may send—and we cannot read a letter of it. The system is capable of a thousand changes and ten thousand shifts of code. And the time is slipping by. It's maddening, maddening... Suggest something, Parkinson, there's a good fellow."

Parkinson might be conscious of a complete mental destitution at that moment, but he had never yet failed to comply with an order reasonably given.

"I recollect, sir, reading about a Bristol baker who murdered his wife because she had been communicating with a young gentleman by means of secret marks on the rolls delivered at the house. He discovered—"

"Enough!" exclaimed Mr Carrados, making for the writing-table with his indecision vanished. "That's it. You were inspired, Parkinson. Clifton Baker, of course!"

"Thank you, sir," replied Parkinson, much gratified.

In those days the name of Clifton Baker appeared on the frosted glass of the outer door belonging to a small top-floor office in Chancery Lane. There was nothing more to indicate who Clifton Baker was or the nature of the business carried on there. Few callers appeared at the dingy office, but those who did almost invariably left instructions to proceed, and as each order meant a substantial cheque eventually, Clifton might be assumed to be not so unsuccessful after all.

In almost every case the new client experienced a mild shock on opening his business. Generally he had been sent there by a firm of responsible solicitors, and the matter on which he required assistance was confidential, extremely technical, and beyond the capacity of any other specialist. He expected to see—well, at all events he did not expect a slight, sallow-complexioned, glad-eyed, deep-browed young woman who dressed rather skittishly and struck him as being more than a shade rattle-pated. He might have left the commission somewhat dubiously, but he did leave it, and it was duly carried out: done to time, done as required, and done perfectly.

At the age of fifteen Clifton Baker had made up her mind—a considerable achievement of itself in that era. At twenty-five she spoke all the most useful living languages and wrote the four most important dead ones. Eight letters (which she never by any chance used) after her hermaphroditic name were some evidence of a scientific grounding, while the recital of her attainments in the higher planes of mathematics made elderly professors who were opposed to the movement ooze profusely in the region of the collar. Then chance, in the shape of a baffling testamentary puzzle, threw destiny across her path, and on the assumption that there was room for one professional lady cryptologer in the world, Clifton took an office and passed the word round among her friends.

Up to that time the girl had never really done her hair, and she regarded boots merely as things to protect the feet. Suddenly it dawned on her that she was considered plain and that she diffused an atmosphere of intellectual frost. A morbid terror of being thought learned seemed from that moment to possess Clifton, and to make up for her neglected youth she began to outflap the veriest flapper in a stern resolve not to be taken seriously. Had she been less brilliantly efficient it might have ruined her business; had she been less impossibly absurd it would have spoiled her pleasure, but the two things simply antidoted one another. Everybody smiled indulgently and said how typical a product of the age Miss Baker was, and how hopeless it would be, except in this London of nineteen-dash, to look for such another.

Thus it came about that Mr Greatorex, dutifully "standing by" on Monday afternoon, was startled to receive a duplicated telegram as follows:

> FIND CLIFTON BAKER AND GET HER HERE ON ANY TERMS BY BREAKFAST-TIME TOMORROW. REPORT PROGRESS. CARRADOS.

"Whew!" ejaculated Annesley, who was not altogether ignorant of the lady's personality, "that puts the top-knot on the pan-lid with a vengeance! Bank holiday, too, ecog!" He went through the various rooms of the almost empty house vainly bleating for suggestions. "Where on earth am I to find Clifton Baker, on this of all days, Auntie?"

The housekeeper looked up over the top of her reading glasses a trifle dourly. She had a niece at school somewhere near Dinant...

"What should you want Miss Baker for?" she asked.

"I don't want her; I fear and shun her. But Mr Carrados does. He's just wired."

"Oh, that will be all right then. Well, my laddie, I can't tell you where Miss Baker is, but I can tell you this; if she's not verra hard at work somewhere she's somewhere verra hard at play."

It was at breakfast-time that Greatorex delivered her. Mr Carrados was standing in the loggia of the Hotel Beverley when a not unfamiliar sound claimed his attention. It announced to him the arrival of his own touring car, and the next moment a squeal of maidenly delight indicated that Miss Baker had espied him.

"You monster!" she exclaimed vivaciously, while a dozen yards away. "To inveigle me into travelling all night with that delightfully wicked-looking young secretary of yours! I declare I don't know what people will say when I get back."

"I thought it better to bring her down by car, sir," explained Annesley in an aside of moody resignation. "I only dug her out at something past eleven last night, and all the trains are at sixes and sevens just now."

"Quite right," assented Carrados. "I suppose you can be ready for breakfast in about ten minutes, Miss Baker?"

Clifton drooped one eyelid thoughtfully as she considered this—a device she had lately taken up.

"Do I really require breakfast?" she confided to the hotel front generally. "Mr Greatorex was most attentive all the way. He insisted on stopping at a charmingly romantic cabman's shelter somewhere, at five o'clock this morning, and we had a surfeit of hot cocoa and currant buns. I simply can't imagine why he should take such enormous care of small me."

"I think I'll go up and wash, sir," announced Mr Greatorex abruptly, "if you don't require me just now."

"Not until after breakfast," said Carrados. "In the meanwhile Miss Baker and I will talk business."

Breakfast at a little table in the Fountain Court provided an opportunity (the discovery of filleted sole *à la Normande* restored Clifton's appetite), for the hotel was no longer full...

"Yes, I see," nodded the girl at intervals, forgetting to be coy, and Carrados deployed the facts. When he had finished she held out her hand for the transcript of the message that he had already made.

"H'm. It looks rather hopeless, doesn't it, Mr Carrados?" she remarked professionally. "When do you want it by?"

"Three o'clock if possible," he replied brazenly. "Six o'clock in any case."

Clifton gave a little shriek of young-ladylike dismay.

"Mercy! Today?" she exclaimed. "Why, you dear creature, do you know— "

"I know what you can do when you like," he got in.

"And I know that perhaps it can't be done at all, sir."

"And I know that Edgar Allan Poe said— "

"He said nothing about doing it in six hours." Miss Baker had had that celebrated dictum quoted to her quite often enough to be able to dispense with it. "Are you sure that you have even got this morse the right way up?"

"Yes, I can guarantee you that. But the message certainly begins incomplete and it probably ends so."

"In German, we assume? Oh, yes; I think it must be. Well— "

"I knew you would. My sitting-room here is at your disposal. You'll find most things you may require already there. Anything else— "

"By the way, was there no later message sent? What was the man doing last night?

"No. I have him watched now, of course. Last night after leaving the Museum he was at Pentland until quite late, and returning he went home and stayed there."

"Then I should like a full list of the warships in Pentland Harbour, recent sailings, and those expected, please. The 'Navy List' I suppose you have here?"

"Good girl!" smiled Carrados approvingly. "You shall have it if it's humanly possible. If I am caught in the act and my motives doubted I shall certainly be shot at dawn—and you will be transported... Will they insist on blindfolding me, I wonder? Probably... Regulations, you know, Miss Baker. Nothing else?"

"No, thank you." Clifton still wriggled about the open door of the private room. "Well—please keep Mr Greatorex away while I am busy, won't you? He will be sure to want to bring me ices and things like that; he's so absurd, poor boy!"

So much for that particular Clifton Baker. About three o'clock Carrados tapped lightly on his own door and a very faint voice bade him enter. Clifton was lying prostrate on the couch, a napkin round her head, and the reek of eau-de-Cologne filling the room. A single written sheet of paper was on the table near her—but there were more than a hundred others, torn across, littering the floor. Without a word she picked up the single sheet and, rattling it slightly to call his attention, held it towards him.

"You have?" he exclaimed, scarcely daring to believe it. "You are really a wonderful woman, Clifton. This is splendid." Neatly set out on the paper were three separate details—the alphabet in morse code as she had finally resolved it; the message William Byles had intercepted (including three textual errors to be discounted), as it was sent in German; and the same rendered into English.

"'— — — instruction. Your presence not yet suspected. *Virulent*, *Delhi*, and *Telemachus* left today for unknown. *Westmorland* for repairs expected tonight. Supply arrangements stand, VJ.372 will be trawling — — —'" he read aloud. "Yes; we have it now. Mr Vangoor's bulletin tonight should be more interesting still."

"I think you really are a wonderful man, Mr Carrados," retorted Clifton, watching his shifting fingers as he touched her firm, bold handwriting word after word without a pause. "I suppose you always get your way? I wonder what you are going to do with me now?"

"I am going to prescribe a cup of tea at once, an early dinner, and twelve hours" good solid sleep after all this excitement.

Tomorrow I shall pack you off back to town by the car again, with Mr Greatorex to beguile the way."

"Oh, please, please, please, Mr Max!" wailed Clifton in appealing tones. "Can't you leave Mr Greatorex here and come instead? I should feel ever so much safer with you in these dreadful times!" But Mr Max laughed indulgently and shook his head. He had heard Miss Baker at work before.

"Not yet, I'm afraid," he said. "I am here for another fish, only Vangoor came along. And while I remember"—he took a slip of tinted paper from his wallet and held it out—"I hope that will be all right."

"Oh, Mr Carrados," she tittered. "Ought I to, really? It doesn't seem at all like business with *you*! I hope no one will think—"

"I should like you to—it's certainly well earned," he said. "But, of course," he added maliciously, "if you prefer the satisfaction of serving your country for nothing you can always burn the cheque."

"Burn it!" shrieked Clifton, scrambling the paper into her handbag. "And my visit to the Cosmo-Croxtons in Scotland only ten days off! Why, you delightfully opportune being, this means four new frocks to me!"

"Well, make the most of them," he advised, a trifle grimly. "There won't be any country-house parties next year."

"Why ever not?"

"When you wake up tomorrow you will find that we are at war. Before long most of your fair friends will be wearing white caps and aprons—or black dresses."

* * * * *

Carrados had quite intended to climb up to Headlam Height on Monday afternoon, he had fully determined to do so on Tuesday morning, but each time the more important post lay elsewhere. When, therefore, taking Parkinson with him, he turned his inquiring footsteps in that direction after leaving Miss Baker, it was his first reconnaissance.

"Admirably chosen, Parkinson," he remarked as they made the circuit of the acre or so of grass and heather that comprised the Height. "No path or roadway near, cut off from Castlemouth's view by cliffs, and not a house or habitation in sight anywhere... And this thing may really be an early British grave for all that we can say."

"Yes, sir," agreed Parkinson. "I have always understood that the early natives of these parts were peculiar in their habits. But if I may mention it, sir, the ground here is very broken and there is little beyond a crevice, almost a yard wide, between us and the edge."

"Quite right," assented the other, turning back; "we must be careful. The British Empire doesn't exactly hang on us today, but a British ironclad may. I suppose that crevice was the unfortunate William's retreat—there seems no other cover that would serve up here. We have a better arrangement for tonight. Now for the excavation."

A couple of rough balks of timber across the entrance were the only barrier. The tumulus itself rose to nearly thirty feet, and the cutting was sufficiently roomy for a tall man to stand in.

"Are we to imagine that our enthusiastic friend contemplated driving an unpropped tunnel clean through?" reflected Mr Carrados, touching the loose earth sides. "What does the view seaward give us, Parkinson?"

"There is a flat-topped rock visible a little way out at sea, and, farther away, the extremity of Pentland Rump—as I understand it is designated, sir." Privately, Parkinson thought the name lacking in delicacy, and he wished to make it clear that the expression was none of his.

"Aye. And the extremity of Pentland Rump and the flat-topped rock line this point of course. Ah, what have we here?"

Evidently the excavator's tools, piled at the far end of the tunnel and covered with tarpaulin: a spade, a pick, a riddle, a wheelbarrow, rope, and the usual odds and ends—that was all; no, there remained a wooden tripod, such as may serve a score of uses, lying with the rest—a tripod with rough, substantial wooden legs but a nicely-finished metal top. Smooth metal is rather pleasant to the touch, and the blind man's hand lingered on its construction thoughtfully.

"We must put all these back just as they were," he observed, busying himself. "Parkinson!"

There was no answer for a moment; then Parkinson appeared at the entrance to the tunnel.

"I was looking out beyond the mound, sir. I felt apprehensive... There is someone coming."

Carrados replaced the last tool and rearranged the covering.

"Von Groot?" he asked quietly.

"Yes, sir."

The two timbers fell into their proper places; everything was as they had found it. They stood, hidden from the land side by the mass of earth rising above them.

"How far off is he?" said Carrados.

"Nearly half a mile, sir. I saw him with the glasses on the skyline of the hill we had to cross. That means ten minutes yet."

"He may have seen you also."

"I was careful to keep in the shadow of the mound. I don't think you need entertain that, sir."

"It doesn't matter." For once the blind man's voice had lost its wonted suaveness. "I've made a hash of it this time, Parkinson. I took it for granted that he'd not venture on anything before it was night again. We were prepared to deal with that, but he's going to steal a march on us. He isn't waiting for the dark—he's going to heliograph. We can stop him, of course," he went on, sensing the unspoken question; "we shall have to stop him. But we lose the message and whatever hangs upon it. No matter how plausibly we put him off it now, after finding us up here he won't risk it again—not on the top of William Byles's affair."

"Excuse me, sir," volunteered Parkinson, "but I see no reason why we should not attempt to obtain the message still."

"We—how?" demanded Carrados sharply.

"I understand, sir, that the system is merely a succession of long and short flashes of a mirror, and that one may commit it to paper without any understanding of the meaning."

"Quite so—as William doubtless did. But where are you going to see it from?"

Parkinson's backward nod indicated the crevice on the very edge of the sheer precipice. "I think it might succeed, sir."

"No, no," exclaimed Carrados, with a sharp pang of misgiving in his voice; "it would be madness in broad daylight. Besides, here am I—"

"There are suitable clumps of gorse a little way back, sir. I anticipate that you would be quite safe there, or I would not suggest it, sir. And lying in the crevice I could watch through the grass and heather."

"I can't allow it," insisted Carrados, moved by the horror of what he saw impending. "The man discovered Byles there even in the dark, and we know how that encounter ended. No, Parkinson, I won't have you sacrificed in the forlorn hope of patching up my bungle."

"I beg your pardon, sir," said Parkinson, without a hair's deviation from his invariable tone of dignified respect, "but I was not thinking of you—or of myself. I understand that we are on the point of war, sir, and that if we lose this message it may involve a misfortune to our arms. And I must remind you, sir, that yesterday you described this affair as mine."

"By heaven, you have me there!" exclaimed his master, in an access of fine emotion. "Go if you must—and God go with you!"

"The gorse, sir." Parkinson took his arm and began to hurry him across the slope that led from the Height to the rolling land behind. "I must be satisfied that you are safe there first."

"Not so fast." Carrados checked his pace to the deliberate walk at which he tried the unfamiliar. "I may need to know this ground again." His hand went to a pocket and came out with something in it. "You are the one to have this now."

"I would rather not, sir", if I may say so," declared Parkinson with naive reluctance. "I have never discharged a firearm in my life and the consequences might be unpropitious." So Carrados retained the weapon, and a moment later he was lying in a natural bower of undergrowth, listening to the swish and crackle of Parkinson's diminishing footsteps.

It was perhaps three minutes before any sound other than the cheeping of a linnet or the rasping of a dead leaf on its bough reached the straining ears. Then, away on the left, Carrados heard the approaching beat of a heavy foot. There was little chance of reading any of the subtler indications on that luxuriant carpet, but the blind listener interpreted haste and the strain of an alert caution. The intruder passed within ten yards of the unsuspected lair—within easy pistol-shot, and the steady hand went again to the pocket, but this time it came out empty.

From the direction of the mound no sound came through; the day was drowsy, with occasional puffs of warm air and the smell of honey, and time began to hang like lead.

"He must get on, from every point of view," argued Carrados to pass the seconds. "Five minutes to fix the rig, ten more to send his message, five to pack up. Heavens! it seems an hour already." He touched the fingers of his watch and found that barely twelve minutes had gone. "But that's only if the submarine is here. He may have to wait... At any rate, he hasn't spotted Parkinson at the outset or I should have heard something."

And then, as if his action had been a continuation of the unspoken words, Carrados was on his feet and racing across the glacis. He had heard "something," and that sound the echo of his worst forebodings, for the sharp crack of a pistol had whipped the flagging afternoon—and that could mean one thing only. It was with this return in view that the blind man had marked his way, and he covered the ground with confidence, making directly for the barrow. When the difference of the air against his face told him that he was by it he dropped into a walk and moved with caution. Beyond it he was in full view, and the sheer drop hardly twenty yards away. Everything was now poised on the edge of chance.

"Damn!" came the low murmur to his ear. "*Ein anderer!*"

It was not the time to ask for explanations. Carrados—conscious even then of the irony of the phrase—had to take the risk. As he once stopped to explain to Monsieur Dompierre, upon an occasion less hurried but quite as tense, he aimed by sound and practised round a watch. He fired now into the centre of the "Damn!" and on the overhanging lip of the cliff there was a little scurry of movement among the loose stones and earth. He did not fire again. He waited, listening...

"Parkinson!" he called, without moving from the spot. "Parkinson, are you—"

There was no response. The disturbed sea-gulls wheeled overhead, raising a plaintive clamour at the violation of their homes; a string of swift shorebirds cleft a zigzag course right out to sea; at his feet the untroubled bees continued in their humble toil.

"Gone!" whispered the blind man to himself. "Gone, and I'm left alone. The best fellow—Good heavens!"

From the bowels of the earth, apparently, a wild echoing sound had come with startling suddenness—a sound so truculent and formless that it baffled perception. The next moment it revealed itself: a human being had sneezed with appalling vigour.

"Parkinson!" exclaimed Carrados, dropping on hands and knees and crawling to the crevice. "Where the devil are you?"

"I'm down here, sir," replied the welcome voice from somewhere below. "I was unable to reply when you called before as I was on the point of sneezing. The dust, sir—"

"Wait; don't try to get out," directed his master. "I'll get that rope."

It was the rope that Mr Vangoor had thoughtfully provided to give an air of conviction to his labours. By its aid Parkinson was soon hauled to safety. Once there he looked apprehensively around.

"Has anything happened to Mr Vangoor, sir?" "Yes," replied Carrados. "He was too talkative. If you do not see anything of him about we must conclude that he has gone down the same way William Byles went... What happened to *you?*"

"Unfortunately, when he had finished his message the gentleman seemed to be looking my way. I endeavoured to obliterate myself more thoroughly and evidently attracted his attention. I infer that he was rather nervous, sir, for he shot at me without saying a word."

"If only he'd had the sense to do that in my case we might both be in Kingdom Come now."

"Yes, sir? I may say that I didn't like it, sir, and as he fired I made a considerable effort to get down still lower. I imagine that something must have given, for the next moment I found myself wedged in some twenty feet down. I believe that the gentleman was much concerned what to do next as he could not discover me... What is that?"

"Back!" cried Carrados. "The cliff is going!"

The cliff, as Mr Lidmarsh had remarked, had been going for centuries—going by inches, by feet, or by yards. Possibly William Byles's activity had started a movement that Parkinson's struggles had consummated; perhaps, even, the pistol-shots had vibrated a responsive tremor. Now the cliff face—all the ground beyond the fissure—began to fall rigidly away from Headlam Height, as a ladder falls; then, as its base gave way, to change and to collapse, in hundreds of tons of shattered rock, upon the beach. In Castlemouth it was thought that the war had begun.

"Excellent," remarked Carrados, when voices could be heard again. "That should save much inconvenient inquiry about Mr Vangoor's unfortunate end. I suppose, Parkinson, that any notes you made are down there also?"

"No, sir. I managed to get the notebook back into my pocket. I trust that my efforts will have been adequate."

"That is easily proved. If you really have got the message, Parkinson, you will deserve a knighthood."

"Thank you, sir, but I hope you won't mention it to anyone. It would be very uncongenial to me to become notorious in any way."

Carrados laughed as he took the notebook. Then he sat down at the base of the mound, and with Miss Baker's key before him he began to test the notation.

"Yes," he reported presently, "you seem to have hit it off all right, '*Kriegserklärung*' this begins."

"I beg your pardon, sir?"

"It's in German of course—'War declaration'. I'll give you the whole thing in a few minutes."

"You left your hat in the gorse, sir," said Parkinson thoughtfully. "I will get it while you are engaged."

"Thank you—do," murmured Mr Carrados, again deep in the code. "Now what—oh, '*hafen*', of course."

When Parkinson returned—he had taken the opportunity to wisp himself down—Carrados was already on his feet and impatient to get away.

"We don't want to be here when the town comes out to find what the row was about," he explained. "We are not going to appear in this, Parkinson. We will make a wide detour—in fact, we may as well make Pentland direct while we are about it."

"Very well, sir."

"The message—you only got two letters wrong, which was better than William and less important, of course, as we have the code now. Well, here it is:

> DECLARATION OF WAR MIDNIGHT. 'INEXORABLE' LEAVES WESTERN HARBOUR ONE A.M. BY VIKING CHANNEL AND FROM GNOME LIGHTSHIP WILL PROCEED S.S.W. RENDEZVOUS AS ARRANGED.

"The *Inexorable* it was to have been, Parkinson."

"Yes, sir. What had we better do now, sir?"

"Nothing, practically. We have done. At Pentland I shall hand this over to the naval authorities with so much explanation as they may desire. It will then rest with them to do the doing. I venture to predict that *Inexorable* will not leave the western harbour at 1 a.m. by the Viking Channel. At the same time I think that a rendezvous will be kept. But so far as we are concerned it is *Finis*. You, Parkinson, have already done your bit."

"Thank you, sir," replied Parkinson, entirely satisfied.

2

THE MYSTERY OF THE VANISHED PETITION CROWN

Max Carrados always seemed inclined to laugh quietly if anyone happened to mention the curious disappearance of the Willington Petition Crown. Why he should have been amused rarely came out at such times, perhaps because it is not expedient for one private collector openly to accuse another private collector of barefaced theft (whatever misgivings the majority may secretly admit of one another's morals), but the extent of his knowledge in the affair will emerge from the following pages.

As a specialist in Greek tetradrachms Carrados would naturally only have a condescending interest in any of the non-classical branches of numismatics, but it was an interest that drew him to every word of coin news that appeared. As his delicate fingertips skimmed the morning paper headings at breakfast one day they "read" for him a line that promised some entertainment, and the item was duly blue-pencilled for consideration later. It was no effort for the blind man to pick out all the essentials of the newspaper's contents in this way; he could even, though not with the same facility, read the ordinary smaller type, but where there was no special reason for this it was his custom to mark off such paragraphs for his secretary's subsequent attention. This was in the nature of their ordinary daily routine, and an hour later Greatorex noticed and read aloud the following extract from the *Daily Record*:

RARE COIN DISAPPEARS
AUCTION ROOM SENSATION

"Collectors and dealers who forgathered at Messrs Lang & Leng's well-known sale-rooms yesterday in the hope of bidding for an exceptionally fine specimen of the celebrated Petition Crown of Charles II were doomed to disappointment. When the lot in question was reached and the coin was displayed at the tables it was discovered that something was wrong. The Petition Crown, which had previously been on view for several days and up to the hour of the sale, had disappeared and a comparatively valueless coin of a somewhat similar type occupied its numbered receptacle.

"Immediate search among the other lots, both sold and unsold, failed to reveal any trace of the missing rarity and the whole affair is so far shrouded in mystery.

"Piquancy is added to the incident by the fact that the last person to see and handle the coin was a well-known lady journalist, who, however, disclaims any numismatic cravings. After inspecting the coin merely as a rare and valuable curiosity the lady in question returned the tray containing it to the attendant in charge, who at once replaced it in the cabinet. As already stated, when it was next required the crown had vanished.

"The Petition Crown holds the auction record among English coins, an example having realized £500 some years ago. It is generally stated that only fifteen specimens of this excessively rare coin were ever struck, and all but two or three are now in public collections and therefore out of the reach of enthusiasts. The crown owes its name to the interesting circumstances of its origin. The English engraver, Thomas Simon, having been supplanted in Charles II's favour by his Dutch rival, Roettier, the former put all his skill and genius into the creating of a super-coin, which took the form of a crown piece, with the following quaint inscription neatly engraved around the edge:

Thomas Simon most humbly prays your Majesty to compare this his tryall piece with the Dutch, and if more truly drawn and embossd, more gracefully ordered, and more accurately engraven, to relieve him.

"Sad to relate, although Simon's work is admittedly superior to that of 'the Dutch', his petition was in vain. Still worse, the royal patron of the arts allowed his 'most humble's' salary and working expenses for several years to remain unpaid, so that after the engraver's death his widow had also to 'petition'—for £2,164 long overdue."

"That's rather like another plant where a string of pearls was changed some years ago," volunteered Greatorex, laying aside the paper in favour of his own reminiscences. He was a cheerful, mercurial youth who conceived that the more important part of his duty was to regale Mr Carrados with his personal views on life and affairs, nor, strange to say, did his employer very often undeceive him. "Do you remember the one I mean, sir?"

"Yes; they mulled that by not copying the sale label closely enough, and the attendant noticed it when the necklace was laid down again. There was a woman in that business also. But the two cases have nothing in common really."

"How do you mean? Both were at auction sales; both—"

"True," interrupted Carrados, "but those things are only superficial. The essential motives fall into two quite different classes. Good pearls are always readily saleable, and it is simply a matter of rearranging them and making them up in a different form. But what is a man going to do with a Petition Crown? Wear it on his watch-chain? As a marketable piece of loot he might as well carry off a Turner from the National Gallery, or, indeed, one of the lions from Trafalgar Square. Its trade value is about one and ninepence for the melting-pot.

"Oh, come, sir," protested Greatorex. "This account speaks of a few other specimens knocking about. Surely in a year or two's time this one couldn't be positively identified as stolen?"

Max Carrados turned to pull open a drawer of his desk and took out the top pamphlet of a number it contained.

"Here is Lang's catalogue of this sale," he said, passing it across. "I haven't gone into it, but very likely that crown will be illustrated among the plates at the end. Just see."

"Quite right, sir. It is Lot 64, and it is reproduced in one of those photographic process types here on Plate 2."

"Take a glass and look into it. It is described as exceptionally fine, but you will almost certainly find a number of small cuts and dents here and there on the surface."

"Yes; I see what you mean. They don't show ordinarily."

"All the same they label the specimen as definitely as if it was a numbered bank-note. The simplest way out of that would be to carry it loose in your pocket for a few years. That would reduce its cabinet value to one-half, but it would effectually wipe out its identity. The trouble would be that whenever you started to dispose of it you would be pointedly asked for the pedigree. What collection had it come from last? All these little details are on record and easily available. No, it's amateur work, whoever it may be, Greatorex."

"I was rather hoping that perhaps someone would bring it round here to offer sooner or later," remarked the adventurous Greatorex, still examining the plate. "I'll bet I could spot it by that scratch over his majesty's eye."

"Then you will certainly be disappointed," was the unpromising reply. "If the coin really has been stolen—

and that's a palpable 'if' so far—ten to one its immediate destination is the private drawer of some collector who will be content to handle and gloat over it in secret for the remaining days of his life."

"And then I suppose it all comes out when he goes off?"

"It may. But I have heard a curious story of an old fellow who had a few pieces in his collection that he never showed. When he thought that he only had a short time left he took a coal hammer and in five minutes the rarities were effectually put beyond any fear of identification."

"My Sunday hat!" exclaimed Mr Greatorex, compelled to a generous admiration. "Some collectors are hot stuff!"

With that decorous epitaph the subject was laid to rest, with no indication that it would ever be raised again. But—just as one may meet three piebald horses in the course of one short walk—the Petition Crown was fated to persist, and before lunch-time a telephone call from Mr Carlyle had resurrected it. The period of interment had been just short of three hours.

"Busy, Max?" chirruped the familiar voice of his friend the inquiry agent—incurably brisk and debonair even after its ten miles" journey along the wire. "Not to me? Dear old chap! Well, I dare say you've read all about the disappearance of Lord Willington's—er—Petition Crown in the paper this morning? I thought you might be interested as it's something in your line."

"Greatorex is, at all events," replied Mr Carrados. "He was half expecting that someone might bring it here in the course of the day. Do you—strictly between ourselves, of course—do you happen to have it for disposal, Louis?"

"Do I happen to have it for disposal?" repeated Mr Carlyle in a slightly mystified tone. "I thought you would have read that the coin has been stolen. However, Max, in my office at this moment there is a young lady who is very much concerned at being implicated in the affair. Frankly, as the auctioneers are naturally doing all that can be done to solve the riddle, I did not see how I could be of any real service to her, and I told her so. But she seemed so disappointed that as a—er—well—"

"As a sort of forlorn hope?" suggested the listener maliciously.

"Not at all; most certainly not!" protested Mr Carlyle indignantly. "I explained that as you were both a keen coin collector yourself and an enthusiast in certain branches of criminal research, if—if, mind you, Max—you cared to hear what she had to say, you would be in an exceptional position to give her a word of advice. And that is really the long and the short of the whole matter, my mordacious friend."

"Very likely, my ingenious sleuth, but I imagine that there is a small piece missing somewhere. You were not wont to turn young and beautiful suppliants from your office door. What is the real reason of this professional reluctance on your part?"

"Max," came along Mr Carlyle's cautiously-restrained voice—the listener could divine how near the moving lips were to the mouthpiece—"I will speak to you as one gentleman to another when there is no danger of being overheard. Miss Frensham is young, but she is not beautiful, and to put it in that way is to pay her a noticeable compliment. She is also, I gather, regrettably hard up. Now, as I never conceal from my clients, my business is conducted on a purely financial basis, whereas you amuse yourself for—the other thing. Doubtless I could earn a few honest but ill-spared guineas at this young lady's expense, but I cannot satisfy myself that she would be any the wiser for the outlay. And so—"

"All right, you old humbug," said Carrados amiably; "send her along. So far as the portents go I am with you in not seeing that there is much to be done for her, but if she finds any satisfaction in talking about it you can tell her that I shall be here for the next few hours."

Miss Frensham evidently did foresee some satisfaction in talking about it, for she came at once. In view of her circumstances, Carrados could not but deem her rather extravagant, for nothing but a taxi from door to door could explain the promptness of her arrival. Mr Carlyle had not maligned her looks: plain she undoubtedly was, not in any sense describably ugly but with a sort of pug-dog grotesquery. Her dress made no attempt to counteract physical deficiences, but when she spoke Carrados's unemotional face instantly lit up with pleasure, for, unexpected in such a setting, her voice had the rare quality of gracious music.

"How good of you to let me come in this way, Mr Carrados!" she exclaimed as they shook hands. "I don't know which I have to thank the more—you or Mr Carlyle."

"I think I shall claim the major share," said the blind man lightly. "Not for any particular merit, but because I am so very pleased to hear you."

"To hear—oh, yes; of course he told me or I really should not have guessed. You know what it's all about?"

"I infer that you are the lady of the paragraph," and the lifted hand indicated the open sheet of the Record lying nearby.

"Yes, in a sense I am." Miss Frensham seemed troubled for a moment. "But I am not really a 'well-known lady journalist', Mr Carrados. I am only a very obscure one—hardly a real journalist at all. That was just swank, and also because I felt sure that under that description no one who knew would ever think of me."

"Oh," said Mr Carrados with an amused and deepening interest, "so in addition to being the heroine of the adventure you wrote it up?"

"Yes, ultimately I did. At first I was too upset to think about that. But I had gone to the place yesterday to see if there wasn't a 'news-story' in this Petition Crown—nothing but 'news-stories' are worthwhile, you know—and it seemed rather a pity to miss it when it turned out to be a very much better 'news-story' than I had ever expected. And then I knew that if I got my 'copy' taken I could keep my own name out. I had particular reasons for wishing that."

Carrados nodded without showing any curiosity about the reasons. "What is it exactly that you want to do now?" he asked.

"Well, I feel that I am really under suspicion of having taken the coin—I don't see how they can think anything else in the circumstances—and the only way of clearing myself is to find out who did take it. Knowing that I didn't, I naturally think that it must be the attendant there, because he seems to have been the only other person who could have done."

"Reverse the argument, and the attendant, knowing that he didn't, naturally thinks that it must be you, because you seem to be the only other person who could have done. And so both sides get into difficulties along that obvious line. Suppose we ignore the two palpable suspects—yourself and the attendant. Now who else might it have been?"

"That is the difficulty, Mr Carrados; it could have been no one else. I returned the coin to the attendant; he put it back in the case and remained on duty there until he displayed it on the tray to show round. Then it was discovered to have been taken."

"I suppose," said Carrados tentatively, "you really were the last to inspect the coin? Sitting there you would probably have noticed if anyone else had asked for it?"

"I only know what they said, but no one seemed to have any doubt about it. I went out to—to get some lunch and when I got back the sale was going on."

"Ah," said the blind man thoughtfully. "Of course you would have to. Suppose you tell me the—the 'news-story' all through."

"I hoped that you would let me," replied the girl. "But I was afraid of taking up too much of your time. Well, I have been living by journalism for some time now. Rather suddenly I had to support myself by some kind of work, and there was nothing else that I seemed able to do. I have always been fond of writing, and I had quite a lot of stories and articles and poems that I had been told by friends were quite good enough to print. I brought them to London with me, but somehow they didn't seem so much thought of here. I got to know one or two other girls who wrote, and they told me that my sort of stuff would be all right when I got into the peerage or became a leading lady, but if I wanted to live meanwhile it was absolutely necessary to cultivate a 'news-nose'. I soon saw what they meant: it wasn't absolutely necessary that it should be news you wrote, but it had to give the impression that it was."

"Miss Frensham, I have been a practical journalist myself," remarked Carrados. "You had grasped the sacred torch."

"At all events, I could just keep the domestic pot boiling after that. It was rather a near thing sometimes, but there was someone—he is a sub-editor on the Daily Record actually—who helped me more than I can ever say. He told me of this sale. "There's a coin to be sold that's expected to break the record,' he said; and he explained to me which it was. 'There ought to be a "news-story" in it if it does—say two hundred words in the ordinary way, four hundred if you can make it kick. I'll try and put it through.' I thought that I had made it kick, so I went to four hundred."

"Yes," agreed her auditor, "I certainly think you can claim that amount of movement."

"I didn't know anything about a coin auction, of course, but I looked up Simon in the biographical dictionary at the B.M. reading-room and then went on to the place. That was yesterday—the morning of the sale. There were two or three others—men—looking at the coins—nothing to what I had expected—and one attendant who gave out the drawers in which they were arranged as they were asked for.

"I expected some sort of formality before they let me see the crown—so valuable—but there was really nothing at all. I just said, 'Can I see No. 64, please?' and he simply pulled one of the shallow drawers out of its case and put it down before me on the table. There were about a dozen other lots in the drawer, each in its separate little box. Then he turned his back on me to attend to something else. I believe that I could have picked up the coin and walked out of the place with it."

"We are a trustful people both in war and peace," conceded Mr Carrados. "But I think you would have found that you couldn't quite do that."

"Well, I didn't try—though it certainly did occur to me that there might be a stunt of some sort in it: You look out for them when one means a week's good keep. I made a few notes that I thought I could work in and then found that it was just one o'clock—the sale was to begin at a quarter past. As the attendant took the coins away I asked him how fast they sold them.

"'If you only want to see that lot sold, miss, a quarter to two will be in plenty of time. If you reckon a hundred lots to the hour you'll be well on the safe side.'

"I thanked him and went out. That was really all I had to do with the coin. I never saw it again. When I got back to the sale room the auction was going on. Even then there were only about twelve or fifteen people there. They sat at the tables—I suppose you know how they are arranged, as a sort of hollow oblong, with the auctioneer at one end and the attendant showing the coins up and down in the middle?—and a few sitting here and there about the room. I didn't sit down; I stood between the table and the door waiting for the price of Lot 64, which was the only thing I wanted.

"When he got to it there was a slight stir of interest, though a more lethargic set of enthusiasts I never saw. I always imagined that collectors were a most excitable race who lost their heads at bidding and went on and on madly. These might have been buying arrowroot for all the emotion they showed."

"Half of them would be dealers who had long ago got over all human enthusiasms; the remainder would be collectors, too afraid lest the others should think that they were keen on something. And then?"

"The attendant was carrying the coin round on a little tray when one man picked it up and looked at it. 'Hullo!' he said and passed it to the next. 'This is the wrong lot,' said that one, and then the auctioneer leaned over and called to the attendant, 'Come, come, my lad—No. 64,' and the attendant said, 'This is No. 64,' in an aggrieved way and showed him the numbered box. Then the attendant and those near that end began to look among the unsold lots, and after that they all turned out the sold lots—they had mostly been put into little envelopes—and when they came to the end of these everyone looked at everyone else and said nothing. Then I think they began it all over again—the hunting, I mean—when the auctioneer hit on his desk.

"'This is an important lot. Very sorry, but we can't go on with the selling until we know more where we are. I suppose someone did see the Petition Crown this morning?'

"Two or three men said that they had, and the attendant, looking round, recognized me.

"'That lady was the last to see the lot before the sale, sir,' I heard him say. 'Better ask her.'

"'Did you—' began the auctioneer, and then, I suppose, recognizing that I mightn't like to carry on a shouting conversation across the room, he added, 'Do you mind coming round here?'

"I went round the tables to where he was sitting, and he continued: "'Did you see this lot before the sale? Our man thinks that you were the last to have it out.'

"'Yes,' I admitted. 'I saw it, and it was there when I returned the drawer. Of course I don't know that I was the last, but it was about one o'clock.'

"'No one had it out later, Muir?'

"'No, sir. I've been on this spot ever since, and that tray hasn't been asked for.'

"The auctioneer seemed to consider, and everyone else looked first at one and then the other of us. I began to feel very uncomfortable.

"'I suppose it really was the Petition Crown you saw at one o'clock?' he asked after a bit.

"'I suppose it must have been,' I replied. 'I copied the "Petition" from the edge into this notebook.'

"'Well, that fixes it all right. You see how awkward it is for us, Miss—Miss—'

"I gave him my name.

"'Miss Frensham. We have to do the best we can in the circumstances. I can't say at the moment on whom the loss will fall—if the coin really proves to have disappeared—but the figure is considerable. Now everyone else in the room is known to us by sight; we have the names and addresses of them all'

"'You have my name,' I said, 'and I am living at the Allied Arts Hostel in Lower Gower Street.'

"'Thank you,' he replied, writing it down. 'But of course that means very little to us. Is there anyone convenient who knows you personally to whom we can refer? You must understand that this does not imply any sort of suspicion of your *bona fides*: it is only putting you on equal terms with the rest of the company.'

"I thought for a moment. I saw a great many unpleasant possibilities. Most of all I knew that I wanted to keep this from my people.

"'The editor of the *Daily Record* knows me slightly,' I replied; 'but I don't see that he can say anything beyond that. And as to suspicion, I am afraid that you already have some. If you have any ladies on your staff I am quite willing to turn out everything I have before them'—I thought that perhaps this would settle the matter off-hand, and I couldn't help adding rather viciously: 'and after that I dare say the rest of the company will do the same before you.'

"'Yes,' he considered, 'but you've been out for half an hour, so that would really prove nothing. At lunch, I suppose?'

"I began to see that things were fitting in rather unpleasantly for me.

"'Yes,' I said.

"'Perhaps I had better note where you went. We don't know where this may land us, and in the end it may be to your interest to have a waitress or someone who can identify you over that time.'

"'I'm afraid I can't do that,' I had to say. 'There was no one who noticed me.'

"'Surely—Well, anyhow, the place?'

"I shook my head. He looked at me for a moment and then wrote something down... You think that was very suspicious, Mr Carrados?"

"Your advocate never thinks that anything you do is suspicious," replied the suave listener. "Probably they would."

"They seemed to. Well, Mr Carrados, I don't mind telling you, but somehow I couldn't say it before that—I felt—unfriendly battery eyes... My lunch consisted of three very unladylike thick slices of bread-and-butter, and I ate them as I walked slowly up and down the stairs at a tube station. So, you see, there could be no corroboration."

"Perhaps we shall do better—not even require it," he replied quietly. "What happened next?"

"I don't think that there was much more. They gave up looking for the coin. The auctioneer said that he had telephoned to someone—his solicitor or Scotland Yard, I imagined, but I didn't hear which—to know what ought to be done, and he hoped that everyone would remain until they knew. The sale began again. I went across and sat down on a chair away from the table. I had no interest in the sale—in fact I hated it—and after a time I took out my pad and tried to write the paragraph. Very soon the sale came to an end and the men began to go—I suppose they had been told to. I waited, for I wasn't going to seem in a hurry, until I was the only person left. After a bit the man who had been selling came in and seemed rather surprised to see me still there. He said he hoped I didn't think that I was being detained, and I said, 'Oh, no, I was just finishing something.' He said that that was all right, only they were going to lock up the room then and have it thoroughly looked over today—it was just possible that something might turn up, though he was rather afraid that it would remain a mystery to the end. He was quite nice about it, and told me several curious things that had happened in connexion with sales in the past. Then I left and he locked the door after us and, I believe, took the key."

Carrados laughed appreciatively.

"Yes, it was rather like the proverb about the stolen horse, wasn't it?" said the girl. "But I suppose they felt that even the unlikeliest chance must be taken. Anyway, they have certainly sent inquiries both to my Hostel and to the Record office. That's chiefly why I want to have my poor character restored. Everyone says, 'Of course, Miss Frensham, nobody would think for a moment—' But what else are they to think privately? The thing has gone and I am branded as the last to handle it."

"Yes, yes," said Carrados, beginning to walk about the room and to touch one familiar object after another in his curiously unhesitating way. "That unfortunate 'last' has obsessed you and all the others until it has shut out every real consideration. Your account of the whole business—quite clear so far as it goes—is entirely based on the fact that you were the last, and the attendant knew you were the last, and the auctioneer was told you were the last, and all the others grasped it, and you all proceeded to revolve round that centre. There stands the man we want, as plain as a pikestaff for us, only you and your lastness get between so persistently that we cannot see him."

"I'm very sorry," faltered Miss Frensham, rather taken aback.

"That's all right, my dear young lady," said an entirely benevolent Carrados. "We are getting on very nicely on the whole, and soon you will begin to tell me the things I really want to know."

"Indeed I will tell you anything," she protested.

"Of course you will—as soon as I have the gumption to ask. In the meantime what do you really think of the celebrated Petition Crown now that you've seen it?"

This light conversational opening struck Miss Frensham as rather an unpropitious way of grappling with the problem of the theft, but she had just professed her general willingness.

"Well," she replied with conscientious effort, "it chiefly struck me as rather absurd that people should be willing to pay so much for this one when other coins, apparently almost like it, could be had for a few shillings."

"Yes; very true." The blind man appeared to consider this naive expression deeply. "As a collector myself of course that goes home. You are not a collector, in any sense, Miss Frensham?"

"No, indeed."

"I was wondering," speculated Carrados in the same idle vein, "how you happened to know that."

"Oh, very simply. There were about a dozen other lots in the drawer the man put before me. One of them consisted of quite a number of crown pieces, and they struck me as being so like the Petition Crown at a glance that out of curiosity I compared them. When it came to the sale they made only a few pounds for the lot."

"You compared them—side by side?"

"Yes. I—I—" As she spoke Miss Frensham suddenly went very white, half rose from her chair, and sat down again. The charming voice trailed off into a gasp.

"You remember something now? You—possibly—changed them somehow?"

"I did! I see it all. I remember exactly how it went. What a dreadful thing!"

"Tell me what happened."

"I was waiting for the attendant to turn so that I could tell him I had finished. It was then that I took up these two coins—the Petition Crown and one from another box—to compare. There was a man near me who had seemed to be watching—at least I thought so—and just then I looked up and caught his eyes on me. I suppose it made me nervous; anyway I dropped one of the crowns back into the drawer. It made a great clatter as it fell among the others and I felt that it would be almost a crime there to knock a coin like that. I just slipped the other into its place and pushed the drawer away as the attendant turned. And now I see as clearly as can be that I returned them wrong."

"That is our real starting-point." said Carrados happily. "Now we can proceed."

"But it must have been found out. All the sold lots were looked over again."

"Oh, yes; it must have been found out. But exactly when? The man who was observing you—did you hear his name?"

"No."

"Where did he sit during the sale?"

"He sat—yes, that's rather curious. You remember that after talking to the auctioneer I went and sat down away from the table? Well, when the selling was going on again this man kept hovering round. Presently he bent down to me and said, 'Excuse me, but you have taken my seat.' 'What on earth do you mean?' I retorted, for it was just at the time that I was feeling exasperated. 'There was nothing on the chair, and there are a dozen others there,' and I pointed to the whole empty row. Then he said, 'Oh, I beg your pardon,' and went and sat down on another."

"Isn't it splendid!" exclaimed Carrados in one of his rare bursts of enthusiasm. "No sooner have we got rid of you and the attendant as the only possible culprits than we find the real man absolutely fighting to make himself known—doing everything he can to attract our attention—struggling like a chicken emerging from its shell. Soon you will tell me that you found his hand on the back of your chair."

"Oh!" cried Miss Frensham in sharp surprise. "How can you possibly know that?"

"I did not; but it was worth while suggesting to you."

"It's absolutely true. I certainly shouldn't have thought it worth while mentioning, but just at the end of the sale, when everyone got up, he passed behind me, and stopping, he put his hand—rather gratuitously it seemed—on my chair and asked me if I had heard what the last lot made. I said that I wasn't taking the least notice, and he went away. What does it mean?"

"At the moment it means that we must telephone to Lang's to keep the stable door locked—don't put your trust in proverbs, Miss Frensham. And there are a few questions I want them to have settled before I call there."

"I dare say I'm an idiot," said the lady frankly, "but I'm beginning to get rather excited. Isn't there anything that I can do to help?"

"Why, yes," he smiled with friendly understanding. "Make out the list for me. We need the catalogue—it's over there. Now which was the lot of crowns you compared with?"

"This one—No. 56," she replied, after studying the pages. "'Charles II, Crowns, various dates, in fine condition generally, 7.'"

"That's sufficient. You have your pad? Now write:

Confidential. Please ascertain

(1) Who bought Lot 56?

(2) What man, if any, left the sale-room about one o'clock and returned before Lot 56 was sold?

(3) What man, if any, returned after the sale for something he had left in the room?

"Of course," he seemed to apologize, "that gives away the whole show to you."

"Ye—es," replied Miss Frensham dutifully.

Mr Carrados insisted on his visitor remaining to lunch. He even arranged that no one else should be present on the occasion, and the guest, justly annoyed at this characteristic masculine act of delicacy, repaid him by discovering the appetite of the proverbial fairy. The ghosts of three slabs of bread-and-butter stood between her and that generous table; and, reflecting on that, the whimsical maiden sought her own means to dispel the spectre.

"It is really my fault that the coin has gone," she found occasion to remark. "Almost as much as though I had taken it. If it never turns up again I can't be satisfied until I have made it good."

Carrados was naturally horrified. Was she mad? Had she forgotten its record?

"My dear young lady, don't be romantic. The coin is insured, or ought to be. Why, it would cripple you for years—for ever."

"Oh, no," she retorted airily. "We all expect to make our fortunes. And I really have some money that I don't use."

"Yes?" he smiled, and in the character of her intimate adviser the words slipped out: "How much?"

"Well," she considered with deliberate effect, "I think it varies... But"—with devastating clearness—"it is somewhere about three thousand pounds a year."

"I beg your pardon?" stammered Carrados. "No, no; don't say it again. I heard perfectly. I see. I understand. You ran away from it?"

"I ran away—if you call it running away—from several things. If you could see me, Mr Carrados, you would understand that I am endowed with an almost supernatural plainness. It is too obvious even for the glass to conceal from me. At school, where politeness is not one of the compulsory subjects, I was

'Pup', 'Puggy', 'Ki-ki', 'Balcombe Beauty', 'Snarleywow', and other shafts of endearment. I was not petted. Even my mother found it a little trying... And yet as I grew up I learned that I could be astonishingly popular with most men. The things I said were witty, the things I did were clever, my taste was exquisite, and they were all prepared to marry me... But when I happened to wander into the society of strange men who had missed hearing of my pecuniary worth, my word! No one noticed that I hadn't a seat, no one thought of asking me to dance, to sing, to skate. They didn't see me. And if I opened my mouth they very rarely even heard me. And then if a really pretty girl happened to come into the circle! What an instant preening up of the fishy-eyed old men and a strutting round of the bored-to-death young ones! They didn't even take the trouble to hide anything from me: I might have been a man too. I could watch them licking their lips and arranging their attractions. Oh—h! Do you wonder that I went sick among it all? There was a man my father wanted me to marry; well, at all events a decent sort of male, it seemed. I was beginning to think that I might as well when that came out. No, it doesn't really matter what. My father thought it needn't make any difference! Mother assured me that it was nicer not to notice these things! When I said that it made all the difference and that I had already noticed a great many things and that I was going away out into the world to see if it was the same everywhere and meant to begin by earning my own living of course I raised a tremendous storm. Then—if I must go—they wanted to arrange things for me, so that everything should be quite nice. But they'd been arranging for me all my life and that was just what I wanted to disarrange. In the end I got my way—you see, I was in rather a strong position—subject to certain conditions. Father stipulated that I didn't get into any 'damned mess', or back I should have to go. Mother hoped that her girlie would remain unspotted from the world. So here I am. And that's the whole story, Mr Carrados, and the reason why I'm so anxious to keep out of what I am sure my father would call a—ahem—mess."

"Poor Louis!" thought his friend. Then aloud, "And is human nature entirely transformed by the five-mile radius, Miss Frensham?"

"No," she admitted seriously. "But at least I know exactly where I am. There is no competition to carry my parcel or to run my errands—I hope I haven't given the impression that I want it?—but if anything I do does happen to get praised I can believe it honest; if I make a friend I can really feel that it is for myself... I am no longer, as I heard of one 'admirer' dubbing me, 'The Girl with the Golden Mug'."

Both laughed. Then he grew almost pensive.

"After laughing at that let me say something," he ventured at length. "When you needn't fear having to meet a man's eyes ever he may be privileged to an unusual frankness... Think as little of looks as you do of lucre, Miss Frensham. I can know nothing of the features you so dispraise: to me you would always be the girl with the golden voice. I am sure that someone else will see you—as you think you are—as little as I do, and to him you will always be the girl with the golden heart."

"You kind man!" she responded. "Well...perhaps there is!"

* * * * *

When Carrados got down to Lang & Leng's a few hours later he found that the seller on the previous day had been Mr Travis, a gentleman to whom he was by no means a stranger.

"Very glad to have your suggestions, of course, Carrados," remarked Mr Travis graciously. "Are you looking into it on Lord Willington's behalf? Miss Frensham's! You don't say so!"

"I have a weakness for being on the winning side," remarked the blind man.

"Well, as to that, I don't know that it's exactly a case of a winning side or a losing side. Unless you call us the losing side, egad! This is the room. You want to look—to go round it?"

"I should like to. One never knows."

"Oh, we've been thoroughly over it this morning. Heaven knows what we could expect, but it seemed the natural thing to do. Yes, it's still being kept locked, since you asked."

"Anyone wanting to go in for anything?"

"No—only Mr Marrabel, who called for his gloves after the sale; they'd been taken to the office though."

"Marrabel!" thought the patient worker in the dark. "Yes, of course—Marrabel the dilettante."

"And, by the way, that reminds me," continued Mr Travis. "Oh yes, sit anywhere you like. That list you sent through. You're not going to suspect Marrabel of any connexion? Because, strangely enough, his name is the answer to each of your inquiries."

"I should scarcely describe it as a case for suspicion," replied Carrados. "Still, one thinks of everyone."

"We can eliminate Mr Marrabel at all events, I think. He did not look at any of the lots yesterday. He only bought No. 56, and both Muir and I noticed that he did not touch the coins when he got them—just put them on an empty chair by his side until the hue and cry was raised, and then he passed the box over to the table for someone to verify—all there and the correct number."

"Very convincing," assented Carrados.

"I mean it rather shows that there isn't much to be gained by looking for so-called 'clues' at this end, don't you think? Marrabel as a case in point. Of course we shall be delighted to put any information or facilities that we may have at your disposal, Carrados, both out of consideration for yourself and as due to your client. But what we chiefly want is to get the coin back. And the people we have put on to it seem to be extending themselves in that direction. By tomorrow every curio-dealer, pawn-broker, and leading collector will be on the look out, America will be notified, for they think that the coin may be quite likely offered there. A reward is being offered to make it worth anybody's while. In the next number of the Bric-à-brac Collector there will be an ingenuous advertisement from a wealthy colonial anxious to buy rare milled silver coins; don't be deceived by it."

"I won't," promised Mr Carrados. "But all this must come rather expensive."

"Doubtless it is. But the fact is, since the thing has gone, Willington's people are persuading themselves that it might have made a fantastic price. That is why we are only anxious to get it back again."

"Oh!" Polite unconcern was Carrados's note. He seldom denied himself these rare moments when, perhaps, a week's patient labour ran down to a needle-point. "Of course I'm more interested in my client. But as the coin is all you want—why, here it is!"

"What—what's—that?" articulated Mr Travis.

"The Petition Crown," replied the arch-humbug, continuing to hold out his hand. "Delighted to be the means of restoring it to you, Travis."

"It is the Petition Crown," murmured Travis. "Good God! You brought it?"

"On the contrary, I found it here."

"Found it? Where?"

"Beneath the seat of this chair."

"You knew that it was there? Do you mean that Miss Frensham told you?"

"I knew that it should be here, and Miss Frensham certainly told me."

"She hid it there?"

"Not at all. She did not know that it was here. She told me where it was, but she did not know that she was telling me."

"Then I'm hanged if I understand," complained Mr Travis. "Can't you be human once in a way, Carrados? Damn it all, man, we went to school together!"

"Sit down," said Carrados, "and I'll be as human as you like... Did you ever commit a crime, Travis?"

"Not really," confessed the auctioneer with admirable sang-froid. "I robbed an orchard when I was ten, but that—"

"Robbing orchards at ten scarcely counts, does it? Well, I have the advantage because there is no form of villainy that I haven't gone through in all its phases. Theoretically, of course, but so far as working out the details is concerned and preparing for emergencies, efficiently and with craftsmanlike pride. Whenever I fail to get to sleep at night—rather frequently, I'm sorry to say—I commit a murder, forgery, a robbery or what not, with all its ramifications. It's much more soothing than counting sheep and it never fails to get me off. The point is, that the criminal mind is rarely original, and I find that in nine cases out of ten that sort of crime is committed exactly as I have already done it. Being a collector myself, of course, I've robbed coin auctions frequently. I know precisely how it should be done and what is to be avoided. Marrabel did the correct things, but he overlooked the contingency of someone else also thinking of them."

"But Marrabel, my dear fellow! He must be almost in Debrett. Think!"

"Oh, yes. But he makes a speciality of getting choice things for nothing, provided there is no risk."

"And is there no risk here?"

"None at all; practically none if he's content to take his loss. But is he? We shall see. However, this is what has happened so far:

"Miss Frenshaw started the business by mixing Lots 56 and 64 without knowing it at the time. She had come to get a newspaper par out of the sale if she could, and was taking an intelligent interest in the subject when she happened to catch Marrabel overlooking her. Well, being nervy and rather touchy she dropped the Petition Crown on to the other crowns in Lot 56 and put the one from that lot into box No. 64.

"Marrabel evidently grasped that. It might prove a golden opportunity. Doubtless he took five minutes to consider the position. Then he hied him off to his Mayfair flat and returned with an appropriate coin in his pocket, well in time to purchase Lot 56. What did it cost him?"

"Three-fifteen," said Mr Travis.

"You know well enough, Travis, that although a single-coin lot is generally taken up by someone as it goes round the table, half a dozen coins, like Lot 56, are seldom touched. At the most they are glanced at. When Muir turned them out on to his tray, what had been at the top naturally got hidden. When he returned them to the box, to hand over to the buyer, the Petition Crown perhaps came to the top again. Marrabel, seated in an unusually retiring position, doubtless received his booty with an appropriate gesture of unconcern and laid it carelessly on the next chair. Good. No risk so far.

"He had at least four minutes in which to act. You and Muir thought he paid no attention to the purchase because he didn't hold the box and examine the contents. Quite natural; but of course you weren't actually watching him and he was out to mask his movements. All in good time the exchange was made. But now the element of risk came in: he had the thing in his possession.

"Your amateur is always self-conscious. Marrabel could have walked off then, but that would certainly have put him in an equivocal position. Yet supposing it came to being searched? And Miss Frensham, you may remember, did throw out the suggestion. Whether he had reconnoitred in advance we need not speculate; but here beneath his chair, without moving,

Marrabel found an ideal crevice for his loot: tight, hidden, accessible.

"He could now move away from the dangerous spot, and he did when the chase began, putting his purchase on the table with a fine indifference for someone else to verify. He stayed away from this chair so long that a curious thing occurred. Miss Frensham took it.

"In one way Marrabel was now on velvet. The leading suspect had drawn a red herring across his tracks, for if by any chance the crown should come to light here Miss Frensham was hopelessly involved. Then presently the situation eased; the sale was coming to an end and there was no suggestion now of search or of anyone being detained. His only desire was to recover the coin and get away. But the lady seemed set here, and Marrabel, ignorant of her intentions, made his first bad move. He claimed the chair, fully expecting to be given it at once.

"As it happened Miss Frensham didn't budge. She is far from being an ordinary meek young person, and the immediate events hadn't gone to soothe her. She was sitting there quietly writing, and, taken on the surface, it was sheerly an impertinence on the man's part. She had had occasion to notice Marrabel already. In strictly feminine terms she told him to go to the devil, and Marrabel, now beginning to feel jerky, veered off.

"The sale comes to an end. Everyone begins to go. Is Marrabel to hang about aimlessly until this chair is vacant and then deliberately come and sit here for no obvious reason? The man's tightened nerves won't hear of it. Act naturally and there is no risk at all. Return later—tomorrow, next week, it doesn't matter, the coin is snugly waiting. And then, good heavens! The thing flashes on him. The chairs are all alike! Next week, tomorrow, even after the sale they may be rearranged, moved, taken to another room, and he will have to go sitting on one after another, an object for all to marvel at. What's to be done?

Why, plainly to mark the chair before it is too late, and here, Travis, under my fingers, is the cross that our man broke his pencil on."

"Very ingenious," admitted Mr Travis, "and in the face of this evidence"—delicately balancing the recovered crown upon a finger-tip—"it would be mean to argue. But, you know, Carrados, Miss Frensham did sit here last."

"Inflexible man!" replied Carrados. "Well, when is your next sale?"

"Friday—enamels. On view for one day only."

"So much the better. You can have it in here? Keep it closed till then and I will be here early. And just make sure that Marrabel is sent his catalogue, won't you?"

* * * * *

There was nothing at all unusal to be noticed about the sale-rooms on Thursday morning, and Mr Marrabel strolled round in perfect composure. With praiseworthy restraint he had not hastened there, and the group of conspirators in the private office had to amuse themselves as best they could for at least two hours.

Marrabel was interested in enamels, as he was in all precious things, and he wandered from point to point consulting his catalogue, examining a piece and marking a price as he had done a score of times before—as everyone else was doing then. Finally he sat down to review his list: nothing could be more natural. Satisfied, he rose to go.

Outside the room an attendant came across to speak to him: the signal had been passed.

"Do you mind stepping into Mr Travis's office, sir? I think he wants to see you about something."

The message was polite and not wholly unusual, but Marrabel's throat went dry.

"Not now," he said, quickening his step. "I have an important—. Back in half an hour, tell him."

It was too late for that easy manoeuvre to carry. Across the hall there was another form between him and the outer door. Nor did the first one obligingly retire.

"Beg pardon, sir, but I understand it's rather particular, sir."

Then Marrabel must have known that something had miscarried.

"Oh, curse it, all right," he snapped and, watched at every step, he went.

"It's about the Petition Crown that disappeared at the last coin sale." The urbane Travis never had a less relished job. "We have received certain information and we may have to take proceedings. Do you wish to make any statement?"

Marrabel had dimly foreseen this possibility and he had given some thought to a satisfactory explanation, but in the end he had left it to be decided by the circumstances of the moment, because there was no perfectly satisfactory explanation to be thought of.

"Well," he said, affecting a light laugh, "that's an unnecessarily brutal way of putting it, because, as a matter of fact, I was bringing the crown to return to you, and I have it in my pocket at the moment. It was only this morning I discovered it when I came to look into that lot I bought. How it got there and how it came to be missed by the dolts who looked I can't say. Personally I didn't examine one of the coins until today."

"I see," remarked Mr Travis. "But I understand that you were leaving the place just now?"

"You understand quite right. I intended handing you the crown, but when I got here and realized how cursed unpleasant it might be I funked it. I decided to send the damned thing back by post without a word."

"At all events you have it for us now?"

"Yes, here it is," and Marrabel took a coin from his pocket with alacrity, and laying it on the desk turned hopefully to go.

"Thanks, but—one moment—what is this?"

The unhappy man looked at the coin he had just produced and turned paler than before.

"I must have picked up the wrong one," he muttered, beginning to recognize the hopeless morass he was floundering into.

"Look again," said a quiet voice as Mr Carrados appeared on the scene. "Look closer at the coin you brought from your room this morning!"

"You blind devil!" Lightly scratched on the surface of the silver he found the signature "Max Carrados" and the date of that very day. "This is your doing all through!"

"If it is it is only to show up a scoundrel. You didn't stick at getting two innocent people suspected by your scheme. Let them see you now."

As if worked by machinery an inner door fell open and Miss Frensham and Muir walked in and stood silently regarding him.

"At the sale," continued Carrados pitilessly, "you were both publicly put in a position of some suspicion by the disappearance of a coin. It is right that you should now know that it was deliberately stolen by Mr Marrabel here. He is the thief and your perfect innocence is established."

"Well, curse it all, it wasn't entirely my fault," snarled Marrabel. "I only accepted what was given me."

"That will be for a judge and jury to assess. You'll give him in charge now, Travis?"

At this prospect Marrabel's last vestige of pretence broke down. All the poltroonery in the man came to the surface with a rush.

"For God's sake don't do that, Travis," he cried, clutching him by the sleeve. "I'll do anything you wish—confess anything you like—only don't have me sent to prison. I'll put all sorts of things your way, and I know crowds of people. Heavens! Man, consider what it would mean to me—one of your own class."

"What shall we do, Carrados? We never like to prosecute."

"I know you don't," replied the blind man. "I've already drawn up his confession. Read this and then sign it, Mr Marrabel, and we will all be witnesses of the spontaneous act of reparation on your part."

"What are you going to do with it?" asked the unfortunate wretch.

"Keep it as a guarantee of future good behaviour, and to vindicate these others if the necessity occurs. And you needn't think of having me knifed to get it back again, because I shan't carry it in my pocketbook."

Marrabel slowly signed and then stabbed the polished desk with the pen he held in a gust of passion that left his fingers pierced and bleeding.

"I'd go willingly to hell if I could first see you skinned alive, Carrados," he said as he turned to leave.

"I am sure you would," retorted Max Carrados pleasantly. "But I don't think that anything to do with me need affect your destination. Now go."

This did not happen last year nor yet the year before. Miss Frensham married her sub-editor, and their children—now old enough to go to school—frequently take prizes at quite important beauty competitions. Mr Marrabel almost immediately left these inhospitable shores, and after a seemly interval appeared in flourishing conditions in New York. Not that American connoisseurs know less than English ones do, but they know less of Mr Marrabel.

3

THE HOLLOWAY FLAT TRAGEDY

A good many years ago, when chance brought Max Carrados and Louis Carlyle together again and they renewed the friendship of their youth, the blind man's first inquiry had been a jesting, "Do you unearth many murders, Louis?" and the private detective's reply a wholly serious, "No; our business lies mostly on the conventional lines among defalcation and divorce." Since that day Carlyle's business had increased beyond the fondest dreams of its creator, but "defalcation and divorce" still constituted the bulwarks of his prosperity. Yet from time to time a more sensational happening or a more romantic course raised a case above the commonplace, but none, it is safe to say, ever rivalled in public interest the remarkable crime which was destined to become labelled in the current Press as "The Holloway Flat Tragedy."

It was Mr Carlyle's rule to see all callers who sought his aid, for the very nature of their business precluded clients from willingly unbosoming themselves to members of his office staff. Afterwards, they might accept the discreet attention of tactful subordinates, but for the first impression Carlyle well knew the value of his sympathetic handshake, his crisply reassuring voice, his—if need be—humanly condoning eye, and his impeccably prosperous person and surroundings. Men and women, guilty and innocent alike, pouring out their stories felt that at last they were really "understood", and, to give Louis Carlyle his due, the deduction was generally fully justified.

To the quiet Bampton Street establishment one September afternoon there came a new client who gave the name of Poleash and wished to see Mr Carlyle in person. There was, as usual, no difficulty about that, and, looking up from his desk, Louis registered the impression of an inconspicuous man, somewhere in the thirties. He used spectacles, wore a moustache, and his clothes were a lounge suit of dark material, cut on the simple lines affected by the prudent man who reflects that he may be wearing that selfsame garment two or three seasons hence. There was a slight air of untidiness—or rather, perhaps, an absence of spruceness in any detail—about his general appearance, and the experienced observer put him down as a middle-class worker in any of the clerical, lower professional, or non-manual walks of life.

"Now, Mr Poleash, sit down and tell me what I can do for you," said Carlyle when they had shaken hands—a rite to which the astute gentleman attached no slight importance and invariably offered. "Some trouble or little difficulty, I suppose, umph? But first let me get you name right and have your address for reference. You can rely on this, Mr Poleash"—the inclination of Mr Carlyle's head and the arrest of his lifted pen were undeniably impressive—"every word you utter is strictly confidential."

"Oh, that'll be all right, I'm sure," said the visitor carelessly. "It is rather out-of-the-way all the same, and at first—"

"The name?" insinuated Mr Carlyle persuasively.

"Albert Henry Poleash: P-o-l-e-a-s-h—twelve Meridon House, Sturgrove Road, Holloway."

"Thank you. Now, if you will."

"Of course I could tell you in a dozen words, but I expect you'd need to know the circumstances, so perhaps I may as well begin where I think you'll understand it best from."

"By all means," assented Mr Carlyle heartily; "by all means. In your own words and exactly as it occurs to you. I'm entirely at your service, so don't feel hurried. Do you care—" The production of a plain gold case completed the inquiry.

"To begin with," said Mr Poleash, after contributing a match to their common purpose, "I may say that I'm a married man, living with my wife at that address—a smallish flat which suits us very well as we have no children. Neither of us has any near relations either, and we keep ourselves pretty much to ourselves. Our only servant is a daily woman, who seems able to do everything that we require."

"One moment, if you please," interposed Mr Carlyle briskly. "I don't want you to do anything but tell your story in your own way, Mr Poleash, but if you would indicate by a single word the nature of the event that concerns us it would enable me to judge which points are likely to be most vital to our purpose. Theft—divorce—blackmail—"

"No—murder," replied Mr Poleash with literal directness.

"Murder!" exclaimed the startled professional. "Do you mean that a murder has been committed?"

"No, not yet. I am coming to that. For ordinary purposes I generally describe myself as a rent-collector, but that is because official Jacks-in-office seem to have a morbid suspicion of anyone who is obviously not a millionaire calling himself independent. As a matter of fact, I have quite enough private income to serve my purpose. Most of it comes from small house property scattered about London. I see to the management of this myself and personally collect the rents. It takes a few days a week, gives me an interest, keeps me in exercise, and pays as well as anything else I could be doing in the tune."

"Quite so," encouraged the listener.

"That's always there," went on Mr Poleash, continuing his leisurely narrative with no indication of needing any encouragement, "but now and then I take up other work if it suits me—certain kinds of special canvassing; sometimes research. I don't want to slave making more money than we have the need of, and I don't want ever to find that we haven't enough money for anything we may require."

"Ideal," contributed Mr Carlyle. "You are a true philosopher."

"My wife also has no need to be dependent on anyone either," continued Mr Poleash, without paying the least attention to the suave compliment. "As a costume designer and fashion artist she is fully qualified to earn her living, and in fact up to a couple of years ago she did work of that kind regularly. Then she had a long illness that made a great change in her. This brings me to one of the considerations that affect whatever I may wish to do: The illness left her a nervous wreck—jumpy, excitable, not altogether reasonable."

"Neurasthenia," was Mr Carlyle's seasonable comment. "The sympton of the age."

"Very likely. It doesn't affect me—at least it doesn't affect me directly. Living in the same house with Mrs Poleash, it's bound to affect me, because I have to consider how every blessed thing I do will affect her. And just lately something very lively indeed has come along.

"There is a girl in a shop that I got friendly with—no, I don't want you to put her name down yet. It began a year or eighteen months... But I don't suppose that matters. The only thing I really think that I'm to blame about is that I never told her I was married. At first there was no reason why I should; afterwards—well, there was a certain amount of reason why I shouldn't. Anyhow, I suppose that it was bound to come out sooner or later, and it did, a few weeks ago. She said, quite nicely, that she thought we ought to get married as things were, and then, of course, I had to explain that we couldn't.

"I really hadn't the ghost of an idea that she'd take it so terribly to heart as she did. There's nothing of the Don Juan about me, as you can see at a glance. The thing had simply come about—one step leading to another. But she faulted clean away, and when she came to again she was like a solid block of ice to everything I said. And then to cap matters who should appear at that moment but a fellow she'd been half engaged to before I came along. She'd frequently spoken about this man—his jealousy and temper and so on—and begged me never to let him pick a quarrel with me. 'Peter' was the only name I ever heard him called by, but he was a foreign-looking fellow—an Italian, I think."

"'Pietro', perhaps?" suggested Mr Carlyle.

"No; 'Peter' she called him. 'Please take me back home, Peter,' was all she said, and off they went together without a word from either to me. Whenever I've seen her since it's been the same. 'Will I please leave her as there is nothing to be said?' and I've been trying to think of all manner of arrangements to put things right."

"The only arrangement that would seem likely to do that is the one that's out of your power to make," said Mr Carlyle.

"I suppose so. However, this Peter evidently had a different idea. This is what happened two nights ago. I woke up in the dark—it was about three o'clock I found afterwards—with one of those feelings you get that you've forgotten to do something. It was a letter that I should have posted: It was important that it got delivered some time the next day—the same day by then—and there it was in my breast pocket. I knew if I left it that I should never be up in time for the first morning dispatch, so I determined to slip out then and make sure of it.

"It would only be a matter of twenty minutes or so. There is a pillar-box nearer, but that isn't cleared early. I pulled on a few things and prepared to tiptoe out when a fresh thought struck me.

"Mrs Poleash is a very uncertain sleeper nowadays, and if she is disturbed it's ten to one if she gets off again, and for that reason we use different rooms. I knew better than wake her up to tell her I was going out, but at the same time there was just the possibility that she might wake and, hearing some noise, look in at my door to see if I was all right. If she found me gone she would nearly have a fit. On the spur of the moment I pushed the bolster down the bed and rucked up my dressing gown—it was lying about—above it. In the poor light it served very well for a sleeping man, and I knew that she would not disturb me.

"In less time than I'd given myself I had done my business and was back again at the building. I was entering—my hand was on the knob of the outer door in fact—when the door was pulled sharply open from the other side and another man and I came face to face on the step. We both fell back a bit, I think, but the next moment he had pushed past me and was hurrying down the street. There was just enough light from the lamp across the way for me to be certain of him; it was Peter, and I'm pretty sure that he was equally sharp in recognizing me.

"Of course I went up the stairs in double quick time after that. The door of the flat was as I had left it—simply on the handle as I had put up the latch catch, never dreaming of anyone coming along in that time—and all was quiet and undisturbed inside. But one thing was different in my room, although it took me a few minutes to discover it. There was a clean cut through my dressing gown, through the sheet, through the bolster. Someone, Mr Carlyle, had driven a knife well home before he discovered his mistake."

"But that was plain evidence of an attempt to murder," declared Mr Carlyle feelingly—he disliked crimes of violence from every point of view. "Your business is obviously to inform the police."

"No," replied the visitor slowly, "no. Of course I thought of that, but I soon had to let it slide. What would it mean? Visits, inquiries, cross-examinations, explanations. Everything must come out. After a sufficient exhibition of nerve-storm

Mrs Poleash would set about getting a divorce and I should have to go through that. Then I suppose I should have to marry the other one, and, when all's said and done, that's the last thing I really want. In any case, my home would be broken up and my whole life spoiled. No, if it comes to that I might just as well be dead."

"Then what do you propose doing, may I ask? Calmly wait to be assassinated?"

"That's exactly what I came to see you about. You know my position, my difficulty. I understand that you are a man of wide experience. Putting aside the police and certain publicity, what should you advise?"

"Well, well," admitted the expert, "it's rather a formidable handicap, but we will do the best for you that is to be done. Can you indicate exactly what you want?"

"I can easily indicate exactly what I don't want. I don't want to be murdered or molested and I don't want Mrs Poleash to get wind of what's been going on."

"Why not go away for a time? Meanwhile we could find out who your man is and keep him under observation."

"I might do that—unless Kitty took it into her head that she didn't want to go, and then, of course, I couldn't leave her alone in the flat just now. After Tuesday night's business—this is what concerns me most—should you think it likely that the fellow would come again or not?"

Mr Carlyle pondered wisely. The longer he took over an opinion, he had discovered—providing he kept up the right expression—the greater weight attached to his pronouncement.

"No," he replied with due authority. "I should say not—not in anything like the same way. Of course he will naturally assume that you will now take due precautions—probably imagine that the police are after him. What sort of fastenings have you to your doors and windows?"

"Nothing out of the way. They are old flats and not in very good repair. The outer door is never kept locked, night or day. The front door of our flat has a handle, a latch lock, and a mortice lock. During the day it is simply kept on the latch; at night we fasten the other lock, but do not secure the latch, so that the woman can let herself in when she comes—she has one set of keys, I another, and Mrs Poleash the third."

"But when you were out on Tuesday night there was no lock fastened, I understand?"

"That is so. Simply the handle to turn. I purposely fastened the latch lock out of action as I found at the door that I hadn't the keys with me and I didn't want to go back to the room again."

"And the inner doors?"

"They have locks, but few now work—either the key is lost or the lock broken. We never trouble about them—except Kitty's room. She has scrupulously locked that at night, since she has had burglars among other nerve fancies."

Mr Carlyle shook his head.

"You ought at the very least to have the locks put right at once. Practically all windows are fitted with catches that a child can push back with a table-knife."

"That's all very well, but, you see, if I get a locksmith in I shall have to make up some cock-and-bull story about house-breaking to Mrs Poleash, and that will set her off. And, anyway, we are on the third storey up."

"If you are going to consider your wife's nerves at every turn, my dear sir," remarked Mr Carlyle with some contempt, from the security of his single state, "you will begin to find yourself in rather a tight fix, I am afraid. How are you going to account for the cut linen, for instance?"

"Oh, I've arranged all that," replied Mr Poleash, nodding sagaciously. "My dressing gown she will never notice. The sheet and bolster case—it was a hot night so there was only a single sheet fortunately—I have hidden away in a drawer for the present and put others in their place. I shall buy another of each and burn or lose these soon—Kitty doesn't keep a very close check on things. The bolster itself I can sew up well enough before it's noticed."

"You may be able to keep it up," was Mr Carlyle's dubious admission. "At all events," he continued, "as I understand it, you want me to advise you on the lines of taking no direct action against the man you call Peter and at the same time adopting no precautions that would strike Mrs Poleash as being unusual?"

"Nothing that would suggest burglars or murder to her just now," assented Poleash. "Yes; that's about what it comes to. You may be able to give me a useful tip or two. If not—well, I know it's a tough proposition and I don't grudge the outlay."

"At least let us see," replied the professional man, never failing on the side of lack of self-confidence. "Now as regards—"

It redounds to Louis Carlyle's credit as an inquiry agent that in an exacting world no serious voice ever accused him of taking unearned money; for so long as there was anything to be learned he plied his novel client with questions, explored surmises and bestowed advice. Even when they had come to the end of useful conversation and the prolific notebook had been closed Carlyle lingered on the topic.

"It's an abnormal situation, Mr Poleash, and full of professional interest. I shall keep it in mind, you may be sure, and if anything further occurs to me, why, I will let you know."

"Please don't write on any account," begged Mr Poleash with sudden earnestness. "In fact, I'd ask you to put a line to that effect across my address. You see, I'm liable to be out at any post time, and if my wife should happen to get curious about a strange letter, why, that, in the language of the kerb, would blow the gaff."

"I see," assented Mr Carlyle. "Very well; it shall be just as you like."

"And if I can settle with you now," continued Poleash; "for of course I don't want to have an account sent. Then some day—say next week—I might look in to report and to hear if you have anything further to suggest."

"You might, in the meanwhile, consider the most practical course—that of having your man kept under observation."

"I will," promised the other. "But so far I'm all in favour of letting sleeping dogs lie."

Not unnaturally Mr Carlyle had heard that line before and had countered it.

"True, but it is as well to know when they wake up again," he replied. With just the necessary touch of dignity and graciousness he named and received the single guinea at which he assessed the interview and began to conduct Mr Poleash towards the door—not the one by which he had entered from the waiting-room but another leading directly down into the street. "Have you lost something?"

"Only my hat and things—I left them in your ante-room." He held up his gloved left hand as though it required a word of explanation. "I keep this on because I am short of a finger, and I've noticed that some people don't like to see it."

"We'll go out that way instead then—it's all the same," remarked Carlyle, as he crossed to the other door

Two later callers were sitting in the waiting-room, and at the sight of them Mr Carlyle's somewhat cherubic face at once assumed an expression of the heartiest welcome. But beyond an unusually mellifluent "Good afternoon!" he said nothing until his departing client was out of hearing. Names were not paraded in those precincts. With a muttered apology Mr Poleash recovered his belongings from among the illustrated papers and hurried away.

"And why in the world have you been waiting here, Max, instead of sending in to me?" demanded the hospitable Carlyle with a show of indignation.

"Business," replied Mr Carrados tersely. "Your business, understand. Your chief minion was eager to blow a message through to you but 'No,' I said, 'we'll take our proper turn'. Why should I interrupt the Bogus Company Promoter's confession or cut short the Guilty Husband's plea?"

"Joking apart, that fellow who just went brought a very remarkable story," said Mr Carlyle. "I should be glad to know what you would have had to say to him when we have time to go into it." (Do not be too ready to condemn the gentleman as an arrant humbug and this a gross breach of confidence: Max Carrados had been appointed Honorary Consultant to the firm, so that what would have otherwise been grave indiscretions were strictly business discussions.)

"In the meantime the suggestion is that you haven't taken a half-day off lately and that Monday morning is a convenient time."

"Generous man! What is happening on Monday morning then?"

"Something rather surprising in wireless at the Imperial Salon—ten to twelve-thirty. I know it's the sort of thing you'll be interested in, and I have two tickets and want someone fairly intelligent to go with."

"An ideal chain of circumstances," rippled Mr Carlyle. "I shall endeavour to earn the price of my seat."

"I am sure you will succeed," retorted Carrados. "By the way, it's free."

To a strain of this intellectual horseplay the arrangements for their meeting were made, and that having been the only reason for the call, Mr Carrados departed under Parkinson's watchful escort. In due course the wireless demonstration took place, but (although an invention then for the first time shown bore no small part in one of the blind man's subsequent cases) it is unnecessary to accompany them inside the hall, for with the enigma centring in Mr Poleash that event had no connexion. It is only touched upon as bringing Carrados and his friend together at that hour, for as they walked along Pall Mall after lunching Mr Carlyle suddenly gave a whistle of misgiving and surprise and stopped a hurrying newsboy.

"Holloway Flat Tragedy," he read from the bill as he investigated sundry pockets for the exact coin. "By gad, if that should happen to be—"

"Poleash! My God, it is!" he exclaimed as soon as his eye had found the paragraph concerned—a mere inch in the "Stop Press" news. "Poor beggar! Tshk! Tshk!"—his clicking tongue expressed disapproval and regret. "He ought to have known better after what had happened. It was madness. I wonder what he actually did—"

"Your remarkable caller of last Thursday, Louis?"

"Yes; but how do you come to know?"

"A trifling indiscretion on his part. With a carelessness that must be rare among your clients I should say, Mr Poleash dropped one of his cards under the table in your writing-room, where the conscientious Parkinson discovered it."

"Well, the unfortunate chap doesn't need cards now. Listen, Max.

"NORTH LONDON TRAGEDY

"Early this morning a charwoman going to a flat in Meridon House, Holloway, made a gruesome discovery. Becoming suspicious at the untouched milk and newspapers, she looked into a bedroom and there found the occupier, a Mr Poleash, dead in bed. He had received shocking injuries, and everything points to deliberate murder. Mrs Poleash is understood to be away on a holiday in Devonshire.

"Of course Scotland Yard takes it up now, but I must put my information at their service. They're devilish lucky, too. I can practically hand over the miscreant to them and they will scoop the credit."

"I was to hear about that," Carrados reminded him. "Suppose we walk across to Scotland Yard, and you can tell me on the way."

At the corner of Derby Street they encountered two men who had just turned out of the Yard. The elder had the appearance of being a shrewd farmer, showing his likely son the sights of London and keeping a wideawake eye for its notorious pitfalls. To pursue appearances a step farther they might even have been calling to recover the impressive umbrella that the senior carried.

"Beedel," dropped Mr Carlyle beneath his breath, but his friend was already smiling recognition.

"The very man," said Carrados genially. "I'll wager you can tell us something about the Poleash arrangements, inspector."

The two plain-clothes men exchanged amused glances.

"I can tell you this much, Mr Carrados," replied Inspector Beedel, in unusually good spirits, "my nephew George here is going to do the work and I'm going to look after the bouquets at the finish. We're on our way there now."

"Couldn't be better," said the blind man. "Perhaps you wouldn't mind us going up there with you?"

"Very pleased," replied Beedel. "We were making for the station."

"You may as well help to fill our taxi," suggested Carrados. "Mr Carlyle may have something to tell you on the way."

On the whole Mr Carlyle would have preferred to make his disclosure to headquarters, but the convenience of the arrangement was not to be denied, and with a keen appreciation of the astonishing piece of luck Beedel and George heard the story of the inquiry agent's client.

"It looks like being simply a matter of finding this girl, if the conditions up there bear out his tale," remarked George, between satisfaction at so veritable a clue and a doubt whether he would not have preferred a more complicated case. "Did you happen to get her name and address, sir?"

"No," admitted Mr Carlyle with a slight aloofness, "it did not arise. Poleash was naturally reluctant to bring in the lady more than he need and I did not press him."

"Makes no odds," conceded George generously. "Shopgirl—kept company with a foreigner—known as Peter. Even without anything else there ought to be no difficulty in finding her."

Sturgrove Road was not deserted, and there was a rapid concentration about the door of Meridon House "to see the "tecs arrive." On the whole, public opinion was disappointed in their appearance, but the action of George in looking up at the frontage of the building and then glancing sharply right and left along the road was favourably commented on. The policeman stationed at the outer door admitted them at once.

A sergeant and a constable of the local division were in possession of No. 12, and the scared daily woman, temporarily sustained by their impression of absolute immobility, was waiting in the kitchen to indicate whatever was required. Greetings on a slightly technical plane passed between the four members of the force.

"Mrs Poleash has been sent for, I suppose?" asked Mr Carlyle.

"We telephoned from our office to Torquay some hours ago," replied the sergeant. "They'll send an officer to the place she's staying at and break it to her as well as possible. That's the course we usually follow." He took out a weighty presentation watch and considered it. "Torquay. I don't suppose she could be here yet."

"Not even if she was in first go," amplified his subordinate.

"Well," suggested George. "Suppose we look round?" The bedroom was the first spot visited. There was nothing unusual to be seen, apart from the outline of the bed, its secret now hidden beneath a decorous covering—nothing beyond the rather untidy details of the occupant's daily round. All these would in due course receive a careful scrutiny, but at the moment one point drew every eye.

"Hold one another's hands," advised the sergeant, as he prepared to turn down the sheet. The hovering charwoman gave a scream and fled.

"That's a wild beast been at work," said Inspector Beedel, coolly drawing nearer to appreciate the details.

"My word, yes!" agreed George, following a little reluctantly.

"Shocking! Shocking!" Mr Carlyle made no pretence about turning away.

"Killed at the first blow," continued the sergeant, indicating, "though it's not the only one. Then his face slashed about like a fancy loaf till his own mother wouldn't know him. Something dreadful, isn't it? Finger gone? Oh, that's an old affair. What're you to make of it all?"

"Revenge—revenge and rage and sheer blood-thirstiness," summed up Mr Carlyle. "Was anything taken?"

"Nothing disturbed so far as we can see, and the old party there"—a comprehensive nod in the direction of the absent charlady—"says that all the things she knows of seem to be right."

"What time do they put it at?" asked Beedel.

"Dr Meadows has been here. Midnight Saturday to early Sunday morning, he said. That agrees with the people at the flat opposite hearing the door locked at about ten on Saturday night and the Sunday morning milk and paper not being touched."

"Milk-can on the doorstep all day, I suppose?" suggested someone.

"Yes; people opposite noticed it, but thought nothing of it. They knew Mrs Poleash was going away on Saturday and thought that he might have gone with her. Mrs Jones, she doesn't come on Sundays, so nothing was found but till this morning."

"May as well hear what she has to say now," said Beedel. "No need to keep her about that I know of."

"Just one minute, please, if you don't mind," put in Mr Carlyle, not so much asking anyone's permission as directing the affair. The sight of a wardrobe had reminded him of the dead man's story, and he was now handling the clothes that hung there with keen anticipation. "There is something that I really came especially to see. This is his dressing gown, and, yes, by Jupiter, it's here!"

He pointed to a clean cut through the material as they gathered round him.

"What's that?" inquired the sergeant, looking from one face to another.

"Previous attempt," replied Beedel shortly.

"There ought to be a sheet and a bolster case somewhere about," continued the eager gentleman, now thoroughly intrigued, and under the impulse of his zeal drawers and cupboards were opened and their contents gingerly displaced.

"Something of the sort here among the shirts," announced George.

"Have them out then. Not likely to be any others put away there." The hidden things were unfolded and displayed and here also the tragic evidence lay clear before them.

"By gad, you know, I half thought he might have dreamt it until this came," confided Mr Carlyle to the room at large. "Tshk! Tshk! How on earth the fellow could have gone—" He remembered the quiet figure lying within earshot and finished with a tolerant shrug.

"Let's get on," said Beedel. These details could very well have waited had been his thought all along.

"I'll fold the things," volunteered Mr Carrados. All the others had satisfied their curiosity by glance or scrutiny and he was free to take his time. He took up the loose bundle in his arms and with the strange impulse towards light that so often moved him he turned away from them and sought the window.

"Now, missis, come along and tell us all about it," called out the young constable.

"No," interposed the inspector kindly, "the poor creature's upset enough already without bringing her in here again. Stay where you are, Mrs Jones, we're coming there," he announced from the door, and they filed along the skimpy passage into the dingy kitchen. "Now can you just tell us quietly what you know about this bad business?"

Mrs Jones's testimony, given on the frequently expressed understanding that she was quite prepared to be struck dead at any point of it if she deviated from the strictest line of truth, did not disclose any new feature, while its frequent references to the lives and opinions of friends not concerned in the progress of the drama threatened now and then to stifle the narrative with a surfeit of pronouns. But she was listened to with patience and complimented on her nerve. Mrs Jones sadly shook her antique black bonnet and disclaimed the quality.

"I could do nothing but stand and scream," she confessed wistfully, referring to the first dreadful moment at the bedroom door, "I stood and screamed three times before I could get myself away. The poor gentleman! What harm was he, for to be done in like that!"

There was a string of questions from one or another of the company before she was finally dismissed—generally from Beedel or George with Mr Carlyle's courteously assertive voice intervening once or twice: the Poleashes had few visitors that she had ever seen—she was only there from eight to six—and she had never known of anyone staying with them; no one had knocked at the door for anything on Saturday; she had not noticed anyone whom she could call to mind as "a foreigner" loitering about or at the door recently (a foreign family lived at No. 5, but they were well spoken of); neither Mr nor Mrs Poleash had talked to her of anything uncommon of late—the gentleman was mostly out and "she" wasn't one of the friendly sort; the couple seemed to get on together "as well as most", and she had never heard a "real" quarrel; Mrs Poleash had gone off for a week (she understood) about noon on Saturday, and Mr Poleash had accompanied her to Paddington (as he had mentioned on his return for tea); she had last seen him at about five o'clock on Saturday, when she left, a little earlier than usual; she knew nothing of the ashes in the kitchen grate, not having had a fire there for weeks past; the picture post card (passed round) from Mrs Poleash, announcing her arrival at Torquay, she had found on the hall floor together with the Sunday paper; she was to go on just the same while Mrs Poleash was away, coming daily to "do up", and so on; it was a regular arrangement "week in and week out".

"That seems to be about all," summed up Inspector Beedel, looking round. "We have your address, Mrs Jones, and you're sure to hear from us about something pretty soon."

"Before you go," said a matter-of-fact voice from the door, "do you happen to remember what you were doing last Thursday afternoon?" It was the first question that Mr Carrados had put, and they had scarcely noticed whether he had rejoined them yet or not.

"Last Thursday afternoon?" repeated Mrs Jones helplessly. "Oh, Lor", sir, my head's in that whirl—"

"Yes, but it isn't so difficult if you think—early closing day, you know."

This stimulus proved effective and the charwoman remembered. She had something special to remember by. On Thursday morning Mrs Poleash has passed on to her a single ticket for that afternoon's performance at the Parkhurst

Theatre, and told her that she could go after she had washed up the dinner things.

"So that you were not here at all on Thursday afternoon? Just one more thing, Mrs Jones. Sooner or later a photograph of your master will be wanted. Is there one anywhere about?"

"The only one I know of stands on the sideboard in the little room. There may be others put away, but not being what you might call curious sir—"

"I'm sure you're not," agreed Carrados. "Now, as you go you shall point it out to us so that there can be no mistake."

"You couldn't make no mistake because there's only that and one of her stands there," explained Mrs Jones, but she proceeded to comply. "There it—"

"Yes?" said the blind man, close upon her.

"I'm sorry, sir, indeed. I must have made a mistake—"

"I don't think you made any mistake," he urged. "I don't think you really think so either."

"I'm that mithered I don't rightly know what to think," she declared. "That isn't him."

"Is it the frame? No, don't touch it—that might be unlucky, you know—but you can remember that."

"It's the frame, right enough. I ought to know, the times I've dusted it."

"Then the photograph has been changed: there's nothing unlikely in that. When was the last time that you noticed the other one there?"

Quite recently, it would seem, but taking refuge behind her whirling head Mrs Jones held out against precision. It might have been Friday or it might have been Saturday. Carrados forbore to press her more exactly, and she departed, sustained by the advice of Authority that she should have nothing to say to nobody, under the excuse, if need be, that she had answered enough questions already for one day.

"While we are here," said the sergeant—they were still in the "little room", the only one that looked out on the front "you might as well see where he got in." He went to the window and indicated certain marks on the wood- and stone-work. "We found the lower sash still a few inches up when we came."

"Went the same way as he came, I suppose?" suggested George.

"Must have done. All the keys are accounted for, and Mrs Jones found the front door locked as usual. And why not; why shouldn't he? There's the balcony, and you hardly have to lean out to see the stairway window not a yard away. Why, it's as easy as ring-a-roses. Might have been made for it."

"Tshk! Tshk!" fumed Mr Carlyle unhappily. "After what I said. And not one of the locks has been seen to."

"Locks?" echoed the young policeman, appearing that moment at the door. "Why, here is a chap with tools, says he's come to repair and fit the locks!"

"Well, if this isn't the fair *nefus ultra*!" articulated the sergeant. "However, show him in, lad."

The locksmith, looking scarcely less alarmed than if he had fallen into a den of thieves, had a very short and simple tale to tell. His shop was in the Seven Sisters Road, and on Friday afternoon a gentleman had called there and arranged with him to come on Monday and repair some locks. He had given the name of Poleash and that address. The man knew nothing of what had taken place and had come as fixed.

"It's a pity you didn't happen to make it Saturday, Mr Hipwaite," said Inspector Beedel, as he took a note of this new evidence. "It might—I don't say it would, but it might—have prevented murder being done."

"But that's the very thing I was not to do," declared Hipwaite, with some warmth. "'Don't come on Saturday because the wife is very nervous, and if she thinks burglars are about she'll have a fit,' he said—those very words. 'She'll be away on Monday, and then by the time she comes back she mayn't notice.' Was I likely to come on Saturday?"

Plainly he was not. "That's all right," it was conceded, "but there's nothing in your line doing today." So Mr Hipwaite departed, more than half persuaded that he had been hardly used and not in the least mollified by being concerned in so notable a tragedy.

"Before I go," resumed the sergeant, leading the way back to the kitchen, "there's one other thing I must hand over. You heard what Mrs Jones said about the fire—that there hadn't been one for weeks as they always used the stove?"

"That's what I asked her," George reminded him. "Someone has had a fire here."

"Correct," continued the officer imperturbably. "It's also what I asked her a couple of hours before you came. Someone's had a fire here. Who and what for? Well, I've had the cinders out to see and now I'll make over to you what there was."

"Glove fasteners," commented the inspector, "All the metal there was about them. Millions of the pattern, I suppose."

"Burned his gloves after the job—they must have been in a fair mess," said George. "'Audubon Frères' they're stamped—foreign make."

"That reminds me—there's one thing more." It was produced from the sergeant's pocket-book, a folded fragment of paper, charred along its edge. "It's from the hearth; evidently a bit that fell out when the fire was made. Foreign newspaper, you will see; Italian it looks to me."

Mr Carlyle, Inspector Beedel, and George exchanged appreciative glances. Upon this atmosphere of quiet satisfaction there fell something almost like a chuckle.

"Did anyone happen to notice if he had written '*Si parla Italiano*' in red on the wall over the bed?" inquired the guileless voice.

The young constable, chancing to be the nearest person to the door, rose to this mendacious suggestion by offering to go and see. The others stared at the blind man in various stages of uncertainty.

"No, no," called out Mr Carlyle feelingly. "There is no need to look, thank you. When you know Mr Carrados as well as I do you will understand that although there is always something in what he says it is not always the something you think it is. Now, Max, pray enlighten the company. Why should the murderer write 'Italian spoken' over the bed?"

"Obviously to make sure that you shouldn't miss it," replied Mr Carrados.

"Well," remarked the sergeant, demonstrating one or two simple exercises in physical drill as a suitable preparation, "I may as well be going. I don't understand Italian myself. Nor Dutch either," he added cryptically.

Mr Carlyle also had nothing more to stay for. "If you have done here, Max—" he began, and turned only to find that Carrados was no longer there.

"Your friend has just gone to the front room, sir," said the constable, catching the words as he passed. "Funny to see a blind man getting about so—" But a sudden crash of glass from the direction referred to cut short the impending compliment.

It was, as Carrados explained, entirely his own preposterous fault. Nothing but curiosity about the size of the room had impelled him to touch the walls, and the picture, having a weak cord or an insecure nail...had it not brought something else down in its fall?

"Only the two frames from the sideboard, so far as I can see," replied Carlyle. "All the glass is shattered. But I don't suppose that Mrs Poleash will be in a condition to worry about trifles. Jolly good thing you aren't hurt, that's all."

"Of course I should like to replace the damage," said the delinquent.

Inspector Beedel said nothing, but as he looked on he recalled one or two other mischances in the past, and being of an introspective nature he continued to massage his chin thoughtfully.

* * * * *

Three days later the inquest on the body of Albert Henry Poleash was opened. It was of the merest formal description, proof of identity and a bare statement of the cause of death being the only evidence put forward. An adjournment for a week was then declared.

At the resumed inquiry the story of Poleash's death was taken forward, and the newspaper reader for the first time was encouraged to see in it the promise of a first-class popular sensation. Louis Carlyle related the episode of his unexpected client. Corroboration of that wildly romantic story was forthcoming from many sides. Mr Hipwaite carried the drama two days later by describing the dead man's visit to his shop, the order to repair the locks, and his own futile journey to the flat. Mrs Jones, skilfully piloted among dates and details, was in evidence as the discoverer of the body. Two doctors—a private practitioner called hurriedly in at the first alarm and the divisional surgeon—agreed on all essential points, and the police efficiently bridged the narration at one stage and another and contrived to present a faithful survey of the tragedy.

But the most arresting figure of the day, though her evidence was of very slight account and mainly negative, was the unhappy widow. As she moved into the witness-box, a wan, graceful creature in her unaccustomed, but, it may be said, not unattractive crêpe, a rustle of compassion stirred the court and Mr Carlyle, who had come prejudiced against her, as an automatic reflex of his client's fate, chirruped sympathy.

Mrs Poleash gave her testimony in a low voice, not particularly attractive in its tone, and she looked straight before her with eyes neither downcast nor wandering. Her name, she said, was Katherine Poleash, her age twenty-nine. She knew nothing of the tragedy, having been in Torquay at the time. She had gone there on the Saturday afternoon, her husband seeing her off from Paddington. Their relationship was perfectly friendly, but not demonstrative. Her husband was a considerate but rather reserved man with no especial interests. Up to two years ago she had been accustomed to earn her own living, but a nervous breakdown had interfered with her capacity for work. It was on account of that illness that she had generally occupied a separate bedroom; it had left her nervous in many ways, but she was surprised to hear that she should have been described as exacting or ill-tempered.

"'Not wholly reasonable and excitable' were the precise terms used, I think," put in Mr Carlyle gallantly.

"It's much the same," she replied apathetically.

Continuing, she had no knowledge at all of any intrigue between her husband and a shop-girl, such as had been referred to, nor had she ever heard of the man Peter, either by name or as an Italian. She could not suggest in what quarter of London the shop in question was likely to be as the deceased was accustomed to go about a good deal. The police already had a list of the various properties he owned. At the conclusion of her evidence Mrs Poleash seemed to be on the point of fainting and had to be assisted out.

There was nothing to be gained by a further adjournment. The cause of death—the real issue before that court—was reasonably clear. The jury brought in a verdict of "Wilful Murder against Some Person or Persons Unknown." Before the reporters left the police asked that the Press should circulate a request for anyone having knowledge of a shop-assistant who had been friendly with a foreigner known as Peter or Pietro, or with a man answering to Mr Poleash's description, to communicate with them either at New Scotland Yard or to any local station. The Press promised to comply and offered to publish photographs of Mr Poleash as a means towards that end, only to learn that no photograph possessing identification value could be found. So began the memorable paper-chase for an extremely nebulous shop-assistant and a foreigner whose description began and ended with the sobriquet "Peter the Italian".

* * * * *

"I was wondering if you or Inspector Beedel would come round one day to see me," said Mr Carrados as George was shown into the study at The Turrets. Two full weeks had elapsed since the conclusion of the inquest and the newspaper value of the Holloway Flat Tragedy had sunk from a column opposite the leader page to a six-line fill-up beneath "Home and General". "Your uncle used often to drop in to entertain me with the progress of his cases."

"That wasn't his way of looking at it, Mr Carrados. He used to say that when it came to seeing through a brick wall you were—well, hell!"

"Curious," remarked Mr Carrados. "I don't remember ever hearing Inspector Beedel make use of that precise expression."

George went a trifle red and laughed to demonstrate his self-possession.

"Well, perhaps I dropped a word of my own in by accident." he said. "But that was what he meant—in a complimentary sense, of course. As a matter of fact, it was on his advice that I ventured to trouble you now."

"Not 'trouble'," protested the blind man, ever responsive to the least touch of diffidence. "That's another word the inspector wouldn't use about me, I'm sure."

"You're very kind," said George, accepting a cigarette, "and as I had to come this way to see another—oh, my Lord, another!—shop-girl, why, I thought—"

"Ah; how is the case going?"

"It's no go, Mr Carrados. We've seen thousands of shopgirls and hundreds of Italian Peters. I'm beginning to think," said the visitor, watching Mr Carrados's face as he propounded the astonishing heresy, "that there is no such person."

"Yes?" replied Carrados unmoved. "It is always as well to look beyond the obvious, isn't it? What does the inspector say?"

"He says, 'I should like to know what Mr Carrados really meant by "Italian spoken", and what he really did when he smashed that picture'."

Carrados laughed his appreciation as he seemed actually to watch the blue smoke curling upwards.

"How easy it is to give a straightforward answer when a plain question is asked," he replied. "By '*Si parla Italiano*' I ventured to insinuate my own private opinion that there was no Italian Peter; when I broke the picture I tried to obtain some definite evidence of someone there was."

George waited in the hope of this theme developing, but his host seemed to consider that he had said all that was necessary, and it is difficult to lead on a man into disclosures when you cannot fix him with your eye.

"Poleash may have been mistaken himself," he continued tentatively; "or he may have purposely misled Mr Carlyle on details, with the idea of getting his advice but not entirely trusting him to the full extent."

"He may," admitted the placid smoker.

"One thing I can't understand is however the man set about keeping company with a girl without spending more on her than he seems to have done. We found a small pocket diary that he entered his current expenses in, and there isn't a single item for chocolates, flowers, theatres, or anything of that sort."

"A diary?"

"Oh, he didn't keep a diary; only entered cash, and rents received, and so on. Here it is, if you care to—examine it."

"Thank you, I should. I wonder what our friend Carlyle charged for the consultation?"

"I don't remember seeing that," admitted George, referring to the pages. "Thursday, the 3rd, wasn't it? No, curiously enough, that doesn't appear... I wonder if he never put down any of these what you might call questionable items for fear of Mrs Poleash seeing?"

"Not unnaturally," agreed Carrados. "You found nothing else of interest then—no addresses or new names?"

"Nothing at all. Oh, that page you've got is only his memorandum of sizes and numbers and so on."

"Yes; quite a useful habit, isn't it?" The long, vibrant fingers touched offline after line without a pause or stumble. "When he made this handy list Albert Henry Poleash little thought—Boots, size 9; hat, size 1/8; collars, size 16; gloves, size 8¾; watch, No. 31903; weight, 11st. 81bs. There we have the man: *Ex pede Herculem*, as the motto has it—only in this case of course the hat and gloves are more useful."

"Very true, sir," said George, whose instinct was to keep a knowing front on all occasions.

When Parkinson was summoned to the room some time later he found his master there alone. Every light was blazing on, and, sitting at his desk, Mr Carrados confronted a single sheet of paper. With his trained acuteness for the minutiae of every new condition, Parkinson immediately took mental photographs of the sheet of paper with its slim written column, of the position and appearance of the chair George had used, of the number and placing of cigarette ends and matches, of all the details connected with the tray and contents, and of a few other matters. It was his routine.

"Close the door and come in," said Carrados. "I want you to carry your mind back about four weeks to the last occasion when we called at Mr Carlyle's office together. As we sat in the waiting-room I asked you if the things left there belonged to anyone we knew."

"I remember the circumstances perfectly, sir."

"I want the articles described. The gloves?"

"There was only one glove—that for the right hand. It was a dark grey *suède*, moderately used, and not of the best cut. The fastening was a press button stamped 'Audubon Frères'. The only marking inside the glove was the size, 7½."

Carrados made a note on the sheet before him. "The hat?" he said. "What size was that?"

"The size of hat, printed on an octagonal white ticket, was 6¾, sir."

"Excellent, so far. When the caller passed through you saw him for a moment. Apart from clothes, which do not matter just now, was there any physical peculiarity that would identify him?"

"He had a small dark mole beneath the left eye. The lobe of his right ear was appreciably less than the other. The nail of the middle finger of the right hand was corrugated from an injury at some time."

Carrados made a final note on the paper before him.

"Very good indeed, Parkinson," he remarked. "That is all I wanted."

* * * * *

A month passed and nothing happened. Occasionally a newspaper, pressed for a subject, commented on the disquieting frequency with which undetected murder could be done, and among other instances mentioned the Holloway Flat Tragedy and deplored the ease with which Peter the Italian had remained at large. The name by that time struck the reader as distantly familiar.

Then one evening early in November Beedel rang Mr Carrados up. The blind man happened to take the call himself, and at the first words he knew that the dull, patient shadowing of weeks was about to fructify.

"Yes, Inspector Beedel himself, sir," said the voice at the other end. "I'm speaking from Beak Street. The two you know of have just gone to the Restaurant X in Warsaw Street. The lady has booked two seats at the Alhambra for tonight, so we expect them to be there for the best part of an hour."

"I'll come at once," replied Carrados. "What about Carlyle?"

"He's been notified. Back entrance in Boulton Court," said the inspector. "I'm off there now myself."

It was the first time that the two the blind man "knew of" had met since the watch was set, and their correspondence had been singularly innocuous. Yet not a breath of suspicion had been raised, and the same elaborate care that had prompted Mr Carrados to bring down a picture to cover the abstraction of a small square of glass had been maintained throughout.

"Nice private little room upstairs, saire," insinuated the proprietor as "the two" looked round. He guessed that they shunned publicity, and he was right, although not entirely so. With a curt nod the man led the way up the narrow stairway to the equivocal little den on the first floor. The general room below had not been crowded, but this one was wholly empty.

"Quite like old times," said the woman with an unmusical laugh as she threw off her cloak—there was little indication of the sorrowing widow now, "I thought we had better fight shy of the 'Toledo' for the future."

""M yes," replied her companion slowly, looking dubiously about him—he no longer wore glasses or moustache, nor was his left hand, the glove now removed, deficient of a finger. "The only thing is whether it isn't too soon for us to be about together at all."

"Pha!" she snapped expressively. "They've gone to sleep again. There isn't a thing—no not a single detail—gone wrong. The most that could happen would be a raid here to look for Peter the Italian!"

"For God's sake don't keep on that," he urged in a low voice. "Your husband was a brute to you by what you say, and I'm not sorry now it's done, but I want to forget it all. You had your way: I've done everything you planned. Now you are free and decently well off and as soon as it's safe we can really marry—if you still will."

"If I still will," she repeated, looking at him meaningly. "Do you know, Dick, I think it may become desirable sooner even than I thought."

"Sssh!" he warned; "here comes someone. You order, Kitty—you always have done! Anything will suit me." He turned to arrange his overcoat across an empty chair and reassured his hand among the contents of the nearest pocket.

Downstairs, in his nondescript living-room, the proprietor of the Restaurant X was being very quickly and efficiently made to understand just so much of the situation as turned on his immediate and complete acceptance of it. In the presence of authority so vigorously expressed the stout gentleman bowed profusely, lowered his voice, and from time to time placed a knowing finger on his lips in agreement.

"Hallo," said the man called "Dick" as a different attendant brought a dish. "Where has our other waiter got to?"

"Party of regular customers as always has him just come in." explained the new one. "Ope you don't mind, sir."

"Not a brass button."

"It's all right, inspector," reported the "waiter". "He has the three marks you said—mole, ear, nail."

"Certain of the woman?"

"Mrs Poleash, sure as snow."

"Any reference to it?"

"Don't think so while I'm about. Drama just now. Has his little gun handy."

"Take this in now. Leave the door open and see if you can make him talk up... If you two gentlemen will step just across there I think you'll be able to hear."

Carrados smiled as he proceeded to comply.

"I have already heard," he said. "It is the voice of the man who called on Mr Carlyle on September the third."

"I think it is the voice," admitted Mr Carlyle when he had tiptoed back again. "I really think so, but after two months I should not be prepared to swear."

"He is the man," repeated Carrados deliberately.

Inspector Beedel, clinking something quietly in his pocket, nodded to his waiter.

"Morgan follows you in with the coffee," he said. "Put it down on the table, Morgan, and stand beside the woman. Call me as soon as you have him."

It was the sweet that the first waiter was to take, and with it there was a sauce. It was not exactly overturned, but there was an awkward movement and a few drops were splashed. With a clumsy apology the waiter, napkin in hand, leaned across the customer to remove a spot that marked his coat-sleeve.

"Here!" exclaimed the startled man. "What the devil are you up to?"

It was too late. Speech was the only thing left to him then. His wrists were already held in a trained, relentless grasp; he was pressed helplessly back into his chair at the first movement of resistance. Kitty Poleash rose from her seat with a dreadful coldness round her heart, felt a hand upon her shoulder, cast one fearful glance round, and sank down upon her chair again. Before another word was spoken Inspector Beedel had appeared, and the grip of bone and muscle on the straining wrists was changed to one of steel. Less than thirty seconds bridged the whole astonishing transformation.

"Richard Crispinge, you are charged with the murder of this woman's husband. Katherine Poleash, you are held as an accessory," The usual caution followed. "Get a taxi to the back entance, Morgan."

Half a dozen emotions met on Crispinge's face as he shot a glance at his companion and then faced the accuser again.

"You're crazy," he panted, still labouring from the effort. "I've never even seen the man."

"I shouldn't say anything now, if I were you," advised Beedel, on a quite human note. "You may find out later that we know more than you might think."

What followed could not have been charged against human foresight, for at a later stage it was shown that a certain cable failed and in a trice one side of Warsaw Street was involved in darkness. What happened in that darkness—where they had severally stood before and after—who moved or spoke—whose hand was raised—were all matters of dispute, but suddenly the black was stabbed by a streak of red, a little crack—scarcely more than the sharp bursting of a paper bag—nearly caught up to it, and almost slowly to the awaiting ears came the sound of strain and the long crash of falling glass and china.

"A lamp from down there!" snapped Beedel's sorely-tried voice, as the ray of an electric torch whirled like a pygmy searchlight and then centred on a tumbled thing lying beyond the table. "Look alive!"

"They say there is gas somewhere," announced Mr Carlyle, striking a match as he ran in. "Ah, here it is."

No need to ask then what had happened, though how it had happened could never be set quite finally at rest; for if Kitty Poleash was standing now, whereas before she had sat, the weapon lay beyond her reach close to the shackled hands. A curious apathy seemed to fall upon the room as though the tang of the drifting wisp of smoke dulled their alertness, and when the woman moved slowly towards her lover Beedel merely picked the pistol up and waited. With a terrible calmness she knelt by the huddled form and raised the inert head.

"Good-bye, my dear," she said quietly, kissing the dead lips for the last time; "it's over." And with a strange tragic fitness she added, in the words of another fatal schemer, "We fail!"

She seemed to be the only one who had any business there; Beedel was abstracted; Carlyle and Carrados felt like spectators walking on a stage when the play is over. In the street below the summoned taxi throbbed unheeded; they were waiting for another equipage now. When that had moved off with its burden Kitty Poleash would follow her captors submissively, like a dog without a home.

"It isn't a feather in our caps to have a man slip away like that," remarked the inspector moodily as the two joined him for a word before they left; "but, of course, as far as they are both concerned, it's the very best that could have happened."

"In what way do you mean the best?" demanded Mr Carlyle with a professional keenness for the explicit.

"Why, look at what will happen now. He's saved all the trouble and thought of being hanged, which it was bound to be in, the end, and has got it over without a moment's worry. She will get the full benefit of it as well, because her counsel will now be able to pile it all up against the fellow and claim that he exercised an irresistible influence over her. Personally, I should say that it's twelve of one and thirteen of the other, and I don't know that she isn't the thirteen, but she is about as likely to be hanged as I am to be made superintendent tomorrow."

* * * * *

"Max," said Mr Carlyle, as they sat smoking together the same night, "when you think of the elaboration of that plot it was appalling."

"Curious," replied Carrados thoughtfully. "To me it seems absolutely simple and inevitable. Perhaps that is because I should have done it—fundamentally, that is—just the same way myself."

"And got caught the same way?"

"There were mistakes made. If you decide to kill a man you must do it either secretly or openly. If you do it secretly and it comes to light you are done for. If you do it openly there is the chance of putting another appearance on the crime.

"These two—Crispinge and Mrs Poleash—knew that in the ordinary way the killing of the husband would immediately attract suspicion to the wife. Under that fierce scrutiny it could not long be hidden that the woman had a lover, and the disclosure would be fatal. Indeed, if Poleash had lived, that fact must shortly have come to light, and it was the sordid determination to secure his income for themselves before he discovered the intrigue and divorced his wife that sealed his fate and forced an early issue.

"If you intend to commit a murder, Louis, and know that suspicion will automatically fall on you, what is the first thing that you would wish to effect? Obviously that it should fall on someone else more strongly. But as the arrest of that someone else would upset the plan, you would naturally make his identity such that he would have the best chance of remaining at large. The most difficult person to find is one who does not exist.

"There you have the whole strategy of the sorry business. Everything hinged on that, and when you once possess that clue you not only see why everything happened as it did but you can confidently forecast exactly what will happen. To go on believing that you had talked with the real Poleash it was necessary that you should never actually see the man as he was. Hence the disfigurement. What assailant would act in that way? Only one maddened by a jealous fury. The Southern people are popularly the most jealous and revengeful, so we must have a native of Italy or Spain, and the Italian is the more credible of the two. Similarly, Mr Hipwaite is brought in to add another touch of corroboration to your tale. But why Mr Hipwaite from a mile away? There is a locksmith quite near at hand; I made it my business to call on him, and I learned that, as I expected, he knew Poleash by sight. Plainly he would never have served the purpose."

"Perhaps I ought to have been more sceptical of the fellow's tale," conceded Mr Carlyle; "but, you know, Max, I have a dozen fresh people call on me every month with queer stories, and it's not once in a million times that this would happen. I, at any rate, saw nothing to rouse suspicion. You say he made mistakes?"

"Crispinge, among divers other things he's failed in, has been an actor, and with Mrs Poleash's coaching on facts there is no doubt that he carried the part all right. Being wise after the event, we may say that he overstressed the need of secrecy. The idea of the previous attack, designed, of course, to throw irrefutable evidence into the scales, was too pronounced. Something slighter would have served better. Personally, I think it was excess of caution to send Mrs Jones out on the Thursday afternoon. She could have been relied upon to be too 'mithered' for her recollections to carry any weight. It was necessary to destroy the only reliable photograph of Poleash, but the risk ought to have been taken of burning it before she went off to establish her unassailable alibi, and not leaving it for her accomplice to do. In the event, by handling the frame after he had burned his gloves, Crispinge furnished us with the solitary fingerprint that linked up his identity."

"He had been convicted then?"

"Blackmail, six years ago, and other things before. A mixture of weakness and violence, he has always gravitated towards women for support. But the great mistake—the vital oversight—the alarm signal to my perceptions—"

"Yes?"

"Well, I should really hardly like to mention it to anyone but you. The sheet and the bolster-case that so convincingly turned up to clinch your client's tale once and for all demolished it. They had never been on Poleash's bed, believe me, Louis. What a natural thing for the woman to take them from her own, and yet how fatal! I sensed that damning fact as soon as I had them in my hands, and in a trice the whole fabric of deception, so ingeniously contrived, came down in ruins. Nothing—nothing—could ever retrieve that simple, deadly blunder."

4

THE CURIOUS CIRCUMSTANCES OF THE TWO LEFT SHOES

At the time when the Enderleighs lost their silver the Monkey Burglar was at the height of his fame. The Monkey Burglar, should you by this date have forgotten, was the one who invariably gained access by leaping from a tree on to an upper-storey window-sill. So strong was habit that there were said to be cases of the Monkey Burglar going through this performance at houses where the front door stood open, or where a builder's ladder, left in position overnight, was reared against the very point he gained by the more sensational flight. During the thick of the burglary season that year each number of Punch regularly contained one or more jokes about the Monkey; no pantomime was complete without a few references to him; and the burgled invariably tried to claim distinction as authentic victims. In this, the Press, to do it justice, worthily seconded their endeavours.

The Enderleighs lived near Silver Park at that time, in one of the old-fashioned cottages that have long, delightful gardens running down to the river edge. They were a young couple, setting themselves a very moderate standard until the day when Enderleigh's wonderful qualities should be suitably recognized by a partnership. In the meanwhile he was something exceptionally responsible but not so exceptionally rewarded in connexion with a firm of estate agents and surveyors. Max Carrados had heard of him favourably from one or two friends and was not unwilling to put business in the young man's way. An opportunity came when the blind criminologist had, as trustee, to deal with an estate down in Warwickshire. He ascertained that Enderleigh was not debarred from doing work on his own account, and gave him a commission to inspect the property and make a general report. Business being slack, there was no difficulty in arranging a few days" leave of absence from the office, and the proposal was gratefully accepted.

On his return—he had conscientiously managed to cover the ground within two days—Enderleigh looked in at The Turrets before proceeding home and found Mr Carrados at leisure.

"I thought that I would leave the report with you now," he explained, "in case you cared to glance over it and ask me about any details while it's all fresh in my mind. I wrote up my notes in the train on the way back."

"Good man," smiled Carrados, accepting the docket. "I should have liked you to stay while we discussed the matter, but I am afraid that someone else has a prior lien on your time."

"In what way?"

"A few hours ago Mrs Enderleigh rang me up on the phone, and there is what I might describe as a standing order for you to communicate with her from here at the earliest moment."

"Good heavens!" exclaimed Enderleigh in some trepidation. "What's up, I wonder? Nothing wrong that you know of?"

"Nothing at all," replied Carrados with reassuring unconcern. "Your wife was in exceptional spirits, I gathered, but somewhat cryptical. However, there is the means of setting your mind at rest," and he indicated the instrument. "I'll leave you to it."

"Please don't go." Enderleigh seemed to be toying with the moment as if rather unwilling to set his mind at rest. "I was startled for a second, but if my wife herself spoke to you there can't be anything much the matter. The fact is," he confided with a certain shy complacency, "she has been getting rather fanciful of late—not an unusual phase of the situation, I understand."

Mr Carrados murmured his discreet congratulations, and his visitor summed up enough indifference to make the call.

"Holy Moses!" the blind man heard him mutter, and there followed a rapid fusillade of "How?" and "When?" and "What?" and "You don't mean it!" all indicating consternation and surprise, as long as the colloquy lasted.

"Here's a pretty go," announced Mr Enderleigh, hanging up the receiver. "We've been burgled!"

"The deuce!" exclaimed Carrados sympathetically. "I hope your wife isn't much upset?"

"No, I don't think so. In fact, she seems rather set up, because some of our neighbours were robbed in a very commonplace way lately, and she's determined that this must have been the authentic Monkey."

"Much taken?"

"Apparently the silver chest and nothing else. Myra rather fancied that I would call here on my way from something I had said—that's why she rang you up—and she wants me to go straight on. I hope you don't mind?"

"Of course not. I had hoped that you would keep me company for an hour or two, but that's out of the question now... I'll tell you what, though: I will make a bargain with you. Stay another fifteen minutes, in which we can have a snack of some kind in place of dinner. In the meanwhile I will have a car got out that will land you at your place quicker than any other way you could go; and in return you shall invite me to inspect the depredation."

"That's certainly a bargain from my side of the transaction," replied Enderleigh. "If it isn't putting you out, I'll accept like a shot."

"Not a bit," declared his host with more than polite formality. He moved across to the house telephone and quickly distributed the necessary orders. "I love anything that comes suddenly along. It may be the beginning of—what adventure?"

"Well, as to that, of course there are two sides," said the domesticated Enderleigh. "This is quite sudden enough for men, but I certainly don't love it."

Carrados was as good as his literal word, and fifteen minutes after he had spoken the lean form of his speedy Redshank car glided down the drive into the high road and then stretched out for Silver Park.

"Now that it's come to this, I may as well tell you about our silver," explained Mr Enderleigh to his companion, on a confidential impulse. "We happen to have rather a lot—more than people in our modest way generally sport, I mean. Myra's father was a fruit-grower and won a lot of cups and plates in his time. I used to be something of a runner and I amassed a few more, and when we got married our friends showered cruets and cake baskets down on us galore. The consequence is that there was a solid half-hundredweight of the metal reposing in a specially made case in the dining-room at Homecroft. Of course it ought to have been kept at the bank, and at first it was, but Myra liked to see an assortment out on the sideboard, so that it got to be a nuisance sending it backwards and forwards. Then I said that if we had it in the house it ought to be kept up in the bedroom for safety, and Myra found that she couldn't even lift the chest and decided that it would be too inconvenient to have it there. What with one thing and another, the confounded silver got to become a bit of a sore point between us—it brought on the first unpleasantness we had. Then, as bad luck would have it, just when I was leaving the other morning to go on this job we must needs get arguing about it again. I suggested that as there would be only two women alone in the house—herself and the servant—it would be safer if I carried the box up and hid it under the bed. Myra—God know why—

retorted that if the silver was the danger-point it wasn't very kind to want to put it just under where she would be. One silly word led to another until I finally went off saying that I wished the damned stuff was at the bottom of the river."

"You seem to have got the next thing to what you asked for then," remarked Carrados. "The silver apparently won't trouble you again." But Enderleigh demurred at this cheerful summary and shook his head.

"Oh, yes," he replied, "but when you wish a thing like that you don't really mean that you want it to happen."

"You are insured, I suppose?"

"Only partly, I'm afraid, because the value of the silver now exceeds the percentage allowed. And of course a lot of the things have associations, although there is nothing of antique value. I'm really wondering how Myra will take it when the excitement wears off."

But so far the excitement was on, and she welcomed them radiantly, albeit a shade mystified that Mr Carrados should have chosen that moment to pay his call. It does not say much for the criminal expert's sense of publicity that neither his host nor hostess had the faintest idea of his uncanny reputation. To them he was simply the rich blind man who seemed as though he might be useful to Guy.

"But isn't it a shame, Mr Carrados?" she cooed, when the first round of wonder and exclamation had been gone through. "Sergeant Lapworth declares that it can't possibly be the Monkey Burglar. And I was so relying on that to squelch the Higgses with."

Carrados divined an exchange of private glances, expostulatory from the husband, playfully defiant on her part.

"I have met Sergeant Lapworth once or twice and he seemed to know his work," said the visitor. "Did he say why it couldn't be?"

"Well, the only way they could have got in was by the side door. No fastenings have been forced or windows opened. And the Monkey wouldn't ever dream of using a side door."

"But how on earth could they do that?" demanded Enderleigh. "I mean without using force. Chloe fastens the door at night, doesn't she?"

"I'll show you if you don't mind accompanying me to the nether regions," said the light-hearted girl. "Chloe only locks the door it seems—the bolts are too stiff to work—and Sergeant Lapworth says that these people—he's almost sure he knows the gang—have all manner of ingenious tools. There's a sort of pincers that you catch hold of a key with from the other side and turn it quite easily. You can see that the lock has been oiled to make it go."

"You found the door unlocked this morning?"

"No—I don't know. I never thought of that. But I suppose they could just as easily lock it again to cover their tracks, and as it happened it was not until this afternoon that I missed the silver chest. Then there are footprints on the bed from the gate to the side door. He found those as well. It's most wildly exciting discovering clues; I've been looking for some all the afternoon, but so far without success."

"Come on then," suggested Enderleigh. "You have a lamp or candle, I suppose?"

"Yes. Do you care to see our private morgue, Mr Carrados—oh, I am sorry: I forgot!"

"That's very nice of you—to forget," smiled the blind man. "It shows that I'm not so helpless after all. Certainly I should like to come; I'm as keen on clues as you are."

The side door was the chief point of interest. It opened on to the garden from the scullery. The scullery—a dank and forbidding chamber that almost justified its epithet—in turn led into the kitchen, and the kitchen into the hall. But there were other ways of getting about, for it was an old house with many passages and on various levels. Most of the rooms appeared to have at least two doors. "I think that the man who built it must have been fond of French farces," remarked Mr Enderleigh, pointing out this feature.

But even at the side door there was very little to see, the Enderleigh burglary being chiefly remarkable for its negative features. There was the oiled lock, and the key bore certain recent scratches, and that was all.

"If the bolts had been shot this would never have happened," said the master of the house. "Perhaps in future—"

"But the bolts can't be stirred, dear," protested Myra. "I've tried myself until my poor thumbs are nearly dislocated. And every one says that if burglars want to get in they will, even if they have to come down the chimney."

"I think the bolts might move if they were simply oiled," suggested Carrados. "The level is all right, you see."

"Chloe," called out Mr Enderleigh—the kitchen door stood open—"is there any oil about?"

A young girl in cap and apron—a girl of quite unusual prettiness—appeared at the door.

"Oil, sir?" she repeated faintly, and she continued to look from one to another of them as though something was amiss.

"Yes, oil—ordinary oil—the sort you oil with, you know. There must be some about somewhere."

"Oh, yes—for the sewing machine," she replied, and disappeared to return with it in a moment.

"Now a feather."

The girl's eyes shot to a bucket holding kitchen refuse that stood beneath the sink; then rose to the level again as she continued to stand there.

"Feathers: in the middle dresser drawer, Chloe," prompted her mistress tartly. "Bless me," she confided to the others, "the girl's going dotty, I believe. Over-excitement isn't good for our poor sex."

"Now we want a chair or something for the top bolt," said Enderleigh.

"I think I can do it without, if you will allow me," put in Carrados. "I fancy that I am just a few inches to the good in that respect."

"But really, Mr Carrados," protested the lady, "won't you get it on your clothes—or something?"

"That is only a matter of carelessness, not vision," replied Carrados. He gave the feather a dexterous turn in the neck of the bottle to remove the excess of oil before he withdrew it. "Children have the keenest sight, Mrs Enderleigh, and yet look how they drop the jam about!"

"It's quite marvellous," she murmured, watching him apply the oil and then work the action until the bolt slid easily.

"Not so much as you might think," he assured her. "Frequently you are indebted to other senses when you think you are using your eyes, and they get all the credit. Several men have told me that they always close their eyes when they are doing certain delicate adjustments."

"I once knew a lady who always shut her eyes before she fired a gun off," contributed Enderleigh. "Yet she was fond of shooting, and often hit things."

"Dogs or keepers?" inquired Myra politely.

Certainly the burglary did not seem to have damped anyone's spirits. Presently they went out to look at the incriminating footprints—"viewing the body" Myra called it—by candlelight until they were tired of striking matches and the friendly darkness put Carrados at liberty to go down on hands and knees and touch the well-marked impressions with his eerily perceptive fingers in his own peculiar way.

"What's this—snowing?" Enderleigh had exclaimed as he opened the door to lead the way into the garden. A sprinkling of white showed on the bare earth before them.

"Goose!" retorted Myra fondly, "it's lime, of course. Old Benjamin—he's a sort of local unhandyman, Mr Carrados, whom Guy employs one day a week to sit in the garden and smoke shag—put it on only yesterday. He said the soil was too 'thodden' for bulbs: it's always too something for Ben."

"It came in useful, all the same," said her husband. "You see, the lime being crushed down in the footprints shows that they were made after it was put there. That's important."

"Lapworth the Sleuth had already diagnosed that, O Fountain of Wisdom," mocked his wife. She leaned forward and struck him lightly on the arm. "You're it! Race you to the river, Guy!"

"Ssh!" warned Enderleigh with a nod towards their guest.

"Go, children—run," urged Carrados benignly. "I will follow at a pace more suited to my years."

"Hold up!" cried Myra, limping into a walk before they were fairly off. "I forgot; my feet are as soft as mush today. Besides, I oughtn't to now."

"No, of course you oughtn't to," said Guy severely. "And we oughtn't to leave Mr Carrados like that. God knows what sort of a lunatic asylum he'll think he's dropped on."

"Never mind: I got you away. Just one, Guy. And don't worry about him. He said his ears, but he meant his eyes, of course: his ears are sharp enough. That old man wouldn't take any harm if you put him down in the middle of a sawmill."

"Old!" exclaimed Mr Enderleigh indignantly. "Great Scott! What next?"

They walked back to meet the advancing Carrados, and then they all strolled soberly down to the extremity of the garden and stood contemplating the slow, muddy river before they turned back again.

"You take Mr Carrados into the dining-room, Guy," said Myra, hastening on ahead as they neared the house. "I'm going up to change my shoes—these are soaked."

"Yes, my lady, you are pretty high up already. I'm afraid," apostrophized her husband as they followed. "That's the way of it, Mr Carrados. I shall think myself lucky if she isn't down below zero before the night is out."

"I've taken hot water up to the spare room, sir," said Chloe, as they passed her in the hall.

They washed their hands leisurely and went down to the dining room. The maid had lit the lamp and was replenishing the fire. Still Mrs Enderleigh did not appear. A few minutes passed rather flatly. Enderleigh made a half-hearted show of asking his guest if he was fond of this and that, but Carrados divined his vague uneasiness and soon they both frankly waited.

"Guy," said a queer little voice just outside the door—it had been left somewhat ajar—"do you mind coming here a minute."

Enderleigh threw a quick, inquiring look across, and the blind man—informed by what sense, who shall say?—nodded mute assent. Then the door closed and Carrados slowly turned his face to the four points of the room.

It was perhaps five minutes later that Enderleigh returned. He came thoughtfully across the room and stood close to his guest's chair.

"It's just as I was afraid," he said, pitching his voice cautiously. "Myra is now at a very minus stage indeed. And a curious thing—curious and trivial, and yet, I must admit, extraordinary—has happened to upset her. It's mixed up with one or two other matters, and I suppose that this burglary also—although that has nothing to do with it—has helped to put the emotional screw on. If you care to hear I will tell you with pleasure, especially as you have seen how bright she was a few minutes ago, but I don't want to bore you."

"Go on," said Carrados. "Curious and trivial things that are extraordinary have never bored me yet."

"Well, you shall judge. I indicated, over at your place, that we are expecting our little household to be increased in the course of a few months. Not unnaturally, Myra has to pass through a variety of new emotions on the subject, and she also has an unfortunate misgiving. It happened that her father was born club-footed and his father was disfigured in the same way. Of course, we tell her that it's all nonsense, but there is undeniably an element of heredity in that sort of thing, and she knows it well enough. Just now she is doubly prone to take notice of any kind of suggestion or premonition that may come along, especially on that one unlucky possibility. You heard her say that she was going up to change her shoes? Well, this is what has happened: she went upstairs, kicked off her wet shoes, and proceeded to pull on another pair. They are shoes that she has worn quite comfortably at intervals for the past few weeks, but now one—the right foot—would not go on. Thinking nothing of it, she picked up a shoe-lift and tried again. Still it refused to accommodate, and then she went to the light and looked more closely... It wasn't likely to fit, Carrados, for the extraordinary thing is that those shoes, which she has worn quite easily and naturally a dozen times in the last few weeks, are both for the left foot!"

There was a rattle of cups and glasses as the attractive maid nearly dropped the tray she was bringing in. Enderleigh looked sharply round, but the girl kept her face averted and quickly went out again.

"There's another who's certainly got the jumps," said her master. "But about those shoes. Of course it's ridiculous, but you see the inference? In each forerunning case it was the right foot that was wrong, and so poor Myra is miraculously endowed with two left shoes at this moment as a sort ol admonition than an ordinary right will not be needed... But you don't see anything in it, I expect?"

"On the contrary," replied Carrados slowly, "I see so much in it—so many thousand possibilities, all wrong but one—that I should like to go up into a very large, perfectly bare attic, lit by several twenty thousand candle-power arc-lamps, and there meditate."

"And the nearest thing I can offer you," said Enderleigh, "is the coal cellar. It's roomy as such places go and certainly practically empty now. For the rest—" He found the pleasantry difficult to sustain.

"So," continued the blind man seriously, "we must still proceed on directly material lines. I should very much like to handle the pair of shoes that has caused the trouble. Do you think Mrs Enderleigh would allow me?"

"Why not?" assented the lady's husband. "I'll go and get them."

He went, and returned almost immediately—but empty-handed.

"She's coming down now. Much better," he whispered in the voice of a conspirator. "Bringing them." And almost at his heels a sobered Myra reappeared.

"I'm a hopeless little rabbit, Mr Carrados," she apologized. "Please don't say anything nice about it, because I am."

"Rabbit!" ejaculated her natural protector loyally; "Rabbit! Why, Mr Carrados, that—that sylph has the heart of a—a—well, I'm not strong on the faunas, but of whatever is the antithesis of rabbit."

"That would be a ferret, wouldn't it?" asked Myra in her funny way. "What a sad flatterer you are, Guy!"

"Go on," said Guy happily. "So long as you can laugh—"

She waved a reassuring hand to him across the room as she addressed their guest again.

"Of course, I know that he has told you all about it, Mr Carrados," she said. "Because when I taxed him he began by saying, 'I only just—' Here is the mystery."

It was a pair of pretty bronze shoes, neat yet not fragile, that she put into the blind man's hands. He held them one by one, and as his long, delicately-formed fingers brushed across their surface the two watchers received a curious impression of seeing something read.

"I shouldn't mind—I shouldn't mind the shoes a particle," declared Myra—she felt compelled to speak to break the almost hypnotic quest of those understanding hands "though, of course, they're no earthly use. But for weeks I've been wearing them all right, and now I know perfectly well that I couldn't. There's something wrong with me somewhere, don't you see?"

"But, dearest," pleaded Guy soothingly, "there's some perfectly simple explanation if only we could see it. Why, only just now you said that your feet were tender. That's probably it. You've got them sore, and so you can't put on the shoe. If they were all right you'd jump into them and not notice that anything was the matter, just as you have been doing up to now."

"Don't talk tommy, Guy!" she exclaimed half wrathfully. "As if I could possibly put on two left shoes without knowing it, even if I could get them on. And yet," she wailed, "I have been putting them on—that's the horrible thing about it."

Carrados had apparently finished his scrutiny, for he was listening to this exchange in his usual benign complacency, and as he listened he absently rubbed his nose gently with the polished toe of a shoe.

"Set your mind at rest, Mrs Enderleigh," he remarked quietly, as he offered her the other one. "There is nothing wrong. You have never worn that shoe."

"I have never worn it?"

"Neither you nor anybody else. The shoe has not been worn."

"But look at the wear," she persisted, displaying the scarified sole. "Look at this worn lace."

"The lace, yes," he admitted, with unshaken confidence. "But not the shoe."

"But how can you possibly know that?"

"In exactly the same way that I could oil the bolt—by using other powers than that of sight."

"Do you mean—" began Enderleigh, but Carrados interrupted him with uplifted hand.

"If I may suggest, please don't say anything more about the shoes just yet. At this moment Sergeant Lapworth has come to the door and your servant is admitting him. Let us hear what he has to say."

Myra and Guy exchanged looks of bewilderment—almost of alarm—and then the girl's face cleared.

"Yes," she exclaimed, "I had forgotten to tell you. He did say that he would look in again after you got back, Guy."

"If you please, m'm," said Chloe at the door, "there's the detective here again, and he would like to see the master if it's convenient."

"Quite right," replied Myra. "Show him in here."

Sergeant Lapworth was a plain-clothes man of the local staff. If he had a fault it was that of giving the impression of knowing more than he would tell, a suggestion that resulted in people sometimes finding him less omniscient in the end than they had expected. The Enderleighs were rather surprised at the sudden respect that came over him when he recognized their blind visitor.

"One or two small matters I thought I'd like to see you about, sir," he said, addressing Mr Enderleigh. "Those footprints by the side gate. I understand that no one came along that way between the time your gardener put the lime there yesterday and my seeing them this afternoon?"

"That is quite right," agreed Myra. "We allow the milkman to come in at the front gate and go to the side door, to save him carrying his can right round the other way. No one else came; I asked Chloe particularly."

"You see the point, sir?" continued the sergeant, directing his voice at Mr Carrados this time. "Whoever left those footprints is the man we want to put our hands on. We should like him to account for his movements last night at all events. Old Ben certainly never made those prints, sir. Now, I wonder," the sergeant's voice became softly specu-lative as he leisurely felt in one or two pockets and finally produced a neat paper template of a boot, "I wonder if this suggests anything to either of you?"

Myra shook her head and passed the paper on to Enderleigh.

"It's a man's boot, I suppose," she said. "It is broader than a woman's and the heel is twice as large. It's much smaller than any of yours, Guy."

"Lord, yes," he agreed. "I'm miles beyond that."

"Perhaps," continued Sergeant Lapworth, becoming almost dreamy in his quiet detachment, "perhaps this might help you more if you should ever have seen the original." It was a small fancy button that he mysteriously produced this time from the Aladdin's cave among his garments. Myra's spirits went up.

"What a splendid clue, Mr Lapworth!" she exclaimed. "Where did you find it?"

"I don't want anything said about it just yet," he stipulated. "As a matter of fact I picked it up in your scullery this afternoon."

"It is a boot button, I suppose?" questioned Enderleigh. "It strikes me as rather dressy."

"It is the top of a pearl boot button undoubtedly, I should say," pronounced the sergeant. "One of those metal-shanked things that they wire into the boot nowadays. First question is, Does it belong to anyone of the house? I dare say you have plenty of pairs of fancy boots and shoes in use or put by, but it isn't a button that you would readily forget."

Myra breathlessly agreed that if she had had boot buttons like that she would never have forgotten it, and added that if Guy had appeared with them she could never have forgiven it—a sotto-voce effort that elicited nothing more than an anxious look from her husband.

"And how about the young person in the kitchen?" suggested Lapworth.

"I know Chloe's boots, and it certainly doesn't come from there," replied Chloe's mistress. "However, you had better ask her, to make sure. Shall I ring now?"

"Don't trouble," he replied, with a quite spontaneous glance towards the decanters on the table, as he returned the precious relic to its hiding-place. "I can have a word with her as I go out. Now as regards the silver. Your good lady said that you would be able to make me out a list, sir."

"Of course," assented Enderleigh; "that's got to be done, hasn't it? And then there'll be the insurance people. And then a young man introducing himself as 'The Press'. I'll tell you what, sergeant, this being burgled isn't such a soft thing after all."

"I don't know, sir. It strikes me that you have come off uncommonly easy, seeing as how things were. No mess, no breakages, no odds and ends from every room that you can't remember until it's too late to claim. Just one big lot taken clean."

"It would be about as much as he could take, anyway," said the owner. "I shouldn't like to heft that case far." He casually indicated the group of liquors. "What shall it be, sergeant?"

"I'll leave that to you, sir," said the sergeant modestly. "Yes, it would be a tidy load. I don't know that I ever remember the case being taken before. Reckon they had a car somewhere near."

"Anyway, nothing was overlooked," said Myra. "There were some tankards out on the sideboard here, and three dozen spoons of various sizes in the drawer, and they went too. I put them—"

"You put them what?" prompted her husband, for Myra had stopped as though she had said her say.

"I haven't the faintest notion, dear," she replied frankly. "To tell the truth I think I was half asleep. Put what what?"

"Well, I think I'll be getting on along, sir," said Lapworth, reading in this a pretty obvious hint. "As soon as we hear from you—"

"Nonsense," interposed Enderleigh, rather put out at the turn; "have another first," and he refilled the not altogether inflexible sergeant's glass.

There was a hesitating knock at the door and Chloe entered with a card.

"Please, m'm," said the girl—Mrs Enderleigh happened to be seated nearest to her—"there's a gentleman would like to see the master for a minute."

"'Wich'—'Mr William Wich'," read Myra. "Isn't there a Lady Wich a few houses away?"

"Trefusis—Lady Wich, madam," volunteered Lapworth. "There is a Mr William, the son."

"I'd better go out and see what it is," said Enderleigh. "Probably only a minute—excuse me, won't you?"

For so short a gap it did not seem worth while discovering a topic of conversation, and so no one broke the minute's silence. If they had spoken their thoughts the exchange would have been something after this fashion:

"I wonder if Lady Wich ever intends to call—city knight's widow, I suppose. Now will Mr Carrados go when the fat sergeant leaves, or does he expect that we have proper supper?"

"Bit of a card this Mr Willie Wich from what I hear. Old party keeps him in pretty tight by all accounts. Larky; girls. Damn fine stuff this Scotch here. Wonder if it'd be all right, if he does give the nod again, for me to—"

"She must stand five feet five—possibly six. At that, with the tread she has, she will take a 4½ to 5. Yes, under any vigorous exercise she might reasonably split a pliant 3½. There were certainly two definable personal exudations about the other shoe, and associable with them syringa—that's the girl—and cheiranthus—this one."

The door opened and Enderleigh entered, then standing aside he waited for someone else.

"Rather curious," he announced. "Mr Wich has come to give us some information about our friend last night; so as we are all here—My wife; Mr Wich; Mr Carrados; Sergeant Lapworth."

"It's really from my mother, you know," said the dapper youth who followed the host in. "She's a frightful invalid—heart and all that—so she sent me to tell you. We only just heard of what had happened: beastly shame—"

"We didn't know that you'd be interested," ventured Myra graciously.

"Eh? Oh, I mean rotten luck being burgled like that. Well, it seems that last night the mater was having a bad turn and she had to get up and sit at the open window to have air. That's how it takes her. It seems that from her bedroom window one can see most of your garden—we live a couple of houses along: Trefusis, you know—and as she sat there she distinctly saw someone go down your garden towards the river and disappear among the trees. She says she wasn't taking much notice of it at the time, because there was no reason why there should be anything wrong in that, and it being dark she didn't see a lot, and she was feeling pretty washed out as well. But she did notice that it seemed to be a man carrying something large and heavy, and when she heard of this she thought you'd better know."

"It's most awfully good of Lady Wich to send," gushed Myra; "and of you to come. We are just celebrating the event with frugal hospitality. Will you drink the toast 'Our Absent Friend' in whisky, port, or coffee, Mr Wich?"

"Eh? Oh, I don't mind. The first for choice, thank you."

"The river," mused Lapworth. "That's certainly an idea now: we couldn't find any likely motor wheel-tracks down the side road here. A boat waiting, you see. What time about would this be, sir?"

"Oh, about half-past twelve, she said."

"Ah!" The sergeant continued to regard Mr Wich with an air of distant speculation while at the same time his hand went mechanically to his mysterious pocket. "I suppose you didn't by any chance happen to be in the neighbourhood yourself at about that hour, sir?"

The perfect respect of the tone could not wholly disguise a certain significance in the question, and Willie Wich looked up to meet the sergeant's eyes on level terms. Enderleigh also found something arresting in the sudden tension that seemed to have involved two of his guests, while Carrados continued to gaze into unseen space with the faint half smile of placid contemplation. Myra alone appeared to have no interest in the passage, and her face was turned away, but her lips were tight pressed to hold back a cry of generous warning and her heart was thudding like an engine beat, for in a flash her eyes had followed Lapworth's and in a flash had seen on her spruce guest's extended foot a boot with identical pearl buttons, of which the upper one was missing.

The gap between the question and the answer was almost as long as it takes to tell of it, for with their eyes meeting Wich paused to consider his reply as though a thought urged caution.

"What do you quite mean by that?" he asked guardedly. "You know, of course, that I live in the neighbourhood. Do you mean, was I at home?"

"Not exactly, sir," replied the sergeant. "You might have been passing this very house on your way home and thought you saw or heard something suspicious here and come nearer to investigate. Or you might have had a dog stray into this garden and come in to call it back, or a dozen things. What I should like to know is, did you come into this house or garden last night for any purpose?"

"I did not," said Wich, his face relaxing into something like an amused grin. "What is more, sergeant, I have never before been in this house or garden in the course of my long and industrious life."

"That's quite definite, sir," Lapworth admitted. "In the circumstances would you mind stating where you were between the hours of eleven last night and two o'clock this morning?"

To those who knew him pretty well young Mr Wich was something of a puzzle, and they complained that you never knew how he would take it and whether the fellow was quite the fool he sometimes seemed.

"'In the circumstances', sergeant, seems to imply the existence of certain conditions of which I have no knowledge," he now replied. "Should I ever find myself in the dock of the Old Bailey, charged with the murder of a constable, or before the Surrey Petty Sessions accused of appropriating Mr Enderleigh's ancestral plate, either of those eventualities would constitute an aggregation of circumstances that would enforce my acquiescence. At present I fail to see any reason why I should render an account of my trivial life and movements."

Sergeant Lapworth took out an irreproachably white pocket handkerchief and wiped his face profusely.

"Very good, sir," he remarked with dark significance. "Should you have any objection to my comparing this form"—here the sergeant dramatically produced his first exhibit—"with the boots you are now wearing?"

"Not the least," replied the buoyant young man, raising his right foot to facilitate the operation; "though I must protest against the attention thus gratuitously directed to my very unprepossessing footwear. Anything to assist the legitimate ends of justice. But not," he added severely, "of mere vulgar curiosity."

Without deigning to reply, Sergeant Lapworth went down on one knee and from that position fitted the paper impression against the proffered boot. It was at once plain to everyone that the two outlines coincided perfectly. But an even more significant piece of evidence was to emerge, for as the sergeant performed this office he slyly inserted a nail in the angle of the instep and an appreciable sprinkling of white-peppered soil fell down into his hand.

"I must call your attention, sir, to the fact that this earth from your boot appears to correspond with the soil of the garden here."

"I say!" exclaimed Mr Wich aghast, "I am sorry, Mrs Enderleigh—bringing stuff like that into your pretty room!" Then with a bright look of toleration, "But I expect you know what servants are!"

"Lastly," said Sergeant Lapworth with admirable composure in spite of a rather flushed complexion, "I shall be glad if you will look at this button which corresponds exactly with those on your boot, where one is missing."

"Thank you," replied young Mr Wich, passing it back again; it's very good of you to have kept it for me, but it's really no use. It isn't a button you sew on, but one of those metal-shanked affairs and the shank is broken."

"Then I understand, sir, that you decline to assist us with any information?"

"Oh, no, you don't, sergeant—not if you understand the common or vernacular tongue, that is," retorted his antagonist. "So far, what I have declined is to give an account of my movements on the strength of an old button hypothetically lost at some time from my boot and a little piece of paper traced to measure. It may be the law that I have to if anyone shows me those: I must look that up. But you may remember that the only reason for my being here was to bring you information."

"Oh, yes," exclaimed Myra, completely won over by the suspect's ready nonchalance, "we are all sure that Mr Wich is quite all right, Sergeant Lapworth. Aren't we, Guy?"

"Mrs Enderleigh," put in Wich, gazing at her with melancholy admiration, "before I go I must unburden my mind, and I'm afraid you may think very poorly of me in consequence. I did not purloin your silver and I have not the faintest idea who did. Good-bye."

"Must you really go?" she asked. "Please be sure and thank Lady Wich from me, won't you? And any Thursday."

"If you would be so kind as to help a blind man to his car, Mr Wich," interposed Carrados, and Enderleigh found his own proffered services quietly brushed aside.

"You don't say you are!" exclaimed Wich. "I never tumbled to it. And that's your little jigger waiting then? I'm looking forward to something on four wheels myself, but so far I have to be content with two."

"It's hardly worth while offering you a lift," said Carrados, when they were in the road, "but if you don't mind I should like to walk with you as far as your gate."

"Right-o," said Mr Wich, wondering who this queer customer who had made up to him might be. "Lovely night, isn't it? What about your car?"

"It will follow presently; my driver understands. I have been trying to think where we have met before. Are you by any chance the Wich who made forty-nine for The Rest against Lord's Schools five years ago?"

"Oh, I say!" exclaimed his companion, becoming quite boyishly shy at the reference to this exploit. "You don't mean to say that you remember that? Were you at Lord's?"

"Yes. I am fond of the minor fixtures; I can hear more play in them than often comes out in first-class matches. We did not speak, but you passed, and I thought I recognized your step again. A Winchester fellow was commenting on the game for me. You were given run out."

"You must simply be a walking Wisden, sir." said Wich, brimming with admiration. And then with a curious intonation in his voice he added, "But why 'given'?"

"I remember some reference to it... Were you out?"

"As a matter of fact I was not," he admitted.

"I don't think you made any fuss about it—quarrelled with the umpire or groused about the pavilion?"

"Well, should I be likely? It was cricket."

"Yes... And now about this business?"

They had reached the gate of Trefusis, but the young man made no movement towards it, and presently they fell to walking slowly on again.

"That isn't so easy. Not by a long, long way. I was taken by surprise, I must admit; I hadn't a notion that there'd be any trace. Of course it would have been simple enough to tell the sergeant how it came about, if that was all."

"You mean the lady in the case; or shall we say the girl in the shoes?"

"Partly; and then there is my mother. She would certainly have a heart attack if she found that William had been taking her neighbour's hand-maiden out to midnight carnivals and other forms of penance."

"Is that quite—cricket?"

"Not absolutely M.C.C., perhaps, but it isn't to be inferred that I had the inklingest of who she was at first. And Chloe really is an awfully pretty girl, you know. What has she let out?"

"Nothing at all, so far as I am aware."

"Then how on earth do you come to know of her—and the shoes?"

"Very much, I suppose, in the same way that Sergeant Lapworth has come to know of you and the boot—because the traces are so obvious."

"I must say I think Chloe was a bit of a mutt to walk on the bed and then leave a button somewhere about. She might have learned better than that from the pictures surely."

"Chloe naturally had not foreseen that the escapade would coincide with a burglary. But I would not be too ready to blame her, my young friend," advised Carrados dryly. "The most disastrous blunder of all was made by someone else."

"That's a straight one," said Mr Wich. "What did I do?"

"Suppose you tell me about it?" suggested Mr Carrados. "Under the seal of confidence."

"I don't mind. I was going to see a lawyer first thing tomorrow to find out what I'd better do to circumvent the forces of law and order. Perhaps you could advise me?"

"Perhaps I could," admitted Carrados. "At all events I will."

"There really isn't very much to tell," said young Mr Wich pensively. "I happened to be on the river alone a few months ago when I noticed a dazzling creature watching my feeble efforts from the bank. To have a nearer look I landed and asked her if she was not, excuse me, Miss Prendergast? She said no, but, how curious, she had been almost sure that I was a certain Mr Johnson. This constituting a deputy introduction on established lines I prevailed upon the bright vision to go for a short cruise and even to accept some slight refreshment of a light and portable nature.

"Under the auspices of the gods the idyll proceeded with exemplary propriety to run its normal course. So far as I was concerned the chief attraction was the extreme likelihood of detection and the certainty that everyone concerned would impute the very worst motives to my conduct when they did find out.

"On our usual 'evening' last week I was indulging the delightful being's passion for a harmless beverage known as Tango Teaser when she espied a handbill announcing a cheap fancy dance at one of the public halls a few miles away and artlessly exclaimed:

"'I should love to go to one of those.'

"Of course there was only one humanly possible reply to a heart-cry like that, and I gallantly made it.

"'And I should love to take you. Why not?'

"To this she said that it was absolutely impossible and we fell to making the arrangements. She was to creep out quietly by a side door after the others had gone to bed, lock the door after her and bring the key, and meet me at our usual trysting place—a spot a few hundred yards from our respective abodes. I would be there with my iron steed, and on the pillion thereof would whirl her into fairyland.

"Everything went off as per schedule. The only contretemps was that Chloe—have I mentioned that the heroine was Chloe, by the way?—ripped one of her shoes across and thus passed automatically into the retired list. I confess that I was surprised at the consternation the mishap occasioned the sweet chit, and then she told me. Ashamed at the deficiency of her own pedal outfit she had surreptitiously 'borrowed' a pair belonging to her mistress. Detection would now inevitably follow, disgrace, possibly dismissal. Sighs, tears—heavens!—reproaches. Again I did the insane chivalrous thing and swore to replace the shoe within twelve hours or perish."

"The rest is obvious. Chloe knew where they had been bought—a shop in Oxford Street—and I was to his me off at dawn and duplicate them. As there would be the business of giving the shoes the necessary 'wear' it would be simpler to keep only one, and this I was to put into a clump of ivy on the garden side wall. But when it came to parting a difficulty arose: it was essential for me to have the split shoe as a pattern; I could not allow the fair penitent to walk stocking-footed along the stony road; and it wasn't wise to risk being seen together any nearer our houses. The simple way out was for me to lend her one of mine, and this I recovered from the ivy bush when I put the other one in. And there, Mr Carrados, you have the whole egg in a nutshell."

"Everything went off all right then?" inquired Carrados maliciously.

"Like a clock. I obtained the exact thing in the exact size, scrubbed it down to the exact appearance of the other and put in the old lace. The superfluous shoe was flung over into an orchard somewhere Isleworth way. There was nothing much in all that. But now you see why it was impossible to satisfy Sergeant Lapworth's inopportune curiosity."

"You may perhaps find it difficult to satisfy one or two other people as well. Did Chloe say anything when she let you in just now?"

"Why, yes; it struck me as ungracious at the time. The angel looked at me very weirdly and just said 'Idiot!' I thought she must be overwrought."

"I think it very likely. I told you that there had been other blunders besides Chloe's. What she wished to indicate by a single appropriate word, my budding Lothario, was that you had thrown away the wrong shoe, with the consequence that Mrs Enderleigh is now on the verge of hysterics at an apparent miracle."

"No!" exclaimed Wich incredulously, "I could not. And yet, surely... Oh, good Lord, I did! I kept them to make a pair—the new one and the other, instead of... Well, I am a prize fathead! What will happen now?"

"What? Why the extreme probability that you have had your trouble for nothing and that Chloe will be sacked after all."

"Oh, I don't think that—not after seeing Mrs Enderleigh. You and Chloe both misjudge her strangely. She seems the jolliest sort of girl to me. I bet she'll understand."

"I'll bet she will," assented Carrados grimly. "And when she understands that her pretty servant has been wearing her things, sneaking out at nights (to say nothing about giving burglars the chance of sneaking in) to foot it at dance-halls with the young spark from next-door-but-one, you may not find her quite so sympathetic as she was half an hour ago. If she doesn't take the opportunity of calling upon Lady Wich about it I'm badly out."

"It's a mug's business," said Mr Wich with a qualmish note in his voice. "What had I better do?"

"What you had better do is to leave it in my hands and agree to my condition."

"What condition?"

"That you never go gallivanting with Chloe again. You both 'don't mean anything', but suppose you did happen to get the girl discharged with a very dubious character? Should you see any alternative to behaving either as a fool or a knave to put it right?"

"Whew!" exclaimed Mr Wich, easing the collar against his neck, "that's heart-to-heart stuff. Well, if you can bring it off I'm good for my part. Chloe certainly is a dazzling thing, but, strictly between ourselves, her mind is little more than an assortment of obsolete film captions."

* * * * *

When Mr Enderleigh returned from business the next day Myra greeted him with a subdued note. It was plain that the excitement had quite worn off.

"If Mr Carrados is really going to be useful to you, Guy, of course I shall do my best to amuse him. But I wonder all the same if he is going to make a practice of dropping in every evening."

"How so?" demanded Guy.

"He rang me up this afternoon and hoped that we should both be in later as he would like to call. I had to say we should be charmed."

"Just as well you did, my lady," remarked Guy. "Do you know that quite important people have a most extraordinary opinion of the man, and I am told that Scotland Yard will do anything to oblige him. That's what I've come across today."

"My gracious!" said Myra, deeply impressed; "It's just as well I fawned. Talking about police, I met Sergeant Lapworth in the road this morning and he seemed very odd. He said they had received instructions to go slow in taking any steps."

"That ought to suit them down to the ground," suggested Guy pessimistically. "We don't look like seeing any of our plate again, old girl."

"I don't know, Guy. It struck me that Sergeant Lapworth knew more than he would tell. He said that they expected developments."

"It used to be 'were investigating a clue'," said the unimpressed gentleman.

Mrs Enderleigh had named nine o'clock as a convenient hour and with the busy man's punctuality nine o'clock found Mr Carrados walking up the Homecraft garden path. Looking out, the lady of the house felt a pleasant access of importance, arising from the notable proportions of the car waiting at her gate.

"How nice of you to come again!" she exclaimed playfully. "After the alarms and excursions of yesterday I hardly dared to hope it."

"Oh, yes," he replied prosaically, "your husband and I have some small business details to discuss."

"Of course," she assented quickly. "I am going to leave you at it."

"But first," he continued, "I have a bargain to offer you."

"Offer me? How exciting! Whatever can it be?"

"You really want to get your silver back again?"

"Why, naturally. Guy tells me that we shall only receive about half the value the way our policy goes—isn't it, Guy?"

"I'm afraid it is," admitted her husband.

"And that's only money. To both of us many of the things are priceless."

"While you have no particular affection for that odd pair of shoes?"

"Shoes? Oh, *those*! How ridiculous, Mr Carrados! You are not coming like an up-to-date genie to offer silver plates for old shoes, are you?"

"You have guessed. But there's always a catch about these attractive bargains, you remember. If you agree to let the shoes go, everything connected with them goes also. You have no curiosity, make no inquiries, entertain no suspicions: it is to be as though they and all that appertains to them had never been."

"I wonder if I understand?" mused Myra with a sharp little look in his direction.

"I think you do," replied Carrados. "You are—forgive the homely phrase—no fool, Mrs Enderleigh. If you do not quite understand yet it's only because you have not had time to think about it. You soon would."

"All right; I'll take it," said Myra, with a very sporting air.

"But do you mean that you actually know now where the silver is?" demanded Enderleigh.

"I know where the silver is," Carrados admitted.

"Where?" exclaimed two simultaneous voices.

"When you went off a few days ago, you expressed a wish as to where it might be, Mr Enderleigh, didn't you?"

"What was that?" asked Myra, from whose mind the malediction had apparently faded. Her husband, on the contrary, remembered very well and he coloured at the recollection.

"I am sorry to be reminded of that," he said moodily. "Something happened to put me out, Myra, and in a moment of irritation, without meaning it, I said I wished the stuff at the bottom of the river. That's all."

"Yes; that's the way with you impulsive people, as we genii are always finding. You want a thing and then discover that you don't. Well, my friend, you have got your wish, willy-nilly. The stuff is at the bottom of the river."

"What a lark!" exclaimed the lady.

"The burglars dropped it or hid it there?" said her husband, keenly intrigued. "How on earth did you find that out?"

"The burglars had nothing to do with it, because there was no burglar—no burglary," was the reply.

"Oh, but I say! Besides, it's gone. No, Mr Carrados! And then the side door key, you know."

"Hush!" said Carrados mysteriously. "That doesn't count. The side door key went, according to our bargain, with the shoes."

"Very well," acquiesced Myra, with something very like a giggle, "but if there was no burglar how did the silver get into the river?"

"How?" Carrados raised an accusing finger and slowly brought it dead level on his hostess. "How? Behold the culprit! You, my dear lady, threw it there!"

Moved by a common impulse Guy and Myra came slowly to their feet. Looking at Max Carrados's quietly smiling face it seemed impossible to believe that he—to doubt that he—to know what to think.

"I—threw—it—there?" articulated Myra queerly.

"You deliberately cast the 'damned stuff' in. Rising in the dead of night, without staying to put on slippers or to cover those inadequate garments that are no longer the prerogative of my sex, you crept down, carefully replaced the silver lying about, took up the burden, let yourself out by the french window in the drawing-room, crossed the lawn, reached the silent river, and with a sigh of relief at accomplishing so meritorious a task, tipped the whole bag of tricks into the water. All in a profound sleep, of course. By the way, I hope your feet are better today?"

Myra sat down again with a strange look in her eyes.

"But I could not—I could not even move the box," she whispered.

"Not when you are awake," he replied, becoming grave again. "And do you know why that is? It is because you know that you cannot, and so, your slavish body assenting, you really cannot. But in your sleep you do not know it; your unbound mind admits no limits, and so—"

"Do you know," interposed Enderleigh sagely, "I've heard something like that several tunes lately. I suppose there may be something in it after all."

"Anyway," said Mr Carrados, "there is one thing you can congratulate yourself on. A wife who carries out her husband's slightest wish even in her sleep is a woman in a thousand."

5

THE INGENIOUS MIND OF MR RIGBY LACKSOME

The mysterious affair of the anatomical subject, that ended in a Great Western corridor express, really began in a New York Mansion when Mr Hiram S. Nogg, wearing noiseless slippers, inconsiderately wandered into the remotest of his five palatial drawing-rooms, to the embarrassment of his niece Sabina and the even more pronounced dismay of Rigby Lacksome. In the terms of Mr Lacksome's unspoken comment, the premature discovery of the idyll "knocked a piece of varnish off the mudguard," and he rapidly speculated that unless something drastic and convincing could be brought into the situation not only his excellent chance of winning Miss Craddock's hand, together with a reasonable settlement, but even his tenure of usefulness as Mr Nogg's third secretary stood in jeopardy. But having been modelling himself on the strong silent pattern for some time past, nothing really useful occurred to him.

"Well, Pop," remarked the maiden, after she had nicked her hair into position (long residence in the Nogg household had led to the adoption of this unpleasant form of endearment at her lips), "what you gotta say about it?"

"Rainproof" Nogg fingered his scanty goatee dubiously and looked from one to the other of the young people in mild reproach. He had been warned by his private specialist that strong emotion consumed tissue, so he never ran to it now that he was seventy-five. He just acted in the same way, but without the excuse of deep feeling.

"Don't know that I've anything much to say, Sabbie," he replied guardedly. "Leastways, not in words. Rigby was going to Europe for the sales next week. Reckon he'd better go over just the same—and maybe stay there."

"I guess not," speculated Miss Craddock in an equally level voice, "England's all right for a trip, but I don't congeal to the idea of a permanency. I must have room to reverse in."

"I wasn't exactly thinking of you, Sabbie," said the old man.

"No," agreed Sabina. "But from a child onwards I've always been encouraged to think for myself. And from what Rigby's just said I understand that if he went he'd wish to take me with him."

"I hope, sir, you won't consider that there's anything clahndestine in my cawnduct beneath your roof." Bracing himself against the Sicilian marble mantelpiece Rigby began to recover something of the attitude of the Noble Lover, a pose necessarily checked as yet by the uncertainty of the old man's real feelings. "For some time past I have regarded Miss Craddock with sentiments of respectful admiration, but until this morning, when speaking of my forthcoming trip to Yurrup, I have never—"

"That so?" interrupted Mr Nogg enigmatically. "Well we'll leave it there. Now, did that Shrubworth sale catalogue come in from Sotheby's by this morning's mail?"

"Yes, sir," replied Rigby rather blankly. That was old Nogg all over—until it suited his own convenience the young man wouldn't have the least indication whether it was going to be the foot of ignominious expulsion or the hand of golden blessing.

"I want to go through it with you then," said Hiram briskly. "Bring it to my room when Johnson leaves." He slid noiselessly away again, and after a very subdued exchange of protestations with his inamorata Rigby followed him. As he went to find the catalogue of the celebrated Shrubworth collection of Shakespeariana he was thinking harder and more rapidly than he had perhaps ever done before.

* * * * *

Max Carrados, you may remember, had some connexion with the United States. He had inherited his not inconsiderable fortune from an American cousin, who had in his time been a successful speculator—a speculator not exactly in crops, which are notoriously kittle-cattle, but in official crop reports. With a select few of his friends out there the blind man endeavoured to hold for a little longer a solitary outpost of the lost cause of polite correspondence. It is to be inferred that his contributions were acceptable; in return he certainly learned much that even the sleuths of American journalism failed to get on to, and once or twice his information was curiously effective.

"I doubt if you will ever have met 'Rainproof' Nogg," wrote one about this time—a shrewd old lady whose Dutch-sounding name caused pushful young hostesses to prick up their ears even when it reached them at third hand. "Not a great many years ago he was living precariously on the crumbs that fall from rich men's waste-paper baskets, but during the last decade or two he has shot forward amazingly. I don't quite know what he does, but if I had a son—no, I should prefer it to be my grandson—I think I would put him to it. We have wheat 'kings' and cotton 'kings' and coal 'kings'; railroad 'kings', stationary engine 'kings', and Mr Ford; 'kings' in the realms of hardware, software, sectional bookcases, crime, and canned tomatoes. But all these sovereigns have some connexion with the domains they represent. I have never heard that Rainproof Nogg had any connexion with anything. I believe that people just bring schemes to him and if he approves of them they give him a share of the scheme for approving. It seems an easy way.

"At any rate, Mr Nogg is vastly wealthy, but he is growing old. This disease, I am told, has brought a morbid affection in its train: a dread that when he is dead he will be forgotten. It has become a terrible thing that in spite of his power and influence now, when he is gone his memory will soon be utterly effaced. I suppose he has been thinking. True, he has three thin-lipped, razor-jawed, stern-faced Wall Street sons, who will doubtless go on gathering more and more moss around the name of Nogg until the Constitution is amended to suppress them. ('So long as I can keep the money-making in the family, I can afford to pay other people to do the spending,' is a golden Noggett.) But that only raises the problem one power higher: Rainproof, poor romanticist, wants to be remembered in the way that George Washington, Col. W.F. Cody, Pocahontas, and Mary Garden will always be.

"You have heard of his National Temple out in Virginia? That we possessed no Westminster Abbey must have touched his native pride somewhere, and he has set out to remove the slur by building and endowing a lordly private Valhalla on one of his seventeen estates for the last sleep of the great. Eminent Americans are to be invited to direct by will their interment there; and in the case of Americans not so eminent as to be invited, but who have nevertheless expressed a wish to join the others, a committee will decide. It seems a touchy business all along... One cannot but think that Rainproof will have established a lien on the verdict of that committee when his own case comes up. A long shot, it may be, at immortality, but longer ones have hit; or Guido Fawkes, William Tell, and Samuel Pepys were forgotten now.

"In another direction Mr Nogg has found what I imagine has been signally lacking in his life hereto—amusement. And this brings me at last back to my original sheep—a fleece in which you may discover the predatory Rainproof's lupine form. You collect something I know, but what it is between cigarette pictures and stuffed mammoths I can plead the most benighted ignorance. But I know that you will have the best of them whatever they are—and so, hark ye, my friend, a word in your judicious ear. If-if they should be Shakespeariana by any chance, lock them up until you hear that a young man called Rigby Lacksome has returned to the land of his fathers.

"For by this time Rainproof is quite slightly Shakespeare mad. A while ago he was advised by a prominent nerve and stomach consultant (the two things go together here it seems) to 'cultivate more interest outside business'. Rainproof made the one recorded joke of his existence then, but let that pass. Whether the poor old gentleman heard the Bard's curious name for the first time about that period, or whether it was because his great financial rival 'Slogger' Macmahomet was commissioning Frissman to corner First Folios matters not. At all events, Rainproof went down into the Shakespeariana pit and became a bull power.

"His first acquisition was a wistful young expert who had been in the ancient book business but who was quite content to get out of it—Mr Lacksome, to wit. He was to be Rainproof's librarian and Shakespeare secretary. This, I glean, is how they got to work.

"'See here,' said Mr Nogg, 'I hear that fellow on the other side the street has just given fifteen hundred dollars for a book called Hamlet, printed way back in the Dark Ages. Now I shall expect you to go one better.'

"R.L. considered.

"'I know of a copy that might be got,' he replied. 'But you would have to go at least two hundred dollars more because it is half an inch taller than Macmahomet's example.'

"'Inch!' snapped Rainproof, 'I don't do things by inches now, young man. Find me one that's about half a yard taller and I won't jib at two thousand dollars more.'

"He has been put wiser since then. You will have heard of the anonymous purchase last fall of the Croxton Park First Folio for four thousand guineas (he buys anonymously on Wall Street principles). Yes, like Macheath's Polly, Mr Nogg by now is 'most confoundedly bit.'

"Will I bring this disquisition to a seemly close? I will, sir, and then only will you plumb its dark significance. R.L. is on his mettle, and the attitude of Rainproof is that of an expectant child with its mouth open and its eyes closed. For the engaging young librarian has fallen beneath the charm of Rainproof's not wholly guileless niece, and in return has found favour in her eyes. But what, everyone will naturally ask, what about the expression of old man Nogg's eyes, for on that the exact complexion of love's young dream must turn? Well, our quite astute Romeo has thrown out a very effective fly and the poor fish has risen. It is to be something so rarely and preciously Shakespearian that our hero begs the continuance of his employer's confidence until his return. Is this mere bluff for time? Or what—a manuscript, a signature, another portrait, a counter-cryptogram? However, young Lochinvar has gone out of the West—*verbum sap*.

"For you collectors are—well, how shall I put it? Rainproof will do it for me.

"'Reckon even in England they take some stock of W. Shakespeare as an asset. So if you get a safe chance at anything unique, Rigby, don't think that I shall worry you any about just how it happened—so long as I don't come in it,' he remarked.

"'I just bet you won't sir,' replied R.L. frankly.

"So now you know."

* * * * *

Mr Carrados dropped the copy of the Pall Mall Gazette that he had been reading and turned to light a cigarette.

"Greatorex," he remarked across the room; "this is the Suffragettes" latest: they have tried to blow up Stratford-on-Avon Church."

"My Sunday hat!" exclaimed the secretary, deeply impressed. "So that was it!"

"Was what?"

With no particular appearance of regret Annesley Greatorex detached himself from the cocupation of typing letters and came across to his employer's chair.

"In a sort of way I suppose I am an accessory before the fact," he remarked with some complacency. "At least, I knew that they were up to some special brand of devilment from Moya's hints and general air of mystery and triumph. Began about last Friday."

"Moya?" repeated Mr Carrados. "Do you mean to say that your shy little sister has become a 'militant'?"

Mr Greatorex essayed a hollow laugh with considerable success.

"'Shy,' you said, sir! And I think you saw Moya less than six months ago? Well, the shrinking violet has been 'had' twice since then for brawling, and if her mother hadn't contrived influenza in the very nick of time I understand that the timid fawn had arranged to chain herself to the minute hand of Big Ben."

"To prove that women are moving with the time, I suppose? Fine spirit, Greatorex."

"Moral hashish, I tell her, sir," amended Annesley with severity. "It's a pretty grey outlook for England if these are a sample of the mothers of the coming generation."

Max Carrados turned away from his ingenuous young assistant in order to strike a match for which he had no use.

"What did you hear about this business?" he asked, indicating the open paper.

"Well, you know what these young women are. I won't say they can't keep a secret, but at the same time they like to let it out on a string and then pull it back again. Now that Moya is on the active list of the precious 'cause' she and half a dozen other hectics are in and out of our place like rabbits all day long. And ever since Friday there's been a sort of 'We could and if we would' innuendo in the air."

"Hallo!" exclaimed Mr Carrados with interest. "Shakespeare again. How the Bard persists."

"Force of example, sir. Moya and her new friend Mamie have been shrieking appropriate quotations at one another, upstairs and down, for days past. Of course, I didn't see the exact point of the various shafts of wit until now, but this is evidently what was brewing."

"Oh," thought Mr Carrados speculatively, "Mamie! Trust an American," he said aloud, "to know more Shakespeare than nine out of ten of us. I suppose your sister's friend is from the States?"

"She just is sir," replied Mr Greatorex, pitching his voice into what he considered an appropriate twang. "And devoted to the emancipation of her downtrawd'n Bri'sh sisters. Says they are real ladies but want gingering some. Seems to be doing it too. I'll bet this last affair was her idea."

"Do you know what she is doing here?"

She says she is the European representative of the *Bluff Folly Weekly Rapier*. My holy aunt!"

All rather slack and jejune doubtless. But Annesley Greatorex was no fool despite his occasional lapses of exuberance. He knew precisely to the dot of an "i" and the crossing of a "t" where he stood with Mr Carrados, and when the blind man merely indicated the newspaper paragraph that had started the digression it was read aloud to him with excellent clearness and diction by an entirely staid and businesslike assistant.

"ATTEMPT TO BLOW UP
STRATFORD-ON-AVON CHURCH
SUFFRAGETTES" LATEST OUTRAGE

"Shortly after midnight a determined attempt was made to wreck a portion of Holy Trinity Church, Stratford-on-Avon, by means of an explosive bomb. Many residents in warious parts of the town were awakened about that hour by a loud report, and on investigation being made it was discovered that a sensational attack had been carried out with the parish church as its objective. Both the fire brigade and the police were quickly on the spot, but the services of neither were immediately required, for no conflagration resulted from the explosion and the dastardly perpetrators of the outrage were clear of the scene before the earliest investigators arrived. Copies of suffragette leaflets strewn about clearly indicate the purposse of this discreditable affair.

"Detailed examination made when it was light reveals the extent of the damage is less than might have been expected. The spot chosen for the attack is on the north side of the chancel, and here several courses of masonry are shattered, much glass—fortunately all modern—broken, and the tracery of one window destroyed. The exact point of the explosion was against the walled-up doorway of what is known as the old 'charnel house', and here the force of the bomb is shown by the dummy door on the interior being blown out. Those familiar with the sacred edifice will recognize from this description that the explosion tock place within a few feet of Shakespeare's monument. It may be assumed, indeed, that this was the real objective, and that nothing but a slight miscalculation due to the darkness of the night, and, possibly, the nature of the explosive used, saved it froom destruction. Fortunately we are spared this crowning act of vandalism; the monument is absolutely untouched and the actual damage can be made good without any loss of historic association.

"That is all, sir—no, here is something more about it in the 'fudge'."

Greatorex rearranged the paper to display the "Stop Press" space and read on.

"STRATFORD-ON-AVON EXPLOSION—LATER

"A representative of Mr Hiram S. Nogg, the American millionaire and Shakespearian enthusiast, who happens to be staying in the town, communicated with his principal as soon as the news of the outrage reached him. As a result of this timely intervention Mr Nogg has generously undertaken to defray the entire cost of repairs. The work will be put in hand immediately, the chuch meanwhile being closed to the public.

"I think that really is all, sir."

"Thank you, said Mr Carrados; "that will do. Now bring me Valp's *First Empire*, will you. I want a reference."

Greatorex stared at his employer almost with concern.

"I'm sorry, but don't you remember? You advised me to read it and—"

"True. I told you to take it home with you. It's still there?"

"Yes, sir... But I could cut out and be back under the hour—time to do these letters for the post."

"No; I want you for something else... And Parkinson is out. I wonder—"

"I could phone to some people who live next door. They'd take a message in, and if Moya is about she'd bring it like a shot."

"Do you think so? That would be very convenient, but it seems rather too bad—"

"Not a bit, sir," declared Annesley with easy generosity. "She thinks no end of you; in fact, only the other day she said that if she was put on to set this house on fire she wouldn't—"

"Really?" said Max Carrados, much gratified apparently.

"Yes; she said she'd certainly persuade someone else to do the job. But, of course, at this hour it's just a toss up—"

As it happened, however, Mr Carrados might be said to have won the toss, for Miss Greatorex was discovered to be at home, and as she arrived at The Turrets within forty minutes she may be judged to have come "like a shot". She was a small, elfin creature (the good looks of the family had begun and ended with Annesley), who in intimate political circles was generally referred to as "The Vole".

"Come and have some tea, Miss Greatorex, and tell me all the Secret History of the day," suggested Mr Carrados, and grinning amiably the Vole complied—to the extent of taking tea, at all events.

"I know that you don't quite approve of us yet, Mr Carrados," she remarked, "but that's only because you've never really thought it out. None but the very young and the very stupid are actually hostile."

"They're all as pert as poll parrots, sir," apologized Annesley. "That's a fair sample."

Moya showed her splendid little teeth at him across the table, but refrained from any of the half-dozen appropriate retorts provided by the textbook for the occasion. After all, there would be no particular sense in exposing Annesley's intellectual shallowness to his employer; and she was quite reasonably fond of her brother—although he would come on the forthcoming Register, with lodger qualification.

"I suppose this is some of your fatuous work?" he remarked presently, pointing to the open evening paper. "I hope you are proud of it."

"Officially, I know nothing of it, Buttons," she replied graciously. "But it seems to have made some stir. Good heavens! Can that possibly be what the idiots intended?"

"Well, for mercy's sake don't call me by that ridiculous name, now we're grown up," he besought. "At least, I am."

"You certainly came within an ace of making a much greater stir," interposed the host, as peacemaker. "I wonder how your friends came to miss the monument."

"Perhaps they didn't want to hit it," suggested the girl cryptically.

"Don't you believe it, sir," put in Annesley with vigour. "They'd blow up old Shakespeare himself, if they could, to keep in the limelight."

"Mr Carrados, do you think that the man who created Portia would object in the least to having that smug, fat-headed image of a retired pork-butcher blown into atoms, if it would help to get her the vote?"

"I think," replied Mr Carrados with a laugh, "that he would recommend you to make better bombs—if you want to prove that you can do anything."

"Hear, hear," applauded Annesley, somewhat at a venture.

Moya Greatorex shot a curious little glance at the smiling Carrados and a quizzical expression twisted her small face.

"I don't mind telling you something, Mr Carrados," she remarked, looking down upon her plate demurely. "It was a man who contrived this particular demonstration."

"Oh, we Englishmen can't," he hastened to declare. "Too law-abiding, I suppose. You ought to get an Irishman—or an American—to do that sort of job."

"How sharp you are," she laughed. "Well, as it happens, he is an American!"

In the pause—of indignation on one gentleman's part but of signal complacency on the other's—that followed this little note of triumph, Miss Greatorex rose to go.

"Good-bye," she said, giving Carrados her hand. "I'm very glad to have been of this slight service to you."

"Thank you," he replied. "It was most good of you to bring the book."

"Oh, the book." She dismissed that casually. "Yes. But of course I was referring to the information that you wanted. Frankly, Mr Carrados, I'm not at all satisfied with the ins-and-outs of that affair myself."

She nodded luminously and under the escort of a rather mystified brother took her departure.

"Greatorex," remarked the blind man, when his secretary returned, "I am not subscribing to a general principle at all, but it would be absurd to deny that your sister ought to have a vote."

It was in this haphazard way that Mr Carrados was fated to be drawn into the curious Shakespeare case—a gossipy letter from an American friend coupled with the Stratford-on-Avon outrage, and the contiguous circumstance that his secretary's sister happened to be in the council of the "militants". Personally, it was no affair of his: Whatever Rigby Lacksome had in mind, a cabinet of Greek tetradrachms did not attract him; and it would be idle to pretend that the amateur criminologist was stirred by public spirit to interest himself in a felony that he saw impending. He would be just as likely to assist in it if his sympathy went that way. No, as he himself would be the first to admit, it was nothing but the element of mystery that attracted here; until that had been set at rest something unsatisfied would continue to disturb the even balance of his mind.

"That is well enough, my friend," he said to himself that night, "but you have precious little to go on. Coincidence is simply the meeting of two straight lines, and they, we all know, can never enclose a space. Before going any farther on a wild goose chase I should advise you to verify the admitted American influence in the affair as connectible with Rigby Lacksome, the get-Shakespeariana-anyhow figure in the drama. Until that point is settled both wings of your deductions are purely in the air."

"All right," replied the other moiety. "I will. That strange young creature certainly will know, and if I ask her nicely (as I might have had the sense to do before) I think she may have enough originality to tell me."

"Do you?" scoffed the negative participant. "Well, I very much doubt it,"

Without wasting any more time in arguing, Mr Carrados sat down and wrote his diplomatic little note. He had to wait several posts for any answer—he heard incidentally from Greatorex that his sister was "out for scalps" somewhere—but one at length arrived. This was the form it took:

> DEAR MR CARRADOS,
> *In reply to yours, the reference you require would seem to be in Brutus's third speech, 'Julius Caesar', Act i, scene 2.*
> *Yours truly,*
> MOYA GREATOREX

"Reference I require?" pondered the recipient dubiously, walking to a bookcase. "Now, did I—" By this time his hand had gone unerringly to the book he sought, and he was turning the pages among the Tragedies. "Well, anyhow, here is the reference I require, whatever it is:

> *Brutus*: I am not gamesome; I do lack some part
> Of that quick spirit that is in Antony.

A sudden light broke upon him and he repeated the first line with expression.

"'Lack some part.' Lacksome, of course. That girl is a born conspirator, I'll take oath. In fifteenth-century Italy she'd have been up to the neck with some ring-and-dagger party... In these prosaic days she has to be a militant suffragette... Well, that settles it."

But what did it settle, after all? Assuming the accuracy of his information, the curious fact was established that Mr Rigby Lacksome, ostensibly in England to attend the book sales, had prompted a convenient organization to carry out a raid on a certain historic building, while he himself immediately appeared on the scene with an arrangement to make good the damage. It could scarcely be an elaborate plan to get Rainproof's name associated with Stratford; that result could have been obtained in a hundred showier and less expensive ways. There was also a detail that might begin to assume significance: one gathered that on the whole the demonstration had somehow missed its full point. The local reports suggested so much, and Moya's suspicions might very well have been awakened by that very fact. Carrados was inclined to agree with his outspoken secretary that the "militants", then at the apex of their frenzy, would be much more likely to blow up the poet's tomb itself, rather than to spare his effigy. Was there, indeed, some double purpose here at work?

In a reflective mood Robinson Crusoe made a tabulated statement of the prospects of his case. In much the same vein Max Carrados now drew a sheet of foolscap before him and stated the position:

"What does Rigby Lacksome need?

"He must procure an incomparable Shakespeare item before he returns—fair means or foul allowed.

"What has he achieved already?

"He had gained the most privileged access to Stratford-on-Avon church under unique conditions. The church and grounds will be closed against further 'militant' attacks. The portions under repair may be screened off if he requires it, and there is no reason to suppose that he cannot introduce workmen of his own selecting.

"What special points will be under his direct control?

"Shakespeare's monument and Shakespeare's grave are both at this spot."

Carrados creased and recreased the sheet of paper a dozen times with absent-minded precision as he began to pace the room, making his way among the scattered furniture with startling certainty; pausing now and then to touch a special piece of ivory or bronze, just as another's eyes might linger for a moment on a possession in half-unconscious satisfaction.

The monument; the grave... The grave; the monument.

Among the many very baffling inconsistencies of Shakespeare's life the outstanding mystery is surely this: That of all his prolific work ("in bulk almost equal to the English Bible; in importance second only to that book"), not a line of manuscript is known to exist today. Nothing approaching this complete effacement can be paralleled in literary history, and to equip legend, when the poet who scrupulously particularized his worn wearing attire and his second-best bed came to the making of a will, not the obliquest reference to the contingencies of thirty-seven dramas finds a place therein. If William Shakespeare had been the greatest exponent of the modern method he could scarcely have planned a more effective "stunt". The Baconian heresy is one of its first-born—certainly the lustiest of its offsprings—but the curious inquirer among the byways of literary credulity will start many another hare.

The monument; the grave...

What, for instance, was that American theory (most of the Shakespeare heterodoxies spring from that vigorous soil) that in the poet's tomb, secure beneath the everlasting curse—though too much strain should not be put on that protection in these material days—the missing manuscripts may still be found, in extenso and intact? Well, as to that, both before Shakespeare's time and after, poets have buried their lyrics in their own graves or someone else's—and one at least of the greatest of the latter has repented and dug them up again.

"I don't feel drawn to that particular line," mused the blind man, wheeling short on his beat to seek his bookshelves again. "No one believed it here, and I doubt if anyone now does in the States. No, Judith made greased cake-papers of the sheets of *Romeo and Juliet* that she found about, and practical-minded W.S. nodded approval. But, ye gods! Imagine a complete and original MS. of, say, *Hamlet* today! Would gold, literally in millions, buy it?" He drew from its shelf a volume of that useful series "The American Catalogue" and soon found the entry he required.

"'Where are Wm. Shakespeare's Manuscripts?' By Hasdrubal Pott. Philadelphia. 1866." it ran. "It might be worth while to look it up. Lacksome will certainly know of it, and one must be on equal terms with him."

He copied the details with his invariable precision and added a line for Greatorex's guidance: "Shadrock, of Museum Street, will be the likeliest to have this."

"It's wrong, wrong, wrong," he repeated softly as he put back the book. "I should feel it down to my finger-ends if I was going right; but what else can there be? The monument... no earthly use or chance there. After all, Lucy Heemskerk did specify manuscript, and she may have had an inkling. Perhaps I'd better make sure of what she really says."

It was easy in that room of perfect system to refer to anything, and in another minute Carrados was reading again the faintly ironic commentary on Rainproof Nogg's lamentable ambitions. At the time that he had received the letter he had attached only the interest of amusement to a warning that was plainly half or wholly jest, but now, as he touched line after line, his long delicate fingers seemed to linger for an inspiration.

And then in a flash it came.

"... You have heard of his National Temple out in Virginia... a lordly private Valhalla... for the last sleep of the great... For by this time Rainproof is quite slightly Shakespeare made..."

The paper fell unheeded from the blind man's hand; he was caught up in the magnificence of the brazen enterprise.

"My gosh!" he exclaimed at last; "But that would lick creation, wouldn't it, Uncle Sam?"

* * * * *

It is one thing to "know" that you are right; it is rather another to go to the length of putting your entirely unsupported conviction into practice. Before he had bargained for quite so astonishing a revelation, Mr Carrados had pledged himself in his note to Moya Greatorex that there should be no prosecution. He nearly always kept that sort of undertaking, and in the present case he had no intention of departing from it, but it might mean that he would be able to avail himself very little of any official help.

But in the first place it would be desirable to strengthen the case somewhat, not so much on his account as against the contingency that he might have to lay his suspicions before other and less romantic-minded people before he had done with it. If he had entered upon the adventure casually he was now in it up to the neck, and with no intention of being left behind.

There were two ends at which he could begin—in London or in Stratford. The latter was the more conclusive ground, but at the same time the more delicate. No harm would be likely to come of any sort of indiscreet move made here in London, but on the scene of the exploit a single false step might easily be fatal. For, be it noted, with his keen appetite for crime, Max Carrados was not so much concerned to scotch a plot before it came to fruition as to demonstrate—if only to himself—that his deductions had been correct. In the meanwhile he took certain simple precautions against being forestalled by

Lacksome's sudden departure, and then, satisfied that he had made the position safe, he turned with leisurely deliberation to the more delicate lines of investifation.

For this theoretical side of the business there was one formula alone. To the extent that Carrados was able to merge himself within the skin of Rigby Lacksome would success or failure attend him. Rigby Lacksome, arrived in London, his plan well in train, certain things assured, certain difficulties ahead, a keen appreciation that the stake was a high one, and that at the last moment, when it might be touch and go, no untoward irregularity must arise to rob him of the prize with the goal in sight. Come now, what would Rigby do?

From this starting-point Carrados launched four entirely different lines of inquiry. Not one of them came to anything and the time was slipping by. It looked very like having to go on to Stratford and take up the case by the thick end. Before admitting this measure of defeat the blind man sent the arrow of venture on one more flight.

"I want you to hunt round and see if it's possible to pick up a fairly complete human skeleton," he said to Greatorex the next morning. "I shan't need you again today, so you can go off and let me know tomorrow how you got on."

"Right-o," assented Mr Greatorex cheerfully—he had "hunted round" after rather out-of-the-way things for his employer too often to be startled. "What about the price?"

"There won't be any price. I don't propose to go to the length of buying one—but you needn't let that out. Just talk to anyone who seems to have anything to say. Even if you come across one for sale you can go on trying, all the same. I want to cut across a similar inquiry—successful or unsuccessful—in the past few weeks. It is not impossible that Lacksome may have bought one. If you strike that, get all you can about it. Anyone who's been asked for another skeleton so recently is sure to want to mention it."

Annesley smiled his usual happy smile of charmed agreement and got as far as the door.

"Oh, where had I better try, sir?" he asked, pausing there.

"That's just what I'm not going to tell you," replied Mr Carrados with decision. "Your chief asset in this business is that you know nothing about it and you are quite likely to go where any other stranger in the same position might get. Now see what you can make of it."

The wanderings of Annesley Greatorex throughout that livelong day (he was a generous worker on occasions) might be treated from a variety of dramatic standpoints, being tragic, comic, farcical, melodramatic, or extravaganzic alternately—or even several at once—nor could the claims of pantomime and mystery justly be omitted. Annesley's own considered verdict was that any account, from its lack of cohesive plot, its tenuous thread of connecting interest, and its wealth of varied and irrelevant detail, could only be done justice to as a musical comedy. It began in the back parlour of Miss Poppington's surprising establishment in Putney High Street and ended in the Lost Property Office at London Bridge. Between those limits Annesley visited two general hospitals, a phrenologist off Fleet Street, an eminent naturalist in Piccadilly, a metal dealer down the Elephant and Castle way, Madame Tussaud's, a theatrical costumier in Convent Garden, a wholesale toy merchant near Aldgate Pump, a Harley Street specialist, a firm of auctioneers, a museum in Lincoln's Inn Fields, a housebreaker (the legal variety), a retired conjurer and about eight other people less easy to define. In most cases he had sought these at someone else's suggestion, and the abiding impression he retained of that wonderful day was of the extraordinary good-nature of nearly everybody. Annesley certainly had a pleasant way with him.

And in the end he had the most astonishing success. It came as the result of one of these kind suggestions—the housebreaker's, in point of fact.

"Look here, mate," said the giant in charge. "What about the big west-end stores? Tried any yet?"

"No," admitted Annesley, who had come on there from an educational appliance maker. "Do you think it would be any good?"

"Why not give it a run? I should. There's Blackley & Whiteing now, up Kensington way. My missus isn't an easy one to please and *she* says they have nearly everything there that she can even think of. Can't do no harm, anyway."

Annesley thanked the dusty giant gracefully and withdrew. Blackley & Whiteing, whose proud boast it was that anything from a troupe of performing earwigs to a desert island would not find them wanting, ought certainly to be on his list. None the less he felt some of the diffidence of youth at stating his business when ah unconsidered entrance brought him face to face with a tall, blonde lady in the glove department. These big, busy shops, thought Annesley, expect one to be precise, and yet... The tall, blonde guide would probably, he feared, emit a piercing shriek. He asked to see the manager.

It would be meticulous to cavil about a definite article. Annesley, at all events, saw an important-looking gentleman with a managerial air. He listened gravely and patiently to his visitor's recital and then struck a desk-bell.

"Mr Chadbeate!"

That is the worst of these big, busy shops. Annesley had imagined that he was getting on. He now had to repeat word for word to Mr Chadbeate all that he had just said to the manager. Mr Chadbeate listened gravely and patiently and then with a dignified "Kindly step this way, sir," led the inquirer to a third compartment.

"Mr Noate!"

"Heavens," murmured Annesley, as the prospect of an unending recital faced him. "I ought to have got it printed."

Mr Noate, however, really was the man. He understood. He even sympathized. It was like that. You never could tell. Curious, too. Within the past few weeks they had had a similar inquiry. Yes, in that case they had been able to supply the order...

"Really? Then there is a sort of demand?"

Scarcely that—not so far as Blackley & Whiteing were concerned, at any rate. Of course they had a reputation, and jokers now and then... But it must have been years ago that the last—

"Scientific requirement of course?" suggested Annesley.

"Oh, yes. An American. Singular idea. Theory that the English and American races, starting from a common stock, are diverging structurally. Wants to be able to demonstrate it by an English skeleton."

"I recently struck a man," volunteered Annesley, "who was on that tack. Fellow called Lacksome; sort of confidential secretary to old Nogg, the U.S.A. millionaire."

"That *is the* chap," cried Mr Noate joyfully. "So you know him? Well, it just happened that we were able to meet his requirement."

"Quite casually," admitted the caller. "He didn't mention this to me. Awkward piece of luggage, won't it be?"

"Of course we had a proper box made; and nicely packed... What he seemed most concerned about was the idea of trouble with the steamship company or at the customs somewhere. Didn't know anything about that sort of thing, and appeared to have an idea that someone might think it fishy and hold him up."

"Yes; that might have occurred to me."

"Quite an ordinary matter, of course. We obtained and filled up a special customs declaration form so that there will be no trouble on that score, and as he still seemed anxious we wrote to the Cunard Company and got their express acceptance of the freight on our voucher. Now as regards—"

"Thank you," interposed Annesley with a grateful air. "I think that should be something for my people to go on. It's a little doubtful, as I said, but if anything—"

"We should do our best, rely on it," acquiesced Mr Noate, with suave dignity.

* * * * *

Carrados retrieved a creased sheet of foolscap from his waste-paper basket, thoughtfully straightened it out, and added a few more lines of writing to round off the new position.

"What precaution has he taken against inconvenient curiosity?

"He has provided himself with a perfectly *bona fide* receipt for what he may be suspected of unlawfully possessing, and he has insured against an unusual property leading to awkward inquiry. He has created a sort of proprietorial alibi, which, like all fictitious alibis, may prove disastrous when it begins to crumble.

This time he burned the sheet. The précis was complete.

The last up-train from Stratford-on-Avon with any tolerable connexion for Paddington (the 6.32 in those days) had just pulled out of Leamington. There was no lack of accommodation and the single occupant of a smoking compartment well towards the rear was congratulating himself that he would be undisturbed for the remainder of the journey when two men passed slowly along the corridor, dropping an occasional word of comment.

"This will do quite nicely," said Mr Carrados, stopping at the compartment indicated and Parkinson slid the door open for him. "Come back as we reach Westbourne Park."

"Very well, sir," replied Parkinson, as he closed the door and moved on again.

The blind man settled down in his corner seat and lifted his face towards the other passenger.

"Ah, Mr Lacksome, I believe," he remarked sociably. "Delightful old place, Stratford, isn't it?"

Rigby Lacksome lowered the late evening paper that he had provided himself with at Leamington station and favoured the intruder with a long, cool stare.

"That's my name, sir," he replied with deliberation. "But you have the advantage of me."

"Scarcely," smiled Mr Carrados. He appeared to be in excellent spirits, as though the interview promised some entertainment.

"I mean," explained the other man distantly, "that I have no recollection of ever having seen you before."

"That gives me no advantage, for I do not even see you now."

"What do you mean?"

"Simply that I am blind." Mr Carrados beamed benignly on his startled fellow-traveller. "There is no question of who holds the ace, you see, if it should come to violence."

"Just a modicum of breathing time, sir," pleaded Mr Lacksome. "You cut the ice considerably quicker than I can stack it... Why violence?"

"One never knows... I was talking to a man about a murder recently—just as casually as I am talking now to you. He became very violent."

Lacksome's vaguely calculating glance went round the narrow place they were enclosed in and came back to the self-possessed figure in the other corner without losing a shred of its own slightly arrogant assurance.

"There's some mistake, I guess," he remarked. "Are you one of the Scotland Yard outfit?"

Mr Carrados laughed appreciatively. "No, no," he said; "you mustn't poke fun at our national institutions, Mr Lacksome. I am really no one. I ought to have introduced myself before.

My name is Carrados—Max Carrados. I am just interested in things."

"I see," commented the other reflectively. Then he added, "Any particular sort of things, might I inquire, sir?"

"Crime in general, if it promises originality. At the moment I am curious to clear up one or two points in what I might call the Mystery of the Anatomical Specimen."

Rigby Lacksome stretched his limbs and yawned slightly to demonstrate indifference.

"It sounds like a three-reel thrill all right, Mr Cahrados," he said. "What does it hinge on?"

I'm afraid," apologized Mr Carrados, "that it hinges on one of your own articles of luggage... No, the communication cord, if that is what you are looking for, is on your side."

"I guessed you were trying to put it across me about being blind," said Mr Lacksome cutely. "I don't want the cord, but I want to know right here before we go any further how you come into this."

"It's a detail of our old-fashioned judicial system," explained Mr Carrados. "According to these antiquated laws it is the duty of the merest outsider—myself, for instance—to arrest and give into custody anyone whom he reasonably suspects of having committed a felony."

"Is that so?" drawled Mr Lacksome, moving a careless hand. "How does he get on with it if he finds himself looking down the barrel of a gun?"

"What, violence already!" chid Mr Carrados amiably. "And after I had warned you, too! But the answer to that, Mr Lacksome, is that a blind man—and you may take my word for it—never knows, of course that he *is* looking down the barrel of a gun."

Rigby Lacksome's hand went back again to its former position.

"Excuse me relapsing into the vernacular, Mr Cahrados," he remarked, not without a streak of admiration, "but you certainly are the gelidest brand of guy I've ever struck."

"Of course," assented his companion; "why not? I am sure it would shock you immeasurably if you met an Englishman who began to show traces of emotion under any circumstances whatever. You, for your part, are the most accomplished body-snatcher I have so far had to do with. Something like an hour must elapse before we reach Paddington. Why should we not entertain one another like two travellers in a mid-Victorian Christmas Annual?"

"Preparatory to being handed over to a posse of the station police at the terminus?"

The blind man raised a deprecatory gesture.

"Surely you must have misunderstood me, Mr Lacksome. I said that such was the *duty* of every citizen... Alas; how few of us do our duty nowadays!"

"Just put it into English for me, sir," said Mr Lacksome wearily. "I'm late on the gear-clutch, I admit."

"It is quite simple. You will find that at Westbourne Park we shall slow down almost to nothing. There will be a couple of plain-clothes men waiting on the platform. If I show a white handkerchief at the window they will just step on to the footboard and take instructions. If I show a coloured one—a certain coloured one—they will know that the case has dropped through and they are not wanted."

"Great," admitted Mr Lacksome with suspicious fervour. "I had no idea that we were doing this for the movies, sir... And now let me tell you, Mr Cahrados, that you've given yourself the devil of a lot of trouble over nothing. The particular equipment that you seem to have had your nose into when no one was looking is a scientific exhibit that I've bought here for anthropological use in America... Like to see Blackley & Whiteing's receipt for it?"

"Not just now, thank you," replied Mr Carrados. "Mr Noate showed me the counterfoil. And we needn't waste time over the arrangement made at the Claverhill Street branch of the

S.W.L.; or your understanding with Rainproof Nogg; nor the engagement of Sam Barbel to be foreman of repairs."

"Hell!" was wrung from Rigby, "That makes a bobtail flush, I must allow, sir. I can only put up one card against a hand like that, but I guess he is the joker."

"Well?"

"You think I've lifted the mortal remains of old man Shakespeare to join the rest of Great Britain that we've accumulated over there, don't you, sir?"

"I think you set out with that idea."

"Say 'Yes', Mr Cahrados, won't you?" pleaded Lacksome. "I should love you to guess wrong just once."

"Was it the curse you weakened on?"

Mr Lacksome smiled his pagan superiority to such a failing.

"It was not, sir. I wouldn't deviate one jot, tittle, or iota for a sackful of best assorted medieval curses. Besides, do you think that the man who heart-throbbed to the tune of Romeo and Juliet, of Rosalind and Orlatido, and of Florizel and Perdita would care a banana-skin what became of his loose parts after three centuries if it would help me to win Sabina Craddock? No, sir; there wasn't a milligramme of gall in old man Shakespeare's constitution."

"It seems to me," remarked Mr Carrados, remembering something very similar not long before, "that whatever anyone wants to do about Shakespeare, it is easy to find authority in his works for doing it."

"That is so," agreed Rigby simply. "W. Shakespeare was not for an age, but for all time; not of one country but common to the world, and he said everything that there is to be said on every subject. That's where old man Nogg left the track. He has worked it out that Shakespeare was an American citizen, and he's tickled to death at the idea of getting him for his National Temple."

"I think someone else has already proved that he was a German," said Mr Carrados. "So why not a German-American?"

"Both wrong, sir," replied Mr Lacksome. "Shakespeare was really a Literary Syndicate. Rainproof is demonstrably *non compos mentis* on that subject, and his infirmity is spreading. My own concern is to get my matrimonial—and I may add financial—arrangements put through before he is actually certified. You see how I am fixed?"

Carrados nodded sympathetically. "But you haven't yet told me how you came to fail," he said.

"Fail..." considered Rigby dubiously. "Well, as to that... You are quite satisfied about it, Mr Cahrados?"

"Life is full of surprises," admitted Carrados, "but I must stand by my opinion. The stone had not been raised—the joint wouldn't even take water—and you certainly had not tunnelled."

"You are right sir. The paralysing truth is that the stone can't be raised."

"Can't? Why not?"

"That will have to wait for another generation to find out, I guess. All I know is that we had a patent suction jack—for of course we daren't use leverage—capable of raising five tons dead weight drawing on a stone weighing something less than five hundredweight and it couldn't budge it a hair. No, sir; do what we might it had us beaten to cold cinders. And if you want my *obiter dictum* I should say the biggest thing in W.S. enigmas is waiting patiently there for some bright boy to come along and scoop it."

"Quite likely," agreed Max Carrados. "You aren't the first to have a try by any means. And you are not going away absolutely empty-handed, I imagine?"

Mr Lacksome's face relaxed appreciably from its smart, purposeful expression into something suspiciously like a genial grin.

"Well, come now, Mr Cahrados," he replied. "What should you say! You know that right beneath my feet there, by what they call the old charnel house, there were enough ancient bones of every sort and kind to stock the field of Waterloo. Sculls, arms legs, middles, toes, fingers, ribs and what not. And there on the other side Hiram S. Nogg is lapping up my cables and biting his nails to keep calm about it. Why should we disappoint the poor old mono-maniac in the midst of plenty? Why, I've even rooted out a few odds and ends of antique coffins and a brass plate with something that you couldn't say wasn't a spear cut on it. Oh, Rainproof will be satisfied, never fear, and Sabina will be satisfied, and I don't see why Rigby Lacksome shouldn't be satisfied too. And in about another century there'll be the dandiest Shakespeare mystery spring up at Nogg's National Temple that ever was!"

The suburban lights had been growing thicker for the last few miles and the slackening train now began to dodge its way across the maze of points and switches. Parkinson's restful face appeared at the window and the corridor door was pushed open.

"We are approaching Westbourne Park, sir."

Lacksome started at the name, and despite the amiable relations that had occupied the journey his face was not without a shade of anxiety as he spoke.

"I hope you are satisfied as well, sir. After all—no one's a red cent worse off."

"Rather a fine point though, isn't it?" conceded Mr Carrados. "However—you're on the platform side—perhaps you'll show this from the window."

Rigby snatched the dark silk handkerchief from the blind man's hand and turned to wave it vigorously at the open window.

"But there's not a soul along the platform!" he exclaimed blankly, looking back. "Say, Mr Cahrados, have you been patting one over on me?"

"Dear me," confessed Mr Carrados, quite crestfallen. "Can I have dreamt that part of it, after all?"

6

THE CRIME AT THE HOUSE IN CULVER STREET

The garden gate of Thornden Lodge stood open as the Bellmarks walked past, and from the path beyond there came the sharp aggressive click of decisive shears at work. Elsie Bellmark grew irresolute, then stopped.

"Do you mind if I just pop in for a wee moment, Roy?" she asked. "I expect that it's Miss Barrowford gardening, and it will save me writing. G.F.S. business, you know."

"All right," her husband replied. "Only don't forget me and stay to supper."

"The idea! As if I ever—I'll catch you up—or won't you come in too? You know her."

"No," he decided. "If I do we shall be talking there for an hour. I won't go right on either. I'll just hang about in the middle distance to keep you up to the mark."

With a nod and a smile she left him, and almost immediately the sound of the shears ceased and through the privet hedge came the rather ecstatic interchange of greetings. A grin of affectionate amusement came into Bellmark's face as he slowly lit a cigarette.

"It's long odds on my finishing this undisturbed," ran his speculation; but he was wrong, for before the first ash had fallen an insinuating "Roy!" from beyond the privet hedge summoned him inside.

"All bets off," he murmured, as he cheerfully complied. "That isn't according to the rules, my dear."

"Oh Roy," exclaimed Elsie, signalling. "Sorry, couldn't help it," with her eyes, "Miss Barrowford wondered whether you had seen her brother. He didn't come by your train, did he?"

"You do know Vernon by sight, don't you, Mr Bellmark?" put in the lady of the garden. "It's unusual for him to be so late on Saturday."

"I think I know him," admitted Roy. "First class, nonsmoking; *Morning Post*: never in a hurry; nine-thirty-seven, isn't he?"

"Spats; black tie: neat umbrella," smiled Miss Barrowford. "Has been in the Civil Service. Yes?"

"At all events he didn't come, or he would have been here long ago—this young lady has been shopping as we came along, and leisurely at that. And when I come to think of it, there was only one other man got off the train at Stanthorpe—an oldish fellow, who didn't quite seem as though he knew what he was doing here. Women and children in plenty, but no other man."

"Well, I don't think that anyone would describe Vernon as exactly old," hazarded his sister. "We are neither of us children certainly, but— "

"No, indeed," exclaimed Elsie with great fervour. "I mean," she added hastily, as she realized that her well-meant disclaimer had got belated, "I mean about your brother, of course. Why I feel ages older than he looks, I'm sure."

"All the same, my dear," confided Miss Barrowford dropping her voice, "I think he feels the stress of business life of late. I often wonder if he was quite well advised in giving up the Civil Service for commerce. Somerset House is so assured; the feeling of permanency must be very tranquillizing."

"I suppose he has to work hard now?" suggested Elsie politely. She had very little interest in the absent Vernon and still less in his occupation, but Miss Barrowford was "a dear", and the surest way to her good opinion was to turn a sympathetic ear to amiable garrulities on her two subjects—her wonderful garden and her exceptional brother.

"Yes," agreed the sister with a slightly dubious look; "I suppose he has. But it is more the weight of responsibility that I was thinking of. Vernon, you see, was never brought up to the business—to any business, in fact—and when an uncle left it entirely to him on condition that he carried it on, it was like beginning life over again. His real tastes are literary and artistic, and he had to overcome something like a positive aversion to trade—though it is strictly wholesale trade of course."

"I don't think that I even know what he does," admitted Elsie. "But perhaps I oughtn't to be inquisitive—"

"Oh, yes, my dear; there's no secret at all about it." Miss Barrowford's shrewd, good-natured eyes opened wide at the implication. "It's a wholesale fancy leather business—Widdowson & Stubb in Culver Street, though Uncle Con was the last Stubb and there hasn't been a Widdowson in it for half a century. They do with all the finer sorts of leather. Vernon didn't know the least thing about either leather or business when he took it up, but he had a very capable manager and reliable staff, or I don't know what might have happened."

"It sounds nice—fine leather: bindings have such a lovely smell. Do you ever go and revel among it, Miss Barrowford? I should."

"I have been once or twice, but I am not fond of going," confessed the lady. "The place was formerly a large, rambling old house—it was a good residential district once—and many years ago a very dreadful murder was committed there. Of course"—with an appropriate smile—"it is now haunted. But, seriously, I do not care about the place; it is a little errie after dusk."

"How gruesome! And your brother really likes it now?"

Miss Barrowford indicated the complexity of her opinion by a shrug and a ladylike little mom before she committed herself on this. She even snipped off a superfluous leaf enigmatically as she glanced slyly at her other visitor.

"Men are strange beings, my dear," she replied. "Do we ever know what they really like—or, for that matter, do they know themselves? But who have we here?"

The gate, which had been pushed to on Mr Bellmark's entrance, was very slowly opened by an unfamiliar hand and along the immaculate path there advanced a peculiar figure—curious not by reason of anything outlandish in dress or feature but by his odd detachment from the scene and his pathetic air of being in some way lost. A trite synonym for witlessness is "not all there", and no phrase could better describe the impression that the stranger made: some essential thing was missing.

"Now, who in the world—" speculated Miss Barrowford with a queer afarness in her voice, and then suddenly she gave a startled little cry and ran a few steps forward, only to stop again in a nameless fear.

"Vernon. *Vernon*!" was wrung from her, though scarcely heard. "What is it? Oh, my dear, what ever can have happened?"

"Good God!" whispered Bellmark to his wife. "This is the man I spoke of—the one who came by the train. It isn't the fellow I took to be her brother, and yet it somehow is. Do you catch on to it?"

"I don't know what you are saying," replied Elsie, hypnotized by the two before her. "But there is something dreadful."

"Oughtn't we to go away?" he asked.

"I'm too bewildered to know. I shouldn't like her to think—And yet she may want us."

Very slowly Vernon Barrowford walked up the familiar path to the door of his house, looking to the right and the left occasionally as he seemed to verify some half-forgotten landmark. He passed his sister, he passed the others, without a sign of recognition, but when Miss Barrowford caught him up and took his hand with a passionate cry to be spoken to he did not shake her off. Only he never spoke. Docilely he allowed himself to be led up the steps to the closed front door. Standing there, with the same monotonous precision that had marked his passage through the garden, he took out his bunch of keys, selected the right one with slow deliberation, and unlocked the door.

"I must go in to her," said Elsie, as the two passed out of sight. "Whatever it is, we've seen it now, so it can't much matter. You will wait, won't you?"

"Of course I'll wait," he replied half gruffly. "Tell her we'll do anything—"

In three minutes she was back again. Bellmark had discovered a garden seat and was meditating. He looked at her with inquiry in his eyes.

"He's sitting there in the morning-room, and he does nothing. He won't speak. And, Roy—don't laugh—she whispered to me would I ask you how you can tell if people are drunk or not. She thinks it may be that, but I'm sure it isn't."

"You ask them," replied Roy gravely. "In either case they deny it, but if they are drunk they begin to argue about it and want to prove that they're not, and the more you agree and say, 'It's all right, old man; don't shout and nobody will notice anything,' the warmer they become, until you can hear a very intoxicated man a mile away protesting how sober he is."

"Well, that's no good because he certainly wouldn't speak. She'd be only too relieved if he would, whatever he might say."

"He looked sober enough just now—too sober, in fact. If you want my opinion, it's a doctor's job."

"I think so too, Roy. I'm sure she'd be glad to be encouraged to send, so I'll go in again and tell her what you say."

"Wait a minute," he advised, looking over her shoulder. "I think—yes, here she comes."

"What does he say?" asked Miss Barrowford, as Elsie went to meet her.

"He thinks you ought to have a doctor at once. I think so too, dear. We are afraid that you brother is really ill in some way."

"I am sure that you are right. Yes, I will send for Dr Page at once. It is all very sudden, and for the moment I wished to keep it from the servants if it had been—anything disgraceful. I ought to have known Vernon better, but it is so inexplicable."

"We'll go straight there and tell Dr Page to come. I'm sure Roy will get him as soon as anyone could."

"Would you? That's very kind of you," said Miss Barrowford quite gratefully.

"Oh, how can you talk like that!" exclaimed Elsie, kissing her in a scramble. "It's nothing, and anybody would—"

"I'll go back now and wait, then," remarked her friend. "I must not leave him for long."

"Should Roy go on alone and I'll stay with you until the doctor comes?" suggested Elsie.

"No, thank you, dear. I am not in the least afraid of anything and I shall tell the servants now."

Dr Page must have been immediately accessible, for in less than twenty minutes—he lived half a mile away—his cheerful, commonplace mien and quiet confidence were diffusing a healthier feeling within Thornden Lodge. Miss Barrowford's face lost something of its unaccustomed greyness and the two maids no longer deemed it necessary to talk in whispers. No one ever thought of describing Page as a "clever" doctor; "good" was the word they used, and that meant that you generally got better soon.

"So it's Master Vernon's turn this time, eh?" he remarked, as he walked across to the unresponsive figure sitting huddled in the big easy-chair—he had dosed "Master Vernon" through whooping cough and measles thirty years before. "When I was last here on business it was your turn, I think, Miss Barrowford."

"Oh, then!" she exclaimed disdainfully. "That was nothing—a touch of flu."

"Nothing when you were all right, again, was it?" he acquiesced tolerantly. "That's the way with things, isn't it? No, he'll do very well where he is thanks. Now let us see."

Miss Barrowford stood aside while the detailed examination went on, ready to do just as she was told, and too sensible a woman to interrupt with needless, anxious questions. When he had finished, Page walked thoughtfully to the window and looked out; she followed with her eyes, now definite in inquiry.

"The simple word 'shock' covers a multitude of effects. 'Shock', Miss Barrowford. Does that satisfy you?"

"I don't understand yet. It is all so very sudden—and—terrifying. Is he—is he dangerously ill?"

"Meaning 'Will he die?' No, he is not. You have a convalescent on your hands. All the mischief has been done; the business is to bring him back to normal health."

"But—doctor—what is it—what has happened?"

"Shock. That is what I crudely indicate. There is no external lesion of any kind: no blow has been experienced. Bellmark told me how he arrived. Whether there is any especial reason—business or personal, for instance—why Vernon should be likely to have any very violent mental disturbance just now, you would be in a better position to know than I should."

"I know of nothing—nothing at all. And it's so dreadful, his never speaking."

"You must not ask him. That is the chief thing now—perfect rest. If he begins to wake up don't encourage him to talk. If they send here from the business wanting to know anything they'll have to do without it. You understand that quite literally, don't you. Miss Barrowford? No matter what it is If the office can't go on without him it must stop. Better the business than the man—he's our job."

"Is it so serious then?" she whispered, the clutch at her heart tightening again.

"It might easily become so if we don't take care, In a few days we shall know more about it—whether, for instance, the loss of speech extends to true aphasia or is only the temporary reflex of the first excitement. I should like to get McFlynn here to have a look—it's his especial subject. Tomorrow or Monday, shall I?"

"Certainly," she replied. "Oh, doctor—anything—everything—you can do."

"Yes, yes," he nodded. "I know. You'd better have a nurse in—for a week, at any rate. Miss Hodge is doing nothing just now and she is handy. Shall I ring her up when I get back?"

"If you think I'd better. Of course"—a little wistfully—"you know I *can* nurse fairly well; still—"

"For a week," he said, smiling reassuringly. "Then perhaps—"

"Very well. I will sit on the doorstep like a veritable dragoness and keep intruders off. But are we to do nothing to find out what has happened doctor?"

"Oh, yes; indeed we must. Everything short of asking him about it. It will be the first step towards repairing the damage to find out what has caused it. We know that he arrived at Stanthorpe in this condition, so we must try farther back. He may have had a terribly narrow squeak of some sort."

"There's the warehouse. But everyone will have left long since."

"Still, that's the place to begin from. Isn't there a manager I've heard of?"

"Yes—Mr Pridger. He lives at Croydon."

"You have his address?"

"Oh, yes, Shall I—"

"Yes, wire him to come up and see you as soon as he can get—tonight or tomorrow. Find out all he can suggest, but"—with a warning finger—"don't take him in to your brother. No reminders of the past just yet."

It was the capable manager's long-established custom to escort Mrs Pridger to a theatre once a week, and Saturday evening had come to be the occasion of this rite. It not being a matter of life and death—Miss Barrowford's telegram simply enjoined "as soon as possible"—there seemed no pressing reason why Mr Pridger should set forth on an adventurous journey from Croydon to Stanthorpe after midnight, so that, as it developed, it was not until Sunday afternoon that he learned of his employer's condition.

Turning in at the gate of Thornden Lodge, on her mission "to inquire", Elsie Bellmark came face to face with a departing stranger, and, preoccupied as she was, she wondered vaguely at the queer look his face wore in the momentary flash before he recognized that she was calling there. The front door stood open, and it seemed very quiet within. With a freedom born of the circumstances Elsie ventured to investigate unannounced. The door of the morning-room was slightly ajar and from beyond came a low, intermittent note. She tapped very gently.

"Come in," said Miss Barrowford's voice, and the other sound stopped.

She was sitting on a couch—it was plain that a moment before she had been lying there, and her eyes and handkerchief betrayed the nature of her occupation. Mrs Bellmark was appalled.

"Oh, dear Louise!" she said, and began to back out again.

"Don't run away," called out the occupant. "That was the last of it anyway. Thank you for coming. I was expecting you some time today."

"He isn't worse, is he?"

"Oh no; he is almost the same as you saw. It wasn't that."

"You don't mean that there's something else?"

"Did you meet Mr Pridger as you came in? He has just gone."

"I did meet a man—at the gate. Whatever is it?"

"It feels rather like the end of the world. We've had a fire."

"Here?"

"No—at the office and warehouse. It's practically burnt out, he says."

"Mr Pridger?"

"Yes; that's why he couldn't get here this morning. The police came across his address first and they sent for him. He found the place a wreck. Isn't it disastrous?"

"Had it—the fire—anything to do with Mr Barrowford being ill?"

"We don't see how it could. Mr Pridger knows practically nothing of Vernon's movements yesterday, as he himself had to go to another part of London to see a customer and he didn't think it worthwhile going back to Culver Street afterwards. The fire was not discovered until late on Saturday night, and long before that Vernon was here."

"Yes," agreed Mrs Bellmark; "but it seems funny, all the same. I suppose it's insured anyway, being a business."

"Oh, yes, I'm certain it will be. But it's bound to be unsettling to Vernon, don't you see. Just when he will be getting all right again and wanting to go back to work he will have to be told of this upset. It will take months to rebuild and straighten up."

"It will be a good chance for him to take a long rest, I should say," declared Mrs Bellmark. "And, another thing, dear, from what you said yesterday I imagine that your brother might not be sorry to give up the business. We don't know, of course, but this might be an opportunity—"

"Oh, don't think that," exclaimed Miss Barrowford hastily. "I am sure Vernon would never dream of taking advantage of such a way out."

"Well, I don't know," said Elsie. "It isn't as if he had set it on fire himself. But what's the good of talking about that? You are no nearer getting at what happened then?"

"Not a bit. And I'm beginning to wonder what next to do if, as I expect, he left the office all right."

"I've been thinking," volunteered her friend. "Did you ever hear of Mr Carrados?"

"I don't think so," admitted Miss Barrowford vaguely. And then with the common frailty of mankind she added: "But the name seems somehow familiar."

"He finds out things. He's quite wonderful at it, considering that he's blind. It's a hobby of his, because he is quite rich."

"But if he is blind, dear—"

"You hardly notice it. If you had lost something from here—stolen or disappeared, I mean—and he was helping you, he might come into this room and in a few minutes he would know all about it: the size and where the furniture was and the colour of the wall-paper and when you last had the chimney swept and why you had moved a picture from one place to another. All the time you would be talking about nothing in particular as you thought and then he would pick up an old nail that no one else had noticed or touch a scratch on the paint."

"How could he see the nail to pick it up?" demanded the elder lady practically.

"He couldn't, of course, but he would pick it up all the same. And in a few days or a few weeks it would lead in some absurdly simple way straight to what you had lost."

"It sounds very marvellous," conceded Miss Barrowford dubiously, "but in any case we do not know this Mr Carrados."

"We know him pretty well—from the time when we used to live at Groats Heath," said Elsie. "An uncle of mine is his great friend. I am sure he would come if he thought that it would help us: We are under a very great obligation to him."

"But, my dear," corrected Louise Barrowford precisely, "that's the wrong way about. It would be if he was under an obligation to you."

"Oh, he doesn't do things like that," responded Elsie from the heights. "Besides, if he was I shouldn't like to ask him."

When Max Carrados learned the particulars of the Barrowford case his first proceeding—before he decided whether it interested him or not—was an obvious one. He made inquiry at Scotland Yard and at certain divisional headquarters to find out if anything had been observed on the Saturday that would promise to bear on the mystery. It had not. No trace of Vernon was picked up until Baker Street Station was reached, where a porter who knew him as a "first season" had noticed that he seemed "groggy". The blind man decided that the case offered enough obscurity to attract him.

It was not until the Wednesday after the tragic happening that Max Carrados found leisure to get across to Stanthorpe. Elsie took him on to Thornden Lodge, where Miss Barrowford, now almost accustomed to her silent charge, received him with some trepidation. It was clear that Mrs Bellmark's rather freely coloured portrait had sunk in, and the lady of the house expected curious things to materialize beneath her eyes. Carrados had never seemed more matter-of-fact in his procedure. He betrayed no startling knowledge of the surroundings (to his sponsor's despair) and merely encouraged Miss Barrowford to talk about her brother from every angle. She was nothing loath, but Elsie had heard most of it before. Nor were his inquiries less commonplace.

"You have looked through his pockets, I suppose?" he asked. "You found nothing unusual?"

"Nothing that I had not seen a hundred times before—with one exception. There was a large enamelled badge or check with a number on."

"Perhaps I might see it?" suggested the inquirer. "Oh, yes"—when it was produced—"this is a cloak-room voucher from the reading-room at the British Museum."

"He frequently went to the National Gallery, I know," suggested Miss Barrowford. "Might it not perhaps be from there?"

"No," replied Carrados. "A benevolent authority has arranged that you shall not procure your neighbour's new silk umbrella from one institution by depositing your own worn-out walking-stick at another, and so all the sets of tickets vary. Is your brother absent-minded in a general way, Miss Barrowford?"

"No, indeed; he is one of the most precise of people. Why?"

Carrados held up the numbered badge significantly.

"Whatever that stands for he omitted to reclaim," he explained. "It is generally a stick or umbrella."

"Of course," she acquiesced. "Vernon invariably carried an umbrella, and on Saturday he returned without it. I took it for granted that he had left it in the train."

"If this usually exact man forgot it after going specially to the reading-room—umbrella or whatever it may be—it is assumable that he may have learned something important there, isn't it?"

"Yes, yes," exclaimed Elsie keenly. "Can you find out what?"

"If it turns upon a book it is doubtful. You help yourself to the thousands of more general works of reference. I suppose"—to Miss Barrowford—"you did not come across a cancelled application slip for a book?"

"I know the sort of thing you mean," she replied. "No, he had none about him."

"They are usually torn up," agreed Mr Carrados.

"Apropos of papers now," continued Miss Barrowford, "Miss Hodge—the nurse, you know—found something rather curious this morning. Vernon was sitting by a table on which there happened to be some stationery—a few sheets of paper and a pen and ink. He wasn't looking at it, but Miss Hodge noticed that his hand was moving on the paper. When she went to him she found that he had actually been scribbling there—hardly words, perhaps, and quite unintelligible, but she thought it was encouraging."

"Yes," assented Carrados, speaking so quietly that one might have thought he was afraid of startling so wonderful a thing of promise away, "I am sure it would be. What became of the paper?"

"I think it was left about—or she may have thrown it away. Do you want it?"

"It is not without interest," admitted the blind man. "I think we ought to see it."

It had not been thrown away, though Miss Hodge hoped for much more coherent signs of intelligence ere long. Carrados accepted the sheet and grasped its details of shape, weight, and texture as readily as another would by sight, while the two ladies overlooked his movements curiously.

"I cannot make head or tail of it," confessed Miss Barrowford, as the senseful fingers crossed and recrossed the scrawl, now following a vague spidery line, now drawn where no visible mark appeared to lead. "Is there any meaning, do you think?"

"That little arrangement comes in more than once," said Elsie, indicating a hieroglyphic twist. "I'm sure it must mean something."

"That little arrangement is the word 'red', and it comes in seven times," interpreted the patient seeker. "It is the strongest impression that persists."

"Red! But what—" conjectured the sister with a tremor in her voice.

"Oh, a lamp-post—a sunshade—a picture," reassured Mr Carrados quickly. "Even a lead pencil if it happened to be there at the right moment."

"Or a fire, I suppose?" suggested Elsie unfortunately.

"Here is a test for ingenuity." Carrados was anxious to repair his indiscretion. "That is a single word manifestly, but what?"

"It doesn't make a word to me," declared Miss Barrowford, after a minute's scrutiny.

"'Meou' or 'miaow', if there was such a thing," suggested Elsie.

"Well, isn't there? What does one call a cat noise?"

"But why not write 'cat'?" Miss Barrowford objected. "If that is it."

"Because the noise is the most arresting thing about it," he replied. "A 'miaowing' cat."

"Shut in," contributed Elsie. "Now I wonder what that long scrawl may be?"

"I think I had better take this for detailed tests," said Mr Carrados, coolly transferring the paper to his pocket. He was not anxious for the broken man's sister to discover that the "long scrawl" (twice repeated) stood for "horrible", or that the poignant exclamation "Oh!" had been penned four times. Later search disclosed only one other word. "This," considered Max Carrados as he reviewed his slender clues that night, "this is the flashlight on a man's brain at the moment of its extinction," and he arranged the impressions according to their persistence:

Red Red Red Red Red Red Red
Oh Oh Oh Oh
Horrible Horrible Horrible
Miaow Door

But as yet Mr Carrados was still in Miss Barrowford's drawing-room, and at the moment he was there alone, for, on the question of certain rather delicate G.F.S. procedure, the lady of the house had sought an excuse to carry off her other visitor.

Why Mr Pridger, on being shown in a few minutes later, should have tacitly assumed that the gentleman who seemed so tolerably at home on the hearthrug must be his employer's doctor, does not appear. Possibly there was an ambiguous word in the simple-mannered girl's exclamation of surprise at finding another visitor still there; possibly Mr Carrados's bland air of perfect self-possession lent itself to the idea.

"Sad business, isn't it?" remarked the manager expansively. "Patient any better today, sir?"

So far, although one might hazard a guess, the blind man had no knowledge of his new acquaintance. A wisely professional shake of the head committed him to nothing.

"Ah! Looks like being a long business, I'm afraid. I wonder if you could give me an idea—I'm his manager, by the way—any sort of an idea how long it might be before he would be fit again?"

"That is a difficult question to answer at all, and an impossible one to answer satisfactorily."

"Yes, I guessed as much. But it makes it rather awkward for me, sir. And when he does come, as you may say, to himself—I suppose there have been plenty of other cases similar—what will he be like should you say?" There was a moment of hesitation in framing the crux of what he sought, an assumption of negligence that stood out like the postscript of a lady's letter, but it had to come: "Will he remember what happened to him up to the last?"

"*Will he remember!*" What did Mr Pridger anticipate; what had he to fear? Carrados could not see the respectful, serious-eyed, decorously-attired manager who stood there. The whole of Mr Pridger's eminently respectable appearance went for nothing, but a hundred other indications that he had never taken into account were signalling their message through subtler mediums.

It was a question to which there could be no absolute reply, but it fell in with the investigator's impulse to lull the man's misgivings, and in his impromptu character Carrados spoke to that end of other curious cases. Mr Pridger seemed to breathe more freely.

"So far as the actual business is concerned, of course his being away wouldn't make a ha'p"orth of difference," he confided. "I'm the practical man and the governor looks on. But there isn't any business now; the fire has put the lid on that. And the latest is that the insurance company is going to be nasty."

This was news, and Mr Carrados encouraged its recital by a sympathetic question.

"They don't say so yet, but the suggestion is incendiarism. They sent down a man at once in the ordinary way, and now we've had a notice to leave everything just as it is pending a further examination."

"Why should they think anything wrong?"

"These insurances go a lot by the fire brigade report. I suppose the officer in charge has suggested something."

"But surely he must be mistaken?"

"Well, it isn't for me to say. I'm an employee of the firm and bound to stand by it. Besides, I was away all the Saturday after ten o'clock, so I couldn't say what happened. But it's no secret that W. & S. have been getting short of the ready for more than a year now; it's claimed that the fire began in three or four places at once; and Mr Barrowford was the last to leave the premises. We've got to make the best of that whether we like it or not."

"How gratuitously a rogue gives himself away; every clumsy insinuation is a window to his mind," ran the hearer's thoughts, while his commiserating voice was saying, "Dear, dear me! This is very surprising."

"Of course"—implied the loyal manager, and "Oh, of course; not a word," assented his confidant. He had at that moment picked up the returning footsteps on the stairs and the *tête-à-tête* was at an end.

"I don't altogether trust that manager," confessed Mrs Bellmark as she carried the blind man off a little later. "I came suddenly face to face with him here a few days ago and he was grinning in a most sinister fashion. Why should he seem so taken aback that you were not a doctor?"

"People get such curious ideas, don't they?" agreed Mr Carrados. "I thought that he seemed annoyed about something when your friend said who I was. And yet he had been talking quite confidentially to me just before."

"You hadn't misled him about being the doctor, had you?" asked a rather startled Elsie.

"Misled? I! Good gracious no; I wouldn't mislead a tortoise."

"No, of course I didn't actually mean that you would," said the amiable girl almost penitently. "But really and truly I don't always quite know what to say about you, Mr Carrados. I was trying to tell Miss Barrowford what you would do and I could think of nothing better than to say that you might pick up a pin or a needle and that would be sufficient clue for you, and, do you know, all the time we were there she was craning her neck to see if you picked one up!"

"I wish I'd known," he chuckled. "I certainly would have done."

"I wonder," mused Elsie artlessly, "if you did pick anything up?"

"No needles," he replied lightly. "A few loose threads at the most."

It was in pursuit of the other ends of those same threads that Mr Carrados motored up to Culver Street on the next day. It was a neighbourhood of small industries with their contiguous offices, almost deserted after business hours and a wilderness at week-ends. Such shops as appeared to exist there were those supported by a special and assured clientage, with here and there a modest establishment of the humbler catering class. Widdowson and Stubb, not being in need of even such publicity as that peaceful thoroughfare afforded, had been thrust into the background by more assertive neighbours and had to be reached along an inner passage. A back entrance with a trade approach was discoverable in a cul-de-sac that seemed to have no name.

Parkinson accompanied his master, and with the perfect understanding of long association he reproduced from time to time just those details of the surroundings that he knew to be required. So much was routine, for any special need a word was enough to direct his peculiar talent for observation into the desired channel.

Interest in No. 33 as the scene of the fire had passed away—indeed nothing of the premises involved could be seen from Culver Street. The door, the sole evidence on that side of the existence of Widdowson & Stubb, opened to a push and the visitors found themselves in a long, bare passage, where a notice painted on the wall directed the inquirer onward to the office.

"We will wait here a moment and consider the circumstances," directed Mr Carrados.

"Very good, sir," replied Parkinson. He knew that at those close quarters his descriptive powers were not required unless to some specific end, and the blind man's interest in the floor and walls did not concern him. He sauntered down the passage and then back again.

"I imagine that Mr Carlyle is in the room beyond, sir," he remarked. "I can hear what I apprehend to be his voice."

"Yes," assented Carrados. "He is part of the circumstances."

They found the inquiry agent dominating the ruin of what had been the principal's office, and with him Mr Pridger. The manager's greeting was not by any stretch of imagination cordial, but Mr Carlyle's triumphantly assertive cry of welcome drowned the other's formal inquiry as to how he could serve the visitor.

"You, of all men, by the immortal powers!" he proclaimed enthusiastically. "What piece of luck brings you this way, Max?"

"I scarcely think that the Barrowfords would describe it as that," replied Carrados, indicating their surroundings. "Do you happen to know that Elsie is quite a friend of theirs?"

"What, my niece?" exclaimed Mr Carlyle, with a sudden drop in his elation. "No, by gad, I didn't. To be sure, they all live at Stanthorpe, don't they? I shall get into hot water over this, Max; I'm here for the Business and Domestic Insurance people."

"I may as well go on with my own work now, Mr Carlyle," interposed the manager, with severe formality. "For any other particulars you may require I'm entirely at your service."

"Queer affair," explained the professional investigator, with a gracious gesture of assent towards the departing Pridger. "Shocking barefaced attempt, Max, if ever there was one. And now, I hear, this Barrowford is playing possum to avoid explaining things."

"Oh, have you extracted that admission from the reluctant Pridger, Louis?"

"Egad, the fellow feels it, being connected with such a job; but he sees that there's nothing to be gained by piling perjury on the top of arson. Four separate fires, all starting about the same time, figure in this remarkable outbreak, and the first things to be consumed are the firm's books."

"That was very unfortunate," admitted Max Carrados.

"It was, when you consider. Books, Max, are about the most stubbornly uninflammable things that you find about an office. So long as it remains closed it is next to impossible to light a solidly-bound ledger; what happens is that it slowly chars for an inch or two inwards all round. These"—indicating the heap of soaked debris on the floor—"have been deliberately thrown open, drenched with some spirit, and set fire to."

"Turpentine," declared the blind man, picking up the relic of a volume. "All this must have taken time, Louis."

"Undoubtedly; the preparations were thorough enough for anything."

"Vernon Barrowford—the last to leave as you very naturally insist—locked the Culver Street door after him at half-past twelve. The general office clerk was here certainly up to twelve-twenty. Ten minutes at the outside, Louis."

"I haven't gone into that yet. He may have returned again. We learn that he did not reach home until rather late that day."

"I think he very likely did return, and my interest lies in what he found here. He certainly went meanwhile to the reading-room of the British Museum—I have his umbrella in my car at this moment."

"To pass the time until it was safe to return here? The brigade think half-past twelve too early to assume this fire which was not discovered until about ten at night."

"The place is shut in all round and a moderate fire might go on for a long time unseen, but three or four o'clock would suit me better than half-past twelve," agreed Carrados. "What case of motive are you making against him, Louis?"

"The suggestion is that the stock has been going down ever since this Barrowford took on the business—five years ago—and the insurance has remained the same. The concern is practically bankrupt now, and the manager admits—"

"Don't say 'admits', Louis; I have already conversed with that good, and faithful servant."

"Well, I am only dealing with facts, whatever we call the source of our information. For months past Barrowford has been trying to get in capital. Lately he found some people who were not unwilling, but of course they stipulated for a proper stocktaking and an independent audit. Now that's just what—"

"I say," came a plaintive voice from outside the door, "I don't want to intrude, but—"

"Come in by all means," called back Mr Carlyle. "The formalities of office routine are suspended for the nonce. But if you want to see the manager—"

"No, I don't want to see good old Pridger," said the visitor, disclosing himself as an elderly young man of rather languid aspect; "I just drifted across, *en passant*, for a nod and a sympathetic word with dear old Vernon, but the bright young Frederick intimates that he hasn't arrived—"

"We are afraid he isn't likely to arrive," volunteered Mr Carrados. "Your friend is rather seriously ill at present."

"You don't say so," replied the caller, balancing himself against his walking-stick after looking vainly round for an unburnt piece of furniture to lean upon. "Nervous breakdown and all that, I suppose? The fact is, dear old Vernon wasn't cut out for the turmoil of modern business competition. It was a fundamental error for him ever to have crept out of his cosy corner in Somerset House, where he really was integral. He didn't fit the wall space here."

"I understand that his tastes were literary and artistic," remarked Mr Carrados.

"Literary and artistic? Literary and artistic!" repeated the new acquaintance, with some play in emphatics. "Certainly, the dear old somniloquist achieved an occasional letter to the Moribund Review on "Telepathy among Cab Horses", or something of that sort, but, my good Lord, artistic! And that reminds me—what has become of the Van Doop amid the cataclysm?"

"The Van Doop?"

"Yes; you've come across the atrocity, haven't you? He had it hung up there when I was last in—Saturday. You don't mean to say—"

"If it was anywhere in this room on Saturday last it has certainly gone the way of all flesh," declared Mr Carlyle briskly. "A painting, I suppose? Those may be the remains of a frame where you are looking. Was it valuable?"

"If the dear old chap has had the mental acumen to insure it for what he claimed it to be worth I should say it was very valuable indeed," was the sage reply. "If not— "

"There is no picture of any sort in the schedule," declared Mr Carlyle, after consulting his papers.

"Then I don't mind telling you that it was rotten. Under the impression that anything signed 'Van Doop' was by Van Doop, and that anything by Van Doop was worth about the level thousand, the poor old haddock seems to have let a gang of Bond Street rooks put it across him to the tune of some three hundred. Of course it was easy, because he thought that he was a born judge, and that is the beginning of ignorance."

"Was he likely to find this out on Saturday?" asked Mr Carrados.

"Well, I told him. I don't see that you could have anything more conclusive than that," explained the gentleman with some complacency. "'My dear old image,' I said quite plainly. 'Van Doop painted only one "Portrait of a Father-in-Law" and that's in the Eremitage and has been for the last half century.'"

"The where?" inquired Mr Carlyle with alert curiosity.

"Eremitage—the Hermitage Museum at St Petersburg, you would probably call it."

"Yes, of course," assented Mr Carlyle hastily. "I didn't quite catch the word, that was all."

"'As for this mutton-faced adventurer,' I told him; 'he is probably a worked-up piece by Jan Van Doop—an obscure relative of the man. As a matter of fact, I think Lenlau disposes of this canvas in his list of spurious Van Doops.' 'Lenlau?' he said helplessly, and I saw that the unfortunate oyster had never heard of the one man who wrote intelligently on the subject of Van Doop. 'Good heavens, old thing!' I said, being really too overcome to rub it in, and then, as he asked me, I gave him the details of the work, and that's about all there is to it."

"I think that explains why Barrowford came back," said Carrados when the two were alone again. "That egregious *poseur* knew what he was talking about, at all events. Our man went to the reading-room, got out "Lenlau", and then returned here to verify some point of description."

"More desperate than ever," remarked Mr Carlyle significantly.

"Not desperate enough to burn a picture that he hasn't had the prudence to insure, especially as there might be a chance of getting something back yet," replied his friend. "Did he find the place on fire when he got here? It is difficult to imagine anything particularly 'horrible' about the redness of a burning room. Did he surprise Pridger, who attacked him? Then the cat? Of course it might—"

"One moment, Max, one moment," cut in Mr Carlyle's assertive protest. "It is very nattering of you to credit me with a supernatural intuition, but it makes your monologue unnecessarily cryptical. If this is a case of incendiarism—and, by Jupiter, on the evidence lying round I shall advise my clients to resist the claim tooth and nail—who is the perpetrator if not Barrowford?"

"Who?" said Max Carrados, and then his attention suddenly faded. With one of his disconcertingly exact movements he went direct to the mantlepiece, skirting a heap of debris in his progress, and picked up a few letters that were ranged there. "Oh, Louis, Louis, and we two sleuths are asking, you 'Who?' and I 'How?' and here are Barrowford's neglected letters."

"Pshaw!" fretted Garlyle impatiently. "What business are they of ours, Max? Besides, the fellow is too ill to deal with them by your account."

"And no letter-box to the door."

"Well, what of that?"

"The letters fall upon the floor." The blind man's inquiring fingers were touching off every word and sign accessible to them as he threw aside one packet after another. "What do you make of this, Louis?"

"A post card. Not very confidential that, eh? 'Thanks for your kind inquiry. At the moment we have not—' This is merely formal."

"Try the other side."

"Ah, the post mark, 'London, E.G., 12.30 p.m., 25 May'—Saturday last. You mean that if this was picked up on Saturday it indicates that someone was about after—let me see, twelve-thirty, say two-thirty delivery, say three o'clock here—and if it wasn't picked up—I see."

"Not exactly that. Isn't there a sort of a—" and he indicated the cancellation.

"A mere pinkish smudge from something. Do you mean that?"

"What one might perhaps describe as the faint impression of a cat's paw transferred in red. Now, Louis, what was the office cat—"

"But, good heavens, Max, seriously, what have we to do with the peregrinations of this feline marauder? You are not suggesting that the abandoned quadruped deliberately set fire to the establishment, are you? My only concern is who—"

"Oh, who, of course," apologized his friend. "You asked that before, didn't you, and I got led away to something else? Naturally, Pridger set the place on fire—hasn't he told you that yet?"

"The manager?" Louis Carlyle stared hard and incredulously for a moment, and then swung half round to Carrados's lead with his usual mental agility. "Do you know, Max, I always had an underlying instinct that there was something fishy—but so long as it is incendiarism I don't suppose it matters to my clients who the criminal is."

"Oh, don't you, my friend?" retorted Max. "It may considerably."

"How so?"

"Barrowford is the sole proprietor of this concern. If he sets it on fire that naturally invalidates his insurance. But if someone else does—"

"His manager," the other reminded him. "His confidential employee, Max."

"True. But you don't suggest that burning the place down is 'in or arising out of' his duty, do you?—especially as it was after hours! If you are thinking of your clients, Louis, you had much better stick to Barrowford."

"Well, after all, I shall keep an open mind on the subject yet. I have still to question some of the men—only Pridger and a boy come here now, and I must hunt the others up."

"And I must hunt the cat up. We won't trouble Pridger about it, but the boy might be worth seeing."

"Extraordinary fancies you sometimes get, Max," said Mr Carlyle, regarding this whim with benevolent toleration. "I believe half of them are to mystify the simple-minded. The curious thing is that now and then they seem to lead—indirectly, of course—to something we've been looking for."

"You've noticed that?" responded Carrados. "I thought that perhaps it was only my imagination."

"If you really want the boy I'll call him," preferred Mr Carlyle. "But I should warn you that even as boys go, he doesn't seem to be a very intelligent member of his tribe."

The blind man nodded a smiling assent, and Mr Carlyle, going to another door across the way, sent out his ample authoritative voice in a call for "Fred".

An undersized, weak-eyed lad of about fifteen emerged unwillingly from a secluded lair, and stuffing an untidy paper-backed book into a pocket as he came he greeted Mr Carlyle with a boorish "Well?"

"This is the brilliant individual, Max," said the inquiry agent with elegant disdain. "Democratic education, egad!"

"Can you tell me where we are likely to find the cat, Fred?" asked Mr Carrados persuasively. "Perhaps there is more than one kept here?"

"Cat?" repeated the unwholesome-looking boy stupidly. "The cat isn't none of my business."

"But you might perhaps know where it usually is," suggested the inquirer mildly. "Cats have habits, you know." But Fred was not to be cajoled by mildness, and turning away he muttered something of which only the words "if you use your eyes" emerged.

"You young ruffian!" exclaimed the irate Carlyle; "Is that the way to reply to a gentleman—and a blind man, too! If I were Mr Carrados I'd have you skinned, by Jupiter!"

Mr Carlyle was not unaccustomed to his impressive voice and forensic manner carrying effect, but he was hardly prepared for the dramatic change that his words produced.

"Mr Carrados, did you say—blind!" came from the boy in a wholly different tone. His doltish look was gone, his sulky bearing had given place to lively excitement, and his dull eyes were now charged with intelligence—almost with cunning. Coming nearer he laid a hand eagerly on the venerated sleeve, and dropping his voice to the tone appropriate to melodrama, "Are you Max Carrados, the blind "tec?" he demanded.

"Come, come; really!" protested Louis Carlyle, scandalized by his familiarity, but his friend only laughed understandingly.

"Was that 'Jake Jackson, the Human Bloodhound' you were reading just now?" he asked. "Pretty good, isn't it?"

"I'll tell you about the cat, sir," whispered the boy. "It was suffocated by the smoke on Saturday, and it's out at the back by the dust-bins now. Is it the fire or embezzlement you're on to now, sir?"

"Fred!" sounded the manager's voice not so far away. "Fred, where are—"

"Look out, sir," cautioned the boy, as he made for the door. "Old Pridger half suspects it's not going smooth. Bins straight through warehouse—yellow jinny cat." Then his former lethargy descended on him and he lounged into the passage muttering, "Electric fuses? "Ow'm I to know—"

"Oh, Fred," said the manager sharply, "why the devil can't you come when—Here, get your hat at once and take this note across to Marchmont's and wait an answer. Well, gentlemen—"

Two minutes later, as the three walked towards the warehouse, they encountered Fred on his way out. The loutish youth, not dreaming of giving way, barged into Mr Carrados and earned a reprimand for clumsiness and a further word for the whistle of studied disrespect with which he artistically rounded off the affair. When the opportunity came the blind man smoothed out the screw of paper that the encounter had left in his hand and read as follows:

If you want to know more about it meet me at twelve tonight (mid-night) on Waterloo Bridge. Boss is all right, but old P. is a churlish swine. I've been dogging his footsteps for months and can put you on to two banks where he goes in different names. What ho!
(Signed) FREDERICK THE BOY DETECTIVE.

"Frederick will probably be heard of again," speculated Carrados as he slid the message into his wallet. "All the same, I wish that his taste in appointments had not been quite so inconveniently dramatic."

* * * * *

"Dear Louis," wrote Max Carrados some time later, "I will redeem the promise made when you were called away in the middle of the Barrowford affair. You complained that I did not seem to take much interest in that conflagration, and you were right, for a mere straightforward piece of incendiarism offers nothing new. But the mystery of Vernon Barrowford's condition struck quite another line. Whether we should ever have reached a true understanding of that curious case without the miraculous intervention of Frederick is beside the question. That boy, Louis, is in his way a masterpiece. Do you know, every article of clothing that he wears is reversible, so that he can present quite a different appearance at the shortest notice!

"You will have seen that Pridger got five years. It might well have been more if Barrowford could have appeared, but that was out of the question, and so, much against the man had to be ignored. His is quite an ordinary case. His nature is not essentially criminal and he had no expensive tastes. For twenty years he had been an exemplary servant under the eye of old Conrad Stubb; but Stubb knew the business to his finger-nails, while Vernon never really touched it with a long pole. His coming was the beginning of Pridger's downfall. The man saw—it was, indeed, thrown at him—how easy peculation was. Everything was left to his unsupervised control. In five years, out of a salary of six or seven pounds a week, he had 'saved' at least eight thousand pounds!

"This wholesale success was the manager's undoing. The business grew poorer and poorer until it could no longer turn. Then Barrowford bestirred himself to get in outside capital. He found someone not unwilling to go into it, but that entailed a thorough audit. So far as Pridger was concerned the game was up. He had cooked the buying, he had cooked the selling, he had systematically pillaged the stock. He could, of course, have bolted—all his booty was conveniently arranged for that—but the man's conventional nature shrank from such a break with respectability. A fire was obviously the solution, and, as luck would have it, a fire just then might very easily be made to look like Vernon's expedient.

"This brings us down to the Saturday of the deed. For some time Pridger had been waiting and watching for the occasion when his employer should be the last man to leave. In pursuance of this scheme it was his custom to announce that he was going and then secrete himself. This is what happened on the day in question, and when Barrowford saw all the others off and himself locked the outer door on his departure the manager decided that his chance had come.

"He was in no hurry. There was the bare possibility at first that someone might return for something, while as the afternoon wore on the footstep of the occasional passer-by would get even rarer, and it was no part of the plan that the fire should be discovered by some premature busybody. Mr Pridger leisurely consumed his simple lunch and re-read through his morning paper. Then at about three o'clock he began work seriously.

"We know now what had happened to Barrowford meanwhile. He had, I have since discovered, been the victim of a quite elaborate 'plant' over the Dutch old master—thinking by his 'connoisseurship' to improve his position—and he could not afford it. Whether the proof of the deception was quite such a simple affair as it pleased that debonair sprig to affect need not trouble us; at any rate, Barrowford found some reference so disconcerting at the British Museum that he hurried back to his office to verify the worst.

"Three-thirty, let us say. Pridger had been burning books and other incriminating matter now for half an hour. Then on his startled ear there falls suddenly the sound of someone unlocking the outer front door. No need to think twice who. Only one man beside himself possessed the keys.

"For this emergency the guilty knave had no plan ready. He had gone too far to make extrication possible; the evidence of his intention lay about in every room, and however slack a master Barrowford had been he would certainly read the plain riddle of the scene that met his eyes, and then Pridger was lost.

"Flight was no longer possible; for even to reach the warehouse and the back he must have recourse to the long passage. It was then that Pridger's eye fell on the door of a small store closet—he was in the general office now—windowless and dark. I think that the man's impulse was simply to hide himself and gain a breath of time. But as he stumbled in there flashed to his mind the desperate expedient of this last chance. It was no sooner grasped than acted on.

"A few months before a handy fellow among them had offered to paint the place and the materials were bought, but something intervened and the project hung. The tins of paint still stood there, already mixed, and it was to a lurid crimson that Pridger's mind had leapt. There was no subtlety—there was no time for it. He stooped, dipped both hands into the fluid, and simply laved his face with it. Then throwing completely round his form a sable cloth—one of those to be spread over the goods—he stepped out to meet his unsuspecting victim.

"How they met—whether the dreadful apparition leapt out as the man drew near, whether it stood silently awaiting him, or whether it rushed shrieking down the passage threateningly—we shall perhaps never know. But reconstructing the scene among those silent walls in the precarious light, with the unforgotten ghosts of other crimes ready to emerge from every shadow, I can conceive that no more frightful spectre than this sombre being, dripping red from hands and face at every step, has ever walked. Its effect on a rather soft and just then greatly harassed mind was tragic. Vernon Barrowford has brought from that shuttered past just one vivid lightning flash—the ghastly, all-pervading redness of the Thing; his own paralysing sense of helpless terror; the panic-stricken howling of the flying cat; and the safety of the distant door that he must—must—reach. He did reach it, but he left something there behind."

7

THE STRANGE CASE OF CYRIL BYCOURT

"I Knew you in a moment, Mr Carrados. But I expect that you haven't the very faintest idea of who I am?"

"No," admitted Max Carrados pleasantly; "I am afraid that I must plead guilty. But," he added, in his usual matter-of-fact, effective way, "of course I know well enough who you were. Twenty years ago—at least, twenty to my account—we acted charades together and you were Gertie Hamilton."

"I still am," admitted the lady, with a suggestion of resignation in her voice. "And it's every bit of twenty years as far as I'm concerned."

That evening Mr Carrados (duly announced by an occasional small bill in the windows of dairies, fancy wool shops, and other refined establishments) had been delivering an address on "Premonition, Hallucination, and Autosuggestion" at the Corn Market Hall in Overbury. It had amused the blind man to accept the invitation to give the annual Stalworthy lecture, as it frequently did amuse him to do unexpected things—sheerly to experience—but more than once before he was through the unentertaining business he cursed the moment of good-natured assent.

The last formal word of compliment was spoken and the audience dribbled away with a sense of having performed a duty only slightly less meritorious than that of going to church. Parkinson, at all events, in the glory of being seated on the platform, had thoroughly enjoyed himself. It was then that the lady, who had occupied a retired seat well down the hall, summoned up the resolution to approach the lecturer and to challenge his recollection.

"And you really do know me by my voice! How wonderful! I had been told—but you never know what to believe."

"It does depend somewhat on the teller, doesn't it?" agreed Carrados.

"Well, it was chiefly Lydia Murgatroyd, I think. You remember her? Lydia married a drawing-master who had a pupil whose father—a wholesale druggist, you know—got into a case and employed a Mr Carlyle, who said—"

"Heavens!" interposed Carrados, "That's five removes already. You can only believe a fifth of what you heard. Much better expect to find me as you found me in the past."

"Well, we were always quite good friends, weren't we? You were Mr Max Wynn in those days, and you—you—"

"I had to trust my poor misleading eyes then? Yes; I wonder if I should have known *you*, Miss Hamilton, at sight."

"Oh, I hope not!" she exclaimed ingenuously, and disclosing that train of thought she added, "but my sister Mildred was the pretty one, you know."

"Mildred; yes, I remember her very well indeed," replied the blind man thoughtfully. "We were all her devoted slaves. And she died?"

"You heard?"

"Not until now. Your voice told me that."

Miss Hamilton's look expressed surprise, but she accepted what he said unquestioningly; it agreed with much that she had heard.

"Yes; she died five years ago. And, curiously enough, it has to do with that in a way that I am here now. I came"—she suddenly found her diffidence returning—"I came to see if the Mr Carrados I'd heard so much about really was the Max Wynn we used to know, and if so to ask your advice."

At the back of the hall a sad man was already putting out the lights; in the neighbourhood of the platform another coughed hopefully from time to time. No one else remained; even the young lady who had played selections from Bach and Schumann before the lecture and "God Save the King" after it had closed the hired piano, rolled up her music, and stolen silently away. At a suitable distance apart, exercising his unique gift of being profoundly impressed by a subject that he had no interest in whatever, Parkinson was deeply immersed in a chart illustrating a century of wheat averages of the British Isles.

"I suppose that I oughtn't to detain you here," continued Miss Hamilton looking about. "I wonder if you could spare the time to go back with me and tell me what you think. I live just outside Overbury—quite a short walk."

"If you knew anything of life in the 'Mitre' smoking-room you wouldn't sound so diffident about offering an alternative for an hour or two," replied Carrados.

"That's just like you used to be," she commented. Thanking me for asking you to do something."

As they walked through the silent and deserted streets of the little market town, Carrados was reviewing his memories of the past. Twenty-five years ago (he had given the lady the benefit of five) he had been of very small account indeed—an unknown youth in a strange city, with the wealth that had afterwards suddenly descended on him as remote then as if it had been buried in the mountains of the moon. The Hamiltons had let him understand that he need not be solitary if he cared to accept the simple, kindly entertainment they dispensed. It had not lasted very long; promotion to another town had cut across his path, and the Hamiltons had never become more than an incident, but, a little tardily perhaps, he recognized that at the time their friendliness had meant much to him.

The now middle-aged Gertrude, padding rather heavily by his side as she guided his course, had been the elder of the sisters. The other—Mildred—had more than merited Gertie's claim and his own prosaic tribute. Her memory stirred no heartbeat now, but he could very well recall the shy wonder with which the adoring youth had watched her movements. Then there had been a brother of whom he was yet to hear. Both parents would be dead...

"Here we are at last," exclaimed Miss Hamilton with determined sprightliness, and Carrados heard the latch of a gate lifted. The garden they passed through was of the cottage order, but trimly kept; the blind man checked off one old English flower after another, and divined the care lavished on them before the door was reached.

"I wonder if Mr Parkinson would mind sitting in the kitchen with my old servant?" whispered Miss Hamilton. "I am rather afraid of him, do you know!" The little grimace accompanying this indicated that the idea was to be regarded humorously, and Carrados understood that what she really doubted was the extent of Parkinson's discretion. "Nothing would suit him better," he replied. "If he happens to approve of my address he will give your servant a selection of extracts from it, only in much superior language."

"Then I will take him through, if you will excuse me." She lingered at the door and laughed a little self-consciously. "And generally—though of course you wouldn't remember a thing like that—we used to have just coffee and cakes as a sort of supper. But I hardly expect that now—"

"Do you still make the cake with pink icing and the orange flavour?" he inquired.

"Well, really, I wouldn't have believed!" she exclaimed, and bounced away like a delighted schoolgirl.

A little later, having successfully introduced Parkinson and arranged for the appearance of the celebrated cake, Miss Hamilton launched upon the subject of her trouble.

"It's really about Cyril I meant when I said Mildred," she explained. "Cyril is Mildred's son, the only child she had, and so, of course, my nephew, the only one *I* have."

"Then Tom—"

"Tom went to South Africa ten—twelve—oh, fifteen years ago. We never heard from him after the war there; I think he must have been killed. You see, Mr Carrados, I'm quite alone except for Cyril now. Father—Mother—Tom—Mildred—all I had: all gone."

"Your nephew lives with you here?" prompted Carrados. He was sorry for the poor lady, forlorn and rather unwieldy among the buffetry of circumstance, but he began to foresee that it might be necessary to keep her to the point.

"No; I'm coming to that. You must forgive me—I know I'm slow and tiresome. I can do nothing but think about things now, hour after hour: moping I suppose others would call it. It's so dreadful if it's true that I can hardly believe it possible; and yet, there it is. I must do something about it."

"Yes," said Carrados, smiling away the edge of his retort, "you must really tell me about it."

"There I go again!" confessed Miss Hamilton with a gesture of despair. "How can I expect you to advise me? Well, Millie married a Mr Bycourt—Mark Bycourt—who still lives a few miles from here. He was quite a nice sort of man, but a little old for her, I thought, considering her looks and chances, and he really doesn't appear to be interested in any subject except water beetles. It seems a strange taste for a man. He might have taken up golf, or prize poultry, or politics, or lots of things, I mean, that would have seemed more—well, gentlemanly."

"Quite a number of people are interested in water beetles," observed Carrados mildly.

"So I am given to understand," she admitted, "and I suppose that I must be narrow-minded. But don't think that I have anything against Mr Bycourt; he made what I should call a good husband, though it must undoubtedly have been a little dull for Millie at times. When they had been married about three years Cyril came... Did you ever hear of an Uncle Stace when you knew us at Midchester, Mr Carrados?"

"Stace? No, I have never heard the name before," replied the blind man.

"I don't quite know where the relationship came in or if he really was any relation at all. I have heard that he had been very fond of mother years ago and wanted to marry her, but when we children knew him he seemed quite old and was said to be very rich. Well, all that he has to do with it is this: Millie was his favourite—as she was everyone's—and when he died it was found that he had left everything—almost everything—to her, and to Cyril afterwards."

"To her and to her children generally afterwards?" suggested Carrados.

"No, just to Cyril by name. There were no other children, you see."

"Quite so," agreed the listener.

"Millie died when she had been married about eight years—it was appendicitis. Then Mark asked me if I would keep house for him and look after Cyril, and I did—for four years. Of course I got very fond of the child, especially after I had mothered him through his little troubles and illnesses; he was all that was left to me of the old days at Midchester. It was a great blow to me when Mark married again."

Carrados contributed only a sympathetic nod; Miss Hamilton seemed fairly well set on her subject now.

"I should not have minded so much if the new Mrs Bycourt had been what I would call a suitable person, but really, one could hardly describe her as a lady. She was the very opposite of

Mildred, and what Mark could have been thinking of I cannot imagine."

"Some people are like that," admitted Carrados diplomatically.

"Well, I suppose so; but it is a great pity. She was the widow of a sort of small country gentleman who owned one or two racehorses and came to grief, and she really seemed to have absorbed the atmosphere of the stable and the farmyard. Not that I mean there was anything definitely wrong about her—but the whiskies-and-sodas, the cigars, the slang (to call it nothing worse), the slap-dash of everything!—and Mark was such a refined man, whatever else he was. I really couldn't stand it for more than a week, although they both pressed me to remain until I could make my own arrangements; it was a sudden marriage, you know. That was about a year ago.

"It really was very terrible for me, Mr Carrados, to have to give little Cyril up. He was such an affectionate, dear little boy, and for four years I had been neither more nor less than his mother. But there! I took this cottage partly so that I could get across to Stacks—that's their house—from tune to time, and of course I have to consider ways and means as well: Papa was unfortunate towards the last. In the meanwhile Cyril goes daily to a small school kept by a lady in the village; he is delicate and rather too young to leave home yet. Mrs Bycourt has two boys of her own, a few years older than Cyril and perfect young ruffians. Fortunately, they are generally away at boarding-school."

"And now?" prompted Carrados, for Miss Hamilton's silence was becoming rather strained, and, after maintaining an admirable control up to this point, the poor lady, brought face to face with her immediate distress, suddenly brimmed over.

"Oh, Mr Carrados," she wailed appealingly, "don't laugh at me, but I'm sure the woman's murdering Cyril by degrees so that her own will get his money. I know she is, and what am I to do?"

Now with regard to murder, experience had imbued the blind man with two convictions: the first that it is a very easy thing to do, and the second that it is a very difficult thing to do properly. If this inauspicious Mrs Bycourt actually succeeded in removing her young stepson, Max Carrados did not doubt that the chances were on the side of justice overtaking her, but the more pressing need was to find out if she had any such intention, and if so to frustrate it.

"Would the money go to her if your nephew died?" he asked.

"Oh, yes. I saw our old solicitor about that. As I said, it was left to Millie and to Cyril after her. It is really Cyril's now, but held in trust for him until he comes of age. Of course he can't make a will yet, so that if he died the money would pass to his father, and he naturally would leave it to his wife."

"He probably would," agreed Carrados. "How much is there?"

"It was about thirty thousand pounds. I understand that by the time Cyril could touch it there would be more than fifty thousand. That seems a lot to people like ourselves. Mark is quite comfortably off, I suppose, but by no means wealthy, and his new wife will have brought him little. If she is determined to get rich or to provide well for her own awful children, Cyril's fortune—"

It was quite clear that Miss Hamilton had definitely settled the offending Mrs Bycourt and Cyril in their respective roles of murderess and victim, but when the patient investigator brought her up against the test of concrete facts he felt that the most useful purpose he could serve would be to discount her fears.

"But I feel so absolutely convinced that something sinister is going on," pleaded the distressed lady. "Oh, Mr Carrados, the boy is growing thinner and more lifeless week by week, the woman is capable of any villiany, the inducement is plain before our faces—"

"Then why not persuade the father to get a doctor in?"

"The doctor has seen him already. I insisted on Dr Huntley being called in some time ago."

Carrados passed the revealing word "insisted". "And he said?" he inquired.

"Oh, he said that there was nothing really the matter. Of course he meant that Cyril hadn't measles or chicken-pox, and we knew that well enough already. He recommended a little change. Cyril went with me to Eastbourne for two weeks. There he improved wonderfully. Then we came back and he went down again."

"Could he not live with you here for some time?"

"I should love it. But Mrs Bycourt won't hear of such a thing—naturally. She says that the boy has been coddled enough already—me, of course—and that the sooner he gets over his morbid fancies the better, and that in any case if the air of Stacks doesn't suit him, it's hardly likely that this will as it's only five miles away... Now whatever can that be at this hour? Did you hear a knock? I didn't, but Susan has gone to the door."

"I heard a footstep outside and then a knock," replied the blind man. "It is a child who is uncertain."

"Please, m'm," said the elderly servant, opening the room door and standing there a little fluttered, "here's Master Cyril from Stacks and in a pretty pickle."

"Do you mean he's alone?" exclaimed Miss Hamilton, jumping up and making for the door. "Oh, my poor lamb!" For the next half minute there was alternate rattle and murmur in the hall, while the staid Susan continued by the door, regarding Mr Carrados with a fascinated interest. Parkinson had undoubtedly been enlarging. Then Miss Hamilton returned, leading in a little boy who clung to her, his pale, over-refined young face not yet wholly reassured.

"This is Cyril, Mr Carrados," she explained, patting the hand that gripped her protectively. "He tells me that he has run away from home and walked all the way here, but I know nothing more because I thought that you had better hear it with me."

"Well, he seems to have come just in time for some coffee and cake, unless the signs deceive me," remarked Carrados with encouraging levity. "Fond of cake with plenty of pink icing on it, Cyril?"

"Yes, thank you, sir," replied the boy politely, as he took serious stock of this new grown-up.

"So am I," confessed the friendly stranger. "And I don't mind telling you, Cyril, that when I was ten—that's older than you perhaps—I ran away, because there was a very fat big boy who used to wait for me every morning and punch my head."

"I *am* ten," protested Cyril; "and I am not much afraid of boys. But I am frightened of the man who comes to me in the night and is going to take me in his cart." A look of pitiable terror came into his eyes and his voice rose almost to a scream. "Don't let him; oh, don't let him take me, Auntie!"

With a croon of horror and affection Gertrude Hamilton flung her arms protectingly about her darling child and shot a meaning look of triumph at her unbelieving guest. "*Now* what do you think?" it seemed to say, and, for all the world as if he had met it, the blind man's scarcely-moving hand mutely signalled back, "Quietly. Be careful now!"

"He shall not touch you," he said reassuringly. "You are going to stay here tonight. Now tell us what this man is like, so that we shall be able to prevent him from ever coming again."

"He is a big man and very strong, so that he can carry people. He stands by my bed looking down; and there is a nasty smell comes with him."

"What does he wear?"

"It is a long brown thing with a belt, and a queer high hat, not like men wear now. And he has a staff."

"Can you tell us what his face is like? Have you ever seen another that reminds you of it?"

"It is only his eyes that you can see," replied Cyril, in a voice low with the memory of his terror. "There is something like a cloth over his face."

"Oh, my precious!" was wrung from Miss Hamilton, but Carrados's insistent gesture cut shot her passionate outcry.

"It is a dream," said the blind man quietly, taking up his patient again; "a bad black dream. You are really asleep at the time, Cyril?"

"I am not quite awake," admitted the boy consideringly, "but I am not really asleep. It is very queer and—different. And he mutters."

"Do you remember anything that he has ever said?"

"Only a little bit now and then. Last night he said, 'He has the—the'—I forget the word; oh, yes—'the tokens on him, but he is not dead yet. I will come again tomorrow night'. That was why I dare not stay any longer."

Miss Hamilton left Cyril on the couch where they had been seated and crossed the room.

"Is it necessary to distress him any more with this?" she whispered. Her face was white and scared, but there was the ring of defiance in her voice. "Whatever happens, he shall not go back while I'm alive."

"It's extraordinarily fascinating," replied Carrados in the same guarded tone, "and we ought to get at the bottom of these things. On the face of it this is plainly nightmare—he has read it all. Do you ever," he continued, turning to the boy again, "do you ever hear a bell ringing while this goes on?"

"Yes," was the reply, given without hesitation, "it rings sometimes outside. That is before the man comes in or after he has gone."

"You see," explained Carrados aside; "that bears it out. If this were someone got up to terrify the boy it's absurd that he should take the extra risk of having a bell rung outside, merely for a point of extra realism, but it is just the sort of detail that sticks in the imagination and reproduces in a very vivid nightmare."

"But what is it?" demanded Miss Hamilton, beginning to be shaken in her high attitude. "What is it that he is supposed to dream about?"

"What? Why the Plague to be sure; the Great Plague that furnished nightmares for many a generation in the past. Let me see, Cyril, you are fond of reading, aren't you?"

"Well, yes, sir," said Cyril. "If it's tales," he added conscientiously.

"Oh, of course; we don't mean lessons, do we? Have you ever read *Robinson Crusoe*?"

"Rather! I've got it at home—with pictures."

"Man Friday and the parrot and all? Do you remember who wrote it?"

"Yes; Daniel Defoe."

"Bravo! Well, he wrote other books. Can you tell me any?"

Apparently not. Cyril considered, but remained dumb. "Something about a 'Journal' and a 'Year', eh?" prompted the questioner. "No? Well, never mind."

"But why not ask him outright if you think it's that?" put in the lady. "Shall I?"

"It is liable to suggest," was his reply. "But try."

"Once upon a time a lot of people got very ill," said Miss Hamilton coaxingly, "and they called it a plague. Have you ever heard of it, my pet?"

"Yes, Auntie," said Cyril, his large, considering eyes incapable of jest. "It's what papa calls me when I ask him things."

Miss Hamilton so to speak "stood down" and Carrados resumed.

"Did you ever see a picture of a man in a long brown dress—"

"Like him?" interrupted the child with a shudder. "No—and—please, sir—"

"My dear lad," anticipated Carrados, going to the couch and laying his hand unfailingly on the boy's shoulder, "we are going to help you. We intend that you shall never, never see the man again. But sometimes the doctor has to give you nasty medicine for your good. It isn't always pleasant to be left in the dark, even when you are ten, is it?"

"No, sir."

"Well, when you feel like that, Cyril, you can think of me being in the darkness with you too. I am always in the dark because, you see, I am blind."

"Oh, I didn't know, sir," said the little boy with quick feeling. "I am very sorry, but"—consolingly—"you look all right."

"Thank you," replied Mr Carrados gravely "Generally speaking, I feel all right. But we all have our moments in the dark."

"Cyril has a little light always in his bedroom," volunteered Miss Hamilton. "Don't you, dear?"

"Quite right," said Carrados idly. "A nightlight?"

"Yes, but electric light, you know. A tiny bulb. It's new there. Mrs Bycourt said she couldn't stand lamps, and so Mark has recently put up an installation for the house."

"Electric light, and recent?" mused Carrados. "How long ago?"

"About, well—how long have you had the electric light, Cyril? A few months, isn't it?"

"At Christmas, Auntie. We had all the lights on at once on Christmas Day. Don't you remember; you were there?"

Miss Hamilton nodded assent, her eyes on her guest's impenetrable face. "Yes, that is right," she said.

"Let me see"—a most disarming unconcern had come into the blind man's voice—"was it before or after Christmas that the bad dream first came?"

"It was just after Christmas," replied the boy.

"Quite sure?"—a little more insistent now.

"Oh, yes; I remember by my presents. And then he began to come oftener, and then he stayed away a bit, and—and I am frightened, but I'm glad I told you."

"My treasure!" cried the fond lady, "Why didn't you tell Auntie sooner?" and for reply Cyril hung his head and whispered the fatal insuperable excuse of childhood:

"I didn't like to."

"Another time you must," she enjoined. "And do you always sleep on your right side, as I told you?"

"Yes, Auntie."

"And the bed is still pushed to the farther wall, away from the draught, where I arranged it?"

"Oh, yes Auntie. It is right up to the little pull-thing in the wall that does my light. I can send it in and out while I'm in bed."

"And the best place for you to be now, young man," said Carrados, taking out his watch and touching its fingers. "Eleven-fifteen."

"Yes, indeed," chimed in Miss Hamilton. "If you don't want another piece of cake Susan will take you up. I suppose"—turning to her visitor—"that I ought to let them know somehow at Stacks where Cyril is tonight?"

"I have been thinking of that. Are they on the telephone?"

"No—what a pity. You would have told them from your hotel, I'm sure."

"Yes, but as they're not, so much the better. Just write them a line and I will take it round there now."

"You, Mr Carrados? At this hour?"

"Why not? All hours are alike to me. Then we needn't disturb them if they know nothing of the escapade as yet. If I find the place in darkness I shall leave the note to be discovered with Master Cyril's absence in the morning. I have a fancy to 'see' Stacks in my own particular way, Miss Hamilton, and, lo and behold! The Fates arrange it."

Less than half an hour later a motor-car skated down the long, slight hill that ended in the village street of Irling and drew up before the cottages began. Mr Carrados and Parkinson got out, and leaving the hotel chauffeur to doze across his wheel they set out on the adventure of discovery.

"The turning to the left before the baker's shop," directed the leader of the expedition. "That must be it ahead, Parkinson, although the rural baker does not seem to bake by night. Edwards should be the name."

"There is a shop, sir," assented Parkinson, peering across the way. "But I am unable to distinguish the name. If I may—" He was away a moment. "Perfectly correct, sir, and there is the lane. The people hereabouts, sir, would seem to dispense with street illumination, and it is very dark tonight."

"True," replied Carrados, "and fortunately there is no moon."

"Yes, sir," agreed the faithful servitor, catching his toe against the kerb and recovering by his master's guidance; "I appreciate that it gives us the initial advantage."

A short half mile, another turn, and presently a darker mass emerged lying back upon their left.

"That should be Stacks," conjectured Carrados, when Parkinson gave him this information. "Now is the murder out yet?"

"We are coming to the gates," reported the proxy "eyes". "There is a small lodge immediately inside. The gates, of open-work iron, are closed. The drive—"

"Wait," interrupted Carrados. "Any lights showing at the lodge?"

"No, sir; not on this side."

"Have a look farther on."

Parkinson walked fifty yards along the road and then returned.

"No lights anywhere," he reported.

"Then the murder is probably not yet out. With so good an excuse for being on the premises, and every opportunity for losing ourselves if need be, I begin to despise the front way, Parkinson. Let us investigate."

They continued along the road away from Stacks. Parkinson soon reported a small door in the garden fence, but this proved to be locked. A little farther on a lane gave promise on their left. A few stars had risen and the seeing eyes were more accustomed to the darkness. After a single futile cast a path was discovered through the fields that now separated them from Stacks, and with scarcely the tribute of a scratch they forced a likely hedge and fell through into what was unmistakably a private garden.

"Never mind the rhubarb plants," said Carrados—his follower was standing rather aghast at the extent of their devastation. "They made capital landing and usefully indicate that we are in an obscure part of the kitchen-garden. Can you see the house? Well, we will take a stroll round."

Progress was slow and vicissitudinous. "The advantage of beginning operations from here is obvious," expounded the specialist. "If we walk across a bed of onions—as we are, in fact, doing at this moment—we create an aromatic fixed point, so to speak, to which it is easy to return again whenever it becomes prudent. It is a line that holds."

"I have always understood that onions possessed certain medicinal properties, sir," replied Parkinson sagaciously, and heaven knows what profundities the ingenuous creature might not have advanced had not a parallelogram of emerging blackness disclosed the position of the house. Here also, ran the report, no lights were visible.

"Then the murder is certainly not out," decided Carrados. "We can resume out leisurely survey. But not, for preference, along their celery trench, Parkinson."

"I am very sorry, sir. For the moment my attention was distracted. I have just observed another building, much nearer than the house, where a light is showing."

"Make for it then. A light means someone, and we must put ourselves right by getting in the first word."

But he was wrong. The place, a small, well-built shed standing in a remote corner of the grounds—half shrubbery, half waste, they judged—was deserted. Machinery, now idle, proclaimed its use; the light that had attracted them a single indicator lamp glowing above a switchboard.

"The dynamo house, of course, and now they're on the battery," explained Carrados when they had investigated. "I heard that they made their own light, but who would have expected to find the place down here."

"I had some general conversation with the elderly person at Miss Hamilton's," volunteered Parkinson tolerantly; "and after the arrival of the young gentleman she expressed her opinions about the family living here. Mr Bycourt is a very nervous, irritable gentleman, it would appear, sir, and cannot put up with any noise or distraction. Perhaps on that account—"

"Aye, that will be it," agreed Mr Carrados. "The beat of the engine will scarcely be heard up there; but ssh! What the deuce is coming now?"

Someone was approaching at all events, and the two intruders shrank back into the readiest cover.

"A woman, sir," whispered Parkinson.

"An old woman," amplified his master. "She carries something, and she's in a hurry. Also, she has no business here: Which gives us a great advantage, because we have."

At the threshold of the little house the burden was shot down. The watchers knew already that the door was fastened and looked for the unknown to produce a key. Instead, there was a sudden scrunch of iron, a splintering of wood, and the door swung loosely open.

"Forced, egad!" thought Carrados. "Our lady is determined." Then as she passed in, dragging along what now appeared to be a sack, he touched his attendant's arm and together they crept forward to the half-open door.

"It's shavings and wood she's brought," conveyed Parkinson, his eye to a convenient chink. "And, blow me, sir," he added a second later, stirred to this deplorable lapse irom his usual diction, "but she's drenching the place with petrol! She means mischief!"

"Stop!" cried Carrados, disclosing himself in the doorway. "Haven't you the sense to know that you'll blow yourself up too?"

The startled creature—never was there a meeker-looking *pétroleuse* than this tidy, grey-haired cottager—dropped the box of matches she was handling and literally fell upon her knees among the mess she had contrived.

"Oh, the dear Lord preserve us all!" she gasped in terror. "Who are ye?"

"Never mind that. The question is who are you and what are you doing here?"

"Sure I'm only Mrs Laffey from the lodge just by, sir. Indeed I wasn't doing no harm at all, but you gave me a great turn—just a bit of arranging and tidying up, as you may say. I dhropped a spot of oil an"—"

"Parkinson," threw out Carrados in a sufficient whisper, "the police."

"Oh, don't bring in the polis on me, kind gentleman," implored Mrs Laffey with redoubled fluency; "the dirty, thievin" sergeant that set the lie against me a short while back over Mister Johnson's sthrayin" pullets, it's little justice I should ever see. Be the good kind gentleman—"

"You have just one chance," Carrados took out his watch and displayed it upon his outstretched hand. "Get up and tell us the exact truth, no matter what it is. Come, out with it."

"Indeed an" I will, sir an" your honour, for I'm sure ye'd not be after bethraying a poor old widder woman. "Tis for me boy I'm doing of it, and that's the blessed truth this minnit, though nothing but black words and the lift of a hand maybe would be me thanks if he did know."

"Your boy? Your son, you mean?"

"Me boy Jim, and he the only one I've got and me husband gone this seventeen years. Ever since he has left school he's worked in the garden, with a thing here and there maybe in the house beyond and a bit extry for it of a Saturday. Well—and it's the stark truth I'm telling ye the blessed knows—last back end the master calls him by and said, 'Jim,' he said, 'the missis is determined on this electrey light and it's all arranged for. You'll have to learn to handle the dynamey an" what not, but "tis no matter at all—an hour here and there maybe and a grand learning for you for to be an engineer'. 'Jim,' I said when I hear of it, 'don't do it. For "twas handlin" of that stuff hoist your granda out of Donegal in the old days'. 'Oh, bother,' he says, 'how am I to say I an't when himself has said I am? Twould be the marching order I should likely get instead'. 'An" if you should,' I up and said, 'aren't there plenty other jobs as good in the long breadth of the land and you a handy thrifty chap?' 'Have done,' he says, souring on me, and—God forgive him!—well I knew the reason why he'd stay, eating the very dirt if need be and she little better than a pagan deity, as you may say."

"He had charge of this place then?" said Carrados with a patience that Parkinson could not but disapprove of. "Well, go on."

"He had indeed, sir, and never a restful moment has he known since. First his bright pretty colour goes, and soon his appetite, and he that would eat me out of house and home now touching no more'n a sup of tay and fiddling with a little thin piece of currant cake maybe. And all the while he taking great store of the dynamey and that, and would spend long hours polishing and oiling up here alone. Then the sleep forsake him, or it'd be one sweaty terror of the livelong night the way he'd fetch likely a groan in his dreams or a curse at the long, still blackness stretching to the dawn, and me listening at the latch-hole of his door."

"What did he dream?" asked Carrados.

"We made no talk about it, sir, him being that stubborn. But many's the queer word he's let out in his sleep, the same as if he'd claim that one was waiting there to fetch him in a cart. But give notice to himself he would not, as I am tellin" yous, and the very grip of death closing in upon him plain for eny to see, until I knew. "Tis either Jim or that rampageous divil that's somehow desthroyin" him up there. And that's the sacred truth itself, God help me!"

For a full minute the blind man remained silent, prodding the loose earth with his walking-stick as he pondered. When he spoke, instead of any of the things that Mrs Laffey had hoped, or perhaps feared, it was to put an idle question.

"Did this part of the ground have any special name?" he asked. "Before this place was built, I mean."

"They did used to be calling it the Bone Mound, so I've heard," she said, trying to catch his mood with surreptitious glances. "There was a little hump, you'll understand, but they thrudged the top off ut for to make a level space."

"Yes, of course they would. And now, Mrs Laffey, you'd better go on home again. Show this man the way to the front gate as you go. We'll leave that way, Parkinson, but don't come back to me for half an hour."

"Very good, sir." Parkinson knew of the times when his master would have no human eye upon him as he worked, and he had ceased—if, indeed, he had ever begun—to feel a trace of curiosity.

""Deed an" I will," said Mrs Laffey cheerfully. "The gentleman is welcome to me little front room too until your honour's ready. And, begging your pardon, sir, you'll overlook to mention what's passed tonight?"

"So far as I am concerned you can set your mind at rest," was his reply; "but you'll have to explain one or two things in the morning, it seems to me. I dare say you can put a very good face on it somehow."

"I might contrive," replied Mrs Laffey hopefully.

* * * * *

Mrs Laffey did indeed contrive to put a very good face upon it, as Mr Carrados found when he visited Stacks openly the following day. It was not Mrs Laffey's fault that she missed seeing them, and doubtless dropping a word of timely preparation, but their own in discovering a wicket gate that saved the bend of the road and brought them upon Mrs Bycourt, who was exercising a pair of young hounds on the lawn.

"If ever there was a good Samaritan this side the Jordan it's surely you, Mr Carrados!" exclaimed that athletic lady when she had identified her caller. "And"—she felt that she ought to indicate some concession to his infirmity—"in spite of your—"

"Or because of, perhaps," he suggested, coming to her rescue. "You got the note anyway?"

"Oh, yes. In fact, it was our first intimation that the bird had flown. It really was a great kindness because my husband fidgets so over little things, and if he had found Cyril gone and no trace of him, heavens knows what! And then this other business coming on the top of it!"

"You mean the incident down the garden?" asked Carrados tentatively.

"Good gracious, yes! I hope there isn't anything else? Not that *I* mind a bit of a shindy any time, but I have my poor dear's nerves to consider. He is most tremendously indebted to you; it really was sporting in the circumstances. Mrs Laffey gave us a most glowing account of your exploit."

"Oh, did she?" Carrados considered a little. "I rather wondered what she would say."

"Well, she said—as near as I can remember—'The way the sthranger gentleman, and he not seeing, put the shame of terror into the trapesin' interlopin' blackguards, who would wring the neck of their own father for a minted sixpence, is a walking masterpiece,' only much faster and a great deal more of it. I am dying to hear all the details, but we concluded that you must have heard them down the garden as you came across to leave the note. Of course you could get no idea of what sort of men they were?"

"No," admitted Carrados. "I certainly could not."

"Mrs Laffey says she arrived on the scene too late to be any use at all. Sometimes, do you know, I've been a wee bit sceptical of Mrs Laffey's romances, but in this case she is singularly modest about her own share in it. What gets me is why anyone should want to destroy our property."

"Yes, that is the mystery, isn't it?"

"Of course we have enemies here and there I know. It seems strange that anyone who behaves in a perfectly simple, straightforward way, just saying exactly what you think of people, should be received with enmity, but there it is. We've found where they broke in—it's easy to see that they knew their way about—and they have deliberately trampled on the planted beds..."

"Disgraceful!"

"Yes, but unfortunately there's nothing positively to identify any of them by. Well, you'll come in, Mr Carrados, and—and meet my husband?"

"With pleasure, but can you guess what it is that chiefly brought me to Stacks today?"

"No. What?"

"Cyril's bedroom."

"Oh," pondered Mrs Bycourt, pausing in their progress. "I wondered what tale Cyril told."

"You are not going to be angry with him for running away?"

"Angry? Good Lord, no! It's the best thing I've known him do yet. I'm delighted to find that he has that much spirit left in him. The fact is, Mr Carrados, ever since I've been here I've had to be a bit hard-cased towards Cyril, simply to counteract the 'come-to-mammy-and-let-her-kiss-it-better' ways his dear

Auntie Gertie had got him into. But I forgot—you are Miss Hamilton's friend."

"All the same I want to understand just how matters are."

"Then I'll tell you this. Do you know what was the deciding thing made me marry Mark Bycourt in the end? Yes: Cyril. I'm fond of boys, Mr Carrados, and I want them to have their chance in life. I have two dear little scrubby ragamuffins of my own—they're called Bob and Jack. Cyril was being brought up on *Eric*, *Misunderstood*, and *Little Lord Fauntleroy*, and Cyril will have more need of red stuffing than most people because when he is twenty-one he will come into a great deal too much money. You know that, perhaps?"

"I understood so much from Miss Hamilton."

"Yes; and I dare say Miss Hamilton indicated that I was capable of dark designs on Cyril's fortune? No? Well, if she had, it wouldn't have been wonderful. The fact is, Mr Carrados, Gertrude is a misfire. It was the surprise of her life (if I said 'disappointment' you'd think me catty) when Mark married me, and she didn't set out to be pleasant to the interloper. When I saw that, I—well, I certainly laid it on a bit thick for Gertrude's benefit. I'm not really a he-woman or a vamp, Mr Carrados. I'm watching Cyril very carefully, and—if I may confess it to you—rather affectionately. I hope that in the end I, with the unconscious help of my two ragamuffins, may make a man of him. Now we have reached his room. Is there anything particular that you want to—to—"

"To see? To see in my own way? Well"—pointing—"the bed is there?"

"Yes. But how on earth do you know?"

"To make no mystery, by the familiar process of putting two and two together. And on the wall, quite near to the bed-head, is an electric light plug?"

"Yes, there is."

"So that Cyril, sleeping dutifully on his right side, as he has been taught to do, will be lying with his face quite near that plug?"

"Within a foot or so certainly. It seems to be a fad of Miss Hamilton's—sleeping on the right side. I suppose she was taught to as a child."

"I was, too. But I've grown out of it. Now I will look into this fitting, if you don't mind." He put his hand with baffling exactness on the rail of the bed and drew it from the wall so that he could approach the plug—approach it so closely indeed that to Mrs Bycourt's mystified curiosity his face appeared to touch it. "Yes, there it is," he remarked, as one who has brought a delicate experiment to a successful end.

"But what?" demanded the lady, not unreasonably. "Why this hanky-panky, Mr Carrados? Nothing wrong, is there?"

"Forgive me, I really didn't intend to seem mysterious. There is nothing wrong, and if there had been we have got to the root of it at last. But there is something very curious, and there is something—I was, in fact, trying to break it to you mildly—something rather horrible."

"But, my dear man, people don't break things to me—they throw them at me solid."

"I'll be as brutal as you like then. You know that Cyril has been having nightmares lately?"

"Oh, yes. That is not unusual for a boy."

"Not at all. Nor is the menace of a man standing by his bedside uncommon. What is significant is that it always takes the form of the Plague cart come to fetch him, and what is doubly significant is that your man James Laffey passes through exactly the same experience."

"Cyril never told me what it was; but we all knew that Jim Laffey was pining for the blue eyes of my housemaid. But what a dreadful dream, and what a strange coincidence!"

"In my experience," replied Carrados, "coincidence—as we call it—is often merely a key I find that fits a lock I have. Laffey, spending long hours in the new building there, but not, I ascertain, with the electric light fitted in his cottage; Cyril, sleeping here with his face turned to that wall, but not, I learn, allowed to put his foot inside the dynamo-house. What is it, Mrs Bycourt, this strange coincidence?"

"I don't know," she replied, awed in spite of her lavish spirit. "What?"

"I will tell you. Over two centuries ago the Plague—the Great Plague of London as some histories call it—came to Irling, brought by a fleeing pedlar, and nearly wiped the village out. You have heard perhaps?"

"No, I don't think so. I don't remember anyway."

"I find the tradition of it is almost lost here now. There are a few forgotten graves in the churchyard—but after the first weeks the dead were not buried there. It took too long to dig single graves and soon there was neither parson, clerk, nor sexton to perform the office of the Church. So a great pit was dug, well away from the houses of the living, in what was then an open field. But it is no longer that."

"Oh!" exclaimed Mrs Bycourt, with the nameless horror beginning to take form before her eyes, "do you mean—"

He nodded assent to the unspoken question.

"Yes; what was the distant grassland field is now your lower garden. The Bone Mound marks the hasty burial-pit, and right upon it they have built your power house."

"But how does that—why does it—" she stammered.

"Who can say? It is easy enough to reply that you have stirred up the buried corruption of that dreadful place, but how is it that there have been awakened again the groans and the fears and the agonies of those heart-rending times?"

"Oh, how horrible—how horrible!" she cried. "Is it true—can it be really true?"

"Is what true?" he asked. "Do you mean—which detail?"

"I don't know," she said. "I mean any of it—all of it. It is like a nightmare in itself; it is so loathsome—so incredible. Why should it result in that?"

"That is the really interesting thing about it," he replied. "Your—"

"Interesting!" she retorted sharply. "This!"

"To me," he admitted mildly. "I am merely an investigator, Mrs Bycourt. Your dynamo, designed to transform mechanical force into electrical energy, has here in some obscure way also changed physical effect into psychological experience. I dare say you know that in the house"—he indicated the wall plug—"the wires are carried through iron piping, and outside the cable is brought underground through drain-pipes. The lie being uniformly upwards, a warm room like this would create a slight but continuous current, so that, you see, Cyril has really been breathing direct—Yes, it is rather uncanny, isn't it? Laffey, of course, has been in more direct but shorter contact. Actually, we might have expected them both to contract the plague—there is record of that happening to some men who dug into a similar pit rather more than a hundred years after the interment. Instead, they caught the emotions of the victims. It will seem quite simple and obvious some day, but we know so lamentably little of that side of electrical energy yet. Even as it is I shall have to rewrite my lecture."

But Mrs Bycourt had no interest in his lecture. "Oh, the dreadful, dreadful thing!" she moaned. "What should one do? I shall have that horrible place razed to the ground—I can't rest until it's gone—and then I shall have a great fire heaped on the spot and burned and burned for weeks until every trace of those poor creatures is reduced to decent ashes."

"Yes," assented Mr Carrados. "That does seem to occur to one, does it not?"

8

THE MISSING WITNESS SENSATION

In its earlier stages the Ayr Street Post Office robbery had attracted little notice. Afterwards, owing to causes with which this narrative has to do, it achieved the distinction of passing into the grade of what Detective Inspector Beedel was wont to refer to with quiet professional enthusiasm as "First-class Crimes". But so meagre was public interest in the initial proceedings that when Mr Carrados looked in at the magistrate's court purely for old acquaintance's sake one stifling afternoon, he found the place half empty.

"Post office hold-up—Ayr Street case, sir," explained the officer on duty at the door. "Party named Rank charged. Pretty nearly over now, I should say."

"Philip Thaxted!" cried a voice across the court.

"New witness for the defence," whispered the policeman. "Like a seat, sir?"

"Don't trouble—I may only stay a minute. Who are conducting?"

"Mr Booker's for the Public Prosecutor. I don't know the defence—not one of our regular people here."

"He is speaking now?"

"Yes, sir."

Published in Pearson's Magazine, London, July 1926.

A plainly dressed man with a firmly lined and rather artistic face, iron-grey hair, and a quiet, self-confident manner, had gone into the witness-box. The formal oath had been administered and the preliminaries were being rattled through. Yes, his name was Philip Thaxted and he lived at such an address at Kingston-on-Thames. Formerly in the lace business, both as manager and on his own account, but now retired.

"On the afternoon of Wednesday, the seventeenth inst, you were taking a walk in Richmond Park?" suggested the defending counsel.

"That is quite correct."

"Tell us what occurred."

The blind visitor leaned across and touched the attendant lightly on the arm.

"I should like to hear a little more of this evidence," he remarked with lowered voice. "Perhaps I had better have a seat."

As he moved quietly to a place, piloted by the officer's unobtrusive hand, someone in making way dropped a stick with an exasperating clatter. The man in the witness-box glanced sharply across in the direction of the noise, and something almost as perceptible as a start touched him, and for a word or two his voice rang flat. The next moment the flicker, such as it was, had passed and he was continuing his story as evenly as before.

* * * * *

"I suppose, inspector," said Mr Carrados, "it might seem rather unreasonable of me to ask you to come down here after being in court all day, eh?"

"Well, no, sir," replied Inspector Beedel with his usual unpenetrable candour; "I can't exactly say it did. You see, Mr Carrados, you've asked me to come and talk to you on one occasion or another a good dozen times now, and it's always been—as they say in the advertisement—'to hear of something to my advantage'."

Carrados laughed as he pointed to a chair and pushed the cigars across the table.

"Don't be too confident this time," he advised. "Can you give a guess what it's about?"

Beedel raised his slow, meditative eyes and wondered for the hundredth time at the strangely alive expression in the gaze that really seemed to meet his own.

"I may say that I noticed you in court today, sir, and putting one thing and another together—"

"Quite right," assented Carrados. "It is about today's case. These post office hold-ups are getting beyond a joke, inspector."

"This one has certainly been beyond a joke for Lizzie Baxter, sir. We have it privately that the poor girl hasn't one chance in a thousand of pulling through. Then—"

"Aye. Then the case against Rank will not be one of Robbery with Violence, but Wilful Murder. That determined a special effort to get him off if possible before the graver charge came in."

"The alibi, you mean, sir?"

"The alibi, yes. What did you think of that timely encounter at the exact minute that the job was taking place?"

A brightly-coloured band had adorned the cigar that Inspector Beedel was appreciatively considering. He smoothed out the pretty scrap and put it, carefully flattened, away in his notebook for the benefit of a stalwart young Beedel now rising five.

"It certainly staggered me more than a bit to hear that evidence this afternoon," he replied. "The man who comes forward and testifies that he was talking to Dennis Rank at half-past four that day isn't one of the sort that bob up after every assault or accident, prepared to swear anything for half a quid and a pot of beer. He has been in a good way of business, and so far from anything being known against him, inquiry goes to show that he has a creditable public record extending over twenty years. A police magistrate is a bit wary, and, as you know, Mr Lipscott committed, but if this chap sticks to his tale at the Old Bailey I doubt if any jury will convict."

The blind man nodded weighty acquiescence. Plainly there could be no question about the importance of the Kingston evidence.

"He was walking in Richmond Park—quite a likely thing for a middle-aged gentleman who wants a little exercise to do—when this happened. A little dog coming out of a clump of bracken barked at him furiously, and he swished back with his walking-stick. Then it seized one of his trouser legs and tore it. The dog's master appeared on the scene and they fell to abusing one another, the owner accusing him of savaging the dog and he accusing the man of keeping a vicious animal. In the end he demanded this fellow's name and address, and there it is, written in his notebook widi the date and the exact time of the occurrence."

"That's it," assented the inspector. "All very reasonable and circumstantial."

"Yes," agreed Mr Carrados. "More than that: almost providential one might say. Had it been one of Rank's friends the evidence might have been open to suspicion, but our Mr Thaxted appears as a total stranger. Had they met, say in Hyde Park, a very slight discrepancy of time might have made the alibi unconvincing, but Richmond is too far away to consider that. And then under how few circumstances are you likely to ask a total stranger for his name and address, to write them down, and to note the time and date of the occurrence?"

"There is no doubt that Rank had a small terrier that might have acted like that," admitted Beedel.

"And certainly Mr Thaxted will be able to produce a pair of trousers that would prove to have been torn," said Carrados dryly. "Come; what is behind this business, Beedel?"

"Behind it, sir?" repeated the inspector with the utmost innocence.

"The Ayr Street Post Office hold-up wasn't an ordinary outrage at all. You know that as well as I do."

"It's a funny thing," remarked the visitor introspectively. "Here for the last week I've been trying to persuade one or two up at the Yard to regard it in that light and almost your first words—"

"Of course I really know nothing about it," qualified Mr Carrados.

"It's my belief," declared Inspector Beedel with sombre relish, and repeating the expression of faith to emphasize it, "it's my belief that there's a secret organization at work in the background somewhere. I've never thought that Treasury notes were what those two fellows were after, though they certainly grabbed all they could as they went through it."

"What then?" prompted Mr Carrados, for Beedel had relapsed into a keen professional abstraction.

"Something political, I'm pretty sure, sir. A lot of those Sinn Feiners are out to make trouble systematically just now. And you'd be surprised to find who are more or less in with them—all sorts of people."

"The retired gentleman from Kingston, for instance?"

"I have no doubt he may be one. But people you'd never think of as, well, I mean—professional men and soldiers, civil servants, society ladies, dock labourers, skilled artisans. I dare say a good many of them wouldn't go very far for 'The Cause', but some of them would, and then on the edge of it there are the usual crowd who are always keen to make something out of whatever's going on."

"It's likely enough," conceded the blind man. "What were they after here?"

"There isn't a great deal of business generally at this Ayr Street Post Office, but it lies handy for certain public offices. Anything that had been registered would be lying beyond the counter, handy for collection, at the time of the raid. My idea is that they knew of something being posted that they were desperately anxious to secure or to stop. Lizzie Baxter wasn't shot holding on to the notes but because she got between Rank and the letters."

"She hasn't spoken?"

"No; she probably never will. She is the only one who could identify the men, and without her the case against Rank is purely circumstantial; that's what makes it safe for Thaxted to come forward now."

"Perhaps not entirely safe, after all, inspector," remarked Mr Carrados with significance.

"How do you mean, sir?"

"I mean that as it happens on the seventeenth—the day concerned—Mr Thaxted and I sat on a retired seat in Kew Gardens from four to half-past and discussed carnation-growing and other impersonal topics. Afterwards we walked together as far as the Lion Gate and parted at about ten minutes to five."

"Oho!" Inspector Beedel swung his shrewd but not very agile mind round to review the position created by this new factor. "That's something of a facer for the defence, isn't it, sir? Do you mean that you know this Mr Thaxted?"

"Not at all. We were perfect strangers who just met and chatted a little and then went on our separate ways. I didn't know him from Adam until I recognized him in court today."

"I see. Of course if he wasn't quarrelling with Rank in Richmond Park at half-past four he must have been somewhere else. But still, you would think—Well, he took a fairish risk."

"Don't we all do that if we decide to commit perjury, inspector? After all, the man never mentioned his name, his business, any tangible personal detail; and he knew that it was a blind man who had sat by his side and talked with him. When—as we may assume—a volunteer was called for to save Rank by providing an alibi, it may have seemed to Mr Thaxted that the half hour or so that he must compromise himself over was pretty well secured."

"Yes, yes," agreed Beedel, rounding up the situation within his orderly mind as a rather slow but capable sheepdog brings in stragglers; "it's all reasonable enough... There's one weakness ahead—if you don't mind my mentioning it?"

"Let us examine the thin places, by all means," encouraged Carrados.

"You are willing to give evidence, sir?"

"I suppose I must. I know nothing of Rank one way or the other, but I must either come forward or let an appalling perversion of justice go on. It may also help to clear off a trifle of my debt to you, inspector, eh?"

"Thank you, sir, but I think that's pretty good weight already. Still, I don't deny that it would do me a bit of good to produce evidence to upset that alibi. And that brings me to what I was saying."

"Yes; only you seem rather reluctant to say it."

"Well, it's like this, Mr Carrados. In the ordinary way you would give your evidence, and then the question would be put: 'Do you see that man in court?' Now here—"

"When counsel says, 'Have you heard that man in court?' and I reply, 'Yes; when Mr Thaxted was speaking', you think it would fail to carry conviction?"

"I don't think the ordinary jury would see that it's as satisfactory to identify a man by his voice as by his face."

"I am inclined to agree with you. If I said, 'The man who sat with me bit his finger-nails, smoked Algerian cigars, and wore an elastic stocking', do you think it might impress the court?"

The inspector laughed rather contentedly.

"Why, yes, sir; I can't but suppose it might. We could challenge Mr Thaxted to show his finger-nails, produce his cigar-case, and pull up his trouser-leg. It ought to be a fair bombshell."

"Then I must consider myself booked for Tuesday fortnight and as many days afterwards as the case lasts."

"The fewer the better, sir," replied Beedel cryptically. "To tell you the truth, I shouldn't be sorry if tomorrow was Tuesday fortnight. It's a good thing that none of the lot know that you have anything to do with the case, and I hope you'll keep it close, up to the very last minute."

"Oh!" Mr Carrados felt a trifle guilty, remembering that moment when the witness paused and faltered, but Beedel was quite solicitous enough already. "Any particular reason?"

"One of our witnesses has already had the misfortune to be rather badly run down while cycling, and I've had a natty-looking box of chocolates by post from an 'unknown friend' myself," replied the inspector. "I imagine this Rank must be something of a top-hat among these people."

* * * * *

There was a form overlooking a deep expanse of country where Max Carrados often sat when he took a walk in that direction. Indeed, a mild pleasantry current at one time among park-keepers and their kind credited him with a weakness for pointing out the things of interest to any passing stranger who happened to share the seat with him, and the prospect threatened to become mysterious to posterity as "Blind Man's View".

One breathless July afternoon (the drought and languor of that summer have become a record) about a fortnight after Inspector Beedel's visit, Carrados was sitting there alone when his ear picked up the footsteps of two men approaching. In a minute he knew that one man led the other, and with that came the intuition that the second man was blind. Then he found that they were making for the seat.

"This will do," said the leader. "You don't mind?"

"No, no; not at all. Only don't be long," replied the other. "I shall get anxious if you are and I—I feel so confoundedly helpless by myself."

"There is a gentleman already on the seat," dropped the voice warningly. "That will be all right; I won't be long. I must have lost the damn thing within the last three minutes."

His footsteps sounded on the turf, and then grew less along the gravelled road. The stranger turned to Mr Carrados.

"Could you give me the time, sir?" he asked, and at once enlarged the opening sociably. "You'll have noticed that I'm blind. Helpless, of course. My friend dropped an important pocket-book some way back. Three minutes he said—say three minutes there, three back, and three looking about. Ten minutes at the outside... I'll time him if you're staying so long. I don't mind being left in an ordinary way. but I get so confoundedly anxious if anything goes different. You see... If anything happened and he didn't come back for a long time—or at all! Well—"

"That will be all right," said Carrados. "I shan't be going just yet. Ten minutes..."

"I daresay it doesn't seem very long to you, but it's different when there isn't a single blessed thing for you to do... Just to sit and smoke and think... Oh, and talk, of course, when you're lucky enough to get anyone who will... But it's a pretty dull outlook. You normal people have no idea—"

In all this there was, as it happened, an insidious temptation. "You are as fond of showing off, Carrados, as a child with a recitation", had been the piqued barb flung across by a man at whose expense the "showing off" had been effected and there was in the jibe just enough truth to twist the blind man's habitual suaveness for a moment. Max Carrados was admittedly prone to a certain vein of superiority, and his demonstrations were occasionally timed to achieve a theatrical effect, but all sprang from a not unworthy root—from a passionate insistence on being treated as an ordinary human being. To take in a seeing man—to outwit five senses by the use of four—was well enough, but might not the opportunity be at hand of demonstrating to another sufferer that his life need not be so empty as he pictured? He waited.

"The war?" he hazarded.

"Nothing so romantic. Cataract. I suppose I shall get used to it in time... Surely it must be ten minutes now?"

"No—eight." Carrados referred to the fingers of his watch. "But don't think too much of the time. There may be a hundred things to cause delay. Ten minutes...that was altogether too fine a margin."

"That's just it—a hundred things. Anything might happen to a man going along the road looking for a pocketbook... and then where should I be? I was a mug to let him go... Suppose—"

"Don't suppose. I'll stay here till your friend comes back... At all events I'll see you through."

"That's most confoundedly good of you... I must strike you as a poor sort of wash-out..."

"No." The situation was beginning to endear itself to Carrados's mind. "I am interested in the blind... Like faith, blindness moves in a peculiar way..."

"Faith?" mused the stranger vaguely. "Yes; I suppose so... What's that—a car?"

"No," replied Carrados." A plane going south. Queer how the sound varies, isn't it?"

"We left our taxi somewhere near—Heriot Lane the driver called it. I thought that perhaps—A flier, eh? Wings—'The wings of the morning', doesn't old Shakespeare or someone say? Suppose I shall never see a plane travelling again. Used to give me a funny touch sometimes, that. Just as if I was on the point of finding out what this old caboodle is all about anyway—only I never quite got it. Seemed as though I just needed that extra push through that I could never raise. Sounds mushy rot to you, I expect."

"No," admitted Carrados; "most of us have been there. Seeing 'through a glass, darkly', said the Jewish tent-maker of old."

The other man gave a nod of ambiguous agreement. "How's the time?" he asked. "Confound Stringer; he ought to be here by now."

"Going on for twenty minutes. But I don't suppose that it will have seemed like ten to your friend."

They talked again and Carrados tried to interest his companion to make the time pass inperceptibly. Half an hour went by and still there was no sign of Mr Stringer. When three-quarters had been reached, Arnold—he had incidentally dropped his name—could stand it no longer.

"Look here. Something must have happened. I can't stay here for ever. And you—you've been most confoundedly decent, but you must want to be moving. Can you put me in the way of getting back to the taxi? Then I shall know where I am, whatever's gone wrong."

"Certainly," replied Carrados. "I know Heriot Lane well enough. I'll take you there with pleasure. It isn't ten minutes" walk from here. What do you say to pinning a line here on the seat, so that your friend—"

"No, confound him!" exclaimed Arnold with sudden warmth. "He's left me in the lurch all right. Let him do a bit of guessing."

It wasn't an outsider's affair either way. Carrados took the blind man's arm and led him from the seat. Out of consideration for his charge the pace was about half that at which the more experienced man usually walked. There was also still the chance that Stringer might appear. But he did not, and they reached Heriot Lane without incident.

"Is it far down?" asked Carrados. He knew that the lane was a winding little byway where even the humblest sort of traffic might not pass from one hour to another. He could take Arnold along it with a fair amount of confidence, but detection might come at any moment now. He had set himself to pilot the blind man right up to the door of the cab before he revealed the true situation—anything short of that failed to drive home the moral of his achievement. "I don't see a taxi yet," he added.

"A bit along, I suppose," said Arnold. His eyes were open and he was looking sideways into his guide's face with an expression of peculiar and private amusement that did not carry into his voice. "He may have drawn on..."

"Ah," exclaimed the blind leader as they cleared a bend, "there's something at last." Ear and nose told him so much, and it would be an easy matter to bring his charge right up to the car. But—the chance of so inglorious a fiasco was small in that infrequent place—but how to be sure that this was indeed the taxi?

"Back again, sir?"

That settled it. Carrados moved on by the light of his own intuitive judgement. When he knew that he was three yards from the car the door was opened. He had reached the goal.

"Now!" said another voice in sharp command.

Before the word was spoken Carrados had had a flash of realization. It came with the nature-sense of overhanging danger, with the subtle change of intention in the arm that touched his own, with the slight chirrup of a stoppered phial being opened—but it came too late. Arnold's light pressure on his right suddenly became a pinioning grip, another pair of arms closed on his left and a saturated cloth not unpleasantly odoured, was pressed against his face...

"It worked?" remarked one, rearranging himself after they had bundled the senseless form into the car.

"Like a charm," replied the man called Arnold, smiling at a thought.

"Change that plate again, and move about it," said the third of the gang shortly.

A minute later the renumbered car slipped out of Heriot Lane without any superfluous parade of warning, and taking on a pace much too moderate to suggest the remotest connexion with things sensational, it was soon swallowed up in the stream of evening traffic flowing eastward.

* * * * *

"Ah. So ye're com'n" round now, aren't ye?" said a not unfriendly voice, as consciousness began to trickle at first and then rush into Max Carrados's perceptions. "Feelin" just a thrifle sick, too, at first, I don't doubt."

"Where am I?" asked the blind man mechanically. Sick he certainly did feel in more ways than one, for the stuff that had been used to drug him with was of an unholy texture that left nausea and headache in its wake, while to be drawn into so guileless a trap outraged his most vulnerable susceptibilities. "Where am I and who are you?"

"Now don't be troublin" ye'self about things like those that don't really matter at all," replied the other persuasively. "Ye're right enough now, and so long as ye don't sthruggle, so to speak, ye can be as comfortable as a dormouse in a haystack."

"I quite understand," retorted the captive. "And if I struggle, as you are pleased to call it, I may infer that I shall be treated as Lizzie Baxter was?"

""Tis a great mistake to dhrop from the exthract on to the conkrate, as the man remarked whin he fell from the distillery window down into th" sthrate. Ye'll understand that whin there's a war goin" on there's likely to be cashoolties. Ye're a cashoolty just at the moment, Mr Carrados, but whether ye're ultimate destination is to be the recooperation camp or the wayside simitry is a matter entirely awaitin" ye're own personal convenience."

"I have an idea," replied Carrados, "that it will turn out to be the witness-box."

"I shouldn't build on that now," said the Irishman speculatively. "With all due respect to the three classical females who arrange the destinies, I can see no indication of anything like that on the immedjet horizon. Doubtless if ye were to consult the mysterious lady who prognosticates through the mejum of a chrystal sphere, or the obliging wizard who for the small consideration of haf a crown tells you what he sees in the smoke of an aromatic pastille, something in the nature of a witness-box might possibly be adumbrated; but for all practical purposes I should eliminate it from ye're calc'lations, Mr Carrados."

"You appear to be a pleasant and ingenious gentleman, Mr—?"

"Murphy is a very handy name for the purpose of short reference."

"Mr Murphy, then. You appear also to have a general knowledge of me and my movements, while I, unfortunately, know practically nothing of you or my surroundings. As a guest, enjoying your hospitality, that naturally puts me in a very humiliating position. You see—"

"I appreciate the delicacies of the situation," replied Mr Murphy in the same vein of guarded satire to which they had fallen. "I should dearly love to act as a general vade-mecum, who's who, and illustrated gazetteer of the situation if it could be done. But ye'll understand there may be sthretegic reasons aginst lettin" on which end of Park Lane this mansion is situate in, or whether ye're host is a blue-blooded aristochrat or merely a Labour member."

"Perhaps," suggested the blind man, "it would be permissible to say why I have been carried off in this outrageous manner and what you imagine you are going to do with me?"

"There's no harm at all in tellin" ye what ye know already," replied Mr Murphy, with a sudden loss of geniality in his manner. "Ye're here because ye intended giving evidence in a case that was no airthly concern of ye's, and ye'll stay here, or in some other suitable place of retirement, until that little matter's satisfactorily disposed of. What call had ye to go acting otherwise than sthrictly as a nootral if ye're not prepared to take the consequences?"

"A neutral!" repeated Carrados in amazement. "Good heavens, man, neutral in what? This was simply a case of elementary justice. But perhaps," he added pointedly, "you have never heard of that?"

There was a movement of anger from more than one part of the room, and the man who had been carrying on the conversation strode across and stood over the captive. The taunt had served a useful purpose, for Carrados had learned a little more.

"I should advise ye to keep that sort of remark in ye're breeches po'k"t while ye're here, Mr Carrados," said Murphy. "This once ye're blind eyes protect ye."

"They often do," replied Carrados imperturbably. "I am confident that they often will."

"Don't be too sure while ye are here, that's all."

He heard the man turn sharply on his heel and walk across the room. The door banged and silence lengthened out, but the prisoner knew that unfriendly eyes still watched him and that he had not been left alone.

Nearly a week went by and nothing happened. Max Carrados was as completely cut off from the world as if he had been carried away to Mars. Food was put before him on a generous scale and his ordinary needs were attened to, but conversation with those who moved about was not encouraged. Mr Murphy seemed to have disappeared after the first evening.

From the moment of his recovering consciousness Carrados began to construct the details of his surroundings and to examine his prison. It was, he learned within a day, a spacious, old-fashioned house of three storeys and a basement, detached, and standing in some private ground. The rooms were generally large and lofty, but their former state was not kept up; several were empty and the furniture of the others was miscellaneous and haphazard. Gas was used, the telephone bell often rang, and a silent elderly woman did the cooking and attendance. The captive soon discovered that he was never left alone, and at night he slept in a room where the window was barred from top to bottom and the chimney blocked. The blind man smiled as he realized that an alarming reputation must have preceded him.

It was not until the second night that he could definitely locate his prison. How long the journey in the car had been he had no means of knowing, but the taste of the air, the touch of the water in which he washed, and the distant noises of the street were all unmistakably of London. It was a quiet and secluded back-water to which he had been brought, and at no great distance from the house he soon knew of a park-like space where thrushes sang at dawn and the owl proclaimed the night, but a great highway of traffic lay extended on the south and another, rather less busy, on the north. On the second night he heard Big Ben slowly booming out the hours on a line almost directly east, and applying to the sounds his own peculiar methods he found that he could assume the space between them as just about three miles. The next day he dropped a simple test.

"I suppose I can have a certain book I want? I think it could be got—"

"A book?" repeated the man who was then in charge of him, dubiously.

"Yes, from Mudie's in the High Street just below here"—nodding direction—"you know."

The sharp breath of surprise confirmed what he had already guessed, even without the attendant's belated and rather hurt protestation that he "could say nothing about that." The matter of the book progressed no further.

For a couple of days Carrados had been speculating rather poignantly about his position. A crisis of some sort must, he conjectured, be at hand. Even if the trial of Rank lasted three days—a generous limit—the verdict was now due. He had, he assumed, been carried off purely to suppress his fatal evidence, but if the case went against the prisoner—how then? He had no illusions about the methods of the desperate little band of extremists into whose hands he had fallen, and, without flurry or visible concern, there were very few minutes of the day when he was not considering plans of escape. But so far the strength of his prison was unassailable, the guards not to be drawn by casual hints of gold.

It was on the evening of the sixth day of confinement that the expected crisis came. All that afternoon there had been less movement about the big house than was usual, but towards dusk men began to arrive by ones and twos until Carrados had accounted for at least a dozen above the usual company.

"They have all been to hear the verdict given," surmised the blind man. "Now for it."

He was right. An hour later he was curtly summoned to another room—"the council chamber," as he had always mentally described it from the meetings that obviously took place there—and found himself before an informal court.

"This is the man Carrados?" inquired someone, with brusque authority.

One of Carrados's regular custodians replied.

"He is blind, captain, though you mightn't notice it," he added. "Shall I give him a chair?"

"Was Dennis Rank given a chair once during the three days of his trial?" demanded the voice.

"He was not," came the hearty response from half a dozen.

"Let the prisoner stand."

"A prisoner," remarked Carrados mildly, "is usually charged with an offence. May I ask what mine is?"

"Conveying information to the enemy," was the answer, rapped out with domineering harshness. "It concerns you to learn, Carrados, that Dennis Rank was pronounced guilty this afternoon and sentenced to death."

"That would be the very natural result of carrying me off, wouldn't it?" insinuated the blind man. "You had surely thought of that."

"What do you mean?"

Carrados was almost tempted to shrug his shoulders to underline the obviousness of what had happened.

"If I had appeared and given evidence it would have been perfectly easy to suggest that I was either mistaken or a liar—one man's word against another's. As it was, there was nothing on which to suggest that I was mistaken or lying. You simply advertised that my evidence was correct and true and that you daren't allow it to be given at any price."

"There now, captain, what did I tell ye?" muttered a malcontent.

"Stow that," commanded the man in authority. Then he turned to the prisoner again. "You are not before us to express your own personal and private views on this or that, Carrados, but to hear the decision of this court. Needless to say an appeal is being lodged against the bloodthirsty tyranny of Dennis Rank's sentence. If you can suggest anything to help that along you'd do well to get busy right now and let us know."

"Theoretically," admitted Mr Carrados, "I've never been in favour of capital punishment."

"That's vurry opportune," remarked the captain dryly. "But there are exceptions, and possibly this may be one of them."

"Oh, it may, you think?" roared the astonished inquisitor. "Wall, let me tell you this: The hour the black flag goes up at Brixton Jail for Dennis Rank your family will have cause to go into mourning too."

"What good will that do?"

"It will do this good, that you may as well begin to get a move on you to dodge it. We opine that you have a pull in more than one direction, Carrados, and pawsably your Government may cawnsider your neck worth saving. Wall, you know the price, and you'd better make out the best case you can for the exchange when you let them know. You can have pen and ink and paper and—under suitable examination, so don't try any of your slim tricks here—you can communicate with your own lawyer or anyone else you like."

"Thank you," replied Mr Carrados, "but I won't trouble you."

"Won't trouble! Hell! What d'ye mean?"

"Just what I say. I have no intention of writing. Of my own free will I might in ordinary circumstances sign a petition against Rank being hanged. As you put it, I am much more likely to sign one against his being reprieved. You'll have to do your own unpleasant work yourself."

"The man's clean daft," sighed one of the court in helpless bewilderment. "What'll there be unpleasant in saving your nut?"

"Merely a point of view," remarked Carrados, turning towards him quite courteously. "There are things that we all stick at doing at any price... Or, at all events"—his face was again in the direction of the president of the court—"most of us."

For some reason, in the five minutes that they had been together there had sprung up between these two men a deep and corrosive antipathy. Towards all the others of his captors Carrados bore little beyond a philosophic tolerance, with an occasional lapse into mild annoyance. But here each felt the other's hatred, and recognized that between them there would be no accommodation, no compromise. The only difference was the way the motion showed—in the captain it produced a tendency to shout, in the captive an icy quietness.

"So you think you can ride the high horse here, do you?" exploded the leader, flashing out passionately. "With ya blasted 'point of view' and ya infernal five-cent style. Remember that ya're not dealing with any of ya're own shilly-shallying Dublin Castle trash, but with men that mean what they say. And show proper respect to the court ya're up before or, by heaven! The crack of a fist'll teach you."

"I can't defend myself." Carrados turned towards the others and held out his groping hands with a plaintive helplessness. "Is there any man here who can strike me across my sightless eyes?"

"God know that's true!" murmured more than one.

"Then how are you going to hang me?"

The captain summed up his stalwarts with a cold, contemptuous glance.

"Leave that to me," he said more quietly., "when the time comes. There's a proverb about killin" a dog, Carrados, you'll maybe know. In the meanwhile you'll have a few days to think better of it. Bear in mind that it's not to hang you for preference that we're out, but to save Dennis Rank. Remove the prisoner."

When Carrados was removed he guessed that the eventuality had plainly been foreseen, for he was not led back to his former quarters. Instead, he found himself traversing parts of the house where he had never been allowed before. Then came a downward flight of steps and a cooler atmosphere. He was to be imprisoned in a cellar.

His treatment, as he learned presently, was to be in keeping with the place. All the contents of his pockets were taken from him, but being now in close confinement he was left alone. Doubtless it was considered that forcible escape was impossible, and when he came to examine his surroundings he saw no reason to dissent. It was not so much a cellar as a blind passage to which a massive door had been fitted. Probably at the time of its conversion there had been some special use in view. Every quarter has its vague, half-forgotten legends of mystery and crime. The house was old, and who could say now why the remote, unwanted passage should have been so strongly turned into the semblance of a dungeon? The prisoner paced it and examined its every corner with investigating hands. Five ordinary strides took him from one end to the other, and standing there he could without shifting his position touch its two long walls at the same time-with outstretched hands, and then the ceiling. Less than five yards in length it would seem to be, two yards across, and seven feet in height. The walls were stone, the floor was stone, and ceiling stone or concrete. Its most dreadful feature—the total absence of window or any source of light—did not trouble the man who now sat down to review his rather desperate plight. A single chair had been provided and a small pallet with a couple of rugs.

With the prison went prison fare—three very plain meals a day—enough, but far from lavish. It was perfectly indicated what this rigorous system meant: Each day his jailer asked whether he wished for writing material, and each day he returned a negative. The odds were rather heavily balanced, but if it came to a test of mere obstinacy between the man they called "Captain" and himself, Carrados was quite inclined to fancy his own chances. After the execution, or the reprieve, of Rank there would be no sane reason for detaining him. And somehow at the back of his mind the blind man could not abandon the feeling that even in the last extremity his star would see him through.

Three days passed. Carrados was not unendurably bored, for his mind was an inexhaustible storehouse, and with the unconcern for surroundings that was one of his assets he at once resumed the composition of a monograph on "The Persian Archer on a Unique Tetradrachm of Corinth," an entertainment that his capture had interrupted. But on the evening of the third day something occurred to make the Persian archer rather less interesting than he had been up to then. Night came, but no supper was brought, and as the hours went on and Carrados failed by the most delicate tests of hearing to discover any movement in the house above, a sudden misgiving shook him. What if... He put the thought aside and went to bed as the simplest way of ignoring the situation.

But the next morning there was no breakfast. Again an unnatural silence lay upon the place. With his ear to the wall, the blind prisoner had been able to follow a footstep from his door up to the distant kitchen, but not the faintest echo now reached him. He took off a boot and beat a crescendo of remonstrance upon the door... He might just as well have flicked it with his handkerchief for all the attention it provoked. Yet it could scarcely have failed to be heard, remote and subterranean as his prison was, if there had been anyone... If there had been anyone! The thought suddenly developed and spread in half a dozen directions like a flame among dry shavings: Was it part of a plan to starve him to submission—had some been arrested and the remainder fled—was there some ghastly misunderstanding, everyone leaving his care or release to someone else—had they suddenly given up all hope of influencing Rank's disposal and in revenge had left him there to die? In less than five minutes he was speculating on the probable discoverer of his body and how long hence the event would be a month, a year, or so remote that he would be referred to as "a shrivelled skeleton." He cursed his imagination and forced his mind back to the Persian archer and his significant appearance on a Greek tetradrachm.

But at noon there was no dinner. Hunger now began to make itself really felt, but more than that, a tormenting thirst had come over him. He raved a button off and kept it in his mouth to induce secretion, but it was a poor pretence. At measured intervals he beat upon the door as he had done before; to attempt to make himself heard by the outside world was, he knew, hopeless...

That night Carrados again went supperless to bed. He had been without food for a day and a half, but that was a small consideration beside the awful thirst that now possessed him. Those were the hottest days of an exceptional summer, and though the cellar was cooler than the house above it was also closer. A neglected drain somewhere near had given the prisoner "a throat" which ticked and throbbed for relief in vain. His mind turned to innumerable tales of shipwrecked sailors dying of thirst, to accounts of men cut off and driven to frenzy through lack of water in the trenches, to the parable of the Rich Man and Lazarus, to a memory of a nauseous passage in Robinson Crusoe, to the awful case of... Would it end in madness with him also? Before that... he had no weapon, but there were the blankets of his bed, and he had touched a substantial pipe running in the angle of the wall and ceiling of his cell that would surely bear his weight.

It was to escape these thoughts that he lay down and tried to sleep when his time-sense told him that it was something short of midnight. He still clung to the hope that morning would bring relief, and if so he was in the mood to write anything to avert another day of thirst and torment—even the ink, he reflected grimly, would be a godsend at that moment.

Thinking of the ink—the ink—ink—the door opened miraculously and Parkinson came in. "What a horrible dream," thought Carrados. "I fancied that I was shut up in a cellar, and here I am sitting down to dinner at some nice restaurant. What soup have you got there, Parkinson?" "I beg your pardon, sir," replied his attendant, putting a large bowl before him, "but I understand that the custom of this house is for a dish of water to be left at night on every table; otherwise, I am told, the rats will gnaw through the lead pipes in search of it." "Very well," replied Mr Carrados. "But this is ink that you have brought." "I'm extremely distressed," stammered Parkinson, "I will change—" And as he spoke he changed into the magistrate at Lemon

Square Police Court, and Carrados found himself listening to a case about a fountain-pen. "Your worship," pleaded the plaintiff, "the pen was in perfect condition when I sold it. I would respectfully suggest that it was damaged by—" "Rats!" interposed the defendant contemptuously as he proceeded to light a cigar. "Silence in coort!" roared his worship. "What this poor, honest man says is very true, belike. Sure, the craytures'll do anything for dhrink. Why, every morning don't I find the ink on me desk here lappit up and—" Again the court shook with laughter, and in the middle of it Carrados suddenly awoke—still in his cell and more thirst-racked than ever, but with a new hope to inspire. As he sat up he heard the rats outside scampering past his door.

"Idiot!" he apostrophized himself; "not to think of that. You are certainly getting old and stupid. Dying of thirst with a water pipe—oh, my God, suppose it isn't! If it should be the gas!"

But it was not the gas. One tap with a finger-end set that at rest. In an old, rambling house it might have been anything, but an inch pipe giving the resonance of liquid contents could indicate nothing but the supply—an inexhaustible stream, of pure water was his for the taking. But how? His mind accounted for one useless article after another in a vain search for any kind of makeshift tool. Not a scrap of metal, not even a serviceable edge of broken stone or brick, had been left to suggest escape. Still, there must be something—must—Yes; the boot! His frequent poundings on the floor had already strained a heel; one sharp wrench against the other boot and the loose heel came away. In his hand he held a slab of leather bristling with rows of pointed nails: as effective a file as one could wish for.

In less than three minutes Carrados was drinking—drinking gloriously. He had rubbed through the soft metal of the pipe until the water began to jet, then he dropped the boot heel and used his hands to form a cup. He had no means of stopping the leak now; it might flood the cellar and ultimately drown him, but even if he had known that that must happen it would not have held him back—not at that moment.

When he had drunk sufficient for the time he took his handkerchief and held it to the stream, intending to sponge his face. On that slight incident—even on the hazard of the position he took up—depended all that happened after; for as he waited there—crouching rather on the uncertain chair and steadying himself with one hand upon the pipe a faint but distinct tremor passed beneath his hand. It was so trivial in itself, so barren of suggestion, that not one man in a thousand—even among desperate prisoners—would have given it a thought. But to Max Carrados his fingertips were eyes, and to him that slight vibration flashed a ray of hope. It told him little—definitely there was little it could tell—but he knew that somewhere someone was within reach of a signal in reply. The supply pipe would lead to a cistern up above, and at that hour—about daybreak now he judged—it was unlikely that anyone should be moving there. But in the other direction—out, through the garden, and along the streets? For months past now no rain had fallen, and the air was full of the talk of great droughts and threatening water famine. Every wasted drop was grudged, and by day and night—especially by night when the streets were quiet—the company's inspectors made their rounds, tracing every suggestion of a leak, raising the little traps that give access to the mains, and stick to ear for the faintest distant sound, listening—oh, ray of hope, Max Carrados!—listening!

A second gone, perhaps. Still lightly touching the pipe to take up any response, the blind man dropped the unheeded handkerchief and with the strong bare knuckles of his other hand he began to spell out into the unknown the universal message of despair: short, short, short; long, long, long; short, short, short—S.O.S.; S.O.S.; S.O.S.

* * * * *

About the time that Mr Carrados awoke and thought of a boot heel two men in the chaste blue attire favoured by the Metropolitan Water Board stopped at a small iron plate let into the road and prepared to enter upon the cabbalistic ritual of their tribe. The high priest, as it were, of the two carried a wand of office in his hand—a serviceable bamboo rod with a saucer-shaped top, and his ceremonial cap was dignified by the word INSPECTOR blazoned on a neat oval badge above the peak. His acolyte differed from him only in the slight details of appearance, but instead of a rod he affected a dangerous-looking implement that could only be likened to a small—but not a very small—harpoon.

"When we've worked down to the High Street again we'll knock off for breakfast, "Orras," remarked the inspector, speaking as one who conveys encouragement.

""Bout as well," commented "Orras. "My inwards are beginning to inquire audibly whether me throat's bin cut."

"It's queer how young fellows are always thinking of their teeth nowadays," mused his superior. "They don't seem to have no endurance, somehow, "Orras. Did I ever tell you how three of us signallers were up in a tower outside a place called Binchley for the better part of a week—"

"Often; yesterday for once," retorted the younger generation. "Contrive to forget those early days of crime, Father William. The war's over and done with, and we aren't going to have no more."

The inspector sighed and, leaning against a convenient lamp-post, tactfully indicated to "Orras a suggestion to get on with it, while he himself proceeded to write up current record in his book. Disdaining an offer of the listening stick the assistant impaled and raised the lid of the trap with his own sinister weapon, and probing the depths with the business end of it applied his ear to the other.

"Well?" inquired the inspector presently. "All O.K.?"

"Nor yet in sight of it," reported "Orras gloomily. "There's something going on somewhere that's beyond me."

"That's queer." The inspector meant nothing by it, but "Orras twisted his neck to get a sight of his superior's face. "What do you mean it's like?"

"Better have a look yourself," suggested the junior, making way, while the other closed his book and took his place above the trap. "Listening posts are more in your line than mine."

A minute passed in silence as the more experienced man stooped with his ear upon the depression of his stick.

"It's rummy that we should be talking about signalling and what not just now," he remarked, without raising his head. "If such a thing was credible I should have said that someone was talking morse along the pipe."

"Wha'd"z'e say?" inquired "Orras with languid interest, as he rolled a cigarette.

"Nothing what you might call coherent—just a run of letters. Sos; sos; sos all the time. Half a minute though: isn't there something 'S.O.S.' stands for?"

"Yes," agreed "Orras with expression, "there is. Sosagers. And very nice too for breakfast."

"Tchk! Tchk!" clicked the inspector reproachfully. "Can't you never leave off thinking of food for half a minute, "Orras? There! Now I've got it. S.O.S. It's the signal of distress a sinking ship sends out, of course."

"Of course. Submarine must ha" come up the main, and now it can't neither turn nor reverse in the narrows. Why ever didn't we think of that at first?"

But the inspector was not to be put off by the cheap humour of irreverent youth. He had not lived five and forty years and gone through the war without discovering that very queer things do occasionally occur in real life. For a moment he twirled a pair of pliers absent-mindedly in his free hand; then kneeling on the pavement he struck the metal fittings down below a succession of measured taps—a score or so.

"What's that?" demanded "Orras, intrigued in spite of his blase outlook.

"I just sent 'Who's there?'" explained the inspector, returning to the listening attitude again. "They mayn't know the calls and general answer and such like."

"Seems to me this isn't M.W.B. routine at all," said the assistant flippantly. "You must have got through to the cinema somehow, uncle. 'Snatched from Death's Jaws' in seven snatches—"

The inspector's right hand shot out in a compelling gesture of warning and repression.

"Get this down, lad," he said with sharp authority. "You have a bit o" paper and pencil, haven't you? C-A-R-R—You have a bit o" paper and a pencil, haven't you? C-A-R-R..."

"Right-o," responded the other, discovering an old *Star* in his pocket and turning to the "Stop Press" space. "C-A-R-R—Carry on, sergeant."

"-A-D-O-S."

"Carrados! Why, he's the bloke—" The boy dived into the paper until a head-line caught his eye. "MISSING BLIND WITNESS. STILL NO TRACE OF MAX CARRADOS." "You don't mean to say—"

"Shut it!" snapped the inspector fiercely. "Attend, can't you? T-R-A-P-P-E-D P-H-O-N-E N-E-A-R-E-S-T P-O-L-I-C-E S-T-A-T-I-O-N U-R-G-E-N-T L-I-F-E D-E-A-T-H-"

"Phew!" murmured "Orras, perspiring ecstatically. "That's the stuff to—"

"A-M O-P-E-N-I-N-G L-E-A-K G-U-I-D-E P-O-L-I-C-E R-E-W-A-R-D."

"Orras drew his breath in sharply, almost overcome by the vista of gain and glory.

"That all?" he whispered meekly.

"S-E-N-D-R-T-I-F U-N-D-E-R-S-T-O-O-D—you needn't put that last bit in though."

"Let's see you do it." "Orras, subdued by a technical efficiency that lay outside his range, shrewdly foresaw that for the next three weeks at least every word he might condescend to drop would be worth its weight in cigarettes.

The inspector bent down and gave the metal a few considered taps with the pliers.

"That's all. Now slip off into the High Street, boy, and get through on the nearest telephone. And for God's sake don't stop to have your breakfast anywhere on the way, and I shouldn't wonder if this doesn't mean a week's fishing at Southend for us."

"Garn," retorted "Orras, now in a state of giggling bliss. "A day at Barnes Reservoir more likely. What're *you* going to do?"

"Now hop it," said the inspector firmly. "And don't muck up your end of the job. I'm going to look into this leak."

Ten minutes later he was still tapping the road at intervals when two quite unnoticeable gentlemen appeared in sight, walking that way. As they took in his occupation a few words passed hurriedly between them and instead of passing him they stopped.

""Morning, inspector," said one affably—he had shot a glance at the official cap. "Nothing wrong with the water supply up here, I hope?"

"Nothing that I know of, sir," replied the inspector simply. "Just our usual rounds."

"Ah?" said the stranger. "That so? But it's a hell of a summer, isn't it? Keeps you people busy, I bet. I thought you might be making a round to look at our taps and fittings to see there was no waste."

"Everything O.K. so far as I have found," was the reassuring answer. "We don't like to give any more trouble than we need. As a matter of fact, I'm only waiting for my mate to knock off for breakfast."

The two nodded pleasantly and passed on. The inspector threw his stick into the hollow of his arm and strolled idly along the road after them, whistling softly to himself, until they turned in at a distant gate. He had a particularly guileless face and mild, speculative eyes.

* * * * *

As it turned out Mr Murphy and the Captain could scarcely have timed their return better from one point of view. They had just entered, seen that everything was, as the genial Irishman took occasion to remark, "Go'n" on schwimmin"" (there being then about six inches of water in the cellar), and brought up the prisoner to a higher and drier level for a little serious conversation (foreshadowed by certain references to necks and ropes and throats and knives on the Captain's part) when a polite knock on the front door called one of them away for a moment. It chanced that the Captain was the one who went and he did not immediately return. Noticing this, Mr Murphy was seized by a sudden desire to investigate the rear portion of the grounds, and he rather hurriedly opened a window and dropped down, with the evident intention of proceeding there. In his excitement, however, he had overlooked the presence of several policemen, standing in what he himself would have described as "sthretegic attitoods", and he fell into their arms to be escorted ingloriously back again...

"Do you know, Mr Murphy, I still have an idea that it will turn out to be the witness-box," Mr Carrados observed when they all reassembled in the hall—an ignoble thrust admittedly, but much may be forgiven of a man who is carrying half a gallon of cold water after fasting for a couple of days.

THE BRAVO OF LONDON

"Abellino," said the Doge, "Thou art a fearful,
—a detestable man."

—*The Bravo of Venice.**

BRAVO (I) a daring villain. —*The Oxford English Dictionary.*

[* *The Bravo of Venice*. A five-act drama by the German writer Heinrich Zschokke (1771–1848). Original title *Abellino*.]

CONTENTS

1. The Road to Tapsfield 291
2. Joolby Does a Little Business 306
3. Mr Bronsky Has Misgivings 323
4. Cora Larch Is Offered a Good Situation 334
5. The Meeting at Eleven 351
6. Tilehurst Fails to Keep an Appointment 373
7. Dr Olivant Establishes His Bona Fides 386
8. Max Carrados Becomes Interested in Trifles 398
9. In Which the Assurance of the Eye Deceives the Mind 412
10. Nipper Contributes to the Problem 421
11. A Mine Is Countermined 437
12. The Stage Is Set 455
13. Nora Tells the Tale and Carrados Supplies the Music 471
14. A Signal of Distress Into the Unknown 489
15. The Man at the Other End 502
16. Last Laughter 512

1

THE ROAD TO TAPSFIELD

"A tolerably hard nut to crack, of course," said the self-possessed young man with the very agreeable smile—an accomplishment which he did not trouble to exercise on his associate in this case, since they knew one another pretty well and were strictly talking business; "or you wouldn't be so dead keen about me, Joolby."

"Oh, I don't know; I don't know, Nickle," replied the other with equal coolness, "There are hundreds—thousands—of young demobs like yourself to be had today for the asking. All very nice chaps personally, quite unscrupulous, willing to take any risk, competent within certain limits, and not one of them able to earn an honest living. No; if I were you I shouldn't fancy myself indispensable."

"Having now disclosed our mutual standpoints and in a manner cleared the ground, let's come down to concrete foundations," suggested Nickle. "You're hardly thinking of opening a beauty parlour at this benighted Tapsfield?"

The actual expression of the man addressed as Joolby at this callous thrust did not alter, although it might be that a faint quiver of feeling played across the monstrous distortion that composed his face, much as a red-hot coal shows varying shades of incandescence without any change of colour or surface.

For such was Joolby's handicap at birth that any allusion to beauty or to looks made in his presence must of necessity be an outrage.

He was indeed a creature who by externals at all events had more in common with another genus than with that humanity among which fate had cast him, and his familiar nickname of "The Toad" crudely indicated what that species might be. Beneath a large bloated face, mottled with irregular patches of yellow and brown, his pouch-like throat hung loose and pulsed with a steady visible beat that held the fascinated eyes of the squeamish stranger. Completely bald, he always wore a black skull-cap, not for appearance, one would judge, since it only heightened his ambiguous guise, and his absence of eyebrows was emphasised by the jutting hairless ridges that nature had substituted.

Nor did the unhappy being's unsightliness end with these facial blots, for his shrunken legs were incapable of wholly supporting his bulky frame and whenever he moved about he drew himself slowly and painfully along by the aid of two substantial walking sticks. Only in one noticeable particular did the comparison fail, for while the eye of a toad is bright and gentle Joolby's reflected either dull apathy or a baleful malice. Small wonder that women often turned unaccountably pale on first meeting him face to face and the doughty urchins of the street, although they were ready enough to shrill "Toady, toady, Joolby!" behind his back, shrieked with real and not affected terror if chance brought them suddenly to close quarters.

"The one thing that makes me question your fitness for the job is an unfortunate vein of flippancy in your equipment, Nickle," commented Joolby without any display of feeling. "No doubt it amuses you to score off people whom you despise, but it also gives you away and may put them on their guard about something that really matters. This is just a friendly warning. What sort of business should I be able to do with anyone if I ever let them see my real feelings towards them—yourself, for instance?"

"True, O cadi," admitted Nickle lightly. "People aren't worth sticking the manure fork into—present company included—but it's frequently temptatious. Proceed, effendi."

"The chap who has been at Tapsfield already was a wash-out and I've had to drop him. He'll never come to any good, Nickle—no imagination. Now that's where you should be able to put something through, and I have confidence in you. You're a very convincing liar."

"You are extremely kind, Master," replied Nickle. "What had your dud friend got to say about it?"

"He came back sneeping that it was impossible even to get in anywhere there because they are so suspicious of strangers."

"To do with the mill, I suppose?"

"Of course—what else? He couldn't stay a night—not a bed to be had anywhere for love or money unless someone can guarantee you bona fide. The fool fish simply dropped in on them with a bag of golf clubs—and there wasn't a course within five miles. You'll have to think out something brighter, Nickle."

"Leave that to me. Just exactly what do you want to know, Joolby?"

"Everything that there is to be found out—position, weaknesses, precautions, routine, delivery and despatch: the whole business. And particularly any of the people who are open to be got at with some sort of inducement. But for God's sake—"

"I beg your pardon?"

"No need to, Nickle. I only want to emphasise that whatever you do, not a shadow of suspicion must be risked. We haven't decided yet on what lines the thing will go through and we can't have any channel barred. I can give you a fortnight."

"Thanks; I shall probably take a month. And it's understood to be five per cent on the clean-up and all exes meanwhile?"

"Reasonable expenses, Nickle. You can't spend much in a backwash like this Tapsfield."

"My expenses always are reasonable—I mean there is always a reason for them. But I notice that you don't kick at the other item. That doesn't look as if you were exactly optimistic of striking a gold mine, Joolby."

"In your place I might have thought that, but I shouldn't have said it. Now I know that you will make it up in exes. Well, let me tell you this, Mr Nickle: no, on the whole I won't. But what should you say if I hinted not at hundreds or thousands but millions?"

"I should say much the same as the duchess did—'Oh, Hell, leave my leg alone!'" languidly admitted Mr Nickle.

* * * * *

The road from Stanbury Junction to Tapsfield was agreeably winding—assuming, of course, that you were at the time susceptible to the graces of nature and not hurrying, for instance, to catch a train—pleasantly shady for such a day as this, and attractively provided, from the leisurely wayfarer's point of view, with a variety of interesting features. For one stretch it fell in with the vulgarly babbling little river Vole and for several furlongs they pursued an amicable course together, until the Vole, with a sudden flirt like the misplaced coquetry of a gawky wench, was half way across a meadow and although it made some penitent advances to return, the road declined to make it up again and even turned away so that thereafter they meandered on apart: a portentous warning to the numerous young couples who strolled that way on summer evenings, had they been in the mood to profit by the instance. Its place was soon taken by a lethargic, weed-clogged dyke, a very different stream but profuse of an engaging medley of rank grass and flowers—tall bulrushes and swaying sedge, pale flags, saffron kingcups and incredibly artificial-looking pink and white water-lilies, and the sure resort of countless dragon flies of extraordinary agility and brilliance. This channel at one point gave occasion for a moss-grown bridge whereon the curious might inform themselves by the authority of a weather-beaten sign that while the road powers of the county of Sussex claimed the bridge and all that appertained to it, they expressly disclaimed liability for any sort of accident or ill that might be experienced there, and in fact held you strictly responsible and answerable in amercement.

Everywhere was peaceful shade and a cool green smell and the assurance that anything that was happening somewhere else didn't really matter. A few small, substantial clouds, white and rotund like the puffs of smoke from a cannon's mouth in an old-type print, floated overhead but imposed on no one to the extent of foretelling rain. Actually, it was the phenomenally dry summer of 1921.

The single pedestrian who had come that way when the 3.27 down train steamed on appeared to be amenable to these tranquil influences, for he continually loitered and looked about, but the frequency with which he took out his watch and the alert expectancy of his backward glances, would soon have discounted the impression of aimless leisure had there been anyone to observe his movements. And, in truth, nothing could have been further from casualness or lack of purpose than this inaction, for on that day, at that hour and in that place, the first essential move was being made in a design so vast and far-reaching that the whole future course of civilization might well hang on its issue. So might one disclose a tiny rill in the uplands of Thibet—and thousands of miles away the muddy yellow waters of the surging Whang Ho obliterate an inoffensive province.

Presently, following the same route, the distant figure of another pedestrian had come into sight, and swinging along the road at a fine resolute gait (indicative perhaps, since he wore a clerical garb, of robust Christianity) promised very soon to overtake the laggard. It is only reasonable to assume that in his case there was less inducement to examine the surroundings, for while the first could be dismissed at a glance as a stranger to those parts, the second was the Rev. Octavius Galton, vicar of Tapsfield, who, as everyone could tell you, paid a weekly visit on that day to an outlying hamlet with its little tin mission hall, straggling at least a mile beyond the Junction.

With the first appearance of this new character on the scene the behaviour of the loitering man underwent a change—trifling indeed, but not without significance. His progress was still slow, he continued to take interest in the unfolding details of his way, but he studiously refrained from looking round, and his watch had ceased to concern him. It was, if one would hazard a speculative shot, as though something that he had been expecting had happened now and he was prepared to play a part in the next development.

"Good afternoon," called out the vicar as he went past—he conscientiously greeted every wayfarer encountered on his rounds, tramp or esquire, and few were so churlish as to be unresponsive.

"Glorious weather, isn't it?—though of course rain is really needed," The after-thought came from over his shoulder, for the Rev. Octavius did not carry universal neighbourliness to the extent of encouraging prolonged wayside conversation.

"Good afternoon," replied the stranger, quite as genially. "Yes, isn't it. Splendid."

He made no attempt to enlarge the occasion and to all appearance the incident was over. But just when it would have been, Mr Galton heard a sharp exclamation—the instinctive note of surprise—and turned to see the other in the act of stooping to pick up some object.

"I don't suppose this is likely to be yours"—he had stopped automatically and the finder had quickened his pace to join him—"but if you live in these parts you might hear who has lost it. Looks more like a woman's purse, I should say."

"Dear me," said the vicar, "how unfortunate for someone! No, it certainly isn't mine. As a matter of fact, I never really use a purse—absurd of me I am often told, but I never have done. Have you seen what is in it?"

Obviously not, since he had only just picked it up and had at once offered it for inspection, but at the suggestion the catch was pressed and the contents turned out for their mutual examination. They were strictly in keeping with the humdrum appearance of the purse itself—no pretty trifle but a substantial thing for everyday shopping—a ten-shilling note, as much in silver and bronze, the stub of a pencil, two safety pins and a newspaper cutting relating to an infallible cough cure.

"Dropped by one of my poorer parishioners doubtless," commented Mr Galton, as the collection was replaced by the finder; "but unluckily there is nothing to show which. You will, of course, leave it at the police station?"

"Well," was the reply, given with thoughtful deliberation, "if you don't mind I'd rather prefer to leave it with you, sir."

"Oh!" said the vicar, not unflattered, "but the usual thing—"

"Yes, so I imagine. But I have an idea that you would be more likely to hear whose it is than anyone else might. Then in these cases I believe that there is some sort of a deduction made if the police have the handling of it—not very much, I daresay, but to quite a poor woman even the matter of a shilling or two—eh?"

"True; true. No doubt it would be a consideration. Well, since you urge it, I will take charge of the find and notify it through the most likely channels. Then if we hear nothing of the loser within say a week I think I shall have to fall back on the local constabulary."

"Oh, quite so. But I hardly think that in a little place—I take it that this is only a village?"

"Tapsfield? A bare five hundred souls at the last census. Of course, the parish is another matter, but that is really a question of area. You are a stranger, I presume? And, by the way, you had better favour me with your address if you don't mind."

"I should be delighted," said the stranger with his charming smile—an accomplishment he did not make the mistake of overdoing—"but just at the moment I haven't got such a thing—not on this side of the world, I should say. My name is Dixson—Anthony Dixson—and I am over from Australia for a few weeks, a little on business but mostly as a holiday."

"Australia? Really; how very interesting. One of our young men—a member of the choir and our best hand-bell ringer, as a matter of fact—left for Australia only last month: Sydney, to be explicit."

"My place is Beverley in West Australia," volunteered the Colonial. "Quite the other side of the Continent, you know."

"Still, it is in the same country, is it not?" The vicar put this unimpeachable statement reasonably but with tolerant firmness. "However: the question of an address. It is only that after a certain time, if no one comes forward, it is customary to return anything to the finder."

"I don't think that need trouble anyone in this case, sir. I expect that there are several good works going on in the place that won't refuse a few shillings. If no one puts in a claim perhaps you wouldn't mind—?"

"Now that's really very kind and generous of you; very thoughtful indeed, Mr Dixson. Yes, we have a variety of useful organisations in the parish, and most of them, as you tactfully suggest, are not by any means self-supporting. There is the Social Centre Organisation, the Literary, Dramatic and Debating Society, a Blanket and Clothing Fund, Junior Athletic Club, the C.L.B. and the C.E.G.G., and half a dozen other excellent causes, to say nothing of a special effort we are making to provide the church heating apparatus with a new toiler. Still, an outsider can't be interested in our little local efforts, but it's heartening—distinctly heartening—quite apart from the amount and the—er—slightly speculative element of the contribution."

"Well, perhaps not altogether an outsider, in a way," suggested Dixson a little cryptically.

"Oh, really? You mean that you have some connection with Tapsfield? I did not gather—"

"Actually, that's what brought me here. My father was never out of Australia in his life, and this is the first time that I have been, but we always understood—I suppose it was passed down from generation to generation—that a good many years ago we had come from a place called Tapsfield somewhere in the south of England."

"This is the only place of the name that I know of," said the vicar. "Possibly the parochial records—"

"One little bit of evidence—if you can call it that—came to light when I went through my father's things after his death last year," continued Dixson. "Plainly it had been kept for its personal association, though it's only brass and can't be of any value. I mean, no one called Anthony Dixson would be likely to throw it away and by what I'm told one of us always has been called Anthony, and very few people nowadays spell the name D-i-x-s-o-n."

"A coin—really?" The vicar put on his reading glasses and took the insignificant object that Dixson had meanwhile extracted from a pouch of his serviceable leather belt. "I have myself—"

"I don't see that it can be a coin because that should have the king—Charles the Second wouldn't it be?—on it. In fact I don't understand why—"

"Oh, but this is quite all right," exclaimed Mr Galton with rising enthusiasm, as he carefully deciphered the inscription, "It is one of an extensive series called the seventeenth century tokens. I speak as a collector in a modest way, though I personally favour the regal issues—'Antho Dixson, Cordwainer, of Tapsfield in Susex,' and on the other side 'His half peny 1666,' with a device—probably the arms of the cordwainers' company."

"Yes," said the namesake of Antho Dixson of 1666 carelessly. "That's what it seems to read isn't it?"

"But this is most interesting; really most extraordinarily interesting," insisted the now thoroughly intrigued clergyman. "In the year when the Great Fire of London was raging and—yes—I suppose Milton would be writing 'Paradise Lost' then, your remote ancestor was issuing these halfpennies to provide the necessary shopping change here in Tapsfield. And now, more than two hundred and fifty years later, you turn up from Australia to visit the birthplace of your race. Do you know, I find that a really suggestive line of thought, Mr Dixson; most extraordinarily impressive."

"I can hardly expect to discover any Dixson here," commented Anthony, with a speculative note of inquiry, "and even if there were they would be too remote to have any actual relationship. But possibly there are some of the old houses standing—"

"There are no Dixsons now," replied Mr Galton with decision. "I know every family and can speak positively. Even in the more common form we have no one of that surname. As for old houses—well, Tapsfield is scarcely a show-place, one must admit. 'Model' perhaps, but not picturesque. The church is practically the only thing remaining of any note: if you can spare the time I should be delighted to take you over the building where your forebears worshipped. We are almost there now. Was there any particular train back that you were thinking of catching?"

"As a matter of fact," said Dixson readily, "I came intending to stay a few days and look around here. I've always had a hankering to see the place properly, and in any case I don't find that living in London suits me. So I shall hope to see over the church when it's most convenient to you."

"Oh, you intend staying? I didn't—I mean, not seeing any luggage, I inferred that you were just here for the afternoon. Of course—er—any time I shall be really delighted."

"I left my traps up at the station. I must find a room and then I can have them sent over. To tell you the truth, I couldn't stand London any longer. I have hardly slept a wink for the last two nights. Perhaps you could put me in the way of a place where they let apartments?"

It was a very natural request in the circumstances—nothing could have been more so—but for some reason the vicar did not reply at once, nor did his expression seem to indicate that he was considering the most suitable addresses. Actually, one might have guessed that he had become slightly embarrassed.

"Almost any sort of a place would suit me—just simple meals and a bedroom," prompted Dixson, without apparently noticing his acquaintance's difficulty. "On the whole I prefer a private house—even a workman's—to an inn, but that is only a harmless fancy."

"Awkwardly enough, a room is practically unobtainable either at a private house or even at one of the inns," at length admitted Mr Galton with slow reluctance. "It's an unusual state of things I know, but there are special circumstances and the people here have always been encouraged to refuse chance visitors. The consequence is that nobody sets out to let apartments."

"'Special circumstances?' Does that mean—"

"Evidently you have not heard of the Tapsfield paper mill, Mr Dixson. The particular circumstance is that all the paper used in the printing of Bank of England notes is made here in the village."

"You surprise me. I should have imagined that they would be printed in a strong room at the Bank itself or something of that sort. Surely—"

"Printed, yes," assented the vicar. "I believe they are. But the peculiar and characteristic paper is all made within a stone's throw of where we are. It is really our only local industry and practically all the people are either employed there or dependent on the business. Of course it is a very important and confidential—I might almost say dangerous—position, and although there is no actual rule, new-comers do not find it practicable to settle here and strangers are not accommodated."

"Newcomers and strangers, eh?" The visitor laughed with a slightly wry good humour.

"I know, I know," admitted the vicar ruefully. "It is *we* who are really the interlopers and newcomers compared with your status. But the difficulty is that owing to the established order of things it is out of these good people's power to make exceptions."

"But what am I to do about it?" protested Mr Dixson rather blankly. "You see how I am placed now? I can't go back to London for another wretched night, and it would be too late to get on to some other district... I never dreamt of not finding any sort of lodgings. Surely there must be someone with a room to spare, even if they don't make it a business. Then if you wouldn't mind putting in a word—"

"Now let me think; let me think," mused the good-natured pastor. "It would be really deplorable if you of all people should find yourself cold-shouldered out of Tapsfield. As you say, there may be someone—"

Since the moment when chance had brought them into conversation, the two men had been walking together towards the village of which the only evidence so far had been an ancient tower showing above a mass of trees, where a querulous congregation of rooks incessantly put resolutions and urged amendments. Now a final bend of the devious lane laid the main village street open before them, and so near that they were in it before Mr Galton's cogitation had reached any practical expression.

"There surely might be someone—" he repeated hopefully, for by this time, what with one slight influence and another, the excellent man felt himself almost morally bound to get Dixson out of his dilemma. "I have it!—At least, there's really quite a good chance there—Mrs Hocking."

"Splendid," acquiesced Dixson with an easy assumption that this was as good as settled. "Mrs Hocking by all means."

"She is an aunt of the youth I mentioned—the one who has gone to Sydney. He lived there, so that she ought to have a bedroom vacant. And I expect that she would like to hear about Australia, so that might make it easier."

"Quite providential," was Dixson's comment, and rather inconsequently he could not refrain from adding: "How lucky that I didn't come from Canada! I am sure that if you would kindly introduce me and put in a good word on the score of respectability, that—coupled with a willingness to pay in advance—would make it all right with Mrs Hocking."

"We can but see," agreed Mr Galton. "I will use my utmost powers of persuasion. She is really a most hospitable woman—I believe she provides the buns for the Guild Working Party tea regularly every other Wednesday."

"I happen to be very fond of buns," said Dixson gravely. "I am sure that we shall get on together famously."

"Oh, really? As a matter of fact, I never touch them—flatulence. However, her cottage is only just there over the way. Now, had we better—no, perhaps on the whole if you waited by the gate while I broached the matter—what do you think?"

"I am entirely in your hands," said Dixson diplomatically. "It's most tremendously good of you. Is there only a Mrs Hocking?"

"Oh, no. She has a husband and a daughter as well—an extremely worthy family—but as they work at the mill, like nearly everyone else here, she will probably be the only one at home just now."

"Perhaps I had better wait as you suggest then,"—really a *non sequitur*, thought the vicar—"and, if it's any inducement, I'm doing pretty well at home, you know, so that I shouldn't mind something above the ordinary in the circumstances."

The gesture that Mr Galton threw back as he turned into the formal little garden of a painfully modern cottage might have implied that it would be or it wouldn't—or indeed any other meaning. Dixson strolled on as far as an intersecting lane. It began with a couple of rows of hygienic cottages on the severe plan of Mrs Hocking's, but in the distance a high wall indicated premises of a different use, and from this direction came the regular but not too discordant beat of machinery at work. Less in keeping with the rural scene than this mild evidence of industry was the presence of a sentry-box before what was apparently the principal gate of the place. Plainly a strict guard was kept, but the picket himself was too far away or not sufficiently in view for the actual force he was drawn from to be determined. It was the first indication that Tapsfield held anything particular to safeguard and Dixson experienced a momentary flicker of excitement.

"So that's that," he summarised as he turned back without betraying any further symptom of interest. He had not long to wait for his new acquaintance's reappearance.

"Our efforts have been crowned with success," announced Mr Galton, beaming with satisfaction. "Mrs Hocking only stipulates for no late cooking."

"Famous," replied Dixson, a little more careless of his speech now that he had secured quarters. "I never tackle a heavy meal after sunset myself— insomnia."

"The question of terms I have left for your own arrangement. But I do not think that you will find Mrs Hocking too exacting."

"I'm sure. And you'll remember your promise? I'm dying to see the celebrated twelfth century canopied sedilia."

"You have heard of our unique Norman feature? Oh, really!" It would have been impossible to strike a better claim on the vicar's favour. "Really, Mr Dixson, I had no idea that you took an actual interest in ecclesiastical architecture."

"Well, naturally, I felt a deep regard for the church where my forefathers worshipped. Way out at home someone happened to be able to lend me a sort of guide to Sussex. I simply lapped it. Now I want to go over every nook and cranny in Tapsfield."

"So you shall; so you shall," promised the clergyman. "I will answer for it. We'll arrange about the church as soon as you are settled." He had turned to go, but before Dixson was through the gate he heard his name called with a rather confidential import. "And, by the way, while I think of it. We have a little informal entertainment in the school house once a week—a, er, 'penny reading' we call it."

"A sort of sing-song, I suppose?"

"Precisely; but not in any way—er—boisterous. Well, we find it increasingly difficult sometimes—not that everyone isn't most willing; quite the contrary, indeed, but what handicaps us with our limited material is to provide variety. Now I was wondering if you could be persuaded to give a little talk—it need only be quite short, of course—on 'Life and Adventure in the Land of the Wombat,' or naturally, any other title that commends itself to you. You—? Well, think it over, won't you?"

"That was a tolerably soft shell," reflected Dixson, as he discreetly avoided discovering any of the interested eyes that had been following the details of his arrival from behind stealthily arranged curtains. "Now for Mrs Hocking—and the husband and daughter who work at the paper mill."

2

JOOLBY DOES A LITTLE BUSINESS

Strangers who had occasion to visit Mr Joolby's curio and antique shop—and quite a number of very interesting people went there from time to time—often had some difficulty in finding it at first. For Mr Joolby, in complete antagonism to modern business methods, not only did not advertise but seemed to shun the more obvious forms of commercial advancement. His address had never appeared in that useful compilation, the Post Office London Directory, and as yet—surely a simple enough matter—Mr Joolby had not taken the trouble to have the omission righted. The street in which he had set up, while far from being a slum, was not one of the better-known and easily remembered thoroughfares of the East End, so that collectors who stumbled on his shop (and occasionally discovered some surprising things there) more often than not found themselves quite unable to describe its exact position to others afterwards, unless they had the forethought at the time to jot down the number 169 and the name Padgett Street before they passed on elsewhere. "A couple of turns out of Commercial Road, somewhere towards the other end," was as good as keeping a secret.

Nor would the inquirer's search be finished once he reached Padgett Street, for with the modesty that marked his activity in sundry other ways, Mr Joolby had neglected to have his name proclaimed about his place of business or else he had allowed it to fade from the public eye under the combined erosion of time and English weather. Of the place of business itself little could be gleaned from outside, for the arrangement of the shop window was more in accord with Oriental reticence than in line with modern ideas of display. Dust and obscurity were the prevailing impressions.

Inside was an astonishing medley of the curious and antique and in this branch of his activities the dictum of an impressed collector did not seem unduly wide of the mark: that Mr Joolby could supply anything on earth, if only he knew where to put his hands upon it. And if the arrangement of the large room one first entered suggested more the massed confusion of an extremely bizarre furniture depository than any other comparison, it had what, to its proprietor's way of thinking, was this supreme advantage: that from a variety of points of view it was possible to see without being seen, not only about the shop itself but even including the street and pavement.

At the moment that we have chosen for this intrusion—a time some weeks later than the arrival of "Anthony Dixson" in Tapsfield—the place at a casual glance had all the appearance of being empty, for the figure of Won Chou, Mr Joolby's picturesquely exotic shop assistant, both on account of absolute immobility and the protective obscuration of his drab garb, did not invite attention. But if unseen himself Won Chou was far from being unobservant and when a passer-by did not in fact pass by—when after an abstracted saunter up he threw an anxious glance along the street in both directions and then slipped into the doorway—a yellow hand slid out and in some distant part of the house the discreet tintinnabulation of a warning bell gave its understood message.

Inside the shop the visitor—no one could ever have mistaken him for a customer, unless, perhaps, qualified by "rum"—looked curiously about with the sharp and yet furtive reconnaissance of the habitual pilferer. But even so, he failed at the outset to discover the quiescent figure of Won Chou and he was experiencing a slight mental struggle between deciding whether it would be more profitable to wait until someone came or to pick up the most convenient object and bolt, when the impassive attendant settled the difficulty by detaching himself from the screening background and noiselessly coming forward. So quietly and unexpected indeed that Mr Chilly Fank, whose nerves had never been his strongest asset (the playful appellation "Chilly" had reference to his condition when any risk appeared), experienced a momentary shock which he endeavoured to cover by the usual expedient of a weakly aggressive swagger.

"'Ullo, Chink!" he exclaimed with an offensive heartiness, "blimey if I didn't take you for a ruddy waxwork. You didn't oughter scare a bloke like that, making out as you wasn't real. Boss in?"

"Yes no," replied Won Chou with extreme simplicity and a perfect assurance in the adequacy of his answer.

"Yes—no? Whacha mean?" demanded Mr Fank, to whom suspicion of affront was an instinct. "Which, you graven image?"

"All depend," explained Won Chou with unmoved composure. "You got come bottom side chop pidgin? You blong same pidgin?"

"Coo blimey! This isn't a bloomin' restrong, is it, funny? I want none of yer chop nor yer pigeon either. Is old Joolby abart? If yer can't speak decent English nod yer blinkin' 'ed, one wei or the other. Get me, you little Chinese puzzle?"

"My no sawy. Makee go look-see," decided Won, and he melted out of the shop by the door leading to the domestic quarters.

Left to himself Mr Chilly Fank nodded his head sagely several times to convey his virtuous disgust at this pitiable exhibition.

"Tchk! Tchk!" he murmured half aloud. "Exploitation of cheap Asiatic labour! No wonder we have a surplus industrial population and the nachural result that blokes like me—" but at this point the house door, opened again, Won Chou having returned with unforeseen expedition, so that Mr Fank had to turn away rather hastily from the locked show-case which he had been investigating with a critical touch arid affect an absorbing interest in something taking place in the street beyond until he suddenly became aware of the other's presence.

"Back again, What-ho? Well, you saffron jeopardy, don't stand like a blinkin' Eros. Wag yer ruddy tongue abart it."

"My been see," conceded Won Chou impartially. "Him belongy say: him you go come."

"My strikes! If this isn't the nattiest little vade-mecum that ever was!" apostrophes Mr Fank to the ceiling bitterly. "Look here, Confucius, forget yer chops an yer' pigeon and spit it aht straightforward. The boss—Joolby—is he in or not and did he say me go or him come? Blarst yer, which—er—savvy?"

At this, however, it being apparently rather a subtler idiom than the hearer's limited grasp of an alien vernacular could cope with, Won Chou merely relapsed into an attitude of studious melancholy, extremely trying to Mr Fank's conception of the yellow man's status. He was on the point of commenting on Won Chou's shortcomings with his customary delicacy of feeling when the sound of hobbling sticks approaching settled the point without any further trouble.

As Mr Joolby was—ethnologically at all events—white, a person of obvious means, and in various subterranean ways reputedly powerful, Mr Fank at once assumed what he considered to be a more suitable manner and it was with an ingratiating deference that he turned to meet the dealer.

"'Evening, governor," he remarked briskly, at the same time beginning to disclose the contents if an irregular newspaper parcel—fish and chips, it could have been safely assumed if he had been seen carrying it—that he had brought with him. "Remember me, of course, don't you?"

"Never seen you before," replied Mr Joolby, with an equally definite lack of cordiality. "What is it you want with me?"

To the ordinary business caller this reception might have been unpromising but Mr Fank was not in a position to be put off by it. He understood it indeed as part of the customary routine.

"Fank—'Chilly' Fank," he prompted. "Now you get me surely?"

"Never heard the name in my life," declared Joolby with no increase of friendliness.

"Oh, right you are, governor, if you say so," accepted Fank, but with the spitefulness of the stinging insect he could not refrain from adding: "I, don't suppose I should have been able to imagine *you* if I hadn't seen it. Doing anything in this way now?"

"This," freed of its unsavoury covering, was revealed as an uncommonly fine piece of Dresden china. It would have required no particular connoisseurship to recognise that so perfect and delicate a thing might be of almost any value. Joolby, who combined the inspired flair of the natural expert with sundry other anomalous qualities in his distorted composition, did not need to give more than one glance—although that look was professionally frigid.

"Where did it come from?" he asked merely.

"Been in our family for centuries, governor," replied Fank glibly, at the same time working in a foxy wink of mutual appreciation; "the elder branch of the Fanks, you understand, the Li-ces-ter-shire de Fankses. Oh, all right, sir, if you feel that way"—for Mr Joolby had abruptly dissolved this proposed partnership in humour by pushing the figure aside and putting a hand to his crutches—"it's from a house in Grosvenor Crescent."

"Tuesday night's job?"

"Yes," was the reluctant admission.

"No good to me," said the dealer with sharp decision.

"It's the real thing, governor," pleaded Mr Fank with fawning persuasiveness, "or I wouldn't ask you to make an offer. The late owner thought very highly of it. Had a cabinet all to itself in the drorin'-room there—so I'm told, for of course I had nothing to do with the job personally. Now—"

"You needn't tell me whether it's the real thing or not," said Mr Joolby. "That's my look out."

"Well then, why not back yer knowledge, sir? It's bound to pay yer in the end. Say a...well, what, about a couple of... It's with you, governor."

"It's no good, I tell you," reiterated Mr Joolby with seeming indifference. "It's mucher too valuable to be worth anything—unless it can be shown on the counter. Piece like this is known to every big dealer and every likely collector in the land. Offer it to any Tom, Dick, or Harry and in ten minutes I might have Scotland Yard nosing about my place like ferrets."

"And that would never do, would it, Mr Joolby?" leered Fank pointedly. "Gawd knows what they wouldn't find here."

"They would find nothing's wrong because I don't buy stuff like this that the first numskull brings me. What do you expect me to do with it, fellow? I can't melt it, or reset it, or cut it up, can I? You might as well bring me the Albert Memorial... Here, take the thing away and drop it in the river."

"Oh blimey, governor, it isn't as bad as all that. What abart America? You did pretty well with those cameos wot come out of that Park Lane flat, I hear."

"Eh, what's that? You say, rascal—"

"No offence, governor. All I means is you can keep it for a twelve month and then get it quietly off to someone at a distance. Plenty of quite respectable collectors out there will be willing to buy it after it's been pinched for a year."

"Well—you can leave it and I'll see," conceded Mr Joolby, to whom Fank's random shot had evidently suggested a possible opening. "At your own risk, mind you. I may be able to sell it for a trifle some day or I may have all my troubles for nothing." But just as Chilly Fank was regarding this as satisfactorily settled and wondering how he could best beat up to the next move, the unaccountable dealer seemed to think better—or worse—of it for he pushed the figure from him with every appearance of a final decision. "No; I tell you it isn't worth it. Here, wrap it up again and don't waste my time. I'd mucher rather not."

"That'll be all right, governor," hastily got in Fank, though similar experiences in the past prompted him not to be entirely impressed by a receiver's methods. "I'll leave it with you anyhow; I know you'll do the straight thing when it's planted. And, could you—you don't mind a bit on account to go on with, do you? I'm not exactly what you'd call up and in just at the moment."

"A bit on account, hear him. Come, I like that when I'm having all the troubles and may be out of my pocket in the end. Be off with you, greedy fellow."

"Oh rot yer!" exclaimed Fank, with a sudden flare of passion that at least carried with it the dignity of a genuine emotion; "I've had just abart enough of you and your blinkin' game, Toady Joolby. Here, I'd sooner smash the bloody thing, straight, than be such a ruddy mug as to swallow any of your blahsted promises," and there being no doubt that Mr Fank for once in a way meant approximately what he said, Joolby had no alternative, since he had every intention of keeping the piece, but to retire as gracefully as possible from his inflexible position.

"Well, well; we need not lose our tempers, Mr Fank; that isn't business," he said smoothly and without betraying a shadow of resentment. "If you are really stoney up—I'm not always very quick at catching the literal meaning of your picturesque expressions—I don't mind risking—shall we say?—one half a—or no, you shall have a whole Bradbury."

"Now you're talking English, sir," declared the mollified Fank (perhaps a little optimistically), "but couldn't you make it a couple? Yer see—well"—as Mr Joolby's expression gave little indication of rising to this suggestion—"one and a thin 'un anyway."

"Twenty-five bobs," conceded Joolby. "Take me or leave it," and since there was nothing else to be done, this being in fact quite up to his meagre expectation, Chilly held out his hand and took it, only revenging himself by the impudent satisfaction of ostentatiously holding up the note to the light when it was safely in his possession.

"You need not do that, my young fellow," remarked Mr Joolby, observing the action. "I know a dud note when I see it."

"Oh I don't doubt that you know one all right, Mr Joolby," replied Fank with gutter insolence. "It's this bloke I'm thinking of. You've had a lot more experience than me in that way, you see, so I've got to be blinkin' careful," and as he turned to go a whole series of portentous nods underlined a mysterious suggestion.

"What do you mean, you rascal?" For the first time a possible note of misgiving tinged Mr Joolby's bloated assurance. "Not that it matters—there's nothing about me to talk of—but have you been—been hearing anything?"

It was Mr Fank's turn to be cocky: if he couldn't wangle that extra fifteen bob out of The Toad he could evidently give him the shivers.

"Hearing, sir?" he replied from the door, with an air of exaggerated guilelessness. "Oh no, Mr Joolby: Whatever should I be hearing? Except that in the City you're very well spoken of to be the next Lord Mayor!" and to leave no doubt that this pleasantry should be fully understood he took care that his parting aside reached Joolby's ear: "*I don't* think!"

"Fank. Chilly Fank," mused Mr Joolby as he returned to his private lair, carrying the newly acquired purchase with him and progressing even more grotesquely than his wont since he could only use one stick for assistance. "The last time he came he had an amusing remark to make, something about keeping an aquarium..."

Won Chou was still at his observation post when the door opened again an hour later. Again he sped his message—a different intimation from the last, but conveying a sign of doubt for this time the watcher could not immediately "place" the visitors. These were two, both men—"a belong number one and a belong number two chop men," sagely decided Won Chou—but there was something about the more important of the two that for the limited time at his disposal baffled the Chinaman's deduction. It was not until they were in the shop and he was attending to them that Won Chou astutely suspected this man perchance to be blind—and sought for a positive indication. Yet he was the one who seemed to take the lead rather than wait to be led and except on an occasional trivial point his movements were entirely free from indecision. Certainly he had paused at the step but that was only the natural hesitation of a stranger to the parts and it was apparently the other who supplied the confirmation.

"This is the right place by the description, sir," the second man said.

"It is the right place by the smell," was the reply, as soon as the door was opened. "Twenty centuries and a hundred nationalities mingle here, Parkinson. And not the least foreign—"

"A native of some description, sir," tolerantly supplied the literal Parkinson, taking this to apply to the attendant as he came forward.

"Can do what?" politely inquired Won Chou, bowing rather more profoundly than the average shopman would, even to a customer in whom he can recognise potential importance.

"No can do," replied the chief visitor, readily accepting the medium. "Bring number one man come this side."

"How fashion you say what want?" suggested Won Chou hopefully.

"That belong one piece curio house man."

"He much plenty busy this now," persisted Won Chou, faithfully carrying out his instructions. "My makee show carpet, makee show cabinet, chiney, ivoly, picture—makee show one ting, two ting, any ting."

"Not do," was the decided reply. "Go make look-see one time."

"All same," protested Won Chou, though he began to obey the stronger determination, "can do heap wella. Not is?"

A good natured but decided shake of the head was the only answer, and looking extremely sad and slightly hurt Won Chou melted through the doorway—presumably to report beyond that: "Much heap number one man make plenty bother."

"Look round, Parkinson," said his master guardedly. "Do you see anything here in particular?"

"No, sir; nothing that I should designate noteworthy. The characteristic of the emporium is an air of remarkable untidiness."

"Yet there *is* something unusual," insisted the other, lifting his sightless face to the four quarters of the shop in turn as though he would read their secret. "Something unaccountable, something *wrong*."

"I have always understood that the East End of London was not conspicuously law-abiding," assented Parkinson impartially. "There is nothing of a dangerous nature impending, I hope, sir?"

"Not to us, Parkinson; not as yet. But all around there's something—I can feel it—something *evil*."

"Yes, sir—these prices are that." It was impossible to suspect the correct Parkinson of ever intentionally "being funny" but there were times when he came perilously near incurring the suspicion. "This small extremely second-hand carpet—five guineas."

"Everywhere among this junk of centuries there must be things that have played their part in a hundred bloody crimes—can they escape the stigma?" soliloquised the blind man, beginning to wander about the bestrewn shop with a self-confidence that would have shaken Won Chou's conclusions if he had been looking on—especially as Parkinson, knowing by long experience the exact function of his office, made no attempt to guide his master. "Here is a sword that may have shared in the tragedy of Glencoe, this horn lantern lured some helpless ship to destruction on the Cornish coast, the very cloak perhaps that disguised Wilkes Booth when he crept up to shoot Abraham Lincoln at the play."

"It's very unpleasant to contemplate, sir," agreed Parkinson discreetly.

"But there is something more than that. There's an influence—a force—permeating here that's colder and deeper and deadlier than revenge or greed or decent commonplace hatred...It's inhuman—unnatural—diabolical. And it's coming nearer, it begins to fill the air—" He broke off almost with a physical shudder and in the silence there came from the passage beyond the irregular thuds of Joolby's sticks approaching. "It's poison," he muttered; "venom."

"Had we better go before anyone comes, sir?" suggested Parkinson, decorously alarmed. "As yet the shop is empty."

"No!" was the reply, as though forced out with an effort. "No—face it!" He turned as he spoke towards the opening door and on the word the uncouth figure, laboriously negotiating the awkward corners, entered. "Ah, at last!"

"Well, you see, sir," explained Mr Joolby, now the respectful if somewhat unconventional shopman in the presence of a likely customer, "I move slowly so you must excuse being kept waiting. And my boy here—well-meaning fellow but so economical even of words that each one has to do for half a dozen different things—quite different things sometimes."

"Man come. Say 'Can do;' say 'No can do.' All same; go tell; come see," protested Won Chou, retiring to some obscure but doubtless ingeniously arranged point of observation, and evidently cherishing a slight sense of unappreciation.

"Exactly. Perfectly explicit." Mr Joolby included his visitors in his crooked grin of indulgent amusement. "Now those poisoned weapons you wrote about. I've looked them up and I have a wonderful collection and, what is very unusual, all in their original condition. This," continued Mr Joolby, busying himself vigorously among a pile of arrows with padded barbs, "is a very fine example from Guiana—it guarantees death with convulsions and foaming at the mouth within thirty seconds. They're getting very rare now because since the natives have become civilized by the missionaries they've given up their old simple ways of life—they will have our second-hand rifles because they kill much further."

"Highly interesting," agreed the customer, "but in my case—"

"Or this beautiful little thing from the Upper Congo. It doesn't kill outright, but, the slightest scratch—just the merest pin prick—and you turn a bright pea green and gradually swell larger and larger until you finally blow up in a very shocking manner. The slightest scratch—so," and in his enthusiasm Mr Joolby slid the arrow quickly through his hand towards Parkinson whose face had only too plainly reflected a fascinated horror from the moment of their host's appearance. "Then the tapioca-poison group from Bolivia—"

"Save yourself the trouble," interrupted the blind man, who had correctly interpreted his attendant's startled movement. "I'm not concerned with—the primitive forms of murder."

"Not—" Joolby pulled up short on the brink of another panegyric, "not with poisoned arrows? But aren't you the Mr Brooks who was to call this afternoon to see what I had in the way of—"

"Some mistake evidently. My name is Carrados and I have made no appointment. Antique coins are my hobby—Greek in particular. I was told that you might probably have something in that way."

"Coins; Greek coins." Mr Joolby was still a little put out by the mischance of his hasty assumption. "I might have; I might have. But coins of that class are rather expensive."

"So much the better."

"Eh?" Customers in Padgett Street did not generally, one might infer, express approval on the score of dearness.

"The more expensive they are, the finer and rarer they will be—naturally. I can generally be satisfied with the best of anything."

"So—so?" vaguely assented the dealer, opening drawer after drawer in the various desks and cabinets around and rooting about with elaborate slowness. "And you know all about Greek coins then?"

"I hope not," was the smiling admission.

"Hope not? Eh? Why?"

"Because there would be nothing more to learn then. I should have to stop collecting. But doubtless you do?"

"If I said I did—well, my mother was a Greek so that it should come natural. And my father was a—um, no; there was always a doubt about that man. But one grandfather was a Levantine Jew and the other an Italian cardinal. And one grandmamma was an American negress and the other a Polish revolutionary."

"That should ensure a tolerably versatile stock, Mr Joolby."

"And further back there was an authentic satyr came into the family tree—so I'm told," continued Mr Joolby, addressing himself to his prospective customer but turning to favour the scandalised Parkinson with an implicatory leer. "You find that amusing, Mr Carrados, I'm sure?"

"Not half so amusing as the satyr found it I expect," was the retort. "But come now—" for Mr Joolby had meanwhile discovered what he had sought and was looking over the contents of a box with provoking deliberation.

"To be sure—you came for Greek coins, not for Greek family history, eh? Well, here is something very special indeed—a tetradrachm struck at Amphipolis, in Macedonia, by some Greek ruler of the province but I can't say who. Perhaps Mr Carrados can enlighten me?"

Without committing himself to this the blind man received the coin on his outstretched hand and with subtile fingers delicately touched off the bold relief that still retained its superlative grace of detail. Next he weighed it carefully in a cupped palm, and then after breathing several times on the metal placed it against his lips. Meanwhile Parkinson looked on with the respect that he would have accorded to any high-class entertainment; Joolby merely sceptically indifferent.

"Yes," announced Carrados at the end of this performance, "I think I can do that. At all events I know the man who made it."

"Come, come, use your eyes, my good sir," scoffed Mr Joolby with a contemptuous chuckle. "I thought you understood at least something about coins. This isn't—I don't know what you think—a Sunday school medal or a stores ticket. It's a very rare and valuable specimen and it's at least two thousand years old. And you 'know the man who made it!'"

"I can't use my eyes because my eyes are useless: I am blind," replied Carrados with unruffled evenness of temper. "But I can use my hands, my finger tips, my tongue, lips, my commonplace nose, and they don't lead me astray as your credulous, self-opinionated eyes seem to have done—if you really take this thing for a genuine antique," and with uncanny proficiency he tossed the coin back into the box before him.

"You can't see—you say that you are blind—and yet you tell me, an expert, that it's a forgery!"

"It certainly is a forgery, but an exceptionally good one at that—so good that no one but Pietro Stelli, who lives in Padua, could in these degenerate days have made it. Pietro makes such beautiful forgeries that in my less experienced years they have taken even me in. Of course I couldn't have that so I went to Padua to find out how he worked, and Peter, who is, according to his lights, as simple and honest a soul as ever breathed, willingly let me watch him at it."

"And how," demanded Mr Joolby, seeming almost to puff out aggression towards this imperturbable braggart; "how could you see him what you call 'at it,' if, as you say, you are blind? You are just a little too clever, Mr Carrados."

"How could I see? Exactly as I can see"—stretching out his hand and manipulating the extraordinarily perceptive fingers meaningly—"any of the ingenious fakes which sharp people offer the blind man; exactly as I could see any of the thousand and one things that you have about your shop. This"—handling it as he seemed to look tranquilly at Mr Joolby—"this imitation Persian prayer-rug with its lattice-work design and pomegranate scroll, for instance; exactly as I could, if it were necessary, see *you*," and he took a step forward as though to carry out the word, if Mr Joolby hadn't hastily fallen back at the prospect.

The prayer-rug was no news to Mr Joolby—although it was ticketed five guineas—but he had had complete faith in the tetradrachm notwithstanding that he had bought it at the price of silver; and despite the fact that he would still continue to describe it as a matchless gem it was annoying to have it so unequivocally doubted. He picked up the box without offering any more of its contents, and hobbling back to the desk with it slammed the drawer home in swelling mortification.

"Well, if that is your way of judging a valuable antique, Mr Carrados, I don't think that we shall do any business. I have nothing more to show, thank you."

"It is my way of judging everything—men included—Mr Joolby, and it never, never fails," replied Carrados, not in the least put out by the dealer's brusqueness. It was a frequent grievance with certain of this rich and influential man's friends that he never appeared to resent a rudeness. "And why should I," the blind man would cheerfully reply, "when I have the excellent excuse that I do not *see* it?"

"Of course I don't mean by touch alone," he continued, apparently unconscious of the fact that Mr Joolby's indignant back was now pointedly towards him. "Taste, when it's properly treated, becomes strangely communicative; smell"—there could be no doubt of the significance of this allusion from the direction of the speaker's nose—"the chief trouble is that at times smell becomes too communicative. And hearing—I daren't even tell you what a super-trained ear sometimes learns of the goings-on behind the scenes—but a blind man seldom misses a whisper and he never forgets a voice."

Apparently Mr Joolby was not interested in the subtleties of perception for he still remained markedly aloof, and yet, had he but known it, an exacting test of the boast so confidently made was even then in process, and one moreover surprisingly mixed up with his own plans. For at that moment, as the visitor turned to go, the inner door was opened a cautious couple of inches and:

"Look here, J.J.," said the unseen in a certainly distinctive voice, "I hope you know that I'm waiting to go. If you're likely to be another week—"

"Don't neglect your friend on our account, Mr Joolby," remarked Carrados very pleasantly—for Won Chou had at once slipped to the unlatched door as if to head off the intruder. "I quite agree. I don't think that we are likely to do any business either. Good day."

"*Dog dung!*" softly spat out Mr Joolby as the shop door closed on their departing footsteps.

3

MR BRONSKY HAS MISGIVINGS

As Mr Carrados and Parkinson left the shop they startled a little group of street children who after the habit of their kind were whispering together, giggling, pushing one another about, screaming mysterious taunts, comparing sores and amusing themselves in the unaccountable but perfectly satisfactory manner of street childhood. Reassured by the harmless appearance of the two intruders the impulse of panic at once passed and a couple of the most precocious little girls went even so far as to smile up at the strangers. More remarkable still, although Parkinson felt constrained by his imperviable dignity to look away, Mr Carrados unerringly returned the innocent greeting.

This incident entailed a break in which the appearance of the visitors, their position in life, place of residence, object in coming and the probable amount of money possessed by each were frankly canvassed, but when that source of entertainment failed the band fell back on what had been their stock game at the moment of interruption. This apparently consisted in daring one another to do various things and in backing out of the contest when the challenge was reciprocated. At last, however, one small maiden, spurred to desperation by repeated "dares," after imploring the others to watch her do it, crept up the step of Mr Joolby's shop, cautiously pushed open the door and standing well inside (the essence of the test as laid down), chanted in the peculiarly irritating sing-song of her tribe:

"Toady, toady Jewlicks;
Crawls about on two sticks.
Toady, toady—"

"Makee go away," called out Won Chou from his post, and this not being at once effective he advanced towards the door with a mildly threatening gesture. "Makee go much quickly, littee cow-child. Shall do if not gone is."

The young imp had been prepared for immediate flight the instant anyone appeared, but for some reason Won Chou's not very aggressive behest must have conveyed a peculiarly galling insult for its effect was to transform the wary gamin into a bristling little spitfire, who hurled back the accumulated scandal of the quarter.

"'Ere, don't you call me a cow-child, you 'eathen swine," she shrilled, standing her ground pugnaciously. "Pig-tail!" And as Won Chou, conscious of his disadvantage in such an encounter, advanced: "Oo made the puppy pie? Oo et Jimmy 'Iggs's white mice? Oo lives on black beetles? Oo pinched the yaller duck and—" but at this intriguing point, being suddenly precipitated further into the shop by a mischievous child behind, and honour being fully satisfied by now, she dodged out again and rejoined the fleeing band which was retiring down the street to a noisy accompaniment of feigned alarm, squiggles of meaningless laughter, and the diminishing chant of:

"Toady, toady Jewlicks;
Goes abaht on two sticks.
Toady, toady—"

Sadly conscious of the inadequacy of his control in a land where for so slight a matter as a clouted child an indignant mother would as soon pull his pig-tail out as look, Won Chou continued his progress in order to close the door. There, however, he came face to face with a stout, consequential gentleman whose presence, opulent complexion, ample beard and slightly alien cut of clothes would have suggested a foreign source even without the ruffled: "Tevils! Tevils! Little tevils!" drawn from the portly visitor as the result of his somewhat undignified collision with the flying rabble.

"Plenty childrens," remarked Won Chou, agreeably conversational. "Makee go much quickly now is."

"Little tevils," repeated the annoyed visitor, still dusting various sections of his resplendent attire to remove the last traces of infantile contamination. "Comrade Joolby is at home? He would expect me."

"Make come in," invited Won Chou. "Him belong say plaps you is blimby."

"The little tevils need control They shall have when—" grumbled the new-comer, brought back to his grievance by the discovery of a glutinous patch marring an immaculate waistcoat. "However, that is not your fault, Won Chou," and being now within the shop and away from possibly derisive comment, he kissed the attendant sketchily on each cheek. "Peace, little oppressed brother!"

Not apparently inordinately gratified by this act of condescension, Won Chou crossed the shop and pushing open the inner door announced the new arrival to anyone beyond in his usual characteristic lingo:

"Comlade Blonsky come this side."

"Shall I to him go through?" inquired Mr Bronsky, bustling with activity, but having already correctly interpreted the sounds from that direction Won Chou indicated the position by the sufficient remark: "Him will. You is," and withdrew into a further period of introspection.

In the sacred cause of universal brotherhood comrade Bronsky knew no boundaries and he hastened forward to meet Mr Joolby with the same fraternal greeting already bestowed on Won Chou, forgetting for the moment what sort of man he was about to encounter. The reminder was sharp and revolting: his outstretched arms dropped to his sides and he turned, affecting to be taken with some object in the shop until he could recompose his agitated faculties. Joolby's slitlike mouth lengthened into the ghost of an enigmatical grin as he recognised the awkwardness of the comrade's position.

Bronsky, for his part, felt that he must say something exceptional to pass off the unfortunate situation and he fell back on a highly coloured account of the derangement he had just suffered through being charged and buffeted by a mob of "little tevils"—an encounter so upsetting that even yet he scarcely knew which way up he was standing. Any irregularity of his salutation having thus been neatly accounted for he shook Joolby's two hands with accumulated warmness and expressed an inordinate pleasure in the meeting.

"But I am forgetting, comrade," he broke off from these amiable courtesies when the indiscretion might be deemed sufficiently expiated; "those sticky little bastads drove everything from my mind until I just remember. I met two men further off and from what I could see at the distance they seemed to have come out from here?"

"There were a couple of men here a few minutes ago," agreed Mr Joolby. "What about it, comrade?"

"I appear to recognise the look of one, but for life of me I cannot get him. Do you know them, comrade Joolby?"

"Not from Mahomet. Said his name was Carrados—his nibs. The other was a flunkey."

"Max Carrados!" exclaimed Mr Bronsky with startled enlightenment. "What in name of tevil was he doing here in your shop, Joolby?"

"Wasting his time," was the indifferent reply. "My time also."

"Do you not believe it," retorted Bronsky emphatically. "He never waste his time, that man. Julian Joolby, do you not realise who has been here with you?"

"Never heard of him in my life before. Never want to again either."

"Well, it is time for yourself that you should be put wiser. It was Max Carrados who fixed the rope round Serge Laskie's neck. And stopped the Rimsky explosion when everything was going so well; and, oh, did a lot more harm. I tell you he is no good, comrade. He is a bad man."

"Anyhow, he can't interfere with us in this business, whatever he's done in the past," replied Joolby, who might be pardoned after his recent experience for feeling that there would be more agreeable subjects of conversation. "He's blind now."

"'Blind now'—hear him!" appealed Bronsky with a derisive cackle. "Tell me this however notwithstanding: did you make anything out of him, eh, Joolby?"

"No," admitted Joolby, determinedly impervious to Bronsky's agitation; "we did no business as it happens. He knew more than a customer has any right to know. In fact"—with an uneasy recollection of the Greek coin—"he may have known more than I did."

"That is always the way. Blind: and he knows more than we who not are. Blind: and he stretch out his cunning wicked fingers and they tell him all that our clever eyes have missed to see."

"So he said, Bronsky. Indeed, to hear him talk—"

"Yes, but wait to hear," entreated the comrade, anxious not to be deprived of his narration. "He sniffs—at a bit of paper, let us haphazard, and lo behold, where it has been, who has touched it, what pocket it has laid in—all are disclose to him. He listen to a breath of wind that no one else would hear and it tell him that—that, well, perhaps that two men are ready round the corner for him with a sand-bag."

"Oh-ho!" said Joolby, sardonically amused; "so you've tried it, have you?"

"Tried! You use the right word, comrade Joolby. Listen how. At Cairo he was given some sandwiches to ate on a journey. He did ate three and the fourth he had between his teeth when he change his mind and throw it to a pi-dog. That dog died very hastily."

"Anyone may recognise a taste or smell. Your people mixed the wrong sort of mustard."

"Anyone may recognise a taste or smell but yet plenty of people die of poison. Listen more. One night at Marseilles he was walking along a street when absolutely without any warning he turn and hit a poor man who happened to be following him on the head—hit him so hard that our friend had to drop the knife he was holding and to take to heels. And yet he was wearing rubber shoes. It is not right. Julian Joolby; it is not fair when a blind man can do like that. The good comrade who warned me of him say: He can smell a thought and hear a look. And that is not all. I have heard that he has the sixth sense too—"

"Let him have; I tell you, Bronsky, he is nothing to us. He only chanced along here. He wanted Greek coins."

"Greek coins!" This was reassuring for it agreed with something further about Max Carrados that Bronsky remembered hearing. "That may be very true after all as it is well known that he is crazy about collecting—thinks nothing of paying five hundred roubles for a single drachma... Yes, Julian Joolby, if it should become necessary it might be that a hook baited with a rare coin—"

"Don't worry. Next week we shall have moved to our new quarters and nothing going on here will matter then."

"Ah; that is arrange? I was getting anxious. Our friends in Moscow are becoming more and more impatient as time goes on. The man who pays the piper calls for a tune, as these fool English say it, and the Committee are insist that as they have allow so much for expenses already they must now see results. I am here with authority to investigate about that, comrade Joolby."

"They shall see results all right," promised Joolby, swelling darkly at the suggestion of interference. "And since you fancy English proverbs, comrade, it is well to remember that Rome was not built in a day, one cannot make bricks without clay, and it is not wise to spoil the ship for the sake of a kopecks worth of caulking."

"That is never fear," said Bronsky with a graciously reassuring wave of his hand; "nobody mistrusts you of yourself, comrade, and it is only as good friend that I tell you for information what is being thought at headquarters. This is going to be big thing, Joolby."

"I don't doubt it," agreed the other, regarding his visitor's comfortable self-satisfaction with his twisted look of private appreciation. "I shall do my best in that way, comrade."

"Extraordinary care is being take to make sure for wide and quick distribution in China, Japan and India and everywhere agents signify good prospects. The Committee are confident that this move, successfully engined, will destroy British commercial prestige in the East for at least a generation—and by the end of that time there will not be any British in the East. Meanwhile there must be no weak link in the chain. Now, Julian Joolby, what can I report to the Commissar?"

"You will know that within the next few hours. I've called them for eleven. Larch is working on the plates at a safe place now and as soon as dusk we will fill in the time by going to see what he has done and approve or not according to what you think of them."

"Good. That sounds as business. But why should we go there? Surely it is more fitly that a workman would come and wait on our convenience at your place of living?"

"It isn't a matter of fitness—it's a matter of ordinary prudence. Have I ever been what is call 'in trouble,' Bronsky?"

"Not as far as to my knowledge," admitted the comrade. "I have always understand that you keep you hand clean however."

"So. And I have done that by sticking to one rule: never to have anything in my place that isn't capable of a reasonable explanation. Most things can be explained away but not the copper plate of a bank note found underneath your flooring. That is Larch's look-out."

"You are right. It would never do—especially when I is here. We cannot be too much careful. Now this Larch—was he not in it once before when things did not go rightly?"

Joolby nodded and the visitor noticed that his bulging throat sagged unpleasantly.

"That's the chap. There was a split and Larch didn't get his fingers out quickly enough. Three years he was sentence and he came out less than six weeks ago."

"He is safe though? He has no bad feeling?"

"Why should he have?" demanded Joolby, looking at Mr Bronsky with challenging directness. "I had nothing to do with him being put away. It was just a matter of luck that while Larch had the stuff when he was nabbed nothing could have been found on me if they had looked for ever—luck or good management."

"Good management if you say to me," propounded Bronsky wisely. "Notwithstanding."

"The one who has the plates is bound to get it in the ear if it comes to trouble. Larch knows that all right when he goes in it."

"But you are able to persuade him to risk it again? Well, that is real cleverness, Joolby."

"Oh yes; I was able as you say it, to persuade him. George is the best copper-plate engraver of his line in England; he came out with a splendid character from the prison Governor—and not an earthly chance of getting a better job than rag-picking. I've had harder propositions than persuading him in the circumstances, if it comes to that, Bronsky."

"It is to your good notwithstanding," declared Mr Bronsky urbanely. "The Committee of course officially know nothing of details and are in position to deny whatever is say or done but they is not unmindful of zeal, as you may rely in it, comrade. That is the occasion of my report. Now as regards this business of eleven?"

"You will meet them all then and hear what is being done in other directions. Nickle will be here by that time and we shall be able to decide about Tapsfield."

"Tapsfield? That is a new one surely? I have not heard—"

"Place where the mills are that make all the official Bank paper," explained Joolby. "Naturally the paper is our chief trouble—always has been: always will be. Larch can make perfect plates, but with what we're aiming at this time nothing but the actual paper the Bank of England itself uses will pass muster. Well, there's plenty of it down at Tapsfield and we're going to lift it somehow."

"I quite agree that we must have the right paper however. But this person Nickle—he is not unknown to some of us—is he quite—?"

"In what way?"

"Well, there is a feeling that he appear to think more of what he can get out of our holy crusade than of the ultimate benefit of mankind. He has not got the true international spirit, Julian Joolby. I suspect that he has taint of what he would doubtless call 'patriotism'—which mean that he has yet to learn that any other country is preferable to his own. To be short, I have found this young man vulgar and it is not beyond that he may also prove restive."

"Leave that to me," said Joolby with a note of authority, and his unshapely form gave the impression of increasing in bulk as if to meet the prospect of aggression. "This is London, not Moscow, Bronsky; I'm in charge here and I have to pick my people and adapt my methods. Nickle will fall into line all right and serve us just so far as suits our purpose. So long as he is doing that he can sing 'Rule Britannia' in his spare time for all it matters."

"But in the cause—"

"In the meantime we can not be too particular about the exact shape of the tool we use to open closed doors with," continued Joolby, smothering the interruption with masterful insistence. "We are going to flood China, India, and the East with absolutely perfect Bank of England paper so that in the end it will be sheerly impossible for English trade to go on there, and so pave the way for Soviet rule. But it is not necessary to shout that sacred message into every ear, even if for the time they work hand in hand with us. Let them think that they are out to make easy money. Few men work any the worse for the expectation that they are in the way to get fortunes. Does that not satisfy you, comrade Bronsky?"

"So long as it goes forward," admitted Mr Bronsky with slightly ungracious acceptance, for he could not blink the suspicion that while he himself was an extremely important figure, this subordinate monstrosity would do precisely as he intended.

"It is going forward—as you shall convince yourself completely. In the meanwhiles—you have not, I hope, made dinner?"

"Well, no," admitted the visitor, with a flutter of misgiving at the prospect, "but—"

"That is well—you need have no qualms; I can produce something better than kahetia or vodka, and as to food—Won Chou there is equal to anything you would find at your own place or in Soho. Won Chou—number one topside feed, me him, plenty quick. Not is? Is?"

"Can do. Is," replied Won Chou with impassive precision.

"There you see," amplified Joolby, with the pride of a conjurer bringing off a successful trick, "he can do it all right—take no longer in the end than if you went out somewhere. And," he added, with an inward appreciation of the effect that he knew the boast would have on his guest's composure, "all that he will use for a six course spread may be a gas-ring and two or perhaps three old biscuit tins."

4

CORA LARCH IS OFFERED A GOOD SITUATION

It was a continual matter of pained surprise to George Larch whenever he came to think about it—and owing to the nature of his work and its occasional regrettable developments he had plenty of time for meditation—that he should have become a criminal. It was so entirely different from what he had ever intended when he set out in life. All his instincts were law-abiding and moral and the goal of his ambition from the day when he put by his first saved shilling had been a country cottage (as he conceived it), some fancy poultry and a nice square garden. Not a damp, broken-down, honeysuckle-clad, spider-infested, thatched old hovel of the sort that artists loved to depict, but a really sound, trim little new red-brick villa, standing well up and preferably in the immediate suburbs of Brighton or Worthing.

As a baby, a child, a boy, he had given his mother no trouble whatever, and at school he had always earned unexceptional reports, with particular distinction in his two favourite subjects—Handwriting and Scripture History. Indeed, on the occasion of his last Breaking Up the schoolmaster had gone out of his way to contrive a test and as a result had been able to demonstrate to the assembled boys that, set a line of copper-plate, it was literally impossible to decide which was George's work and which the copy. As it happened, "Honesty is the Best Policy. £ s. d." (the tag merely to fill up the line), had been the felicitous text of this experiment.

Very often in these periods of voluntary or enforced inaction George cast his thoughts back in a distressed endeavour to put his finger on the precise point at which he could be said to have deviated from the strict path of virtue. Possibly it might be fixed at that day in 1898 when a casual but very emphatic acquaintance gave him in strict confidence the name of an unsuspected dead cert for the approaching Derby. Not without grave doubts, for it was quite contrary to his upbringing, but tempted by the odds, young Larch diffidently inquired how one made a bet and ultimately decided to risk half-a-crown on the chances of Jeddah. Still all might have been well but unfortunately the horse did win and—the bookmaker being not only honest but positively delighted—George found himself at a stroke twelve pounds ten (more than the result of a month's conscientious work) the richer.

Then there was Cora. That had been a wonderful thing, so unexpected, so incredible, so tumultuously sweet, and even now, at forty-three, with all that had flowed from it, he would not have a jot of that line of destiny altered if it would have involved losing that memory. Cora was as true as steel and had stuck to—and up for—him through thick and thin, but it was quite possible that her youthful gaiety, her love of pretty, costly things, and the easier views on life and conduct in which she (naive child) had been brought up might have imperceptibly shaped the issue. It was simply impossible for him not to follow in her rather hectic round and as for refusing her anything—why, the greatest pleasure he could win had been to anticipate whatever she had set her innocent heart on. It goes without saying that no more shillings were being saved; instead there were frequent occasions when pounds had to be—on whatever terms—somehow borrowed. Meanwhile there had been other dead certs: one in particular so extremely dead that coming at a critical hour George had been hypnotised into the belief that it would be the merest form to make use of a comparatively trifling sum when it could inevitably be replaced before the accounts were looked into the following morning... So here he was, sitting in the back upper room of an ostensible rag-and-bone shop, fabricating with unmatchable skill the "mother plate" of a Bank of England "tenner" and at this particular moment preparing to unlock the door in response to old Ikey's rapped-out signal that "safe" visitors were below to see him.

* * * * *

Mr Joolby had spoken of visiting Larch "at dusk," possibly on general precautionary grounds, but it did not escape the notice of those who knew him best that most of the outdoor activity of the crippled dealer was nocturnal. Padgett Street rarely saw him out at all for the rear premises of his shop gave access to a yard from which it was possible to emerge in more distant thoroughfares by way of a network of slums and alleys. A pleasantry current in Padgett Street was to affect the conviction that he burrowed.

It was sufficiently late when Won Chou's peculiarly appetising meal had been despatched to answer to this requirement. Mr Joolby glanced up at the deepening sky of spilled-ink blue as seen through an uncurtained pane, produced a box of cigars curiously encased in raffia and indicated to his guest that they might as well be going.

"It's a slow affair with me," he apologised as he laboriously crawled about the room, preparing for the walk, "so you must expect a tiresome round. Now as we have some little distance to go—"

"But is it quite safe—this place we go to?" asked Bronsky who had drunk too sparingly of either wine or spirits to have his natural feebleness heartened. "It would not do—"

"Safe as the Kremlin," was the half contemptuous reply, for by the measure of the visitor Joolby was a man of mettle. "My own chap is in charge there and so far as that goes the place is run as a proper business. Ah-Chou," — raising his voice, for that singularly versatile attendant was again at his look-out—"we go come one two hour. You catchee make dark all time."

"Alle light-o," came cheerfully back and although no footsteps were to be heard Won Chou might be trusted to be carrying out his instructions.

"And makee door plenty fast. No one come look-see while not is," was the further injunction; then piloting his guest into the lumber-strewn yard Mr Joolby very thoroughly put into practice this process as regards the rear premises before he led the way towards their destination. Leading, for most of the journey, it literally was, for much of their devious route was along mere passages and even in the streets Mr Joolby's mode of progression monopolised the path while Bronsky's superficial elegance soon prejudiced him against using the gutter. He followed his host at a laboured crawl, relieving his mind from time to time by little bursts of "psst!" and "chkk!" at each occasion of annoyance. Joolby, unmoved, plodded stolidly ahead, his unseen features occasionally registering their stealthy broadening grin, although he seldom failed to throw a word of encouragement over his shoulder whenever a more definite phrase indicated that the comrade had come up against an obstruction or trod into something unpleasant.

"Well, here we are at last," was the welcome assurance as they emerged into a thoroughfare that was at least a little wider and somewhat better lit than most of the others. "That is the place, next to the greengrocer. When we go back we can take an easier way, since you don't seem to like this one, Bronsky, especially as it will be quite dark then."

"It will be as good that we should," assented Mr Bronsky, still justifiably ruffled. "Seldom have I been through such tamgod—"*

[* tamgod: an old back-slang form of "goddam."]

"Just a minute," put in Joolby coolly. "Better not talk until I've made sure that everything is clear," and they having now come to the rag-and-bone shop he rapped in a quite ordinary way on the closed door. With no more than the usual delay of coming from an inner room and turning a rusty key it was opened by an elderly Hebrew whose "atmosphere"—in its most generous sense—was wholly in keeping with his surroundings.

"Good evening, Ikey," said Mr Joolby, still panting a little now that he had come to rest after an unusual exertion, "I have brought you perhaps a very good buyer. This gentleman is making up a large purchase for export and if it is worth his while—"

"Come in, sirs, come in if you please," begged Ikey deferentially; the door was held more fully open and they passed into a store heaped with rags, bones, empty bottles, old metal, stark rabbit skins and all the more sordid refuse of a city's back-kitchens. Joolby did not appear to find anything disturbing in the malodorous air and even the fastidious Bronsky might have been perfectly at home in these surroundings.

"It is quite O.K, Mr Joolby," said Ikey when the door was closed again, and it could have been noticed that he spoke neither so ceremoniously nor in such very audible tones as those which had passed on the threshold. "If you want him he's upstairs now and there isn't nothing different going on anywhere."

Joolby grunted what was doubtless a note of satisfaction and wagged assurance at Mr Bronsky.

"There you see," he remarked consequentially, "it's exactly as I told you. This isn't the land of domiciliary visits and if the police *are* coming they will always send you printed form giving twenty-four hours notice."

"No; is that rule?" asked Mr Bronsky innocently, and repeated: "Good! good! It is comical," when he saw that the other two were being silently amused at his literalness. "Come, come," he hastened to add, thinking that it was time to reassert some of the authority that seemed to have become temporarily eclipsed by the progress of the unfortunate journey, "this is no business however, and we are not here for evers."

"Tell George to come down and bring pulls of his latest plates," confirmed Joolby. The narrow rickety stairs leading to the floor above—little better than a permanent ladder—were impractical for him and scarcely more inviting to Mr Bronsky. Ikey apparently had some system of conveying this message by jerking an inconspicuous cord for almost at once George Larch appeared at the top of the steps, recognising the two visitors as he descended.

"Peace be with you, persecuted victim. The day dawns!" exclaimed the comrade, bustling forward effusively and kissing Mr Larch on both cheeks—an indignity to which he had to submit or lose his balance among the jam jars.

"That's all right, Mr Bronsky," protested George who had as much prejudice against "foreign ways" as most of his countrymen. "But please don't start doing that again—I told you about it once before, you may remember."

"But—but, are we not as brothers?" stammered Mr Bronsky, uncertain whether or not to be deeply hurt. "In spirit of all-union greeting—"

"Well, I shouldn't like the wife to catch you at it, that's all, Mr Bronsky. I should never think of carrying on like that with a grown-up brother."

"*Catch* me 'at it,'" managed to voice the almost dumbfounded Bronsky. "'Carrying on!' Oh, the pigs Englishmen! You have no—no—" At this emotional stress words really did fail him.

"Come, come, you two—what the hell," interposed Mr Joolby judicially. "We're here to see how you've got on, George. May as well go into the room where we can have a decent light. Did you bring pulls of the latest plates down? Bronsky here needs to be satisfied that you can do all I've claimed for you."

At the back of the evil-smelling vault Mr Ikey had his private lair, a mixture of office and, apparently, a living-room in every function. It was remarkably garnished with such salvage from the cruder stock as had been considered worthy of being held over and, as Joolby had foreseen, it possessed a light vastly superior to the dim glimmer that hung over the cavernous store. Here the three chiefly concerned drew close together, the old man remaining behind to stand on guard, while Larch, with the outward indifference that merged his pride as a craftsman and an ineradicable shame to be so basely employed, submitted an insignificant sheaf of papers. Some of the sheets were apparent Bank of England notes in the finished state, others proofs of incomplete plates and various details; both the visitors produced pocket lenses and Mr Bronsky smoothed out a couple of genuine notes that he extracted from a well-stocked wallet. A complete absorption testified their breathless interest.

"Well?" demanded Joolby when every sheet had been passed under review. "Say what you like, Bronsky, this is as near the real article as—" and he instanced two things which might be admitted to be essentially the same although the comparison was more forcible than dainty.

"It could certainly deceive me, I confess," admitted Bronsky, "and yet in ill-spent youth I have experience as bank official. But see," he added, as though anxious to expose some flaw, and wetting across one corner of a sheet with a moistened finger he demonstrated that it could easily be severed.

"Ah, but you mustn't judge the result by this paper, Mr Bronsky—of course it's no good," put in Larch, carefully securing the fragments. "But if we get some of the genuine stuff, as Mr Joolby will tell you he means to do, not even the

Chief Cashier of the Bank of England could be dead certain which was which—except for one thing, of course."

"And that is what?"

"Why, the numbers to be sure. They can refer to their issue."

"Not so fast, George," objected Joolby, "how is that going to help them? Suppose we duplicate actual numbers that are out in circulation, and perhaps hold over the originals? We can triplicate, quadruple, multiply by a hundred times if it suits our purpose."

"Well, by hokey that's an idea," admitted simple George Larch. "Why, they'd have to pay out on all that come in then or risk repudiating their own paper. It's lucky for the Old Lady of Threadneedle Street that we aren't in the wholesale business."

"Yes, to be sure," replied Joolby, favouring the other conspirator with a meaning sideways look. "Lucky, isn't it, Bronsky?"

"I should think to smile," agreed Mr Bronsky, combing his luxuriant beard for the mere pleasure of verifying that dignified appendage. "Notwithstanding however."

"There's one thing I should like to mention, Mr Joolby, while you're here," said Larch, getting back to practical business. "Do you really mean me to go on with plates for all the high values up to the thousand pound printing?"

"Why not?" demanded Joolby, turning on his props to regard George with the blank full-faced stare that presented his disconcerting features in their most pronounced aspect. "What's the difficulty?"

"None at all so far as I'm concerned. Of course I can do them just the same as the others—technically there's nothing whatever against it. Only no one ever heard of soft flims for anything like that—only for fives or tens or at the most a twenty."

"All the more reason why the big ones will go through then. As a matter of fact, George, our friend here has struck special facilities for putting stuff of that sort about in the East. There'll be no risk to any of us at this end whatever happens."

"But you don't mean that it's going to be negotiable for anything like at value? Why if—"

"A profitable use will be found for all of them, never fear," replied Mr Joolby, evincing no intention of pursuing the subject. "Yes, we're through now, Ikey. You can come off. Well, what is it then?"

"It was Mrs Larch outside at the door," bleated Ikey in his ancient falsetto. "I assure her that the place is all locked up and no one here and she laugh at me through the keyhole. She says she will come inside and see for herself."

"Then she will," remarked George, who might be supposed to know. "So you may as well unlock the door and let her."

"If she is I had perhaps better as well go back into the room," suggested Mr Bronsky—they were again in the front shop on their way to leave, "Your wife, for some reason, cannot endure my presence."

"Oh, I wouldn't go as far as that, Mr Bronsky," protested George guiltily, for he knew well enough that he could go exactly that far. "There must he some sort of a mistake... Still, if you think so, perhaps it would be as well at the moment."

Mrs Larch came breezily in, paying no more attention to the now obsequious Ikey than if he had been one of his own commercial assets—an emaciated thigh-bone. A woman smartly turned out (as she would herself have complacently said) and—if a little floridly—handsome still, she might bear slight resemblance now to the simple angel of George's early dreams, but it was possible to trace something of that unfortunate pilgrim's progress in her rather defiant front, her meretricious embellishment, and in an eye that was not devoid of material calculation. For the moment it was only the unwieldy form of Mr Joolby that stood out in that place of continual shadow.

"Oh, good evening, Mr Joolby," she exclaimed, sparkling triumphantly over her success at the doorway. "Of course I guessed that Mr Ikey was telling fibs but I didn't know that I should find you here. I suppose that George is up in the attic as usual? He might just as well be a member of the Carlton for all that I see of him nowadays."

"No, my dear, here I am," proclaimed George, emerging from his particular shadow. "Only you oughtn't to be, after the place is shut up, you know. It isn't prudent."

"Well, someone had to do something about it. I did go round to Padgett Street first and Mr Peke there—no, that isn't right, is it? but I know that it's some kind of a fancy dog. Anyhow, he seemed to be telling the truth when he said that you 'not is' there, so there was nothing for it but to come on here and chance it."

"But what's the matter, Cora?" asked Larch. "Has anything happened?"

"Only the landlord this time, my lad—the gasman was yesterday and the furniture people—oh, you've been home since then, haven't you, and know all about those beauties."

"But I thought that I left enough to tide over the most pressing. We figured it out, if you remember, and it seemed—"

"So I thought, but unfortunately it didn't turn out quite as we figured, boy, and some of the others got more pressing," said Mrs Larch calmly. "At all events I left the landlord sitting on the landing."

"He means it?"

"I'm afraid he most decidedly does. There was that nasty little air of finality about the way he picked his teeth with a bus ticket as he talked—I think he must save them up for it—that, as the Sunday school poem says: 'Is a certain forerunner of sorrow.' 'Come now, Mrs Larch,' he said, running his suety eye over everything I'd got on, 'you can't be hard up you know and you've had a cart-load of warnings. Doesn't your husband make good money?' 'Better than most husbands at his job do, I will say,' I replied, 'but, you know, it's always the cobbler's wife who has the worst shoes, and just at the moment—'" She finished up with the conventional little laugh and held out a hand towards him.

"Come, George, fork out. I'm sorry if you're rocky too but it's an absolute that it's no good going back without it."

"'Rocky,' my God!" said George, echoing her shallow laugh. "Well—but how much do you need to square it?"

"Oh, a couple might do just to carry on—and of course as many more as you can spare me."

"A couple, eh, my girl?" he replied, fishing deeply into both his trouser pockets. "You don't mean tanners by any chance? Well, that's the state of the exchequer." Two sixpences and a few coppers were the result of his investigation.

"I see. No winners among them today, I suppose, and you'd rather gone it? I might have guessed as much. Well, that being that, Mr Joolby will have to advance you a trifle."

"What me? Two quids?" exclaimed Mr Joolby aghast. "You can't be serious. Everyone know that I never advance anything until afterwards and your husband has been paid for a full week and this is only Friday. Oh, I couldn't—"

"All right; only if you don't our place will be sold up and then where are you going to find George when you want him?"

This was so plainly common sense that there could be only one outcome (to say nothing of the pressure of another development that was duly formulating) but even as he would have capitulated one of the freakish impulses, that occasionally brought out the shifty grin, moved Joolby to change his purpose. Instead of the amount required he slyly picked out another paper and Cora found herself being offered a wholly unexpected five-pound note—in point of fact one of George's most recent productions.

"Oh, Mr Joolby, that *is* kind—" she began gratefully and then flashed to what it was—sensed it in Larch's instinctive frown, in Joolby's half averted face, creased with foolish enjoyment. She bit on to the unpleasant tremor: very well, only Joolby should never again enjoy at her expense that particular satisfaction.

"Well, of all the—" she mock-indignantly declared, and entering into the spirit of the thing crumpled up the note and playfully flung it back at the ogre. "Nice fix it would be for you, Mr Joolby, if I was nicked for planting a snide 'un. They'd be here after George like one o'clock and then what would become of all the work you've paid him for doing?"

"That's all right, Mrs Larch—it was only our fun," protested Mr Joolby, leering like his ancestral satyr. "It isn't likely that we'd risk anything of the sort just now, is it? But I will tell you this: when we get the right stuff you needn't be afraid of walking into the Bank of England with your paper."

"I daresay. But in the meantime I *am* afraid of the bailiff walking into our flat with his paper. George there knows well enough. I must have something before I can go back and that's all there is about it."

"Well, so you shall have," promised Mr Joolby, calling up all the blandishment of his suavest manner. "And that is not all; I may as well tell you now, though I hadn't intended to until it was quite settled. Very soon we shall have a nice regular job for you with good wages—oh, a splendid position in a beautiful house with very little to do and everything found that you require."

If Mr Joolby expected the enchanted lady to fall upon his neck (metaphorically, of course, for physical contact was a thing sheerly inconceivable) he was a little out of his reckoning. Cora Larch had experience of considerable slices of life in various aspects. During periods of George's compulsory withdrawal it had been necessary for her to fend for herself, nor, in truth, had she ever found any particular difficulty in so doing. But as a result of the education that had thereby accrued she now approached Mr Joolby's surprising proposal in the spirit that prompts a creature of the wild to walk all round a doubtful morsel before venturing to touch it.

"Oh, and what sort of a job is it, may I ask?" she guardedly inquired. "And for that matter, what sort of a house where everything is going to be so fairy-like?"

"Well, you see, it's like this," explained Mr Joolby. "The time's come when we must have another place—it's getting too risky for all of them to be in and out so often of my shop, to say nothings about coming direct here when at any time one might be followed. Then very soon there will be others—foreign gentlemen—that we may want to put up for a few nights at a time. Oh, I can tell you it won't be altogether money wasted."

"No, I'm sure it won't if you are doing it, Mr Joolby," agreed the lady. "Still, I don't see—"

"Well, as I'm telling you I've taken a private house in a different name—a furnished house right across the other side of London. It must be conducted quietly on highly respectable lines so that it would never occur to anyone outside that it wasn't thoroughly dull and bourgeois. With the milkman and the baker calling every day that oughtn't to be difficult. Nothing impresses the neighbourhood so favourably as two or three bottles of milk taken in regularly every morning and put out again at night. It must be that crooks aren't supposed to drink it. And any account of yourself that you want to put about—we will make that up—you can safely pass on to the baker."

"Well?" Mr Joolby seemed to think that everything necessary had been said, but Mrs Larch was still expectant.

"Well; don't you understand? You are to be as housekeeper, manage the place and arrange for whoever we send to stay there. All the bills will be paid—only don't be extravagant of course. Deal at the multiple shops and there's a nice street market—and you will have a pound a week for wages."

"H'm; it sounds promising," admitted Mrs Larch. The prospect of being able to cap it by giving notice when the insufferable landlord made his next caustic remark was not without an influence. Still, she had not quite completed the cautionary circle. "But is it part of the—the arrangement that you are going to take up your abode there, Mr Joolby?"

"I?" replied Joolby, with just the flicker of an instinctive glance in the ingenuous George's direction. "What has that got to do with it? I live at my own place as usual, of course. I may have to come occasionally—"

"Oh, all right. I only wanted to understand—*and have it understood*—from the start. Let me know when I'm to begin and I'll take it on for you."

"Of course you will. It's a holiday that you're being paid for having, not a job. What do you say, eh, George?"

"I say that if Cora wants to do it she will," contributed Mr Larch with tempered loyalty. "It's her affair after all, Mr Joolby."

"Eh? Oh yes, of course; but that's settled. Well, what about putting this paper out of the way now that Bronsky is satisfied; and you don't leave any of the plates where they can be found at night I hope? We can't be too careful."

"I'll see to that you may be sure," undertook Larch and he proceeded to satisfy himself that no dangerous paper had been left about and then climbed up to his quarters. Meanwhile Cora lingered on in the cavernous gloom, waiting for Joolby to redeem his promise—a small detail that seemed to have escaped his memory.

"What sort of a house is it that you're taking, Mr Joolby?" she said at last, finding the man's eyes repeatedly upon her and speaking to break a silence that threatened to become awkward.

"Oh, a very nice house in a first-class neighbourhood and quite the swell side of London. There's a garden all round so we can't be overlooked and a back way out into another street, which is always a convenience. It's costing me a lot of money."

"Costing your Bolshie friends, I suppose you mean? What size is this house—it sounds rather a handful."

"Quite a good size. Ten or a dozen rooms, I daresay, and then there are cellars and attics besides. Oh, plenty of room for all that we require."

"Plenty of work for me more likely. I can't do all that myself you know, Mr Joolby. I must have a maid of some sort if the place is to be kept at all decent."

"What! A servant to feed and pay wages into the bargain!" cried Mr Joolby in dismay. "Well, well; you shall have one, Cora. I daresay we can find one of those devoted, hard-working little scrubs who are glad to come for nothing and live on the table leavings. And when there's nothing else for her to do she can always put in some time working in the garden—I have to keep it in order."

"She shall, Mr Joolby; you can have my word on that. Now what about the rent for me to take back? You said you would, you know—"

"So I did, my dear," amorously breathed Mr Joolby, coming nearer as he took out his wallet to comply and dropping his voice almost to a whisper, "and I'm not going back on it or anything else I promise you... You think me a bit—careful I dare say, now don't you, Cora? But if only you'll be sensible and meet me half way you'll have no reason to complain that you're short of money. There's the two pounds, and I'll make it five more—well, say three more for a start; that's five altogether—if you're reasonable—" Amid all this tender eloquence, in which Mr Joolby's never very dulcet voice assumed an oddly croaking tone as the combined outcome of the exigencies of caution and his own emotional strain, Mrs Larch realised that her hand was being held and increasingly caressed under the cloak of passing her the money.

"Oh, you beastly old toad!" she impulsively let out, and tore herself away from those fumbling paws, though, characteristically enough, her fingers tightened on the two notes that were already in her possession. "So it *teas* that, after all!"

Whatever had been Joolby's delusion a moment before, that one word Cora had used brought him crashing back to earth as effectually as if it had been a bullet. For a short minute his contorted face and swelling form grew more repellent still, his hands beat the air for help, and swaying then, with his props laid by, it seemed as though he must have fallen. The effect was sufficiently alarming to blur Mrs Larch's disgust, while fearful of lending any physical aid she began to babble, lamely enough, to turn the edge of her incautious outburst.

"Oh, well; of course I didn't mean anything personal, Mr Joolby. You quite understand that I hope, but you ought to be more careful—steadying yourself by clutching hold of one in this dark hole like that. I declare I thought it was a bogie. Now I'd better be getting on I think. You'll let me know when I'm to start housekeeping, won't you?"

"Go; go; get out! Clear off, you harpy. Never show your ugly face again. I've done with you, do you hear?" spat out the stricken creature, hurling the words like missiles. "Go before I have you thrown out—" Gasping for breath he continued to gesticulate and threaten.

Cora Larch was not particularly long-suffering herself; she had tendered her olive branch and if the beast took it like that he could bloody well go and— A little crude, perhaps, but twenty-five years of her sort of life are apt to take the bloom off even the most peach-like natures.

"Oh, all right, all right," she threw back, almost as vigorously. "Keep your hair—well"—with a significant glance at his skull—"keep your skin moist anyway. You know jolly well there's no one else you can trust to put in that house and I'm quite willing to come still *as a housekeeper*, Mr Joolby. Send word by George when you're cool. Ta-ta." And with an emphatic nod to give point to her self-possession Mrs Larch vanished.

"Cow! Bitch! Camel!" Mr Joolby continued to spit and swell while the distracted Ikey drew near and sheered off again, quaveringly helpless among such violent emotions. "George—Larch—come here at once—I'll let you know—"

Evidently George was to become the whipping-boy for his wife's transgressions.

Fortunately, perhaps, George was just then too remote to hear, but Mr Bronsky heard and it was that dignified gentleman who, emerging from the den and surveying his friend's condition with grave disfavour, brought him at once to recognise the very unfraternal figure he was cutting.

"What is this, Joolby?" he demanded with authority, planting himself resolutely in front so as to pen his irresponsible associate between the mixed rags and the bottles. "Are you crazy? Have you become madman? How is this that has possess you? Do you not understand that the row you is kicking up may bring in police? Or have you taken leaves of your senses?"

"You are right—I must have been off my head, but something happened very much to upset me," admitted Mr Joolby, realising at last how fatuously he must have been behaving. "No, nothing to do with our affairs, I assure you, Bronsky, but—well, it is of no matter. I must not talk of it—not think of such things—or it may bring on an attack of my old trouble. Now we will go back straight at once and I'll take you in a bus. Or no, I think perhaps it had better even run to a taxi."

5

THE MEETING AT ELEVEN

With the distaste for being subject to promiscuous observation that ordered the routine of his movements, Mr Joolby stopped the taxi-cab before Padgett Street was reached and they arrived at the back yard after a complicated but relatively short process of burrowing. Won Chou was patiently on watch and discharged himself of a faithful account of all that had happened in the interval:

"She-Larch come and do plenty talkee. Say he is? Say not is. Make go." The subject not calling for any particular elaboration Joolby merely nodded.

He had recovered his equilibrium now and Cora's ungrateful flout, and the jibe that had been its barb, were dismissed into the category of Chilly Fank's reference once to an aquarium and a thousand kindred insults—contributory drops to an ocean of insensate hatred that took little account of individual scores in its unrelenting vendetta against the entire race that was human.

"So far so well," remarked Mr Bronsky with some complacency when they were again seated in the dealer's private den (though he may have had a still more private one somewhere into which nobody but himself ever penetrated) with cigars and coffee of a very especial flavour before them—

waiting, as the comrade vaguely understood, for the arrival of some others. "The workmanship of itself," he continued, "leave no shadow of doubts that Larch will be able to satisfy us. Then Nickle—no, I cannot like that young man—is to say how the paper may be acquired. But the others of that you speak—where do they, as it goes, 'come in?'"

"Nickle will tell us all about the mill but after that we shall have to decide on the most suitable lines for getting to work there. There must be no hitch anywhere when once we make a move in that direction, Bronsky."

"I think so also," agreed his guest; "and that is why I ask it." Mr Bronsky thought intently for a moment, tapping his intellectual brow with a persuasive forefinger until he triumphantly got the happy instance that he was tracking: "Too many cooks upset an apple cart."

"Nickle will be able to tell us exactly what we need to know but it will take more than one to put the thing through when it comes to the real business," replied Joolby, reflecting that as the time had to be passed there was no point in becoming impatient. "No cause to get anxious on that score, let me tell you, my friend; to all except ourselves this is simply going to be an unusually big and well-arranged plant and their only idea will be to do their share to make it a success so that they can have their pickings. So. But once the paper and the plates are safe with us we can arrange matters according to our own programme."

"I feel sure you may be right," assented Bronsky, with his usual pliant acquiescence. "Now as regards these others who are to come in the swim; it is just as good that I should first be told about them in order to be in a position to judge their ability."

There were moments when Mr Bronsky's consequential little airs of authority made Joolby realise what a satisfaction it would be to pick up the nearest heavy object and bring it wholeheartedly down on this shallow-witted comrade's lamentable cranium. It was never more than a passing fancy, for he had long since realised that with the barest modicum of tact the formidable deputy was as plastic as a stick of putty, and with such contemptuous success had he kept this end in view that Bronsky firmly believed in Joolby's high regard and dependence on his judgment.

"That's chiefly why they're coming; I want you to meet them here and then tell me frankly what you think of their fitness for whatever we decide on doing. Dodger and Klantz you've seen, but another—Vallett—I don't suppose you've ever heard of. Then of course there will be Nickle himself and George was to be here in case anything comes up that touches what he is doing."

"Dodger who was call—" Bronsky's snapping fingers failed to induce the expression. "It was a word for *skoliskiey*."*

"'Slippery?'—no, 'Soapy Solomon,' you mean—yes, that is the chap, and Klantz was the man we pulled out of Hamburg when he got into trouble over the Vulkan Works shindy."

"They should be good men—I would approve them both. But who is this Vallett of what you speak. Is he trustworthy comrade?"

"George Larch picked up with him when he was doing his last stretch, and when Vallett was on his beam ends George sent him round here on the chance that I might find something for him. The fact is, Vallett slipped out of Dartmoor before his time was up and consequently he can't go about much in the day looking for suitable employment."

"I do not like that very well," objected Bronsky, feeling that perhaps he had been compliant long enough; "there is too much of the 'Known by the Police' about so many of your people. If there is a description of this fellow put about and he

[* skoliskiey (*sic*). Bramah appears to be confusing the Polish and Russian words for "slippery" (*liski* and *skol'zkiy*). — RG]

is recognise, they follow him to here and then where is we, to say nothings of our project?"

"Oh, I don't think so, Bronsky," said Joolby in his most amiable mood; "I see your point and I'm all for being careful but even if they did nab Vallett here, what about it? I'd be much obliged to the police for opening my eyes about the chap and there would be absolutely nothing to connect him up with us or what we're doing."

"So far, perhaps—"

"And that's all that concerns us yet—afterwards we may or may not use him. Besides they won't; Vallett can make up very well indeed—before he got tired of work he was on the stage and if he goes about by day his own mother wouldn't know him."

"That puts a different complexion on him, I admit"—unfortunately Mr Bronsky did not recognise his own witticism. "Yes, I begin to think Vallett is all right. What is it that we want him for—what is his way of business?"

"Well, he's tried his hand at several things—from calling to test the gas-meter to posing as a co-respondent. Anything lightly adventurous would suit his book and he has a very gentlemanly manner. That's what I had in mind—we have plenty of heavyweights but we may need to put someone there who can walk plausibly up to the front door. As to his being on the 'wanted' list—well, after all, you can't run a knocking-shop with a bevy of virgins."

This refined adage was entirely to Bronsky's taste and put him in a better humour. "Good, good!" he exclaimed, showing his splendid teeth; "I must remember that one. Is it English saying?"

Before Mr Joolby could explain that it was more probably early Egyptian a little bell conveyed its message, and waving aside such trivialities he briefly informed his guest that this indicated the arrival of one of the expected callers.

"I told the boy to send any of them straight through," he added, "so he needn't come off the door. Ah—our resourceful friend Nickle! Now this is luck. You are a bit early, Nick, and we can find out where we are before the others cut in."

It was Nickle safely back indeed, looking extremely brown and fit, but in contrast to the pair who were all interest and affable expectation *his* manner was decidedly offhand and his expression—possibly a defensive pose—one of seasoned boredom. He greeted Joolby with a careless nod and held up—not out—an admonitory hand as Bronsky rose, whatever may have been the comrade's intention.

"I give you fair warning, Bronsky," he remarked, "that if you try any of your filthy brotherly love on me I shall stab you. It's much too hot to be embraced. I wonder you haven't gone back to hell, Joolby; you'd find it a damn sight cooler there than it seems to be in Stepney."

"Kindly put off trying to be funny, Nickle," said Joolby, beginning to glower. "Coffee?" Already he guessed that the awaited report was not going to be any too encouraging, while this, if it came to the pinch, was certainly not the way to smooth down the already prejudiced Bronsky. Nickle's failing.

"I prefer any other form of poison, since you are so kind," was the reply. "Truth to tell, I'm rather sate of coffee and finger sponge biscuits."

Not troubling to speak, but with a very ill grace at this further lapse, Joolby produced his bottles. Meanwhile, having sat down again, Mr Bronsky confided a succession of "psss's" and "tsss's" into his beard and blew out his cheeks between them.

"Now let's get on to things," said their host, when amid this rather strained atmosphere Nickle had indicated and received his mixture. "Our comrade is here specially to hear your report and, since it lies chiefly with us three, there is no particular object at this stage in waiting for the others. You've had all the time you've asked for, Nickle, and with the information you must have got no doubt you've worked out the scheme. Never mind the considerations now—just the bare facts. In a word, how is it to be done?"

"I can tell you that very simply," replied Nickle, shifting his glass about with trivial deliberation. "Not in a word perhaps but certainly in five at the outside. It isn't to be done."

This was worse than Joolby's worst. At the most he had expected a formidable list of the difficulties to be met but he had never doubted that Nickle—of whose nerve and finesse he had proof—would at least have a feasible plan that would be capable of adaption. At this set-back all the familiar symptoms of anger and resentment began to possess the being, but his first words were moderately composed—merely because he refused as yet to credit Nickle's conclusions.

"What do you mean—'It isn't to be done?'" he snarled. "It must be done. We've got to have that paper."

"Oh, very well," said Nickle, very creditably keeping up his pose of nonchalance; "in that case there's nothing to it but for you to go down there and get it. You take with you my best wishes... Look here, Joolby," he continued, switching on to an entirely different tone, "I expect you to feel pretty sick, but if you imagine that this means nothing to me either, you are hellishly mistaken. The only difference is that you get it all at once while I've been up against it for a month, slowly finding out at every turn and twist that I couldn't get an inch further. You sent me down to find out the conditions, didn't you? Well, you may take my perishing word that in one way or another I found them. You simply can't get in there by force and there doesn't seem the foggiest chance to frame an act and lift a bunch of the paper. That's my considered judgment. You'd better send someone else to have a look if you won't accept it. Bronsky doesn't seem any too pleased—let him have a go and try it."

During this harangue Mr Bronsky had been combing his beard vigorously as a practical outlet for his aggrieved feelings, and he now came to his feet and waved his arms excitedly in several directions as an impressive if otherwise ambiguous summing-up of the collapsed situation.

"If this is all," he proclaimed, "I may as better go—"

"Sit down, Bronsky," thundered Joolby, dragging his great body up and coming to himself at last as he realised the crisis, and Mr Bronsky obediently did sit down. "It isn't all." His baleful eye surveyed them both with impartial disfavour. "We need to have that paper for what we are infallibly going to do and whatever stands between we are going to get it. As you both very well know everything has been worked out on the assumption that we shall, and neither Nickle's cold feet nor anyone else's hot air signify a pestilential... I've fitted in all the arrangements here to absolute clockwork; Larch is cutting perfect plates that will defy every test that anyone can make, and Bronsky's people are ready with an organisation that would distribute in dead safety... And Mr Nickle regretfully informs us"—spitting his concentrated scorn—"'It isn't to be done.'... Now go on and tell us about it, Nickle."

"Quite so," agreed Nickle with commendable restraint; "you've put up the dollars and you're entitled to the change. Well, with a regiment of soldiers forcing your way in would be child's play, wouldn't it? Or if you bought over half a dozen employees there need be no difficulty about lifting half a ton of paper, eh? But we haven't got a regiment as it happens and not a solitary employee is up for sale... Continue in your useful line of cross-examination, Mr Joolby; it's all included in the exes."

"How can you positively say that there is no weak spot you've overlooked or that no one can be got at? How must you *know*? The thing has never even been tried as yet."

"Oh hell, no." Nickle shrugged his expressive shoulders at the futility of the inference. "I know all the ancient history of the place of course and I happen to know that it's simply because they take damn good care that it can never be successful."

"It has never been attempt at all before?" chimed in Mr Bronsky, gathering new hope. "Then I am dispose to agree with Joolby that you have missed what you have not seen. It should not be out of the question."

"Possibly not, Bronsky," admitted Nickle, behaving his best, "but unfortunately it is out. The kink in your point of view arises from the fact that whereas neither of you has so much as seen Tapsfield through a telescope, for the last month or so I've been exploring its rural beauties. There isn't an inch of ground that I haven't been over and I don't suppose that there's a man, woman, or child working at the mill who won't really miss me. I've had supper at the vicarage, played darts at the Crown and Anchor, deputised for the local scoutmaster, put up a special prize for the best collection of wild flowers at the Tapsfield and District Horticultural—"

"What for?" demanded Joolby crossly.

"To award it to Joyce Jones so that I might call and congratulate her mother who lives at the mill gate lodge. My God, Joolby, I even sang 'Dreaming of Thee' at a saturnalia called a 'Penny Reading' there, simply because the young lady who whanged the piano had a job of feeding a machine in the drying-room."

"It was women and young girl you got best on with doubtless?" asked the comrade, screwing up his eyes pleasantly. "You had agreeable time exploring these local beauties in one way or another, Nickle?"

"Bronsky," said Nickle gravely, "you ought to take a fairly strong cathartic immediately before retiring. You have a morbid accumulation of offensive matter somewhere... As an actual fact, the person that I most assiduously worked was a young fellow called Tilehurst who is employed in the mill office. He needed someone to improve his tennis a bit and as I was quite equal to that he simply clung to me and wanted me to go round to their place on nearly every other evening. I got all the routine from him; do you think that if there was any way through I shouldn't have spotted it in those circumstances? I'm as keen in the matter of this loot as any of you are, but you may just as well put it out of your minds—it doesn't go this journey."

"I don't put it out of my mind for the fraction of a second, but I may have to put you out of somewhere, Nickle, if this is the best you can do when you are given a chance of showing. All our work—come in, George" (Mr Larch having that moment made an unobtrusive appearance), "you may as well know what's going—Bronsky's, mine, and Georges—to say nothing of a score of others who are in this thing as well—all this isn't going to be scrapped simply because you, and you alone, have failed in your department."

"Failed? I like that!" threw back Nickle. "How have I failed? I went there to find out the conditions. Haven't I?"

"You have failed because you haven't succeeded; that's how. There are no half ways here. You know well enough that you went to find out the best way of getting what we need from there. You say it can't be done. Very well; as we are going to do it we must fall back on our own methods, with just so much or so little as you can help us... Now this man Tilehurst you struck—I suppose yon know his ways—does he go about alone? Could we hold him up down there if we were fixing it that way?"

"Not the least doubt. He cycles about alone pretty regularly and in those godforsaken winding lanes anything could happen. But—"

"Cut out those 'buts' of yours, Nickle. You're only butting up against a brick wall here."

"And besides, remember, comrade," put in Mr Bronsky encouragingly, "that even if it comes to touch and went and it is not well to stay, you would always find asylum with good friend in Moscow."

"An asylum?" repeated Nickle, with a sufficiently pointed look. "Yes, I suppose that does about describe Moscow now, but I don't want to go into an asylum just yet... And since you dislike the more conventional opening, Joolby—what in hell's name do you suppose is to be got by sticking up young Tilehurst and bringing all the resources of law and order round about our ears?"

"He uses some office keys, one may suppose," continued Joolby, without paying the slightest attention to this objection. "Did you happen to make it your business to find out what he actually carries?"

"Naturally. He has the ordinary desk and inner door keys of his own part of the building. None of these are any more serviceable than a corkscrew for getting you into the place, while meanwhile the guard would certainly express disapproval of your presence by drilling several holes through you. Finally, if by any chance you did get in, how are you going to get off with all the weight of paper that you seem to have set your mind on lifting?"

"'All the weight of paper!' Mark him, comrades. This is our expert adviser who for the past month has been finding out all about it. Do you know, Nickle—no, of course you don't: you're just from Tapsfield where they make them. Acquaint yourself with the interesting fact that bank-notes for a million pounds can be carried quite comfortably in a single coat pocket."

"A million pounds? Oh rats—a million rats just as likely! What do you say, George? Why, even Mr Bronsky—"

Joolby swung himself slowly round towards a shelf, creating by his bulk and laboured effort the impression of dumb physical pain that accompanied all his movements. Selecting a moderately small book he drew it out, verified that it was the one he sought, and flung it across the table.

"That inconsiderable book, Nickle, is the approximate surface size of a Bank of England note. How many pages are there in it?"

"Oh, about six hundred," replied Nickle, his casual manner an ungracious protest against being drawn into this unprofitable discussion.

"'About six hundred'—five hundred and eighty four to be exact, since our friend is not sufficiently interested to be prosaically explicit. That means two hundred and ninety-two bank-note-size sheets of paper. In other words, three little books like that, allowing for the covers and extra pages, represent the bulk of a thousand notes, and a thousand notes, each for a thousand pounds, make a million sterling... Put that fact into your trouser- pocket, comrade Nickle, and sit on it!"

"Notes of a thousand pounds!" This time Nickle had been stirred into something like attention, "My good Joolby, what in the name of sanity—I beg your pardon, Bronsky I—but, seriously, what do you imagine that we are going to do with notes of that fantastic value?"

"A use will be found for them, don't fear. All along, Nickle, I have tried to make you realise that this stroke was not to be a matter of planting a few soft fivers on racecourse bookies—I used to think that you had imagination. We intend to make notes of all the values and chiefly of the big ones. George there will tell you that one is as easy to do as another and it may further interest you to know—you with your 'weight of paper'—that just over two pounds and a half weigh a thousand."

"All this is very interesting no doubt," said Nickle, with an air of polite acceptance, "and might even be useful in appropriate circumstances. But my inherent vein of common sense—flattering as it is to be thought romantic, Joolby—continually brings me back to the bed-rock fact that the first essential is either to get into the place ourselves or to have someone in our pay who will do it for us."

"So. So," agreed Joolby smoothly. "It is one of those that we are going to do—with or without your help, friend Nickle. Now will you take this piece of paper and just sketch for me—quite rough you understand—a plan of the village, showing the mill and the other leading features. We will burn it as soon as I have got it off, never fear."

"Delighted," assented Nickle readily enough. "Only too glad to show you that I know what I'm talking about."

"Shall I as well not stay?" asked Mr Bronsky, suddenly making up his mind. "It is more late than I thought, the other ones has not arrive, and, you remember, my hotel is a little unconvenient—" It was only too plain that the comrade's faith in the enterprise had been sadly undermined by the unfortunate turn affairs had taken.

"Just as you like, Bronsky," replied Joolby, without the least show of ill feeling. "I ought to have thought of your time but I left it rather open with the others—about eleven,' I believe I said, so they naturally won't hurry. However, I'll send round to you soon and let you know how we're going to fix it."

"Ah, you still think—?" In the face of the cripple's monumental calm Bronsky's conviction was again veering.

"That this thing is going on? It's as certain as the day after tomorrow. Everything is shaping splendidly now that Nickle has done just as I intended—found out what precautions they usually take and the sort of impression they want to give strangers."

"You mean that you expected this—that you did not trust of him a way in to discover?"

"Well, scarcely." Joolby's great face was expressive of the most impeccable assurance. "Nickle is hardly the kind of chap to help us in that—*you* guessed what he was all along—but he sees what lies on the surface. There's work for the others now and we'll have it all arranged and go straight forward."

"I begin to think that you may be right. Notwithstanding, my report was to have been off sent—"

"Well, I suppose you can assure them that everything is going very well? In any case, details, even in cypher, could not be put on paper."

Mr Bronsky's wise nods seemed to imply that this was precisely what he had intended. Nickle was still absorbed in his plan, George Larch away in thought, and there appeared to be no further inducement for the comrade to linger.

"Then I may as well—" he resumed, but his voice was now half apologetic.

"Go by all means and get a good snooze," was Joolby's cordial advice. "I'll let you know—a minute, though—here's someone else arriving."

According to the arrangement he came in unannounced and for a moment stood at the door picking up the scene with a quiet, self-possessed look of well-bred interest. Scarcely the type of man to have earned the nickname "Soapy Solomon," while the patronymic "Klantz" would be even less convincing. This, then, must be Mr Joolby's "gentlemanly mannered" recruit, the ex-convict Vallett. Joolby grunted a careless word, Larch contributed a friendly gesture, but it was Nickle, coming to his feet so impetuously that his chair went spinning back, who startled them all into a confused wonder as to what on earth was happening.

"Tilehurst!" he cried out sharply. "What in hell's name are you doing here?" Then, as the new-comer continued to stand, amiably discomposed, and the others began to glance away from the two most concerned and to look at one another: "Why don't you speak? This must be a bloody fine frame-up for you to drop in here. Are all the lot of you in it?" His hand slid to a hip pocket and the blue of steel came level. "By God, Joolby, if you think that you are going to put me away to suit your game, the same as you did—"

"To blazes with ya next!" roared Joolby, towering above the row as the others began to join in, and killing Nickle's voice before the name was spoken. "What's ya crazy notion now, ya rotten-hearted rabbit? What'r the hell ya think ya raisin', Nickle?"

"Why have you brought Tilehurst here?—that's what I want to know," retorted Nickle, still excitedly worked up but beginning to recognise that, as he was hopelessly at sea, he might not have been so seriously betrayed as he had in the first rush of blank surprise passionately concluded. "There must be some funny double-crossing going on for you to let me talk as I did and never say that he was in it."

"Nonsense, Mr Nickle, it's you who're being funny," put in George Larch mildly. "This chap's name is Vallett—both Mr Joolby and I know him. All this rumpus about Tilehurst is something of your own inventing."

"He may be Vallett to you and you may both know him," retorted Nickle. "But I know him just as well and it's as Tilehurst I've known him."

"I've been seeing him pretty well every day for the last month, going there to tea and playing tennis with him—is it likely I don't know the fellow when I meet him the day after? If I stood up here just as I am and someone said: 'No, this isn't Nickle—his name's Jim Snooks'—would that convince you? Look here, Tilehurst,"—turning to the stranger—"kindly put the lot of us wise and explain the mystery of this dual existence."

During all this lively scene Mr Vallett had remained standing near the door. He might, as Mr Joolby had implied, have become too indolent to work but he had the stage aplomb and he waited for the most effective moment to intervene with a natural actor's instinct.

"Thank you all very much indeed for this really fine reception," he said in a quiet and very distinct tone, at the same time advancing a few steps so as to take up the centre of the picture. "Now do you mind telling me what it's mostly about as I seem to have missed the caption?"

"Your voice is certainly miles different," admitted Nickle grudgingly and staring very hard. "Look here—do you actually mean to say that you aren't Geoffrey Tilehurst?"

"Not to the extent of a solitary brace button so far as I'm aware," replied Vallett glibly. "But if there's anything in the nature of a missing heir, or a lonely old millionaire, or even a neglected wife, I'm quite willing to oblige."

"It's simply incredible. Except for the voice—and, yes, perhaps something in the manner—you would deceive the very devil."

"Well, you can quite set your mind at rest about it, Nickle," Larch assured him. "I've known Vallett for the past two years and most of that time we've both been in—in geological research work for the Government—the granite strata of Dartmoor."

"Julian Joolby—" purred Bronsky softly.

"I'm listening," was the reply. Doubtless he was but his deliberate eyes were fixed on Vallett's face and the beat of his throat was distressing.

"If these two peoples are so undissimilar—"

"Crikey!" said Larch, following their thoughts; "that's certainly an idea."

Nickle, who ought to have been the first, was the last to catch the suggestion.

"My hat!" he exclaimed, banging the table with his fist, "if we could put it through, what a dead cinch we should have there!"

"Well, why not?" said Joolby coolly. "A minute ago you were ready to take your oath that he was Tilehurst. Why should anyone else be so much wiser?"

"But the voice?" objected Nickle. "I hadn't heard that then. They're no more alike than a sparrow and a cuckoo. If we could get over that—why, dammit, even now when I look, I more than half believe that he must be!" And Vallett's back being turned just then Nickle went a step nearer and called out sharply, as if to take him by surprise:

"Tilehurst!"

But instead of being startled into admission, Vallett merely turned slowly round and politely smiling said: "Oh, I beg your pardon! What am I supposed to do now?"

"Well, Nickle?" prompted Joolby, with the unspoken insinuation in his tone again, and this time Nickle's vista had responded further to the suggestion.

"Suppose we discount the voice—frankly I haven't a flicker of hope that it could be done, but for the sake of arguing the possibilities... Vallett at the most favourable moment appears there... He'd be walking on a mine... The man's position is technical and detailed; all the coaching that I could give in advance would be general and superficial... He must make a false move—he must give himself hopelessly away before we could profit by it. The chances are too grotesque. And the instant the real Tilehurst appeared—when that happens not only the bottom falls out but the sides cave in and the lid comes down on whatever is left of the situation..."

"Yes—*when*!" Joolby dropped the word significantly and left it at that to develop the implication.

"You mean—?" Nickle stopped wrinkling his brow and biting his under lip in doubt, to challenge, wide-eyed, this masterful solution.

"Again, why not? 'In those godforsaken winding lanes anything may happen.'"

"Quite so. But I draw the line at murder."

"So does anyone but a fool—or a successful hero. Especially when there's no need for it. But gagged men tell no tales and we shall have plenty of nice cellar accommodation... Ten minutes ago I told you, Nickle, that we were going to get that paper—not because I had a glimmering how but simply because we must have it. We are still going to get that paper, Nickle—neither more nor less than we were before but perhaps you are not quite so cocksure now that it's going to be impossible to get it?"

"I should like to think we could—and this Vallett stunt is certainly a miracle. At the same time—perhaps because I know the ropes down there pretty well—I don't see how we are possibly to get over—"

"You are not being asked to see how now—from this point on I propose to do all the necessary see-howing. What you are being asked to do is to obey instructions to the letter and not to get the belly-ache whenever you visualise a copper."

"That's a damned unpleasant thing to say," retorted Nickle—but not so warmly as he could have wished, for the excitement of the project was taking hold of him and intoxication of any kind may equally either quicken or blunt a Nickle's *amour propre*.

"It's a damned unpleasant thing to have to deal with," was Joolby's tart reply; "we must make allowances for one another—Well, comrade, really going?"

It was Mr Bronsky who occasioned this aside—a smooth, complacent, and now wholly reassured Bronsky. Conversation with simple, respectful George Larch and that quite charming fellow Vallett had convinced him that everything was going to turn out finely.

"I may now just as good, since that fool place hotel of mine—" replied Bronsky, vague but unmistakably cordial. "It goes well, Joolby?"

"It goes even better than we thought, don't you fear, comrade. You shall hear at the next stage through one of the usual channels. It may be a week—two weeks—even three or four—but it goes; it goes inevitably."

"I think so too, also, and I shall let headquarter know in like strain," assented Mr Bronsky. He proceeded towards the shop, waving gracious adieux. "God be—no! no! *Au revoir*, comrades."

"Good night, Mr Bronsky," Larch called after him; Vallett bestowed an engaging smile, and Nickle's casual: "Oh, go to hell—comrade!" while conversationally given, had been just too late to create unpleasant feeling.

Won Chou, as spiritually detached as a preoccupied cat, was there to "make unfast" the outer door, and on him the worthy man bestowed a final blessing.

"Hope, class-oppressed little comrade; hope and—!" Mysteriously pressing a finger to his lips Mr Bronsky waited to make his exit.

"Hope some piece silber, alle same, comlade," prompted Won Chou, displaying an expectant palm, but the comrade suddenly became deeply interested in his watch and passed abstractedly into the unstirring darkness.

"We'll let it go at that, then," conceded Nickle, reverting to the subject at the point where Bronsky had interrupted. "You to be solely responsible for the general campaign and the plan of battle. I haven't the slightest objection to the strong, silent man, Joolby, so long as he is silent and doesn't begin to shed sawdust badly towards the finish. Bring it off in whatever way you like provided it shows nuggets, and make no mistake about my being in baldheaded with you. But money I must shortly have or my address will be Young Nick, care of Old Nick, The Shady Corner, Hades. There's one thing though—this coprolite-witted Bronsky."

"What about him?"

Nickle shrugged his shoulders to indicate the inexpressible ambit of Mr Bronsky's obvious shortcomings.

"What not about him if it comes to that, but, specifically, he isn't in it with us. He's got some wild cat scheme of making everybody happy by making everybody else miserable. It won't wash, you know, Joolby; it isn't economically sound. Now you and I and old George and Vallett and the rest are simply out to snatch the oof, I take it, and that's a rational proposition. But Bronsky with his blasted universal brotherhood is as likely as not to queer the show if he thinks it's to the common disadvantage."

"Leave that to me, Nickle," said Joolby, with a reassuring look of mutual understanding. "We are out to make big money this time and Bronsky will be useful. He can give us facilities for getting the stuff away and for putting it about on a scale that no one else could offer. If he fancies that we are doped by his communistic hog-wash so much the better; he won't work for us any the worse for thinking that we're playing his game, instead of him playing ours."

"So long as it goes at that—"

"It does go at that, Nickle. As you say, what other end could you and I have in view except to line our pockets? Now I want you to take Vallett in hand and drill him stiff with everything that has to do with Tilehurst and Tapsfield. Of course he'll have to make up quite different and go down there and work Tilehurst for himself before we put it through but he may as well get all he can from you before he goes there."

"Right you are; I'll put him wise," undertook Nickle briskly. "After all, it's entirely your circus. Shall we stay here and—"

"No, no; take him away now and arrange it yourselves—I'll let you know what the next move is. Go—and take George as well—I want to be alone soon and I have a couple of other chaps due in about five minutes."

"The hell you have!" said Nickle, glancing at his wrist. "At twelve? Klantz and Soapy Solomon, I suppose, but didn't I hear you tell Bronsky that you had called them for eleven? And for the matter of that, my friend, you told me it was ten-thirty sharp and then when I was a shade behind the time chipped me for being early."

"Did I?" conceded Joolby, discreetly vague; "one forgets these little things when there's so much else needed. I think I must have done about enough for one day, Nickle. I'm feeling tired: very strangely tired."

* * * * *

It had been a full and exacting day for Mr Joolby, even touching only so much of it as has been told, and now, Klantz and Soapy Solomon conferred with and dismissed, the uncouth bulk of The Toad lay sprawling in collapse within a great armchair, nothing but the arresting beat of that pendent throat to say whether he was dead or living. He might have slept indeed, but Padgett Street—itself now settled down into an uneasy drowse on a night when its tarred road bubbled—Padgett Street had long averred that Joolby never slept or even closed his eyes, but this was manifestly wrong since closed they were though his restless distempered brain denied him the relief of oblivion. Flashes of memories, doubts, hopes, hates and plans stabbed broken splinters of bright light across his sanely fanatical mind and if these had been patterned into coherent thought this would have been the thread of expression it followed:

Help *you* to wealth and the life of easy pleasure that's your ambition, you venal jackal! And help *you* to power and Soviet rule and Universal Brotherhood, you feeble mountebank!... Money! Would millions buy me an hour of happiness? Power! Would any but a clown dream that such as I would give my back to be his stepping stone? Soviets, England, China, India, all the nations and the earth itself; capitalists, bourgeoisie and slaves; man and gods, I hate you equally! Universal Brotherhood! To me—to me!

You dogs, you curs, you fawning, whining, snarling, mongrel, human pack—ah, but I'll use you to my end. Men, women and children—all, all, all alike: nothing to any but a soulless coldblooded, grotesque toad. No man has ever thought of me with friendship, no woman looked at me without a shudder, no child withheld a stone... And I have waited.

Yes, Bronsky, you shall have your way and play your little part, and after you another, bringing you and your tin-pot state crashing to the ground, and after him another to wreck him, and then another, and another, and another, until chaos meets itself right round the earth and civilization is down at last and no one left to laugh...

And yet that blind man was happy and could smile as though he had lost nothing, while I—have I ever really smiled in all my life? No, I've only pulled a sort of grimace to make them think that I was like themselves. But I'll be even with him yet—that blind man who could be happy—and with Bronsky, the hopeless fool, and with Nickle for his cursed impudence, and with Larch and Vallett and Ikey and Klantz and Solomon and that whore Cora and all the other women who have shuddered and everyone I have ever known. I'll show them...

They've all laughed at me behind my back, mocked and pointed and made signs. I'll see them burn, writhe, and shrivel up. I'll live to see it yet, live to shout out that I—Joolby the Toad-have done it. That will be the best of all—when they look up with their foolish, startled faces and understand at last. Then I can go down among them with a sword in my hand, and stab and slash and spit as I always long to. Oh that the whole world had one single body that I might crush it, that I might tear it with my teeth, that I might smash it into atoms!

A sudden crash snatched Won Chou straight out of his dream of a flower-junk on the Canton river. The simple child of the East slept in a rug on the boards of the shop, wearing the dress that was his everyday garb. With stealthy glide he approached the door of his master's room, listened, cautiously peeped in, then entered.

Mr Joolby lay on the floor beside his special chair, his face doubly terrible in its rigid set, his body writhing this way and that with spasmodic jerks and contortions. An epileptic, like many exceptional personages of all times, he was only experiencing a visitation of his "old trouble." Smashed to a thousand bits—brought down in his fall—the wreck of a rare and delicate Dresden china group lay all about him.

Won Chou took the scene in with a face that betrayed no vestige of emotion. Silently and with neat despatch he pushed the heavy chair out of the way, spread a few draperies about the floor, forced a wad of cloth between Mr Joolby's clenched teeth, turned out the light and left him.

6

TILEHURST FAILS TO KEEP AN APPOINTMENT

"Anything interesting among your letters, Geoffrey?" asked Miss Tilehurst, concealing a protective curiosity under this sociable wile, since she had already inspected the covers. And to show how purely conversational the inquiry was, she reciprocally added: "I've had nothing but a long diatribe from Geraldine Churt about her numerous ills. One would really wonder if the foolish woman thinks that her commonplace symptoms are unique or amusing."

"No, nothing particular, Aunt," replied Geoffrey, immediately putting the one letter that mattered away in a coat pocket. Then with the unpractised dissembler's inability to let well—or, indeed, any condition—alone, he must needs elaborate it.

"Just a bill and a couple of appeals and a line from Mostyn about the tournament, and—er—so on. None of them exciting. And, egad, is that the time? I shan't half have to do some hoofing."

"Don't hurry immediately after your breakfast, Geoffrey. You know that clock gains five minutes every day and it's only—" called out Miss Tilehurst, but Geoffrey was technically out of earshot then and the slam of the front door put a full stop to the unfinished monition.

Of course, even if he had not fled, she could not have pursued the subject after his disclaimer—any more than she could have looked into the envelope with the unrecognised handwriting even if he had left it behind with the others now on the table. No—it was as she had guessed—that was the one that he had slipped away. As for the others—there was no harm in just glancing over them since he had said what they were and, for the matter of that, she had known almost as much before he told her. Ellicott's usual bill; Barnardo's Homes and a hospital for the mentally afflicted; a new edition of some encyclopaedia or other; a Dutch bulb grower's list (she had better look through that) and Mr Mostyn's letter. But the one in the unknown script and with a metropolitan post mark—could it be from some London Woman? In spite of having lived in the country all her life and for the most part in remote Devon, Miss Tilehurst had always understood that such beings really existed.

Meanwhile, the subject of her virginal solicitude—perfectly well aware of the clock's chronic lapse—was proceeding on his leisurely way and even finding time to take out the implicated letter again and verify its contents:

Camperdown Hotel,
London.
Friday afternoon.
Dear Tilehurst,
I hope you haven't been thinking me an awful oaf for not writing to thank you for so many jolly games after I left Tapsfield? To tell the truth, I've been expecting to get down one afternoon to say "Good-bye" before I sailed but instead I've been nearly run off my feet every day what with one thing and another. Now to top it all comes a business cable to return at once and I'm going—first part overland—tomorrow.

Now that I am on the point of leaving—with the extreme improbability of ever seeing England again—I seem to recognise how large a share your—may I say, friendship? has had in making my visit so pleasant.

While looking out my route by that mysterious affair, Bradshaw, I have come across a detail that may enable me to salve my conscience—though it is really putting you to more trouble. The point is that instead of going right through by the connecting train (which stops at Stanbury Junction) I shall travel by the one before and break the journey there. This will give me fifteen minutes at Stanbury—from 2.29 to 2.44. If it is not asking too much I wonder if you would cycle across and test the dubious resources of the station refreshment room in a final? I seem to remember that you are not generally particularly engaged so early on Saturday afternoon and the whole affair need scarcely take up more than half an hour.

The fact is, I have a small memento of my stay that I would like to hand over to you if you will graciously accept the trifle. I would also ask you to carry a little offering from me to Miss Tilehurst—not to repay her charming hospitality, which would be impossible, but to remind her now and then of my existence. But please don't tell her anything of this until you are back again; I should like it to be a complete surprise. In fact I wish you wouldn't mention about my going through to anyone until after—there are at least a dozen people I ought to see and although I can't help it I feel somehow guilty.

Sorry that you won't be able to let me know in any case but I shall have left the hotel for good before you get this and for the rest of the time I am bung up to the eyes clearing off arrears.

Of course if you have anything important on you must let me down but unless it's really impossible I know you are too good-natured to disappoint me.

Yours ever gratefully,
Anthony Dixson.

The terms and tone of this communication made Tilehurst experience a passing sense of dereliction also.

Had he really done so frightfully much to earn Dixson's gratitude? Oddly enough, he had scarcely thought of him again, once he had passed on and out of Tapsfield, while the chap had apparently meanwhile been regarding him as his especial friend and mentor. Actually, it might be thought quite as much the other way since Dixson had certainly put him up to the knack of improving his back-hand game considerably. And in return? Well, a few hours' play each week, tea or supper if it happened to be about and an introduction or two so as to give a stranger with plenty of time on his hands somewhere else to go to. Then—yes, he had shown him all over the works, if one could call that entertainment, and certainly these colonial beggars were pretty keen stuff when it came to technical points and wanted to see and know absolutely everything. However, since the fellow looked at it that way, the least that he himself could do would be to push along and meet him. As he said, it would scarcely mean more than half an hour's time, while so early in the afternoon he could hardly expect to encounter Nora Melhuish about if he hung around on the off chance. An opportunity to take Nipper for a good run on a hard road as well—the dog's claws were getting far too long, doing nothing but lying about all day in the garden. Certainly he would meet Dixson.

* * * * *

Nickle had made a wry face over writing the letter but when Joolby told him, dryly enough, to think out a better way, he had to come back to the admission that he could suggest nothing better.

"All the same, it's a dog's trick, getting a man like that," he commented. "I don't mind cutting him out—that's got to be done and it's all in the day's work, but a damned hypocritical letter like this—well, it's about the limit."

"Don't be a fool, Nickle," replied Joolby, glancing equably over the top of the paper as he considered it. "You talk like as if you were an old, established country lawyer arranging a mortgage. And let me tell you that there are good dogs and bad dogs if you think that way about it. The good dogs get the bones and pats and the bad ones get into the lethal chamber at Battersea. Now this is a pretty fair letter."

"Thanks for the pat, kind master," said Nickle contemptuously. "All the same, if it was not for the anticipated bones I might relieve my mind a little."

"If it was not for the bones indeed, Nickle," was the cool reply, "what might we not all—However, these interesting side issues are never worth exploring. What is probably affecting your humour at the moment is a sort of half suspicion that the letter may implicate you personally, eh?"

"Since you mention it, whether I was thinking so or not, it certainly does have that appearance. If it comes to a *sauve qui peut* you fellows may get away but this connects me up past explaining."

"If it comes to a sauve qui peut, Nickle, you'll admit that I should be a slow away-getter. For that reason I don't go into this with the idea of it turning out wrong but in the conviction that it's going to be stupendous. You're a poor psychologist, Nickle, but never mind; we'll get the letter back and wind up Anthony Dixson past all tracing."

* * * * *

While it was reasonably certain that Tilehurst would respond to "Dixson's" bait, while, also, the general progress of his doings could be plausibly assumed, there were crucial details on which it was vital to be exact and arrangements had been made, and were successfully carried out, for following all his movements and for keeping the directing authority informed of each development. These headquarters were represented by a large closed motor car that had taken up a position in the lane which Tilehurst would probably choose if he cycled direct from his house to the station. But since "Brookcroft" lay half a mile outside the village there were in fact two nearly equal routes and almost the last service of the intelligence section, after their man was seen to be committed to the journey, would be to signal by which approach he was to be expected. Nickle had made a choice of lanes but this at the best was only guess-work and the place had to be selected with an eye to the possibility of slipping round, via the station fork, into the other lane and taking up a position there if need be. In the event this obligation did not arise. Blissfully unconscious of the fact that every step he took was being shadowed, Tilehurst trundled his bicycle out by the side gate of Brookcroft soon after two o'clock, called the overjoyed Nipper to follow, and after pausing to glance at his watch and light a cigarette, mounted and began to pedal unhurryingly towards the anticipated lane, with the easy thrust of a man who has just made a substantial meal and knows that he has plenty of time and to spare for his appointment. So far nothing could have been better.

But at the moment when everything was going so well, there came one of those unforeseeable chances that reduce even the most circumspectly arranged plots to the significance of a mere toss-up.

That grassy cut-across lane was deserted enough at any time and in the early afternoon of a hot summer day the chances were a good many to one against the risk of interruption.

Yet as Tilehurst approached it, from the opposite direction appeared Sprout, the village constable, also a-wheel and bound for the same objective. He touched his hat as he turned into the lane and slackening his pace somewhat looked round to see if the other cyclist was following. With the easy social convention of the countryside (when out of doors) Tilehurst would in the ordinary course have caught him up and they would have progressed companionably wheel by wheel for as far as their way lay together, discussing the simpler aspects of Tapsfield existence. Then in a flash Tilehurst realised that Sprout would quite probably refer to Dixson—possibly to ask if he had been heard from since he had gone, or some equally inconvenient question. The predicament need not have been an embarrassing one, and, given minutes instead of seconds to make up his mind, the Joolby-Nickle plot might have very simply miscarried. But in that ambiguous period, the merest trice, allowed him for decision, Tilehurst only visualised the effect of prevaricating to Sprout about Dixson as they rode along and then—possibly under the policeman's disapproving eyes—being greeted on the platform. In the circumstances he jumped at the easiest thing—he drifted past the lane with an amiable wave of recognition, pedalled slowly along until he had given the other man ample time to have gone well away, then turned and leisurely resumed his interrupted progress in the same direction.

* * * * *

The roomy car now drawn up in the secluded lane had been converted to its purpose by bodily removing the inside seats, but with the blinds drawn against a blistering sun there was nothing in this to detract from its otherwise quite ordinary appearance. The spot it occupied had been picked with every consideration under review and though the available choice of road was not unlimited the place conformed well enough to the necessary conditions. It was in fact a short straight piece of ground with a bend at either end and a comparatively long straight piece of road stretching away from it in both directions. Thus, while screened itself until actually reached, anyone there could command the two approaches by walking the score or so of yards that comprised that section.

In this almost sylvan retreat—a wood behind, in front meadows seen through a grille of hedge—the occupants of the car had decided to halt and picnic, and a real table-cloth spread on the grass by the roadside indicated the thoroughness of the occasion. This development had several effects: it enabled the road to be almost blocked and anyone who passed to be constrained into a desired channel, it explained the presence of as many people lolling about as were required for the venture, and, above all, it allowed the car and its party to remain in that not otherwise very explicable spot for hours if necessary without arousing a scintilla of suspicion.

This was the carefully spread net that Geoffrey Tilehurst approached after he had given P.C. Sprout—his one chance of escape—ample time to get clear of participation. He almost tumbled upon the guileless tableau: the drawn-up car, the two men and the girl talking and laughing around the "table," the third man—and this reduced his leisured pace still more for it was questionable which side he must pass on—the third man moving about what was left open of the roadway. Then this man appeared suddenly to realise his presence, for instead of standing aside he remained obstructively where he was, interrogation in his poise, and Tilehurst understood that he wanted to stop him.

The motor "bandit" had not yet arrived and there was no more on the surface of the incident than if you or I had been asked for a match in Piccadilly. The cyclist obligingly pulled up (indeed, by that time he had no option), dropped one foot to the ground and waited for the inquiry.

"I say, I'm awfully sorry to trouble you like this but we haven't the murkiest idea of where we've got to. Do you mind telling me where we really are?"

"Oh, yes," came a feminine voice from the other side the car. "Do get to know, Tommy. It's about time we pushed off if we're to do any bathing."

Tilehurst was one of those amiable creatures who find an altruistic pleasure in performing these small services—telling the time and the way, guiding a blind beggar across the road, recovering a lost ball, making up the penny deficiency in the bus fare for old ladies who have somehow miscalculated their resources. If he gave a thought to the one weakness of the contrivance—for why had they not asked Sprout, that obvious official fount of information?—he at once dismissed it as capable of some very simple explanation.

"Well, it's about a mile and a half to Tapsfield along the lane," he replied, turning to nod in the required direction. "The way I'm going will bring you to the cross-road near Stanbury Junction and on to Crowgate or Slowcumber according to which you take. Or, of course, back to Tapsfield if you turn sharp at the Dog and Plover."

"Ask him—ask him where we *are*," chimed in the girl's voice again. "I don't know that we're actually pining to get to any of those earthly paradises he's mentioned."

The spokesman smiled apologetically. "You see what it is," said the look, establishing the male understanding. Then aloud: "I wish you'd just pick out the place on the map for us; I've got one here quite handy." Without waiting for the implied assent he opened the near door of the car and disappeared within, reappearing a moment later with a large road map that he spread out, but remaining just inside the car himself so that it became necessary for Tilehurst to go nearer.

One of the other men had meanwhile strolled round and the way was still barred—to use so harsh a term about so fortuitous a happening—against escape in that direction. And now the last man in sight got up from the sward, apparently taking a handkerchief from his pocket to brush stray crumbs away, and casually passing round the car on the unguarded side closed the trap at its final outlet. Still every face had the conventional, agreeable air of those who are being obliged, the girl just across the road began to carol a little popular snatch lightly, and "Tommy," at the car step, following the line of his own finger was murmuring: "Now let me see; we are—where?" as he travelled halfway across the county waiting for the obliging stranger to inform him.

Tilehurst knew that he had plenty of time to the good and he did exactly what had been foreseen he would do. In any case the result would have been the same then, although the details might not have dovetailed quite so workmanly. He swung himself wholly out of his bicycle, propped up the machine against the car wheel and turned to the open door to point out the position on the map now held out towards him. The man with the handkerchief was immediately behind, intending seemingly to look on as well. The third man... The map was a large limp sheet and Tilehurst was constrained to put out both hands to receive it.

What actually happened he never quite knew himself, for the universe of conscious thought rushed to extinction at one unbearably crowded point and afterwards everything to do with that episode was dim and tangled. But in the other participants' sight it was far from being confused, for every detail had been carefully considered and rehearsed and each one did his part in perfect time and precision. "Tommy," holding out the map, closed with a rat-trap grip on the wrists of the two hands coming towards him; the saturated cloth was pressed against Tilehurst's nose and mouth; the other man, practising the simple schoolboy stroke, brought their victim to his knees on the running-board, as helpless as a ditched wether among the three men crowding round him. The girl continued to sing about love and undying devotion. In fifteen seconds the anaesthetic had done its work and the inert body was cleanly lifted into the car, to be stripped, reclothed, bound, gagged and left, covered with rugs, unconscious on the floor. It would scarcely be too much to say that people might have gone by without noticing that anything unusual was happening.

Three minutes later an identical Tilehurst emerged from the car; the others paused in their orderly work—they were removing every tell-tale trace and preparing for return—to inspect him critically.

"Oh, boy, but you sure look some!" was drawn from one in frank approval. "Now that you're in his togs the guy's own mother wouldn't suspish you."

It was possible indeed, but there was one small faithful friend who was not to be duped by clothes or outward appearance. Nipper, having taken the opportunity of his master's inattention to engage in a private rat hunt along a drain, had voluntarily returned, and after puzzling over the situation unnoticed from several points of view, had abruptly decided that there was dirty work afoot and this spuriosity the villain. Uttering foolishly futile yaps of challenge—his sure undoing—Nipper heroically launched himself against the foe, only to be met by a straight deliberate kick that sent him reeling. Before the little dog could collect himself again Vallett had snatched up the readiest tool—a weighty spanner—and with a single vicious blow had settled ail Nipper's doubt and questionings for ever. Four white upraised paws quivered protestingly to heaven, the body shuddered, and a dead dog with a battered skull lay on the reddening herbage. In that moment one seemed to have a glimpse of the cool and desperate convict who had got away from Dartmoor, despite warders' loaded guns, in place of the smiling Vallett.

"Damn you, you brute! Why need you go and do that?" shrilled the girl, suddenly whirled into a flimsy passion. "I'd have taken the little dog and looked after it myself—I'd have loved to... Bloody fine thing being able to out a great big beast like him, I should think...bloody well proud of yourself, aren't you?" For quite half a minute she slanged aimlessly on while the others looked at her with no more than grave disapproval. To tell the truth, the unforeseen tragedy of the loyal little terrier had got them all more than anything that had gone before.

"That'll do, kid; shut up your face now, you've shed plenty," said one of the men with brusque understanding. "Vallett did quite right; the pup was bound to go and that's all that's to it. Rip off the collar, Pips, and shove the rest under some stuff in the wood there."

"Yes, but what'n they find it there?" questioned the man who had used the drug, as he carefully handled the body. "These country birds know all the dogs for miles around so shifting the collar won't help any."

"What the hell then? It's all of a piece, isn't it? Besides, they most likely won't—get it well away into a thick scrub and it'll likely be there for months before that happens. Now, buddy,"—this to Vallett—"Number two's coming in and he'll go on and give Soapy the nod and then pass it back on you when Soapy's planted. We're through here?"

"Not quite," said Vallett, who had apparently been dreaming. "I feel that I ought to carry some marks. The artistic sense demands it. Put me one fairly high—you needn't black an eye or tap the claret—but something that'll show a bruise for the next few days anyhow."

"You mean it?"

"Didn't I speak?" inquired Vallett politely. The other smiled a dour aside and with a clean crisp right laid the artistic conscience sprawling on the level. He got up with no loss of graciousness, dusting his clothes, but on second thoughts left them as they were, to infer the happening.

"Oh my God!" wailed the girl, looking on with tightly clasped hands. Vallett didn't deign to notice.

"Satisfied?" grinned the big man.

"That will do for that I expect but I think I ought to show some scratches." Going to the hedge he selected and hacked out a bramble switch and brought it back; its curved thorns were as formidable as a wild cat's claws. "Put that across my face, will you?"

"Don't!" This time the kid rose to a scream of anguish. "I take it all back about the dog. He had to go I see. Only don't—"

"You?" cut in Vallett with elegant disdain. "What in all creation have *you* got to do with it?"

"I know well enough," she blubbered. "You think you're paying me out—"

"Get on with it," said Vallett curtly. "Shut your eyes then," advised the other, taking the switch, and this time he was not grinning. "I don't want to go and blind you."

"Keep your own open and then you won't," was the unconcerned reply. "I have nothing to shut mine for."

"Look out then." The cane slashed across mouth and cheeks and a dozen points of blood followed the thorns' withdrawal. Vallett forbore to wince. The girl ran back to the car making curious noises.

7

DR OLIVANT ESTABLISHES HIS BONA FIDES

At about the hour when an unobtrusive motor car (its number plate varied for the third time that eventful day) was taking its turn through Reigate, with Mr Geoffrey Tilehurst—now sufficiently recovered to feel extremely sick—a very helpless passenger, and while in Hoggets Lane Mr Vallett was, to use a peculiarly inappropriate metaphor, "cooling his heels" as he awaited an agreed signal, the sun went off the rose bed in the Brookcroft trim front garden and Miss Tilehurst, armed with leather gloves, sheep shears and a Sussex trug, came out to carry on the unending warfare that exists between man (as represented in the amateur gardener) and relentless nature.

"Yes, of course; just as might have been expected," she declared after scrutinising the roses. "Teeming with green fly—and our rates are seven-and-sixpence in the pound! Ophelia!"

It is, to be sure, impossible to predict what lines of growth a child will take from the evidence of, say, the first seven days, and there have been Ophelias and Ophelias. This one, the offspring of an ill-assorted union between a pig higgler and an idealistic lady's maid, clearly belonged to the second variety.

Other mistresses—and the girl had experienced a remarkable succession of these before Miss Tilehurst penetratingly discovered in her certain solid qualities (in the sense of "dense" to most employers) that covered many shortcomings—other mistresses had invariably called her by what they considered more suitable names, generally Jane or Sarah, without reference to her own feelings. Penelope Tilehurst questioned whether this was "quite right" and on the other interested party's vague justification that "some thought one thing and some another," severely retorted that this was not the point and that in any case Ophelia—with appropriate instances—was nothing to be ashamed of.

Ophelia had a way of anticipating wants when she was called. If right, she had discovered that this was regarded as rather clever, but if it happened to be wrong there was no doubt that she was being very stupid. Privately, she thought that a simpler average should be struck, but, any way, she was like that she admitted. She now appeared carrying a filled watering can and, as this happened to be right, she felt that she had established her position sufficiently to remain and sociably discuss botanical prospects.

"That Mrs Buffy I was with was a rare 'un for gardening too," she remarked as a general opening. "Only she was all for snapdragers. Funny she shouldn't know their proper name, wasn't it, mm? She always used to call them Auntie Rhinos."

"Yes, Ophelia, but I shall want several more cans to go on this bed," replied Miss Tilehurst discouragingly. "You had better get the other one out as well and keep bringing them."

"That I will, mum." Hard work had no terror for the simple girl, especially when, as in the present case, it involved nothing with a tendency to "just come apart," and contained easy openings for agreeable conversation. "Oh; what had we better say if they catch us at it?"

"What's that?" demanded Miss Tilehurst sharply. "What do you mean, Ophelia?"

"It's the notice what that man left—I forgot to give it you," explained Ophelia, producing a crumpled printed form from the mysterious depths of her apron pocket. "It says that owing to the draft we shall be incurring a penalty of forty shillings for the first offence and not exceeding fourteen days ever after."

"Nonsense." Miss Tilehurst had a sublime faith in the personal equation, which sometimes worked out but occasionally failed to be quite so successful. "That can't apply to me of course. I pay a water rate and anyone can see that the garden needs watering. Put the notice in the fire and then I shall be able to say truthfully that I haven't seen it."

"That I will, mum," undertook Ophelia stoutly.

"And—wait a minute, Ophelia; don't run away, child, when I'm in the middle of speaking. There's someone doing something in the lane out by the side gate—that tinkering has been going on for the past half hour. On your way back just glance out there—you needn't let it appear that you've gone on purpose: you can seem to be looking up the lane as if you expected the baker."

"He doesn't come till later of a Saturday," objected Ophelia, entering into the spirit of the strategy perhaps even too precisely.

"That doesn't matter in the least. They are not to know or you may be looking for the butcher. But if there are gipsies or tinmen about we shall have to keep our eyes open after anything they can lay their hands on."

Of course it was Ophelia's fault; she ought to have come back with a more coherent tale, but when on her return with the second can she breathlessly reported, "...the man. Something about water. And—look out, mum, he's coming!" Miss Tilehurst not unnaturally jumped—quite literally, indeed—to the conclusion that this man must be identical with "that man" and the reference to water was only capable of one construction. In spite of her assurance of personal immunity from the obnoxious order it began to look more serious when this emissary of injustice would seem to have deliberately tracked her down, and it was her rather frantic efforts to conceal her own can among the rose bushes on his approach, and at the same time to induce Ophelia by vigorous gestures to retire in good order with the other, that prevented her from grasping at the outset exactly what it was that the stranger was talking about.

"I wonder if I might trouble you?" was what he really said. "I see you are busy with it yourself—just a small can of water?" Quite a personable individual he appeared to be—dignified, well-dressed, urbane, and he advanced doffing his distinctive hat with a ceremonialism that could not have failed to impress Miss Tilehurst if she had been composed enough to realise it.

"Oh no, indeed I'm not—I can assure you that I never use a watering can in the garden," she exclaimed, rather remarkably in the circumstances; meaning, as she afterwards assured herself, that she was not actually using one *then* and that in any case she only watered certain special beds and did not—as so many thoughtless people did—waste precious canfulls drenching the entire garden.

"I—I beg your pardon." The intruder was, not altogether unnaturally, for the moment nonplussed by the denial he had occasioned, but this did not in the least affect the magnificent composure of his bearing. "The fact is," he deigned to explain with gracious allowance for any misunderstanding, "my chauffeur happens to be away ill and I'm having some bother with my engines and being held up just outside your gate here."

"Oh. Oh? Oh!" apologised Miss Tilehurst on several notes of emotion. "Then you are not the—er—the water authority?"

"Madam," he affably admitted, with the light touch of a playful buffalo, "I am no authority on water in any form—not even, I regret to find, on the water cooling my own car engines.

I'm afraid that my intrusion rather startled you—I ought to have been more explicit. At least permit me to establish my bona fides before I go. My name is Olivant—Dr Olivant of Harley Street, I am merely a stranger, you see, motoring through your charming district and having, so to speak, fallen by the wayside—"

"Oh, Dr Olivant, I *am* so sorry," protested the lady, deeply mortified at the unfortunate blunder.

"Of course now that I really look at you—" and, without actually being so bold as to put the inference into words, Miss Tilehurst made it abundantly clear that in her opinion no one who really looked at him could by any chance take Dr Olivant for anything resembling a water inspector. "But seriously, you know, in this water famine the company is driving us half crazy with its absurd prohibitions and regulations. That," she explained, speaking with extreme clarity and deliberation, "is what I meant just now when I said that a watering can is never much use in the garden. Of course it needs the hose pipe to be effective."

"Oh, of course—naturally," agreed Dr Olivant. "And they don't permit—"

"Oh my goodness no! It would be a crime of"—the situation had gone a little to her head—"ha! ha! Dr Olivant, a crime of the first water!"

"Ha! ha!" weightily confirmed Dr Olivant. "Very apt, indeed. 'A crime of the first water!' I must tell my colleague, Sir Peter Mullaby, that. He'll appreciate it."

"And I—ahem!—hear," added Miss Tilehurst, determined to clear her conscience thoroughly by the white fire of voluntary confession, "that very soon we *may* not be allowed to use even a watering can."

"Really?" contributed the doctor, suitably impressed. "In the circumstances I scarcely like to repeat my request for a small canful."

"Oh nonsense, Dr Olivant; it hasn't quite come to that yet. Ophelia—give Dr Olivant the can you have. Will that be sufficient for your purpose, Doctor?"

"Oh, quite I think. Thank you; thank you. I won't keep it a minute longer than I can help, I need hardly say."

"Pray don't hurry. And if you should want any more—Of course"—as he reached the gate—"you unscrew the nozzle for pouring."

"Oh quite so," he acquiesced. Really, did the woman take him for a loon or was it that she only wanted to hear the sound of her own silly tongue clacking?

In the circumstances Miss Tilehurst decided to go on gardening there—not watering, which would take Ophelia off her work and could be done equally well later, but just tidying up the beds.

Then if Dr Olivant should happen to need—

A most distinguished-mannered gentleman—a specialist, of course, being in Harley Street—and how immeasurably different from the usual type of country doctor! Dr Tyser, for instance, was well enough but ineradicably commonplace, while this locum tenens he had just got—well, it was *said* that he had been seen buying fried fish himself at one of those malodorous little places in Mutbury. The idea of Dr Olivant going into—

"Coo-ee!" said a voice in playful claim of recognition.

"Well, well; I wondered if you would run round this afternoon, Nora. How long have you been there? I never heard you coming."

Nora Melhuish was, it may be recalled, the speculative element in the time-table of Tilehurst's arrangements, and now that we have been permitted to see her the only possible slur on his taste is that he should have taken even the most infinitesimal risk of missing so delectable an encounter. For the rest, she was nineteen, rather small, rather brown, and rather mysterious in her impressions. On this occasion she wore neither hat nor gloves but carried a moderate basket, and as she had come into the garden by the front, or road, gate and along the further path she had evidently failed to encounter the prepossessing specialist.

"Oh, not long," replied Nora as they went through the ritual of kissing. "Only I heard you talking to someone so I slunk. Who is he?"

"A Dr Olivant—a Harley Street specialist, or at least I suppose he must be. At any rate his car has broken down just outside there and he wanted some water."

"That's what everyone seems to be wanting just now—I feel I'm getting it on the brain myself. Mrs Hattock says that the vicar is doubtful if he ought to go on praying for rain any longer—it seems to be making a fool of him when nothing happens."

"Oh, my dear! Isn't that rather—I mean for a clergyman?"

"Well, perhaps it is but they certainly seem to be getting much more snappy. Are you watering the roses? Haven't they cut off your supply yet?"

"Good gracious no. Are they going to?"

"They say so—all except an hour or two night and morning. And someone goes round listening at those little trap-door affairs in the road to catch you wasting any. And then fine you."

"Can they tell that? My dear! what next? And here that tiresome Ophelia is bringing out another canful! Take that back again at once, Ophelia, and don't draw any more."

"All right," acquiesced the impassive Ophelia. "Good afternoon, miss. Just stepped across to see if we were all alive still? Shall I put this lot on the beans, mum?"

"No, we haven't got to waste any. Pour it down the sink quickly."

"That I will, mum." A rather constrained silence marked the time until Ophelia was out of hearing. "Of course I'm glad to find you alive but I really ran across with a few pears if you care to have them," remarked Nora, displaying the contents of her basket. "Jargonelles. We've got heaps and heaps and I know that yours are all the late kinds."

"Thank you, dear. They look delicious. You must let me reciprocate towards Christmas. But how did you know that ours are only keepers?"

"Oh I don't know. Oh yes I do. Geoffrey must have told me."

"I see. 'You plant pears; For your heirs.' Well, whoever planted ours must have credited his posterity with remarkably good teeth. And speaking of that young man, you didn't happen to see anything of Geoffrey as you came along, did you?"

"No; isn't he here?" said Nora. "I expected to find—At least I thought—What I mean is, if we happen to meet and neither of us is doing anything—"

"That's all right, my dear," said Geoffrey's adopted mother, "—at least I hope that it's going to be. And I'm glad it's you, Nora. It will make me very happy."

"Oh, Miss Tilehurst, do you really mean that you've noticed anything? I thought that we were both being extraordinarily discreet, and for that matter, he—Geoffrey—hasn't actually said anything."

"No; I noticed that you were both rather tongue-tied of late," commented Miss Tilehurst dryly. "Well, my dear, if I am to lose my only nephew—and of course I know that in a place like this a young man's fancy must turn sooner or later to thoughts of either love or golf—I prefer it to be you."

"Oh, you are a dear!" exclaimed Nora, who has been placed at a considerable disadvantage by being introduced just at this stage of her florescence. "It would have been too awful if you hadn't—"

"It's so very handy you living just over the way," continued Miss Tilehurst, pursuing her own line of speculation. "At least I shall always know where to find him."

"Well," laughed Nora, "that's one way of looking at it. But I hope that isn't the only reason."

"No," admitted Miss Tilehurst circumstantially. "Still, it's a great convenience all the same."

"And please, please, don't let Geoffrey know that we have been talking—"

"My dear! I'm not an absolute beginner. I can't think where he can have got to."

"Why; where did he go?"

"That's just what I don't know. He must have gone off somewhere immediately after lunch without saying anything about it. He may have ridden across to Cobbet Corner to see about some repairs to a few cottages I have there, or he may have gone to arrange some details of the Gymkhana Tournament with Mr Mostyn who'd written to him this morning. But's it's so unlike him not to mention what time to expect him back or where he was going—especially on a day when you might drop in and miss him."

"But of course he wouldn't have the faintest idea that I should be here, Miss Tilehurst," protested Nora. "Why, I had no idea of it myself until I happened to think—"

"Well," dubiously agreed Miss Tilehurst, "perhaps he wouldn't. All the same I had a strong presentiment that way myself and there is no reason why the state of his emotions should make him less intelligent."

"Perhaps Ophelia saw which way he went," suggested Nora. "She's just gone across to the coal house."

"It's quite as likely she asked him where he was going if she did," declared Miss Tilehurst grimly.

"At any rate it won't be difficult to find out. I'll warrant she only wanted coal on the chance of a little small talk. Oh, Ophelia; Mr Geoffrey doesn't happen to have come in at the back while we've been here, does he?"

"No, mum, or I should have seen him... He got his bicycle out after lunch and went off with Nipper... He didn't say where he was going... When I just said: 'Going out for a ride on your bicycle, Mr Geoffrey?' he said: 'No, Ophelia, I'm going for a three-legged race only I like to wear this on my watch chain.' I thought it sounded funny."

Presumably Nora thought so too for she found it necessary to turn aside and bury her face in a crimson rambler. Miss Tilehurst found it less amusing.

"Thank you, Ophelia; that will do. Tell him we are out here if he does return that way."

"Yes, mum." Ophelia appeared to weigh the conditions with conscientious detail. "You mean if he returns in a three-legged race?"

"No, no. If he returns without our seeing him—if he comes in the back way."

"Oh yes. That I will, mum."

Ophelia retired in the full assurance that this must be one of her good days as she was acquitting herself so successfully and at intervals snatches of her voice could be heard, subdued by the occasional clatter or bang of domestic zeal, as she confided all that was going on to the cat—sole confidant of her deeper feelings.

"Isn't she too dreadful?" lamented Miss Tilehurst, as Ophelia disappeared towards the house. "But she's really such a good, well-meaning girl that I can't find it in my heart to be strict with her."

"No, indeed; it would spoil a gem—think of all the priceless things you'd miss hearing. But, you know, if Geoffrey is trundling a pushbike on a day like this, that might easily account for him not getting back as soon as he had intended."

"True; I expect that's what it is. And speaking of bicycles, Nora, who was the young lady I saw dashing about the road on a motor cycle when I looked out at five o'clock this morning?"

"Well, what's the use of your brother having a motor bike if you can't practise on it when he's away? It's about the only chance I do get."

"Oh? This is the first I've heard of you taking it up at all. I'm not an authority, I suppose, for I've always been accustomed to regard even a foot tricycle as rather an advanced form of propulsion for a woman but you struck me as being remarkably capable for a learner."

"I am," admitted Nora, with what could only be described as a knowing grin; "—but please don't let on to anyone about it. I mean to surprise them one of these days."

"Them?"

"Yes, all at home—oh, my word! my poor wits must indeed be wool- gathering! Do you know what I came across for?"

"Well," replied Miss Tilehurst, with a spice of affectionate malice, "feminine intuition might be equal to the problem. Put into cold words I should say that you came—not to see Geoffrey, of course, but to afford him the unutterable pleasure of contemplating Miss Melhuish."

"Not at all—that may have been why I came perhaps, but it wasn't what I came for. In spite of that truly feline stroke, dear Miss Tilehurst, I came to do you a kindness. Well, you know all about Uncle Max of course—you've always said how you wished to meet him."

"What—Mr Carrados?"

"Yes, Uncle Max Carrados. Well, he turned up all unexpected this morning in his usual eccentric way. Shall I bring him across for an hour now? I would have done straight off but I thought you'd like to know he was coming."

"Yes indeed," agreed Miss Tilehurst, rather fluttered at the prospect. "I should certainly be glad of a few minutes to make myself a little more presentable. But do you think that he would really care—?" and with almost tragic eloquence the disparaging hands indicated the circumscribed garden in which they stood, the unpretentious little villa.

"But whatever do you mean? Why shouldn't he?"

"Well, I should be overjoyed by the honour of course but I mean—wouldn't it be rather dull for him? I feel that there ought to be something rather special going on to bring him here for—only there never is for that matter."

"Oh nonsense, dear. Isn't he with us now, and what's the difference? He doesn't spend every day of his life tracking murderers down and bearding robbers in their dens. Although he's so jolly well off—and rather clever, I suppose—he's really the simplest old dear in the world."

"Old?" The word was rather startling to Miss Tilehurst. "I didn't know that Mr Carrados was at all elderly."

"Oh yes. He must be quite forty now. That's getting on pretty well in years, I should think."

"Yes, I suppose it is," admitted Miss Tilehurst with a backward glance. "It certainly once seemed so. I'll tell you what we'll do to make it something special, Nora: we'll have tea out in the arbour over there. That will be quite like a picnic, won't it, and Geoffrey is certain to be back in time to join us."

"Splendid!" agreed Nora, already on her way towards the gate; "I'll dig out Uncle Max and we'll dash back in no time."

"But you'll give me just a few minutes to—I'm in the middle of gardening you know; I feel an awful fright," pleaded Miss Tilehurst who was rooted in a more ceremonial age when important visitors were not flung upon one "in no time."

"Right you are—will twenty minutes do? Oh no; never mind the old basket now—I'll take it later on. Cheerio!"

"Splendid!" endorsed Miss Tilehurst to herself as another gate, fifty yards away, reverberated on its sorely tried hinges. "But how very strenuous!"

8

MAX CARRADOS BECOMES INTERESTED IN TRIFLES

With twenty minutes—which probably meant half an hour in the end—up her sleeve so to speak, Miss Tilehurst felt that she had the situation well in hand, and she even stayed to finish off her work of cutting out the faded roses from the central bed before she gathered everything into the Sussex trug and began to think of her own preparations. Otherwise she might have missed Dr Olivant on his second incursion into her domain and although the interest of the afternoon had shifted materially with the arrangement for Mr Carrados's visit, it was not to be denied that the doctor—whom even nineteen would scarcely presume to call old—cut a very personable figure.

"I am returning the watering can with very many thanks," he said in the ceremonious way which Miss Tilehurst thought so distinguished, "but I am afraid that you will think me no end of a nuisance. I find now that if I am to do any good I shall have to borrow a hammer."

"Well, I fancy that the resources of my establishment may be even equal to that," replied Miss Tilehurst with the sort of smile which so arch a reply demanded. "At all events, if you will wait here a minute—"

"I feel that I am giving you a great deal of trouble."

"So far I haven't observed it. And in any case you aren't doing now since my very exceptional maid is evidently hovering about on the chance of being useful. She has the remarkable quality, Dr Olivant," confided Miss Tilehurst, holding up a beckoning finger in Ophelia's direction, "of generally being there if she is wanted—or, indeed, if she is not wanted. Ophelia, bring this gentleman a hammer, will you? I expect that you'll find one in the kitchen table drawer."

"That I will, mum," replied Ophelia, dashing off like a young mustang.

In the circumstances it did not seem quite nice to Miss Tilehurst to leave one who might be technically regarded as a guest standing there alone. Ophelia could be trusted to be back, as she would herself declare, "in half a jiffy," and the doctor would be equal to the conversational moment.

"What a lovely old-English kind of garden you have," he dutifully remarked. "Flowers are a passion of mine, but of course in Harley Street—" a melancholy shake of the head dismissed that famous but unhorticultural thoroughfare from the landscape.

"At all events you shall have one for your button-hole now, Doctor," said Miss Tilehurst, sacrificing a promising young Betty Uprichard without the least compunction. "Yes, it is rather flourishing, but of course this dreadful drought—Still, if you are going for a holiday I don't suppose that you will complain on the score of fine weather."

"I am hoping to reach Eastbourne tonight. Even a doctor—even a nerve specialist—has to knock off now and then—Mrs—er?"

"Tilehurst, Doctor. *Miss* Tilehurst."

"Miss Tilehurst? Curious. A very old patient of mine—Sir Bellamy Binge—had a sister who married—"

"Here you are, sir," interposed Ophelia, breaking upon this momentous reminiscence and thrusting a decidedly infirm-looking tool into the doctor's hand. "Don't think you've gone and done it if the head flies off when you're hitting. It often does."

"Oh, Ophelia," said her mistress in some concern, "surely we have a better—"

"This will do capitally, my dear Miss Tilehurst, I do assure you," professed Olivant. "The strain I shall put upon it is not likely to result in any disaster," and since Miss Tilehurst was not anxious to detain him if it really would do, he retired again to grapple with the intricacies of his car in the quiet side lane while she took the opportunity of apprising Ophelia of the variation in their usual routine as they went up to the house together.

"We shall be having tea in the summer-house this afternoon, Ophelia. Miss Melhuish is bringing a gentleman here and I want to have things a little different."

"Tea in the summer-house, mum! That will be nice, won't it?" Ophelia was intrigued, visibly impressed, but also inconveniently reminded. "Did you ever have tea in a hay-field, mum? I did once and you wouldn't believe—"

"No—yes, but never mind that just now, Ophelia. This gentleman who is coming is blind and so I want you to be very careful."

"That I will, mum. Does he have a toby dog, I wonder?"

"Dog?" repeated Miss Tilehurst vaguely.

"Yes, to lead him about the street. Most of them do. Mother had an Uncle Billy—"

"You must tell me about your mother's uncle—er—William another time—I want you to get on with your work now. Mr Carrados has an attendant, not a dog, but I do not imagine that he will bring him here. Now change as quickly as you can and then put out the things in the kitchen ready."

"Were you meaning to use the company tea set out there—the little old cups with blue and gold things on them?"

"Yes, the Crown Derby service—and please *do* be careful with them, Ophelia. Then you had better cut both white and brown bread-and-butter, some very thin anchovy paste and cucumber sandwiches, and we will have quince jelly and strawberry jam and for cake cherry and almond."

"I say!" murmured Ophelia.

"Anything else I will see to myself and I will look in at the kitchen between now and then to make sure that you have all the things ready. And, by the way, Ophelia, you may as well put out cups and so on for five—one never knows; someone else may drop in."

* * * * *

"You know that I am bringing Uncle Max, don't you, Miss Tilehurst dear? And you know that you are coming to Miss Tilehurst's, don't you, Uncle Max dear? So surely that's enough. I think formal introductions are frightfully stuffy."

Miss Tilehurst, with everything going well, had been out in the front garden again when her visitors appeared. Visualising Mr Carrados's arrival she had rather dreaded the ceremony of getting the blind man into a chair in her crowded little drawing-room and almost immediately getting him out again. On a day like that nothing seemed more natural than to be sauntering about the lawn, and then they could stroll round the garden until tea appeared. After all, what was the good of taking a man who could not see into a drawing-room?

Both laughed as they shook hands but Miss Tilehurst felt that she had been defrauded of something that she had looked forward to by Nora's offhand manner, and she was glad that Mr Carrados took the occasion to rebuke his niece—though of course it was done in the nicest possible manner.

"I am afraid that the rising generation thinks a great deal that we used to set considerable store by 'frightfully stuffy,'" he remarked mildly. "I say 'we' hoping that Miss Tilehurst sides with me."

"So it was, Uncle Max," retorted Nora. "Ghastly stodgy. Family pride and great fat dinners and social tradition. All that hank and bunk and tosh and spludge. Sickening."

"Well, my dear, I hope that I am not too old to learn even yet. I must begin with the New Vocabulary."

"It is not we who are too old to learn, Mr Carrados; it's they who are too young to understand," put in Miss Tilehurst a shade tartly. "Now would you care to walk round the garden and see—oh, forgive me! I—I—"

"You pay me a great compliment, Miss Tilehurst," said Carrados reassuringly. "Already you treat me as an ordinary human being, you see, not as a helpless log. That is what I want people simply to do—flatter me that I'm not a nuisance. Certainly I should like to go round your garden and perhaps I shall not miss much. Here, for instance, at the very start there is something that I haven't come across for years"—he turned to the rose bed near which they had been standing and indicated a particular bush—"you can only find this in an old-established garden nowadays. I hear that it's quite gone out of fashion."

"Why, is there anything special about it?" demanded Nora. "It looks a very ordinary sort of flower as far as that goes."

"Nothing but its extreme rarity: it would almost seem as though modern conditions kill it. Miss Tilehurst knows what it is, I'll be bound. Don't you see: she's laughing?"

"Oh go on, have your little joke, my dears," said Nora benignly. "What is the great scream anyway? I know you're dying to tell me."

"It's only an old-fashioned cabbage-rose, Nora, and it's called The Maiden's Blush. The curious thing is that it has become almost extinct for some reason."

"Ha! Ha!" Nora affected a mechanical laugh such as is current in the schoolroom to express non-amusement. "But there are still red cabbages about. They are the sort that get into pickles."

"Both sorts have their points no doubt. There was a bush of this against the porch of our old home when I was a boy—"

"Now, now, Uncle; if you are going to wax sentimental over a cabbage—well, a cabbage-rose or a rose-cabbage, I don't mind—whatever will you be like when we get to the horse-radishes? Come along, old dear," she prompted, taking his arm affectionately; "I think Miss Tilehurst wants to speak to someone for a minute."

It was, as might be guessed, the punctilious Olivant come to return the tool, for surely it would be extravagant to suggest that he could have any interest in looking into the circumstance of these fresh arrivals in Miss Tilehurst's garden. Nor is it to be assumed that the lady herself had any wish to neglect him, for instead of pleading her guests to get off with a perfunctory "Oh, thank you," she sent them on ahead, saying: "Excuse me just a moment, please. Take Mr Carrados along, won't you, Nora?" and waited for the doctor.

"May I thank you and return the hammer?" he said, with his usual air of raising even the slightest act into a courtly ceremony. "You will be relieved to hear that there was no untoward mishap."

Uncle and niece had sauntered on but at the first words of that distinctive voice Nora found herself gently detained as Mr Carrados paused to "look at" a fine dahlia.

"Who is our friend over there?" he asked, dropping his voice to a discreet whisper.

"Oh, he isn't anybody—I mean he doesn't live about here," she replied, with the same precaution. "Some London doctor or other. Elephant? No, Olivant, a Harley Street specialist she said. That's his car come to grief in the side lane."

"Ah." There must have been some incautious quality in his tone for Nora fastened on the simple interjection.

"Why 'Ah' fraught with all that portent, old dear? You don't happen to know him, do you?"

"I don't know any Dr Olivant, Nora."

"Well then, you don't know him. Why won't you say so in a plain straightforward manner, Uncle Max? I'm afraid you're getting to be rather too fond of being mysterious when there's nothing at all to make a mystery out of."

"Yes, possibly it is becoming a habit with me, my dear," he admitted. "I must reform or I shall become the very worst sort of back number."

"*Dear* Uncle Max!" murmured Nora happily. Life was all such an enchanting game, wasn't it?

* * * * *

Meanwhile, Miss Tilehurst, having received the hammer with due relief, was furthering the little idea that had occurred to her in the kitchen.

"If you don't actually need to drive off immediately, Dr Olivant, perhaps you would take a cup of tea with us before you go on? We shall be having it out here very simply on the lawn presently."

"You are really extremely kind, Miss Tilehurst. I should certainly enjoy a cup of tea after my exertions."

"We are only waiting for my nephew to get back—and if he is much longer we must perforce begin without him. Would about ten minutes—?"

"Admirably for me. I think I've located the trouble but I haven't quite put it right yet."

"Then that is settled," she confirmed. "I will let you know when tea is ready."

* * * * *

"Isn't it really too bad of Geoffrey just on this of all afternoons?" lamented Miss Tilehurst after she had consulted her ancient gold watch for the fifth time within ten minutes. "I can only suppose that he has met someone who has inveigled him in for a few games of tennis."

"Not likely—if he didn't go out in flannels," objected Nora. "Ten to one that he has drifted back to that utterly rancid old office to put some extra work in. On a day like this too!"

"Nora!" exclaimed Miss Tilehurst almost severely—the family woman's inherent reverence for the source of bread-and-butter—"the office is his business. My nephew, Mr Carrados," she explained, "is connected with the paper mills here where they make the Bank of England note paper. It is, of course, a highly responsible position."

"Yes," agreed Carrados, "naturally—where they make the Bank of England note paper. And how extraordinarily interesting his work there must be. Has he to do directly with the paper when it's made or is his department purely clerical?"

"That I cannot say—except that I know millions of pounds worth of bank-note paper is at times in some way in his keeping. I'm afraid you'll think me dreadfully ignorant, Mr Carrados, but I understand very little about such things and to tell the truth I have always scrupulously refrained from seeming to pester Geoffrey with questions about business."

They were gathering raspberries into cabbage leaves then, Miss Tilehurst having asked Carrados if he cared for them with cream and having received an enthusiastic admission. She now proceeded to assemble all their spoil on the largest leaf and was surprised to notice that the blind man's contribution to the stock was rather more than either her own or Nora's. Not for the first time that day she wondered secretly whether it was not all an elaborate piece of bluff, with Mr Carrados able to see just as well as she could. Others beside Miss Tilehurst had in the past experienced a similar misgiving.

"I think we have reached the limit of our patience now; Geoffrey must put up with 'husband band's tea' when he does come," she declared as the raspberry business was completed.

"If you will bring Mr Carrados round, Nora, I'll run on with these and see if Ophelia has got everything ready. By the way, I asked Dr Olivant to join us at tea—the poor man must be feeling exhausted."

* * * * *

With the trifling exception of a mishap to the green dessert dish, Ophelia felt—as she confided now and then to Sultan, the lethargic Persian—that she was doing all that could be humanly expected. The fragments of the dessert dish had been temporarily secreted under some rags in the sink cupboard and for the rest Ophelia put her trust in the frailty of human memory and, when it did come out, the softening hand of time. Unfortunately Miss Tilehurst had this very dish in mind when she came in with the raspberries, so that instead of being able to refer casually to something as having happened in a vague and oblivious past, Ophelia was suddenly faced with the discovery of a fault in which she would be detected red handed as it were, and held doubly blameworthy.

"Green dish, mum?" she replied, becoming goggle-eyed with conscientious effort. "I wonder what can have become of that? I don't seem to have noticed it about lately. I think the last time must have been when Nipper was eating something out of it. I wonder if he can have broke it somehow?"

"Nonsense," retorted Miss Tilehurst briskly; "I saw it myself quite lately. And once again, Ophelia, you *must not* let the animals have our plates and dishes. Never mind looking now"—for the conscientious girl was exploring the most unlikely places—"this one will do instead. Now go and ask Dr Olivant if he would care to wash his hands—they may be dirty after that kind of work—and if he would, show him up to the bathroom and take a can of hot water and put out a towel."

Ophelia was free to breathe naturally once more, the matter of the green dish being dismissed to a wholly negligible morrow.

She sought Dr Olivant in the lane and delivered her message with scrupulous exactness.

"I was to ask you, please, if you'd like to wash yourself after you've done your dirty work, sir."

Looking at Ophelia it was impossible to suspect her of elaborate guile and Dr Olivant did look at her: for fully five seconds he bent a level glance on her unsophisticated features. Then he looked at his own hands and with a short laugh detached himself from the consideration of engine troubles.

"Well, yes; it would be as well perhaps, wouldn't it?" he admitted. "Come now, my dear"—as she stood awkwardly waiting for him to lead the way and he for her—"if we are to get on you must be my cicerone."

"That I never will, sir," appallingly retorted Ophelia, bristling up into virtuous indignation. "The very idea—and a gentleman like you too! I shall leave your water outside the bathroom door now."

"Don't be silly, girl; that only means that you've got to show me where I am to go," explained Olivant, his manner at once dropping several degrees in the social register. And as he followed he privately commented beneath his breath on her inopportune want of sense in terms that would have been surprisingly fundamental for Harley Street.

* * * * *

"I find that we shall have to give up the idea of sitting in the arbour," said their hostess as the sauntering pair appeared. "The table is all right to serve the tea from, but the rustic seats are definitely not equal to the responsibility of being sat on, and I know of nothing more embarrassing than to find one's chair collapsing when you have a cup of tea in one hand and a plate of something in the other."

"I think it rather fun," said Nora. "After all, it helps out a picnic."

"Then you shall provide the fun, dear," declared Miss Tilehurst. "Dr Olivant can do as he likes when he arrives but I insist on Mr Carrados being less humorous. There is a garden form under the catalpa, Mr Carrados, if you prefer the shade, or a chair here in the open—"

"I am all for the sun while it lasts, if you give me the choice," said Carrados, putting out his hand unerringly and accepting the chair Miss Tilehurst had indicated. "We don't get so many summers like this in England that you can afford to throw away a minute of one."

"Heroic man! And you, Nora—seriously, the bench in there is out of the question?"

"Then perhaps I can be useful?" suggested Nora. "If not, I'll be one of the shady ones."

"Useful? Well, Ophelia can take the tea but perhaps you wouldn't mind—when Dr Olivant appears—if you would bring him across—he mayn't quite like—"

"That I will, mum!" undertook Nora playfully.

"Sugar and cream, Mr Carrados?" asked Miss Tilehurst, seeing that Ophelia had arrived at the arbour with the tea tray.

"Cream—no sugar, thank you."

It is as well, since it had some little bearing on the course of events that afternoon, and thereafter perhaps for centuries, to indicate the rearrangements of positions that had come about from so trifling a cause as the dilapidation of the summer-house appointments. The tea, as originally planned, was laid in there, with Miss Tilehurst pouring out and Ophelia acting as a connecting link between supply and demand until her services were dispensed with. Mr Carrados, choosing the sun as we have seen, sat on an isolated chair some little distance from the arbour, while on the other side of the grass-plot in the shade of a catalpa tree, a substantial bench accommodated Dr Olivant when he came out and Nora and Miss Tilehurst in turn as they went backwards and forwards refilling cups and offering the more substantial refreshment. Geoffrey had not yet arrived—but of course he must any minute now, and in the minds of three out of the five people there his absence, as the time went on, was the one thing that engrossed them. Three out of the five: but which three?

"Your cup of tea, sir," considerately announced Ophelia, approaching Mr Carrados and regarding him with fascinated interest. "I was to be careful. You're blind, aren't you?"

"Yes, Ophelia. Quite blind," he replied with a reassuring smile as he took the cup and saucer neatly from her.

"You don't know of things that go on then?" she elaborated.

"Sometimes kind people tell me of them." He stirred in the floating cream deliberatingly. "If they think it will amuse me."

"Amuse!" she giggled at the recollection. "Not half, it wasn't! You ought to have seen him with his moustache coming off when he washed his face there. It did look funny, I can tell you."

"It must have done. Did he know you saw him?"

"Not him! I was looking through the—well, a place where he couldn't see me."

"Ophelia! Come, Ophelia," called out Miss Tilehurst and with a friendly nod and the consciousness that she had done her best to "amuse," Ophelia ambled back to the arbour.

"Bread-and-butter or anchovy sandwiches, Uncle?" inquired Nora, coming round in turn.

"Charming man that—sort I abhor. Makes you feel it must lead up to borrowing a fiver every minute. Or raspberries first?"

"Sandwich, thanks." He dexterously put down the cup on the grass beside him (Nora knew better than to butt in with help) and supplied himself from the plate she offered. "By the way, don't you want to go out into the road to see if anyone is coming?"

"Not particularly. Why?"

"Oh, I think I should... Perhaps because I want you to."

"Uncle Max, what is to be the hocus-pocus now? You've suddenly gone rather serious."

"I don't know that there will be any hocus-pocus, Nora. But I think it may have suddenly gone rather serious."

"Very well. I know that when... Tell me what I am to do."

"Keep your wits about you and don't give anything away. You are going to look down the road to see if Tilehurst isn't coming. Get the number of that car and let me have a description."

Nora passed on, admirably calm, to the other guest and smiled off on him another anchovy sandwich. Then she returned her stock to the arbour, and securing her own tea and plate began to walk across to the shade of the catalpa.

"Oh, I think I'll just give a look to see if Geoffrey is in sight yet and hurry him up if he is," she called back. "He's really naughty."

"Yes, do, dear," approved Miss Tilehurst, following her across, "but don't stay out looking. I'm going to sit with Dr Olivant for a minute now but I feel that we are neglecting our visitors shockingly. It would have been different if we could have all been together in the summer-house. As it is —"

"Have another sandwich, sir, while they're here," croaked Ophelia confidentially at the blind man's elbow. Being unable, as she argued, to look after himself, she was moved to take him under her special protection. "I know these picnic parties: once a thing's gone you're never sure if you'll ever see it again. 'A bird in the hand' is what I believe in being."

"I think you are quite right," he admitted no less confidentially, "but not yet, thank you. This time I'll risk it."

Nora came back from the side gate again and for a moment loitered at the bench, claiming her tea and plate with the light flippancies of the occasion.

"No sign of the defaulter yet," she reported, to Miss Tilehurst chiefly; then nibbling her bread-and-butter she passed on to Carrados to see how he was faring.

"Dark blue Lemartine four-seating tourer; four-wheel brakes; mica screen; disc wheels and carries spare one—

cased—left of engine. Sphinx mascot. And the tool box *has a hammer in it.*"

"Good girl," he commended, taking out a slender note-book and proceeding to make an inconsiderable entry. "Number?"

"PZ 9741."

"Just as well to have it, though for a certainty it's bogus."

"What is bogus for a certainty, you two conspirators?" loudly proclaimed Miss Tilehurst, innocently taking advantage of their absorption and the muting grass to spring this devastating revelation. Carrados felt Nora's sterilised dismay as he smilingly took over the situation.

"My niece thinks she has made a find—one of Wheatley's 'Cries of London' in a Mutbury second-hand shop," he obligingly explained; "but I tell her that there are a hundred fakes for every genuine copy. Still, it might be worth while—I wonder if Dr Olivant knows anything of prints? Some doctors have uncommonly good things on the walls of their reception rooms. We might ask him."

"Oh, Doctor, do you know anything about prints?" called out Miss Tilehurst, glad of the opportunity to make the talk more general and Olivant politely came forward. "Miss Melhuish thinks that she has discovered a rare engraving in a shop somewhere only Mr Carrados is afraid that it may be—what is it?—bogus! We wondered if you knew—"

"I fear I must admit my ignorance," replied Dr Olivant, making the admission sound more weighty than most other people's claim to extensive knowledge. "It is a subject that—I beg your pardon, Miss Tilehurst?"

"Geoffrey at last!" the interruption had been, her mind off like a bird as the front gate clanged and a man was seen through the laurels. "Oh, Geoffrey," she exclaimed in a voice of petulant relief, "you are a—" and then as he came round the bend, in a voice that was drained of every shade of expression but dismay: "*Geoffrey!*"

9

IN WHICH THE ASSURANCE OF THE EYE DECEIVES THE MIND

The man who had come in by the front gate and who was walking up the path, trundling a buckled and deflated bicycle at his side, looked up at the cry but he made no response nor did he evince any appreciable sign of recognition. His face had a grey strained look, not as of fear or apprehension now but as though some terrible experience had come suddenly and passed and left a benumbed and abiding impression. He took in the five people gathered there with an incurious acceptance that passed them by and it was distressingly obvious that if left to himself he would go straight on by the way he knew and not bestow another glance or a thought about what they were doing. When Miss Tilehurst laid an impulsive hand on his arm he stopped, but it was as an obedient cart horse stops and without any personal concern in the proceedings.

"Geoffrey, my dear, what is it? Why don't you speak?" implored Miss Tilehurst rather wildly. "Oh, my goodness, look at his poor face! Have you had an accident, Geoffrey—are you hurt? Do, for God's sake, say something!"

"One moment, my dear lady—you must control yourself," interposed Dr Olivant, coming forward with the quiet authority of his recognised position. "Is this—?"

"Yes, my nephew whom we've been expecting. He must have met with an accident—look at his face, look at the machine. But why doesn't he speak? It's so—so alarming, so inconsiderate. He may be badly injured for all we know and trying to keep it from us by not talking. But I can't let him go on like this. We must find out if there's anything worse and what has happened."

"Yes—yes, of course," admitted Olivant soothingly. "You are naturally distressed although it may not be anything like so serious as your first impression leads you to imagine. It is extremely probable that this is only a temporary phase—a matter of hours, or possibly days, and our young friend will be all right again and even laughing at his curious experience."

"You really think that, Doctor; you aren't just saying it—?"

"My dear Miss Tilehurst, if there were any immediate cause for anxiety I would be the first to warn you. However, at a time like this you naturally don't want a stranger—perhaps I had better go—you will no doubt get along all right. Unless of course,"—a considerate after-thought—"as a doctor who happens to be on the spot you would like me to make a provisional examination? If so—need I say?—I would be only too glad—some slight return—to put my services freely at your disposal."

"Oh, Doctor, would you? It would be such a blessed relief. I don't mind admitting that I've had a terrible fright and I'm still—perhaps unreasonably after what you've said—very, very anxious." Almost resentfully: "If only he would say *something*. Geoffrey, my darling, don't you recognise us here—me—Ophelia—Nora?"

"Geoff, dear," said Nora, going to his side, "can't you tell me? Don't I recall anything at all? Humph and Nobbles, you know." But Geoffrey only looked painfully apart and fixed his eyes on the door for which he had been making.

"Um, yes," interposed Dr Olivant, capably taking charge with the implication that this was all very well in its amateur way but that it was now time for someone who understood diagnostics to adopt proper methods. "This is quite unlooked for, I assume? There has been no previous indication of your nephew being in any way—shall I say strange? Not suffering from any physical or mental shock lately? Not complaining specially of the heat or feeling the sun, for instance?"

"Nothing at all," declared Miss Tilehurst, searching her mind with conscientious detail. "Of course we've all grumbled about the weather in an ordinary way, and he may have done too but it didn't mean anything and he was perfectly happy and normal up to the time I last saw him."

"And that was—when?"

"At lunch today. Afterwards he seems to have taken his bicycle out and gone off somewhere but I didn't know that he was going or see him go, Ophelia was the last who saw him."

"Yes, that's right; I saw him go," confirmed Ophelia, suddenly realising that this trifling circumstance might invest her with a gratifying importance. "Came through the kitchen with his machine when I was washing up the things after lunch he did. 'Going out for a ride on your bicycle, Mr Geoffrey?' I said, and then—"

"Yes, yes; there is no doubt that he did go off," interrupted Miss Tilehurst, recognising just in time that in the eyes of a very literal man Geoffrey's absurd reply might pass for evidence of an existing state of delirium. "You may take it for granted that he was perfectly normal when he set out, Doctor."

"Well, I thought it sounded queer," stuck out Ophelia, tolerantly resentful of being somehow "done out" of her scene, but as no one attached any importance whatever to anything that Ophelia might think her testimony faded into the background.

Meanwhile Olivant had taken his patient's unresisting hand and under cover of a flow of smooth commonplace was feeling his pulse, critically looking into his eyes, and inspecting his bruised condition.

"Now, Mr Tilehurst, you've evidently had something of an adventure; can't you tell us a little of what has happened to upset you? Your aunt is naturally concerned to see you behave like this; surely you will make an effort—just a few words—to relieve her anxiety. You—? Yes—? Nothing to say, eh?" for certainly this bland assumption of ability to comply was no more successful than Miss Tilehurst's frenzied appeal or Nora's more recondite suggestion. "Well, never mind; suppose you simply write down the name of the place where this occurred or even your signature," and producing an impressive memorandum tablet from his breast pocket Dr Olivant offered it, together with a pencil, for the purpose.

A sigh of relief went up from at least two throats. Geoffrey accepted the proffered articles—mechanically, indeed, but at any rate he understood the purport of what was said—and for a moment it seemed as though he was engaged in complying with the requirement. Then he held out the pad again—a few meaningless scrawls were the only result of the effort.

"Yes, yes; exactly," commented the doctor, glancing at the lines and accepting them as if they constituted just what he had expected. "Thank you, Mr Tilehurst."

"Not very much perhaps," he confided to his audience aside, "but still, in the circumstances, something." And to Miss Tilehurst more especially: "Oh, he'll be all right again soon; no need for you to worry."

"But what am I to do?" she asked, swayed between an intense relief that this obvious authority should treat the matter so lightly and a feeling that with Geoffrey like that there must be something more than Olivant would admit behind it. "What is it that has happened?"

"Even without our having anything more than this extraneous evidence to go on"—a gesture indicated his patient's bruised and soiled condition and the damage to his machine—"it is pretty plain what has happened. Your nephew has experienced a severe shock—mental and physical combined—with the not unnatural result that for the time certain functions of the brain have been thrown out of action. Whether he was involved in a collision with someone else or merely had a spill or—what is perhaps more probable—received this damage and at the same time underwent the terrifying experience of what is termed a 'narrow squeak' from something much worse is beside the question. Something happened and as the result he is now suffering from what I should confidently predict will be only a temporary form of motor aphasia."

"My word, but that sounds bad," confided Ophelia—in the absence of Sultan—to herself. "Them motors didn't ought to be allowed—"

"Inability to speak, that is of course," amplified Dr Olivant with dignified severity. "And as we see here"—tapping the pad that he still held—"inability to write: agraphia."

"You don't think that he may be hurt internally somewhere all the time, Doctor, and unable to tell us? It must surely have been a very severe crash—"

"Not at all, not at all. As a matter of fact, physical violence is not necessary to produce the condition of aphasia. Quite recently I was called in to a case where a financier fell into the state as a result of unexpected market reverses. Three days later he suddenly recovered the power of speech completely on seeing his wife breaking some coal with his favourite golf club. Another case I had—a lady saw a ghost apparently coming out of her husband's bedroom. It was really the housemaid, who then admitted that she was a confirmed sleep-walker."

"You have had other cases? Then you do actually know all about it?" suggested Miss Tilehurst, still more reassured though not perhaps choosing her words quite happily.

"My dear lady, I am a nerve specialist; of my standing as a consultant—but that is a matter on which it is more befitting for me to leave others to express an opinion," replied Dr Olivant with a fine discrimination of manner. "In Harley Street I deal with analogous cases practically every day. Your own doctor will doubtless confirm my diagnosis if you think it necessary to consult him."

"I suppose we ought to—he has attended Geoffrey for everything from childhood. But, oh, how very unfortunate! Dr Tyser is away on his holidays and his locum isn't at all—You do think that it would be better for him to be seen by an ordinary doctor as well, don't you?"

"Well, as to that—perhaps you would like me to make a more detailed examination to see definitely if there is any internal trouble and say what I think then? If so—I'm entirely at your service."

"Oh, I should; I should. But it is so very, so *very* good of you, Dr Olivant."

"Not at all. Your own man is away and in cases of emergency professional etiquette is mercifully elastic. The circumstances naturally encourage me to take a personal interest in our young friend here. Besides, I am scientifically concerned in observing the curious and varied effects of these sensory disturbances. Then we will go inside for a few minutes if you will kindly indicate where it will be convenient."

"Yes, yes, certainly, Doctor. You had better be at hand, Ophelia. Dr Olivant may require something bringing."

"That I will, mum," promised Ophelia, one might even say with an anticipatory gloating.

"Now, Mr Tilehurst, we are going into the house," said the doctor; "suppose you show me the way," and obedient to the suggestion Mr Tilehurst did lead the way towards the front door almost naturally. Dr Olivant turned to throw a weighty nod of approval towards Miss Tilehurst at this achievement.

"I'm so, *so* terribly sorry that our afternoon has turned out like this, Mr Carrados," apologised Miss Tilehurst, stopping for a moment beside her visitors before she hurried on to catch up with the others on the door steps. "You won't mind my running away I know but I do hope that you will stay and finish your interrupted tea—you will look after him, won't you, Nora? I'll let you hear what Dr Olivant says the minute I can, dear. I know that you are quite as anxious as I am. It's all so sudden and alarming—but wasn't it lucky that just the one man in a thousand should be here!"

"Yes; wasn't it!" agreed Mr Carrados, but as his hostess was well on her way towards the house, and, further, his remark had more significance than polite assent, it was not surprising that Nora was disinclined to let it pass unchallenged.

"What do you mean by that, Uncle Max?" she flatly demanded.

"Some people don't believe in luck, you know, Nora—I imagine they prefer to regard it as an intelligent anticipation of contributory circumstances. Perhaps Dr Olivant is one of them," he temporised.

"Look here, Uncle, I don't want a fencing lesson just now, thank you. I want to understand things."

"That's what most people really want, Nora. It's what I've been wanting all my life. It's what I go on for. Generally I have to wait someone else's good time for it."

"Well, won't you help me to understand here—or even let me help you? It's all simple and straightforward to Miss Tilehurst; I mean she accepts it just as it appears on the surface. I can't do that because I know that you don't do curious things without some motive behind and now you've started my suspicions and I... It's very strange that Geoffrey shouldn't know even me."

"Are you quite sure that even you know this Geoffrey of yours?"

"That I know Geoffrey—?"

"Well, very often a girl thinks that she knows a man through and through, only to find out that she doesn't... It's even been known to happen with a husband and wife who've lived all their life together."

"No, it wasn't that," declared Nora, shaking her head rather sadly. "You didn't mean that—only you don't quite trust me... Uncle Max, you are going on with this, aren't you? You're thinking and planning and finding clues and putting this and that together. Aren't you?"

"A little time ago I came up against a locked door, and something baffling, perhaps even villainous, was going on the other side of it," vouchsafed the provoking Carrados. "This afternoon I have picked up a key; it fits the lock but it doesn't work the levers—not just yet."

"And I don't even know how to begin to set about looking; but I feel as though a shadow, mysterious and sinister, is creeping up. Something has happened to this bright summer afternoon and to this peaceful garden and—I think—to me. It's that sort of feeling... And you sit there like a heathen idol, turning everything over in your wonderful mind and not letting me share a particle. Uncle Max"—taking hold of his shoulders and all but shaking him in a transport of exasperation—"don't you understand? I must do something; I can't just sit down and wait. I can't have Geoffrey change—I can't lose him like this. Yes, lose, Uncle Max; we were all but engaged lovers. Of course I know it's the doctor's job about treatment and all that, but isn't one of the first things towards putting him right to find out what it was that put him wrong? Suppose it was done by someone deliberately?"

"Yes, there may be something in that—perhaps more than one might think," admitted Mr Carrados.

"Let me help you to do it then. You mayn't find me such an utter little rabbit as you might think after all. There are damned few things that I feel I'm afraid of, let me tell you, Uncle Max, and I'm quite ready to take the risks if it comes to that sort of business."

"My dear," protested the blind man with his incurable air of insouciance, "you seem determined to plunge us both into the thick of battle."

"Well, even you can't be in two places at once and sometimes you have had to make use of other people's eyes to see by. I think I'm up to the intellectual standard of your Parkinson and at any rate you certainly wouldn't miss me half as much as you would him if anything went wrong... Dear Uncle Max, if the chance comes along won't you give me a try—can't you use me?"

"That's all very well, my dear, but I don't want to have to fight a duel with Tilehurst when he comes round if I've led you into any scrape meanwhile," he protested lightly. "Thank you all the same child, but seriously you know if there should be any real unpleasantness ahead it would hardly be the sort of work to bring a young lady into."

"Young lady!" Nora achieved almost a shriek of despair. "Bad language fails me! I always say you are an old dear, Uncle, but you are—oh, you are—you really are—the most utter—"

"Ssh!" warned Carrados. "Someone coming."

"Yes; perhaps I had better 'ssh!'" retorted Nora, subsiding.

10

NIPPER CONTRIBUTES TO THE PROBLEM

"Will it do in here?" asked Miss Tilehurst.

It was the door of the dining-room she had opened. "The morning-room is so dreadfully hot at this time of day and the drawing-room rather overcrowded."

"This will do admirably," he replied, taking a deliberate look round. "Now—"

"There is something you need?"

"A little warm water in a bowl, sponge, towel, and the tincture of iodine if you have any."

This simple list of requirements was passed on to the palpitating Ophelia and in a commendably short time—scarcely more than sufficient, indeed, for Dr Olivant to stroll across to the window and, having ascertained that it was not inconveniently overlooked, commend the prospect—a tray containing them appeared. The doctor turned to Miss Tilehurst with his nicely discriminative lady-side manner.

"Now I shall ask you to withdraw for a few minutes, Miss Tilehurst. After I have attended to these superficial trifles I shall put our man through a pretty thorough examination."

"I quite understand," replied Miss Tilehurst delicately, though, of course, she was yearning to be of some use. "There is the bell by the mantelpiece. You will not hesitate to ring if there is the slightest—?"

"Now my dear sir," directed Olivant, as they were in the process of becoming alone, "I think if you sit down there"—"there" being a severe mahogany chair whose suitability consisted in its position, well out of the line of vision from the door—"it will do nicely. Yes, we will have your coat off for a start. Capital."

The door being now closed and the window reasonably safe—especially as Olivant, with his back that way, stood between it and his patient—the process of sponging away the traces of injury began and this naturally brought the two heads close together.

"O.K.?" dropped from the elder man's lips, but so circumspectly that one might have been in the room and still not heard the whisper or seen any facial movement.

"O.K. And you?"

"Lapped it. But how the hell have you got yourself in this state? You weren't to have any bumps—it was to be all mental. Had a spill actually?"

"Nothing like. I simply thought it better... And then that little s—Mae—oh well, well can all that backwash. I'm here, aren't I?"

"I see. Temperamental. Still, let me tell you, my young friend, it might easily have queered my bit of business. However...want anything doing?"

"Nit. But how about the two extras? They're outside calculations."

"Dropped ins. Man called Carrados; blind. Girl, Nora Melhuish. They'll drift back after a while. They don't matter."

"Not so sure. She looks like being a snag. Side line I hadn't thought to handle."

"Oh-ha?"

"T. was damned close about her, I must say. Neither Nickle nor I had an inkling. We're evidently some distance on, but where? As soon as I pick up I shall be expected to do something."

"Well, that oughtn't to be difficult for you."

"It wouldn't if I knew where to leave off but it's so infernally easy for me to overact the part in a case like that. Anyway, I shouldn't be sorry if Nora vanished. She's safe to be the sharp one—the old geezer wouldn't have tumbled to it if I'd turned up cross-eyed."

"I'll tell J., but we can hardly yank the girl out as well. It would raise fire and brimstone."

"I'm not asking you to. But that's how it stands. You can vamoose now—no question of having to get me out. We've arranged for messages."

"Right-o. Closing down now... Yes, I think we'll be satisfied with that"—this resumption of Dr Olivant's hearty self-confident voice coincided with the completion of the use of sponge and towel and the application of iodine to his patient's scratches. "Now suppose we move across to this couch for the next part of our job. I shall want a little more removed to get on with that. Then you can lie down quite comfortable and it won't take long... You do understand? Oh capital! Capital!"

* * * * *

"He is with Geoffrey in the dining-room now and they don't expect to be very long. It will be such a relief for me to know that there is no internal complication to fear. I do hope that Nora has been attending to you, Mr Carrados?"

"Steadily, Miss Tilehurst. And I have been capably responding. One of the great advantages of eating is that it enables you to disguise emotion. To the cynical observation that speech is given us to conceal our thoughts it might be added that eating and drinking enable us to hide our feelings. I think that is why food is an institution almost whenever human beings have anything to say to one another. A man has sufficient time to pull himself together under the excuse of even so simple an action as drinking from a cup of coffee."

"If he didn't there'd be a spill," said Nora. "In fact there always is when it happens on the stage. The startled man blowing out his drink is one of the surest laugh-getters of the modern drama... Don't think me unfeeling, Miss Tilehurst dear—it's only my way of keeping it up. I must be doing something or saying something very fast and Mr Carrados is considerately giving me a lead."

"Mr Carrados...lead...dog," automatically responded some obscure process in Miss Tilehurst's sorely tried brain. "Nora! Nipper!"

"Nipper? I haven't seen him at all since I came. Why, where is Nipper?"

"No; that's it. He went with Geoffrey this afternoon. But he didn't come back with him."

"Your little terrier, eh?" remarked Mr Carrados. "Yes, Nipper may have involved a certain difficulty, mayn't he?"

"He would never have left Geoffrey of his own free will, whatever it was that took place. He always recognized his footstep long before we even heard it and ran out of the house to meet him. What can have happened to him?"

"I think I can tell you that," volunteered Mr Carrados quietly. "You must be prepared for another shock, Miss Tilehurst, although, of course, it doesn't compare with the other. Nipper is no more."

"You mean—dead?" "Yes, dead, I am sorry to have to tell you. He was found less than an hour ago in Birling Wood and though his collar had seen removed the man who found him recognized the dog as yours."

"But—an hour ago! You were here then, Mr Carrados. How could you possibly know of such a thing happening?"

For an answer the blind man raised his hand in the direction of the house and nodded. Miss Tilehurst turned to see Ophelia coming along the path towards them. She carried something white in her bent arms and the simple girl was crying.

"Oh, mum-it's poor Nipper! Mr Batts, the keeper, has just brought him to the back door. He says he found him, not a hour ago, under a clump in Birling Wood, because his own dog knew there was something there and as good as said so. I thought it sounded queer too, mum, but Mr Batts did say that his dog stood and pointed at the bush and there when he looked was Nipper. At least he guessed it was yours through seeing it about with Mr Geoffrey although the collar was gone, so he brought it round as he thought you'd better know what had happened."

"Dead, killed; run over, I suppose, and then thrown aside to save any unpleasantness."

"Yes, mum, Mr Batts said he reckoned it was one of them hemmed stink kettles on wheels and if he had his way they'd pave the roads with broken bottles 'stead of tarring them. And if you please, mum..."

"Yes, Ophelia?" said Miss Tilehurst, gently stroking dead Nipper and smiling sadly. "What is it?"

"If you please, mum," wailed Ophelia, bringing her resolution to the boiling point so that a rush of words welled over, "it wasn't true what I said just now about that there green dish and Nipper. It was me that broke it—not 'im. There"—with obvious relief—"I hope he's heard me say it."

"Oh, Ophelia!"

"Yes, mum," acquiesced Ophelia to the pained tone of reproach, in penitent agreement.

"Well, leave it here now and go back. There's nothing to be done by talking and Dr Olivant may be wanting something more. And, oh, Ophelia, ask Mr Batts if he will kindly wait for a few minutes longer as I would like to see him. Isn't it unfortunate?" she continued, to the others, "It would be bad enough at any time but coming just at this moment—"

"Poor doggie," said Nora, surrendering the form to Carrados who had stretched out his hands for it. "I never thought about it but I suppose we must all have been fond of old Nipper."

"Yes, I'm sure you were," agreed Miss Tilehurst, "but I was thinking more of Geoffrey at the moment. He isn't one to make a fuss of his affections but I know that, without becoming maudlin as so many doggy people unfortunately do, he thought a great deal of his faithful little companion. He's sure to ask for him as soon as he begins to speak again and I dread to think how it may upset him. Would it be better to tell him now so as to get it over—or not yet? What do you think?"

"On the whole I should say that it would perhaps be unnecessary to tell him," replied Mr Carrados.

"You mean until he asks?"

"Exactly—until he asks. When he does course that will be another matter."

"I expect you are quite right. Then perhaps we ought to bury the little body now—it would be dreadful if he should happen to come upon it without knowing. But I can't just now—"

"We could hide it for the time—somewhere—the tool-shed," suggested Nora, seeing that the usually decisive Miss Tilehurst was becoming painfully uncertain. "Then Draycott could dig a grave when he next comes gardening, couldn't he?"

"Yes, but Draycott only comes two days a week you know, and he won't be here again until Wednesday. I don't know—in this weather—"

"Then why shouldn't uncle and I get it done while we are only waiting? I can't go until I know what the doctor says—oh, but if he is—I mean if he isn't—" Nora began to flounder.

"We cannot possibly go until we hear, no matter how long the doctor may be, Nora," reproved Mr Carrados gravely.

"No, of course we can't," accepted Nora. "And it will be such a relief to be doing something vigorous like digging. We shall find a spade all right. Mayn't we as well, Miss Tilehurst?"

"But your clothes, your shoes, my dear," protested the more experienced gardener. "It would simply ruin those flimsy leathers."

"I will do the actual digging, Miss Tilehurst," undertook Carrados, and rather wanly, since only one thing in the world seemed to matter then, Miss Tilehurst stroked Nipper's chalk-white back for the last time and said it would be a weight off her mind if they really would undertake the disposal while Geoffrey was safely out of the way.

"In the rough grass beyond the espalier would be the most suitable place I think," she added. "Shall I run down and show you?"

"I know where you mean quite well," replied Nora, "and I'm sure you're only worrying if you are away from here for a minute. We'll get on all right, never fear."

* * * * *

Miss Tilehurst had not long to wait; in fact she met Dr Olivant coming down the steps as she was making for the hall, to take up a useless vigil outside the dining-room door, after she had stood for a moment absently following Nipper's last progress down the garden. On his side there was no inducement for Olivant to linger once he had played his part. He had now to cope his carefully built-up fabric and when that was done the sooner he made himself scarce the better.

"Ah, Miss Tilehurst," he exclaimed, with a jauntiness appropriate to the character of the report he brought, "I think now that I can set your mind at rest completely."

"Oh, Doctor—completely," she said quickly. "Does that mean that he is really all right again—that he can speak and answer?"

Dr Olivant made a deprecatory gesture and looked quizzically reproachful.

"Well, no, perhaps not quite all that just yet," he admitted, "but what I meant was that you need have no fear—absolutely no apprehension whatever—as regards the future. I have gone thoroughly over our young friend in there—by the way he seems quite content to sit quietly alone and so you'd better let him—and he is definitely uninjured. With the exception of the trifling facial bruises that you have seen he has not been touched; his condition is purely the result of mental disturbance—he has received a shock to put it simply."

"We have just found out that our little dog that went with him has been killed and the body thrown aside—a man who knew the dog has kindly brought it here. Do you think—?"

"Very likely; very likely indeed. Nothing more probable," replied the doctor, looking extremely sagacious. "These reckless drivers! Full speed along a narrow winding lane—no warning. Your nephew sees the inevitable a yard ahead. He hears the despairing death cry of his unfortunate dog and barely escapes by the merest chance himself—the luck of being flung into the hedge and clear of the rushing moloch instead of into the road and beneath it. Yes, there we have the case in a nutshell I think, Miss Tilehurst. Is it any wonder that he emerges from that hedge with his mind temporarily seared?"

"Temporarily, Doctor? You still think that he will get over it before very long then?"

"I don't think, my dear lady; I know. Such cases are—to use rather a vulgar boast—my speciality, and I can absolutely guarantee it. You will find that gradually the normal faculties will come back. Probably he will begin to write—very shakily and unrecognisable at first—when he wants to communicate with you. As we saw just now he is more disposed to write than to speak when the occasion requires."

"I see. And when he does speak will it be the same as with the writing—not coming back suddenly restored?"

"All experience points that way! Semi-coherent speech at first— stammering and broken you understand—but sufficient to make himself understood and to indicate his requirements. You mustn't be disconcerted if the voice sounds rather strange to your ears at the start—it's only a matter of time, like the writing."

"I won't mind I can assure you. And in about how long—?"

"Ah, that's more difficult to say. These cases vary. But I should expect that you will notice a material improvement within a few days and in somewhere about a week you may have quite a surprising transformation—quite surprising."

"That will not seem so very long. And is there absolutely nothing for me to do to help? No matter what, if it only contributes to his recovery ever so little."

"Nothing beyond what I have already indicated. Nothing active that is to say but a great deal passive. Let him have entirely his own way in what he wants to do. Don't seem to notice him; don't watch him—in fact look at him as little as possible. It's all a reminder that something is wrong, and reminding him of what has happened is the one thing that must be avoided. He'll make absurd mistakes at first no doubt—not know his way about even in places where he is quite familiar; pick up things that don't concern him and, of course, fail to recognise his friends—though as to that I shouldn't make a point of having people in to meet him."

"Oh, certainly not. I should dislike it myself. And his business, Doctor? We must apply, I suppose, for leave of absence now?"

"Ah, his business to be sure. In these charming rural surroundings one forgets that there is such a thing as business. I shouldn't wonder—What does he do, by the way?"

"He is in the office of the paper mills here. You may have noticed them as you drove by. It is where they make the Bank of England note paper."

It appeared, however, that Dr Olivant had not noticed them as he drove in; indeed—and this was the single flaw in the impression left by that delightful man—he did not seem to be aware that special paper was required for the issue of Bank of England notes, ever to have even heard of the celebrated Tapsfield mills, or to have the least interest in the subject of the firm's importance. One point only caught his attention and that was when Miss Tilehurst spoke of the responsibility of Geoffrey's position.

"Just so—responsibility," he commented. "That impression may persist; it is a curious fact, Miss Tilehurst, that a man's vocational claims are often the predominant subconscious impulse. It is quite on the cards that your nephew will set off on Monday morning in the usual way and turn up at the office. Let me see—are you on pretty good terms with the important people down there?"

"Oh yes. I meet them all occasionally. They'd do anything to help us I am sure."

"Very well. As this happens to be Saturday it gives you a day's grace. I should go round and see the chiefs tomorrow. Tell them all about it and what I have said. If your nephew should go to the works the very best thing would be to give him free rein to potter about and try to recall his routine. Of course he can't do anything there at first but the association of the place will be helpful."

"I see. Yes; I quite appreciate that and I am sure that there will be no difficulty in arranging it. They are most considerate and of course they value Geoffrey's services very highly."

"Oh, quite so—naturally. Well, Miss Tilehurst, I think that is about all—"

"But, Doctor, aren't we to do anything to discover the culprits? A harmless dog is killed, an inoffensive man's reason, if not his life, endangered. Surely someone ought to be called to account—"

"Yes, yes; not unnaturally I thought of that and then there arises just this difficulty: do we put our patient's recovery or our own feelings first—I say our own feelings for whatever may have happened (and we cannot exclude, my dear lady, the possibility of contributory negligence) the last thing in your nephew's interest is to recall that disastrous occurrence. Once bring in the police and what is inevitably bound to follow? There will be calls and interrogations and cross-questionings as one wiseacre after another gets what he considers 'a clue' until the excellent chance that our patient has of making a quick recovery—is blown to atoms. But of course it's for you to say—"

"No," replied Miss Tilehurst very decidedly. "Oh no; I could not allow that for a moment. We might make discreet inquiry for ourselves but Geoffrey shall not be worried."

"Then I can confidently leave his future in your hands: and now I must see about my own interrupted progress, A trying afternoon for you, Miss Tilehurst, but he'll go on all right; he'll steadily improve, never fear."

"If I don't fear, Dr Olivant, it is entirely due to you. I think you must have been sent direct from heaven."

"Oh, I shouldn't exactly call it that," protested Olivant modestly. "At all events I have no idea of getting back there tonight. Then good-bye, Miss Tilehurst—or possibly *au revoir* It occurs to me that I may be passing this way back in about a week's time."

"Oh, would you? I should be so very glad—only next time you must really let me accept it as a professional visit. That quite relieves my mind about not saying anything to that dreadful locum meanwhile. No, Doctor—I am coming into the lane to see you off... Oh, the others—my visitors, you know—do you care to see them before you go, or—?"

"I hardly think it is necessary—we scarcely spoke. My apologies, if you don't mind, when you rejoin them."

"Certainly I will. By the way, Mr Carrados is particularly interested in crime and obscure cases. He has quite a unique reputation for a blind man, I understand. If he should happen to speak to me of what took place—"

"An amateur sleuth—as I believe they are called—eh?" Dr Olivant relaxed to the extent of a grimace of good-humoured if contemptuous amusement. "Wonderful fellows, provided everything happens their way, if we are to believe the magazine story writers. Well, the less stir and talk there is in any quarter, the better for our patient, but I quite see, Miss Tilehurst, that it may be difficult for you—"

They passed, by the little side gate, into the lane, still talking.

* * * * *

The soil beyond the espalier fortunately was light and easily dug but, even so, Mr Carrados, divested of his coat and with cuffs turned back, more than once bewailed his pliant good nature in taking on the energetic office.

"Alas, poor Nipper; a dog of infinite zest and understanding. A hundred times hath he buried the bones of others here and now we bury his—pest on it," he declaimed between his efforts. "This grave-digger business is ill suited to the day, Nora. Why didn't you suggest the dogs' cemetery in Hyde Park where he could have been put away in style and to our material comfort?"

"Probably because I didn't know of it. Is there such a place really?"

"Certainly there is, and a very singular institution though I dare say it's full up now. Remind me when I am next showing you the sights of London and I'll take you... Will this about do, quotha?"

"Oh yes, I'm sure it's deep enough now. As you've had all the work so far I'll do my share by filling it up again. Poor old Nipper. And that's the end of him... Uncle Max, was Nipper run over by a motor car and Geoffrey nearly run over and frightened out of his senses? I am sure that's what she thinks and it does look like that, doesn't it?"

"Not altogether, Nora. The dog was killed by the single blow of a heavy blunt weapon. The man...the man is more complicated."

"Oh! You mean that someone killed the poor little thing deliberately? But why should anyone? Why, Uncle?"

"A great deal may turn on that. He might have attacked in defence. But there is an immeasurably subtler line of implication that is dangerously attractive."

"Yes, yes?"

"He could always recognise Geoffrey's step, you know; and, like me, he had a nose that was fatal to deception."

"Oh, but that's no good since Geoffrey would still be the same to Nipper. I mean it brings us no nearer to what really happened, does it?"

"Perhaps a little. Geoffrey was first chloroformed, I think. The hand that picked Nipper up to dispose of him had certainly touched chloroform just before. Drugged; does that bring us nearer by taking us further away, I wonder?"

This, needless to say, was not very helpful to Nora who was all for other people being explicit.

"That's very profound I dare say, but I simply don't understand anything from it. And I feel that it's all getting rather horrible—like a forest in a nightmare and whichever way I turn I'm bound to get more and more lost in it. What is there to do, my wonderful Uncle?"

"Wait," he replied, and she was startled by the feeling—almost bitterness—in place of his usual tempered suavity. "Wait for them to show their hand more plainly. That's a fine thing to have to recommend, isn't it, when just the one clue that may spell all the difference between failure and success is on the point of slipping through our fingers."

"The one clue?"

"The Harley Street specialist who is so familiarly at home in an East End fence's den—where is he making for when he goes from here?"

"You want to know that, Uncle Max?"

"It might ultimately lead us to the answer. Now it's too late to have a hope of following. If only your brother had been at home I could have put him on to it with a fair chance of shadowing our ingratiating friend to the trysting place with his report of progress."

"Motor bike! He must make for the Stanbury fork. Dark blue Lemartine. One could overhaul him."

"Yes, but Tom is somewhere among the Alps just now and there's no one else in this fascinating Sleepy Hollow of yours that we could get in time—even if there is anyone at all who would do it."

"Oh blow!" exclaimed Nora in sudden irrelevance, "there's Miss Tilehurst—I suppose she wants me to do the polite by saying good-bye or something silly. Go on filling up, won't you, old dear? Back as soon as I can," and without offering the necessary opening for the proverbial word that is inserted edgeways, she flew up the garden leaving Mr Carrados still painfully reviewing the circumstances that were leading to the calamity of Olivant's secure retirement.

* * * * *

The engine of the car in the lane gave a few preliminary skirls as the blind man threw back the last spadeful of earth; another minute passed and then the sound grew constant. Nora had not yet returned so presumably she had been pressed into remaining to grace the good fairy Olivant's bouquet-strewn departure. Mr Carrados had no wish to figure in the flourish but, as the measured drone of the unseen Lemartine traced its progress along the lane beyond the wall, he picked up his coat again and sauntered up the path with a passing thought of his usually scrupulous appearance.

"Ah, Ophelia," he said, recognising her presence as he neared the house, "you are the very person I'm wanting. Do you think you could bring a clothes brush out and perhaps—? You see the state I've got myself in, burying poor Nipper."

"Why to be sure I will, sir," replied Ophelia, surprisingly varying her formula. "I'll trim you up like one o'clock if you don't mind waiting a couple of jiffies. I'm looking for the mistress now. That Mr Batts doesn't half give me the shivers. He's in the kitchen there with his pocket full of ferrets and they keep getting out and them and the cat does nothing but put their backs up and swear at one another. Says he can't wait no longer."

"The keeper? Oh, he oughtn't to go until Miss Tilehurst has seen him. I think you'll find her just out in the lane there with Miss Melhuish. If you run across I'll have a word with Mr Batts myself meanwhile and keep him until you come back. He should know a lot about trapping vermin."

"Right you are," said Ophelia, with the easy manner which, we are told, is the universal hall mark of good breeding. "The missis may be there but I don't know about Miss Nora. Not two minutes ago she went through the other gate like a streak of greased lightning and if she isn't at Turnpenny Cross by now she might be."

"She went out—" considered Mr Carrados.

"Now that's rather odd—" but even as he stood, from the road beyond and then from the lane itself there came a possible, if rather fantastic, answer to his deliberation. It approached as a crescendo hum, gathering into a husky roar as it swept by, and in less than ten seconds the beat was faintly drumming the air in the direction of Stanbury Junction. For just a moment a gauntletted hand had shown above the level of the wall in a gesture that conveyed both hail and farewell.

"Mr Carrados! What on earth can it mean?" Miss Tilehurst was hastening back towards the house from the gate, to meet her only remaining guest who was reversing that process. "Did you see—bless us, I should say hear? That was Nora, tearing like a wild thing down the lane on her brother's motor cycle. I wouldn't have recognised her she was so got up if she hadn't waved—and do you know I actually believe that she was wearing Tom's leather trousers!"

11

A MINE IS COUNTERMINED

Mr Carrados's appearance at "Orchard Close" had been in the nature of a week-end visit and on the Monday following Miss Tilehurst's eventful Saturday afternoon tea-party he returned to his own house in Richmond.

So far as he was concerned the circumstances of what might be called the Geoffrey Tilehurst case had progressed little beyond the elementary coincidental. Geoffrey had gone out for a ride and returned suffering from complicated loss of memory. At the same time there had appeared on the scene the soi-disant Dr Olivant. Dr Olivant was either a medical man curiously in touch with Julian Joolby—that bizarre figure of exotic reputation—or else an impostor masquerading as a doctor. It would be easy to establish by the *Medical Directory* whether there was, so far as the current issue went, anyone of that name with an address in Harley Street but the evidence would not be quite finally conclusive. Dr Olivant had, in fact, been faced with the alternative of personating a specialist who could be referred to at any time or of inventing a fictitious one who might be less convincing but who would be more elusive. That he had returned to a sequestered house in an outer London suburb (as Nora had been able to establish) meant little or nothing yet. That house had still to be investigated.

So far it was difficult to suggest what had necessitated Olivant's function in Tapsfield. The result of his framed-up appearance at Brookcroft had only been to put about what any genuine doctor could have established. The measure of disguise suggested that he had been there before or intended to go again or else that there was a chance of encountering someone while on that lay who might recognise him in his fictitious character. Certainly he had gained a first-hand knowledge of the house and grounds; was Mr Carrados rating the incidentals too high and this nothing but the prelude to a commonplace burglary?

A coincidence is the intersection of two lines, neither of which need possess in itself the least significance. When three lines meet at the selfsame point of time or space the laws of chance suggest the probability of some conformable agency. "I suppose this is getting frightfully complicated?" once remarked an interested outsider for whom Mr Carrados was investigating a case, when one baffling circumstance after another was brought to light as the quest proceeded. "Not at all," was his reply. "On the contrary it is becoming transparently simple." One or two lines might establish nothing but when a dozen or a score could be "extended" it was inevitable that they must disclose a centre of origin.

The episode of Nipper's despatch was just one of these detached pointers. In itself it went for little but its line of direction might lead to something and in any case it was the *tertium quid* suggesting that the other incidents were unlikely to be fortuitous.

Nipper had been handled by someone who just before had been associated with chloroform. The dog had not been chloroformed itself for, as Carrados had settled, the head was wholly free from any touch of contact. Mr Batts was also eliminated as a possible conveyer when the opportunity offered.

The supposition that Geoffrey had been chloroformed was a reasonable hypothesis at that stage of the disclosure. Had the dog been brought upon the scene five minutes before he was, the point could have been settled very naturally, but by the time that Mr Carrados's nose had made him a present of that piece of information all chance of such a test had been shattered—quite unintentionally as it happened—by Olivant's effectual treatment of his patient's injuries.

If Geoffrey Tilehurst, Dr Olivant and Nipper were all connected by an impending theft from the Tapsfield mills it should be possible to deduce—if not the actual plan in detail—at least a theory into which all the existing facts would fit and no construction that did not reconcile all that had happened was worth exploring. Tilehurst was naturally the crux, for the parts played by the other two were obviously contingent to his function. Was it possible that this responsible mill employee had been laid out and doped and was now existing in a mentally inert state by which he became an unconscious tool in the hands of those who had the key to his position? The basis was almost good enough to answer to the test but Carrados knew of neither drug nor process that could be relied on to work satisfactorily in practice under such tenuous conditions, and although Joolby might feasibly have access to some useful family hoodoo it was scarcely an assumption on which to conduct a serious investigation.

It would have been a simple enough move to warn the firm, but Max Carrados's interest lay in the phase of crime rather than in forestalling it, and on that score he had little tangible as yet to lay before a directorate of level-headed business men who would as likely as not regard him as an officious meddler. After all, what did it amount to? A dog had been run over through straying on the road. A man had received some sort of nervous shock that had upset his mental balance for the time being, and the good Samaritan who had come to his aid had a voice which the caller thought he recognised as having heard in a second-hand shop some time before and he might not be on the Medical Register. A curious tale with which to convey a serious warning that it all pointed to a sensational robbery!

On the other hand there was Scotland Yard, which would have lent a very attentive ear indeed, but it had always been the blind man's humour to take the official branch into his confidence after he had found out all he wanted rather than in the course of that process. One other detail was not without its influence. On the Sunday afternoon Mr Carrados again went across to Brookcroft and, somewhat to his amused chagrin, found that Miss Tilehurst did not consider it wise that her nephew should be submitted to the possible excitement of a meeting. Olivant had played his delicate part commendably well and although Nora flatly called it desertion of herself, of Geoffrey, and of the case, Uncle Max good-humouredly accepted the taunt but provokingly declined to be either goaded or cajoled into upsetting his arrangements.

"After all, there are two ends to every stick," he reminded her, "and it's quite on the cards for mine to be the one that next waggles. You did finely the other day and it's going to be of very great use, but for heaven's sake, my dear, don't get yourself into any scrape following things up—only if you do, remember that I'm the chap you've always got to fall back on."

"I'm not going to promise anything after the perfectly fetid way you're running off," she retorted. "Still, it's pretty obvious that I shall stay here and do what I can for poor Geoffrey in the circumstances." It occurred to the hearer, who was accustomed to glean much of his knowledge from the infinitesimals of tone, that there was a spice of "It is my duty and I will" in this praiseworthy resolve which fell short of the ecstatic resolution of the Saturday Nora. It was an unwelcome suggestion but was this frank high-spirited niece of his becoming slightly calculating?

* * * * *

Mr Carrados was justified in his assumption that it was his end of the stick that might register the next movement, but it was Nora who supplied the action. And if the sudden and unannounced arrival of Miss Melhuish at "The Turrets" contained any element of surprise for him, his habitual imperturbability enabled him to pass it off with disarming lightness.

"This is uncommonly nice of you, Nora," he said, before she had had the chance to embark on any explanation; "I was just wondering what to do next. The dogs' cemetery of course as soon as we've had some sort of refreshment. I'm glad you've taken me at my word about it."

"Don't," she begged, and immediately his face responded to the need of another sort of mettle. "Miss Tilehurst isn't here now. I came because I was frightened."

"That's even nicer of you, my dear," he replied, and took a seat on the couch close to her. "I expect the pair of us can down it."

"Uncle Max," she said, with a childlike directness that put such courtesies aside. "*Did you know?*"

At this, every instinct in him threw up a guard. There was always the chance of giving something away by taking too much for granted.

"Did I know?" he repeated, conscientiously searching his mind. "Surely, Nora, that's a little vague. Did I know—what exactly?"

"If you do know there's no need to ask," she replied sharply. "It can refer to nothing else—that he is not Geoffrey."

Possibly she had looked for an exclamation, either of incredulity or of assent according to his knowledge, but Mr Carrados merely continued to look pleasantly interested.

"I did not know—I could not really know because I had never up to then met him. I could only admit that such a thing might be, although the chances were a million to one against that explanation. So that is it, actually? How did you find out?"

"I think I must have known all along—without knowing that I knew, if that doesn't sound too silly. You see, Uncle, it isn't anything to do with anything, being in love with a person—no matter how soppy it may sound to you in your wisdom. It's just a sort of Itness to do with one another and it won't work under any form of substitution. At first when I missed something that ought to have been there, I thought that it was just a rather contemptible streak of disillusion that Geoffrey should have been so terrified by anything that could have happened as to be scared into that condition, but of course if Geoffrey really had been it would have only made me care for him all the more."

"And then?" prompted Carrados, for Nora seemed to be in danger of losing herself in retrospection. "Something definite happened?"

"I had seen Geoff—*him* once or twice and tried to get him out of that awful apathy but on each occasion he seemed to fight rather shy of me. Then yesterday I met him in the road—he'd been to the mill, I found—and he more or less *had* to walk with me unless he bolted for it."

"Do you mean that up to then you hadn't been close to him?"

"I don't seem to have been, when I think it over," she assented. "You know that on the Saturday I was with you all the time, and since then it's always been in the house where he likes to keep in the shade and that poor dear tries to make everything go on as though nothing unusual had happened, and at the same time gets between him and anyone else who's there, like a troubled old hen with the last survivor of a brood of chickens."

"Yes, I think Olivant must have been pretty word-perfect with his piece. I must find out where he was educated."

"Well, as I say, we walked along the road on the way back. He doesn't speak yet—he doesn't try to, but I knew from his aunt that he has written a few words once or twice, just as that man said he would begin by doing. So I thought I'd try that."

"Yes?" encouraged Mr Carrados.

"I suppose it must sound terribly sloshy to you, Uncle Max," faltered Nora.

"Never mind that, my dear. I have always understood that under the most sportswomanlike jumper a tender heart might be beating."

"I just wrote, 'Am I still the same to you, dear?' and gave him the piece of paper. He took it and seemed to read it in that dreadfully detached way he has towards everything and then very slowly and shakily—all straight lines and angles you know—he scrawled, 'Dear. Dearest,' underneath the other."

"That was fairly satisfactory at all events. It indicated a sufficiently reciprocal superlativeness of feeling."

"The words didn't matter in the least. I only tell you exactly what took place for you to see that I had a perfect opportunity of noticing... On the Friday—the day before everything happened—we had been playing tennis and in some way Geoffrey jagged a finger nail so that it kept catching in his things whenever he touched it. You know how beastly that feels and it was on the first finger of his right hand, so I took a little pair of nail scissors that I carry in my bag and filed down the corner of the nail for him until the notch was taken out and as smooth as ever. It was hardly anything, unless you looked for it of course, but one corner of the nail was down close and quite unlike the rest...and as I watched him write I found that I was looking at that finger-tip and suddenly it flashed on me that the nail I saw was just the same length all round and it couldn't possibly be the one I had altered."

"Good," commented the blind man, coming to his feet and beginning to walk about the room and in and out among the furniture; "that's the sort of thing that takes *my* eye: *It could not possibly be*—and it couldn't! As evidence I don't suppose that it would be worth mentioning to a jury, who would be perfectly satisfied to convict a man who has been 'picked out' of a dozen on the strength of a small brown moustache and a conspicuous limp, and yet it puts everything else behind it. Forgive me!"

"For just a moment I found myself groping among the background of my mind, trying to drag out a possibility that it might have been another finger or the other hand although I knew perfectly well that it wasn't. Then I looked up and saw his face and although every line and every feature was the same I realised all at once that he wasn't in the least like Geoffrey."

"Did he see that you had guessed?"

"I hardly know. I heard your voice saying: 'Keep your wits about you and don't give anything away!' and I pulled myself together. It was all over in a second or two and I got away as soon as I could then and that's the last I saw of him. Oh, Uncle Max, why ever didn't you tell me?"

"How could I, child? I didn't know myself. I only took into consideration that it might be remotely possible. It was no good putting the idea into your head if it was a false scent but I dropped a hint or two that might back you up if you struck that line on your own initiative. It was really too much to hope for. Consider: of all the hundreds of thousands of pairs who have been said to be 'as like as two peas' not one in a thousand could really pass for another. And yet how beautifully it rounds everything off as no other theory could—the presence and exact role of our providential medical friend, the behaviour and deficiencies of the fictitious Tilehurst, and the necessary immolation of the unfortunate dog that couldn't have been hoodwinked by mere externals."

"That's all very well and I have no doubt that it's frightfully intriguing and all that," said Nora with some impatience, "but it doesn't happen to be the one thing that seems of any importance to me to be doing."

"Implying the real Geoffrey Tilehurst?"

"Naturally—what else? Where is Geoffrey now and what are they doing to him?"

"At all events they are scarcely likely to have harmed him. They took the trouble to drug him to bring off the coup with a minimum of violence. Probably he is being held somewhere until the business is through when they will clear off and release him."

"Or leave him gagged and bound somewhere so that they may get a longer start. The tender mercies of this particular gang are not likely to be very fastidious, I take it?"

"From what I know of the gentleman who is presumably acting as managing- director of the firm I shouldn't describe them as rabid humanitarians," he admitted. "The one thing you can rely on is that they won't do anything unnecessary that is palpably to their own disadvantage."

"That's very consoling," she retorted; "isn't it? Well, Uncle Max, here I am. What do you propose to do to rescue Geoffrey before they happen to find it to their advantage to hold him up between themselves and a splash of C.I.D. bullets?"

"I think you exaggerate the risk, my dear," he protested mildly. "Geoffrey is as likely as not to be very well treated wherever he is, and I dare wager that he'd be perfectly willing to stick it for a few more days if that will mean our netting the whole gang with evidence that will convict them."

"Perhaps he would, Uncle Max, but we can't ask him that and in the circumstances I've got to do what I consider the best thing for his interests. Get Geoffrey clear and then asphyxiate the lot and welcome."

"But, my child, if Geoffrey is to be got out at this immature stage it blows the gaff completely. Half of the crowd will vanish, including all the worst, and we shall have no proof at all of the real depths of the conspiracy."

"Sorry, Uncle; I know how attractive that part of it is to you, but Geoffrey's safety is more important to me than unearthing a plot to bomb the Houses of Parliament."

"Of course, of course," he hastened to assure her; "so it is to me—er, theoretically. The only point of difference between us is that I see the extreme desirability of doing both. Secure the offenders in the act and Geoffrey's release automatically follows."

"It might. On the other hand there might be one of those regrettable hitches where the experiment is perfectly successful only they unfortunately fail to revive the subject. As it is, I have a certain amount of leeway to make up for assuming that Geoffrey had been thrown into a blue funk—perhaps I shan't be quite so heroic about my own nerve until I've shown some."

"Well, you made up a fair share when you got us that house in Maplewood Avenue, I should say," he reminded her. "A good deal may depend on what goes on there before we are through with it."

"I wanted to ask you about that—the house I followed Olivant to. Have you found out anything yet?"

"Nothing at all, for the sufficient reason that so far the action hasn't reached there—the first move must come from Tapsfield. Of course if I had given Scotland Yard the tip they would have picketed the place but I saw no reason to make the Yard a present of the facts until I had a pretty complete case to gloat over them about. So that without letting it go out of my own hands I could only cover your end. I may decide to let Inspector Beedel in sooner than I had intended now—this dual Tilehurst business considerably modifies the outlook. And, apropos egad—that secluded old roomy house—er, yes; it might be as well to."

"Go on, Uncle Max," said Nora pleasantly. "I like to watch your exceptional mind at work. Apropos the disappearance of Geoffrey, and that big old lonely house, you were saying—?"

"Saying, Nora? Only that if one is to do any good there it will be necessary—in due course—to get considerably more assistance."

"Exactly what I was thinking as you spoke, dear. Both thoughts. I'm glad that there are points of the case where we have the same ideas. Don't think me presumptuous, Uncle, but it enables me to leave that part in your hands with every confidence."

"My dear," said Mr Carrados, bringing his involved perambulation to a close in front of her, "I feel in a way responsible for letting you into this and no doubt that makes me seem fussy—"

"That's quite all right, Uncle," replied Nora cheerfully. "Mother would be ever so much obliged to you, I'm sure. If you—at the other end—happen to see her before I do again I know that you'll be able to satisfy her that I'm not likely to get into mischief."

"I don't doubt that I shall," he agreed, with a rueful acceptance of the position. "I only wish I could satisfy myself as well while I'm about it. But you aren't going already?"

"Yes. It is rather a disappointment, isn't it? But I take it that the ordinary social amenities are suspended for the nonce—whatever a nonce may be—and you've given me what may be rather a bright idea."

"Then in return perhaps you will give me just an ordinary one—as to what it's your intention to be up to now?"

"Well, I don't quite know yet or of course I should value your advice immensely. You see, Uncle Max, I rather take after you in one thing that I've noticed about your work—we both like to keep an open mind and to be decided by the requirements of the moment."

"And you are determined to tell me nothing—"

"There's nothing really to tell... But isn't there a sort of Right by First Discovery? And, well, in a way I was the one to discover that house that he went to, wasn't I?"

* * * * *

"It seems to me, Joolby," said Mr Nickle, picking his words with the air of elegant disdain which had the double effect of sometimes making the commonplace sound almost impressive and of always making the cripple secretly hate him rather more than before, "it seems to me definitely to put the final lid on. If you take my advice you'll cut your losses, call everything off, and get Vallett out of the way so as to red herring the trail before they sight you."

"If I took your advice, Nickle, and chaps like you, I should be pushing a little truck about Limehouse selling firewood," replied Mr Joolby. "Your trouble is that you see blue whenever you hear a whistle round the corner. This is going through, whatever happens."

"Amiable lunatic," murmured Nickle, turning again to the cypher message.

There were four of them present in Mr Joolby's back office behind the shop in Padgett Street and to judge by their morose looks things were becoming none too rosy for the Tapsfield undertaking. Joolby himself swelled and fumed in a venomous mood against gods, men, and devils; Nickle stretched his "I-told-you-so" pose to its most offensive power and the other two, mere hirelings of crime on the dealer's long waiting list, bit their lips gloomily and exchanged looks of mutual support and mutual instigation.

"That's all very well, governor—'whatever happens,'" said the more assertive of the two at this grandiose challenge, "but what about we blokes as'll be left in it? You'll take bleed'n' good care to have plenty of time to do a guy when the fuse blows out, but it'll find Snooky and me stuck in a jam all right and no one's going to cut across and drop the signal."

"And how am I going to 'do a guy,' you foolish fellow, if it comes to wrong?" demanded Mr Joolby, glowering heavily. "You talk as if I could hop, skip and jump and leave everything behind me. Aren't I chained to the ground like what none of you aren't? Aren't I so tied to my house and shop here where I have thousands of poundsworth of stuff—though, mind you, I can't sell it—that I should starve if I left them behind me. Was there ever such monkey chatter!"

"All the same, governor, what he says is right," put in the other, anxious to back up his friend now that the first step had been taken. "You're here, aren't you, if it comes to a bunk but we're there, cut off so to speak, and if anything slips, like what that bloke makes out in his letter, we shan't have half an earthly. Any reasonable risk's neither here nor there, governor, but it's no use blinkin' a blinkin' moral."

"'If it go wrong,' 'if something slip,' 'is that a cop?' 'Mammy come and give Bertie his dummy,'" bellowed Joolby, wrought almost to frenzy by the renewed thwarting of his cherished plans. "Suffering Jesus! Am I the only one in the crowd with guts enough to cross a road in the dark or to walk past a police-station in the daylight? Isn't this the chance of a lifetime? Have either of you ever made a couple of quids at once in your puff before—pinching goods from the back of delivery vans and smooching lead off empty houses? And now in less than a week you'll have enough to keep you in beer to the end of your natural. Doesn't that make you brave enough to face even a chained bulldog?"

"That's right enough, governor, and if there wasn't—"

"Oh my God! I'm going out to breathe the pure air of Shadwell," exclaimed Mr Nickle, flinging himself from his chair in an access of fastidious irritation. "It's like being in a gory squirrel cage with you three going round and round and getting nowhere."

"How is there anywhere to get but here?" demanded Joolby with stubborn insistence. "It's going on just as ever, don't I tell you, Nickle?"

"Comlade Blonsky want look-see," announced Won Chou stolidly. As usual he gave the impression of knowing exactly what was going on without being there to see it, and although the ingenuity of his observation posts discounted the latter part of the assumption the former was probably correct enough.

"All right," replied his master, with a painfully uncouth gesture of resignation, for the deputy was the last person he could have wished to have to deal with then, and he was feeling very tired. "Make show glad come in."

"Thank heaven even for Bronsky," remarked Nickle, pausing in his door-ward progress. "Time brings strange revenges!"

If Won Chou gave the impression of knowing everything without the least interest in what it was, Mr Bronsky's bearing was plainly that of a man who had been kept too long in the dark and was now determined to receive his proper meed of due attention. The glossy attire might be slightly less resplendent than when he first appeared, but his entrance had lost nothing of its thick-skinned suggestion that he was there to push his way in and to the front whether he was welcome or unwanted. The kiss of fraternal love had no longer any place in his greeting, in fact the greeting itself was reduced to the most perfunctory word and nod in the host's direction. Social distinctions were indicated by entirely ignoring the presence of both Nickle and the other two worthies.

"What is this which I hear of things going not well, Joolby?" he demanded, coming to the point at once. "I was definitely to have been keep inform of any of the sort happening."

"Ah, comrade, sorry that I didn't notice you had come in—forgive the apparent discourtesy," intervened Nickle in his most offensive vein of politeness. "Well, I can only imagine that the omission has been through some underling mistaking his instructions—though possibly our not hearing anything detailed ourselves until now may have had something to do with the unfortunate position."

"Psss! Tsss!" fumed Mr Bronsky, recognising that he was at a disadvantage in this sort of medium. He accordingly took off his hat and put it on again, sat down at the table with his back towards as many of those present as possible and began to drum loudly and persistently with his fingers.

"I beg your pardon?" remarked Nickle, raising his eyebrows; "I didn't quite catch your remark," but as Mr Bronsky merely drummed with increased vigour, what is sometimes called "an awkward pause" was all that resulted from this brief passage.

"You have the letter, Nickle," said Mr Joolby with conspicuous mildness. He seemed to have exhausted all his fighting spirit. "Let him hear what Vallett says about it."

"It is a message in code," explained Nickle, shelving for the time being the acuter symptoms of resentment. "Joolby here sees in it a promising augury of success; everyone else thinks it means that if we don't get out now we stand an excellent chance of getting about seven years a little later. However, I'll decode the essential part and then you can decide which view appeals to you the more."

"How has this message you say is from Vallett come?" demanded Mr Bronsky with all the importance of one propounding something really vital.

"What the hell does that matter—comrade?" replied Nickle. "Naturally we have our channels and this has come in quite the usual manner. If you think—but perhaps you would raise that valuable point after I have finished. Vallett writes: 'I spotted the girl N.'—by that he means a Nora Melhuish who lives near—'to be the chief danger from the beginning. She is mixed up with a man called Max Carrados who is evidently taking a hand in the game though I don't know yet exactly in what direction.'"

"Ten thousand million tevils!" exclaimed Mr Bronsky, springing to his feet and glaring wildly round at each one in turn. "What did I tell you, Joolby? Max Carrados again, and you would have it that he came to buy some of your junk rubbish. He was here that day I come and now he appear on the scene there. And you believe that all he wants are foreign stamps or is it dried ferns to stick into an album! Oh goddam, nobody can say I never warn you!"

"Quite so," commented Nickle. "Well, to resume the tale: 'Today something missed a cog and whatever it was N. is now all but satisfied that G.T. is not the authentic.'"

"She smell a rat?" propounded Mr Bronsky. "We think he must mean that," assented Nickle, with suspicious gravity. "Unless you can cut N. off before she spreads, the big noise may happen any minute and even then I shall have to make some quick tricks to get clear. This is a pity because in all other directions it was going good and I was fixing for next Saturday when there will be a full stock and conditions easy.' There you have it, Bronsky."

"You shall do as you likes but I am done with it," declared the comrade without a shade of hesitation. "If it is as he says that this girl knows and is about there—why in name of thunder did you not have her taken care of before this happen?"

"Well, you see, Bronsky, for one thing we aren't in Bolivia here—not even in Chicago. People will talk so in the country—especially if it's a young girl—that we might just as well have floodlit the village while we were about it."

"All the same, Mr Bronsky's in the right," chimed in one of the others. "You must either put this here girl away or else call off the whole business."

"Precisely," agreed Nickle. "And as we can't do that it is called off in the general interest."

"It is not called off," spat out Joolby, gathering himself together in a last stand for the glorious hazard that in the course of weeks had become his passionate obsession. "It is not changed one line, one inch, one minute. All this talk about recognising and risk and whatnot else is nothings but funk and fiddle. It is clear the girl did not be sure or she would have said so out and Vallett must have gone then. If she think there is something queer she is only puzzled what it is and days will go while she is making up her mind what has happened. I tell you these big jobs always has their touch and go and it is the side that does not get the jumps that comes away with the parcel."

"Howsoever, I cannot be in it now it has come to this," declared Mr Bronsky, siding with the majority with characteristic firmness. "It would bring ill name with Commission. After all, Joolby, this is only detail—in the one matter of paper. There will yet be other ways—"

"There are no other ways," retorted the other harshly. "It was a perfect scheme and everything hung together. It still is and I'll carry it through myself and be damned to your wet trousers! Remember, Nickle, this was to be in my hands and so long as Vallett stays there—"

"Vallett will not stay there after today," Nickle interrupted coldly. "It's sheer madness to let him stay and be taken like a rabbit. I got him there and I'll make it my job to get him away tonight. So put that in those dry trousers of yours, Mr Joolby, and sit on it."

"You are all against me, so?...and it would have been the most terrific smash..." muttered the cripple, falling back into his chair and seeming to grow less before their eyes as the realisation of failure closed in upon him. "You may as well go away now. I do not want you."

"Well, governor, what else could you expect?" genially put in one of the hirelings, good-naturedly hoping to impart a tinge of cheerfulness to the general leavetaking. "Come to look at it as a reasonable man—blimey, hadn't you better see what the perishing blighter wants before he cracks the ruddy contrivance?"

Joolby turned listlessly towards the telephone on his desk—he did not appear to have noticed the calls up to then—and with his slow elaborate movements got the receiver to his ear.

"*What?*" they heard him say, and above the top of the desk—caught by the intensity of that one word—they saw his face change as he listened and the lethargy drop from it in such a startling fashion that all four stiffened where they stood, frankly waiting for dropped crumbs of enlightenment.

"Yes; yes; yes. Of course she will. Go easy and notice nothing. Here, hold on a minute, though. I want you to repeat what you've just said to Mr Nickle here. Nickle, get this slick and tell them what it means now."

"My everlasting Lincoln and Bennett!" faltered Nickle, after he had complied, listened for a moment, and then hung up the receiver; "this—this is really one beyond the limit! George Larch says that Eliza there has suddenly gone sick and sent a cousin in her place to carry on until she gets over it."

"Go on, go on," blared Joolby, swelling and gasping in his chair as Nickle paused and looked round to gather their attention for his dramatic climax. "Tell them what he said then."

"The 'cousin' is Nora Melhuish from Tapsfield—Soapy recognised her for a cert—and now she's walked in of her own free will and all we have to do is to shut the door and keep her."

"No need to call it off, you see," croaked Mr Joolby, enjoying his little triumph quite good naturedly. "It still goes on, eh, Nickle?"

"Why the hell not?" replied Nickle, with a shrug that might mean anything. "Joolby, I really begin to think that you must be under divine protection—by 'divine' in your case of course I refer to the devil."

12

THE STAGE IS SET

"George, dear," said Mrs Larch, as her husband put his head in at the door of the dining-room to see what was going on there, "do come in for a minute or two and make it a bit human."

"Why certainly; what is it, old girl?" he inquired, amiably complying.

"It isn't anything particular," she confessed. "Only this place—it's like a bloody prison."

"Well, for the matter of that it is one," he replied—still naively pained to hear Cora swear, even as it always came to him as a faint shock to see her drink gin and water. "That young fellow down there—"

"Oh, don't talk about it," she said with a deprecatory shudder. "The way one thing's led to another till we're mixed up in raids and kidnappings and Bolshie plots—! Thank goodness we've nothing to do with what goes on down below. Let his Chinks and dagoes do his dirty dungeon work if he wants it done, I say. It's not what we're paid for. Nothing was said to you about keeping anyone shut up in a cellar when you took it on to come here, was it, George?"

"Not a thing. There was to be more room and it would be safer in a new place for a week or two—that was all I ever heard. I don't like it any more than you do, Cora, but there seems nothing for it now we're here but to hang on for the time and chance it."

"You may well say chance it, lad. From what I see and what I hear it seems to be getting a pretty near thing which side touches down first, but the old geezer's dead set on going through whatever turns up, and God knows that if it comes to a general bunk he's bound to be the hindmost."

"Except that he'd throw everyone else out to the wolves to make time to do a getaway," George amended. "He's always been very lucky at that so far, has Joolby."

"Lucky! He has nigger's own luck if you ask me about it. This thing was absolutely down on the rim over what natty Nora had spotted up there, and then, lo and behold, if my lady doesn't coolly walk in to rescue her boy, for all the world like Glory le Roy in a Wild West three-reeler. That gives you the laugh, doesn't it? As if she could have put it across the cat that she was Eliza's cousin."

"Well, she could have put it across me for that matter if Dodger, who'd seen her up there, didn't happen to call round to do with the business," admitted George simply. "All these finches seem to get themselves up in the same way nowadays, till I can't tell one sort of tart from another. But I suppose there's something you go by."

"There's certainly something I can tell Nora Melhuish by from any cousin Eliza Higgs is likely to have, let alone one who'd be willing to come round here to carry on while Eliza was moulting. All the same, it's none too pleasant for me. I'm used to Elizas. I understand their little ways and if they don't understand mine they pretty soon get to. But this Hilda Kelly as she calls herself knows just how things should be properly done and that puts me at a disadvantage. Now would you say that those chairs ought to be left up to the table between meals, George, or pushed back, and should the cruet be kept on the sideboard or put away in the cupboard? I'm blest if I know."

"I'm damned if I do either. But what does it matter?"

"It doesn't. That's just the silly part of it—running the place for a crowd of crooks and roughnecks. But *she* would know, and if it's not done *à la* Ritz she'd put it right after me and make me feel a mut. Wouldn't say anything of course—just show me how it should be."

"Well it can't be for long now," suggested George soothingly. "After this we'll—"

"And then there's another thing," volubly continued Mrs Larch, to whom the relief of possessing George's ear was scarcely less of a luxury than in the rag-and-bone shop days, "and I like it rather less than all the other. She's not to be out of my sight for so much as a tick, if you please, unless I pass her on to that half-baked Chink, and all the time I'm not so sure that someone else isn't told off to keep an eye on me—and perhaps on you too, George, for that matter."

"They're welcome," said George, with the proud consciousness of innocence. "What I say I'll do I do. Joolby knows well enough that I've never double-crossed anyone."

"At all events we can go in and out and that's more than Hilda Kelly is to be allowed to. Mustn't answer the door, mustn't touch the telephone, mustn't stir out of the house—I ask you now, George, what's likely to be the end of this sort of thing when her people get the wind up? And if the cops begin to take notice what does it look like on a night like this, when everyone else is sitting in their shirt-sleeves with the windows wide open, and all these are shut up as if we expected a siege—well, I ask you?"

At this, George looked dutifully about and with a wise shake of the head admitted that from this point of view it might certainly strike the unprejudiced outsider as "a bit rummy." The place was the dining-room of the old-fashioned, well-retired house in Maplewood Avenue, a spacious, heavily furnished apartment, sufficiently well lit by a single cluster electrolier but with its windows—although they were overlooked from nowhere but its own secluded grounds—not only all scrupulously closed on that torrid summer night but with the curtains drawn, and shuttered. It had been a simple enough matter to keep Geoffrey Tilehurst secure without any elaborate precautions; a cellar, closed by a substantial oak door, and a man deprived of everything faintly resembling a tool could be thrust in and safely left to his own devices. But in Nora's case the fiction of liberty was outwardly kept up and though from the moment of her quixotic intrusion she was shadowed at every step and had not the remotest chance of slipping away if she repented of her boldness, she was even yet unable to decide whether her identity had been discovered or whether the spying and restraint were not merely commonplace details of this very queer household.

"One thing," added George, after the peculiarities of the situation had been sufficiently admitted, "it's going to be the last time I'm mixed up in what isn't strictly on the level. If we get clear this once with anything like tidy, old girl, it'll be that little cottage with the pigs and poultry for a moral."

"Oh, my dear lad, that cottage!" exclaimed Mrs Larch, somewhere between laughing and tears. "I wonder how many times we've paid a pretty price for it already!" and then on a common impulse this curiously simple pair of habitual criminals were in each other's arms and exchanging fond kisses for all the world like honest lovers.

"Hullo, turtle doves," remarked Nickle, stumbling in upon this idyll and accepting it with saving coolness. "Seen anything of Toady since dinner?"

"He was in his own sanctuary about five minutes ago with that latest Alsatian Bolshie. Arranging for the end of the world, I suppose. Did you want him?"

"No, it can wait. It's rather amusing, you know. I'll tell you the very latest."

"If it's one of your funny stories, Mr Nickle," interposed George rather hastily, "perhaps we'd better go—"

"No, that's all right," said Nickle with a comprehensive smile. "This is something that really happened just now—not what the barmaid said about the bathing suit to the bishop. I was going across the Triangle down there and who should I run into but our interesting invalid, Eliza Higgs, making her way towards the Rialto Picture House, with an equally young lady friend, both very superbly dressed for the occasion."

"Well I never!" contributed Mrs Larch.

"Oh yes, I assure you. Jewels flashed and silk garments rustled. Well, seeing that further disguise was useless Eliza capitulated and at the inducement of a strawberry ice—supplemented may I perhaps say by the attraction of my society—permitted herself and friend to be lured into Cushing's Comfy Corner Café where under skilful innuendo she broke down at her third sundae and gave away the whole transaction."

"She would," was Mrs Larch's tart comment. "That's Eliza Higgs all over."

"Oh well; we mustn't be too harsh. The young lady who dropped down on Eliza from the clouds—she'd evidently been watching for the chance—assured her that it was all a joke, in fact that she'd made a bet she could act as a servant for a week in a strange house without anything being spotted. Then she offered Eliza five Bradburys and what she was wearing at the time to co-operate and Eliza, we may imagine, simply leapt at it."

"It was a mean thing to give it away though," remarked George severely. "After taking the money."

"Possibly Eliza misunderstood some of the facts. From what she dropped, apropos of what I had said, I gathered that she may have assumed that I was in the secret, on Hilda Kelly's side, from the start," admitted Nickle glibly. "However, it didn't really matter either way. We knew pretty well how it stood already."

"Still, I think that Hilda might have hit on something better in the way of a fairy tale than what she did," speculated Mrs Larch. "She seems quite a sharp girl in general."

"Oh, I don't know," maintained Nickle impartially. "Of course since it tore one's inclined to say that, but as things stood what likelier tale could she put up at short notice? She might have got away with it, too, if it hadn't been—Oh, all right; I'll take it."

The interruption was a telephone call and Nickle crossed over to the small table by the door while the other two, the subject of Eliza talked out, waited to hear if there was any new development. Most of the calls that came were dead matter, for in the directory their number still appeared against the name of the former tenant and less than a dozen intimates were in a position to get through to them.

"It's 'Soapy,' talking from somewhere down there," rapped out Nickle, covering the mouthpiece as he spoke back into the room. "Get Joolby if you can, one of you."

Mrs Larch nodded to George and hurried out. But Joolby's progress was slow even on the level and this entailed a flight of stairs—or possibly the Alsatian Bolshie was difficult to get away from. At all events the conversation was over and the receiver hung up again before the cripple dragged his trailing feet through the doorway.

"What's this?" he said, the quickened beat of his throat betraying the stress of his exertion. "Is Dodger there speaking?"

"He was," replied Nickle, "but he's gone. He seemed to be pressed for time and I gathered that telephoning at all was rather risky."

"Well, where was he talking from?"

"God knows," said Nickle with a shrug. "Some wayside shrine one would imagine. He is scarcely likely to have rung us up from the village pub and in any case there's no idea of calling on him from our end."

"Well, what was it?"

"He says it's all right for Saturday still. Nora M. doesn't seem to have done any harm so far but he's getting jumpy about that fellow Carrados. He can't make out what's going on in that direction but he wishes you could do something. That's all."

"Oh, it is, is it? That's quite satisfactory, isn't it, Nickle? And he's getting jumpy about Max Carrados, is he? Strange that I'm the only one who never seems to get jumpy, isn't it? I suppose it has something to do with my physical peculiarities, for even as a boy I don't remember ever to have gone in much for jumping. Well, as regards Mr Carrados I have already arranged, as he suggests, to 'do something.'"

"The deuce you have!" said Nickle, staring his curiosity. "How is it to be wangled?"

"All in good time, my friend; you won't be left out of the performance. Now go down and help Won Chou and Jules to get things ready. They know what will be needed. And you bring Hilda up to me here, Mrs Larch. I want to have a little quiet talk with my new maid-servant." He waited until they had gone and then looked significantly at Mr Larch. "You understand all right, don't you, George?"

"Oh yes; I understand all right, Mr Joolby," replied Larch in his transparent way. "And so long as it doesn't go actually to extremes—"

"It shan't go actually to extremes, George." Mr Joolby's voice sounded positively sympathetic.

"I know that it may have to be cut rather fine and stretched rather far at a pinch of course, Mr Joolby. That's in the nature of the business we are on. But I rely on you to give me the nod in time to get Cora clear off whatever happens. I can take my own whack as it comes—as I always have done."

"Of course, George, of course. Women and children first—that's what the Bible says, isn't it? But not extremes on any account, eh? Well, well!"

"You know what I mean well enough, Mr Joolby. I mean bloodshed. I never have—"

"Here is Hilda, sir," announced Mrs Larch, reappearing at the door. "You said you wanted to see her."

"To be sure; to be sure," assented Joolby, plainly in his most benevolent mood. "And you two had better stay as well now you are here. One can't be too careful, I understand, in dealing with emotional young females."

"As you please, sir," replied Mrs Larch, remaining between Nora and the door, while George, painfully wishing that he could be away at the more congenial occupation of forging bank-notes, dropped discreetly further into the background.

"So you are our new help, Hilda Kelly, eh, girl?"

"Yes, sir," she answered rather feebly. It was the first time Nora had encountered Joolby face to face, and at the sight of his monstrous swelling infirmities she realised with a tremor of dismay that unless she could fight it down she might suddenly become faint, or sick, or something discreditably weak, if the ordeal went much further.

"And Miss Nora Melhuish, of Orchard Close, Tapsfield, also?" continued her employer. "Well, well"—as Nora found herself unable to combat this thrust in her agitated plight—"there's no great harm in having two different sets of names, and nearly all of our aristocracy have at least two separate addresses. Some of the most illustrious characters in history have found it convenient to change their identity from time to time. I have myself, and I dare say that Mr Larch there has been described as alias this or alias that on certain state occasions."

"I don't see what my private affairs have to do with my employment here so long as I do the work," she managed to retort, hoping to be let off farther questioning on this tacit admission.

"Very reasonably put," conceded Mr Joolby, still pleasantly tickled by what was going on, "and that brings me to another matter. Hearing that your cousin Eliza was feeling indisposed you came here to take her place so that we should not be inconvenienced, didn't you? Very thoughtful and considerate indeed; so different from what one usually hears of the domestic servant classes."

"If you don't mind I should like to get on with my work, sir," she put in, as unconcernedly as she could. "All this has nothing to do with my duties."

"Your work, eh?" replied Joolby, his mood suffering a remarkable transition as he proceeded. "Why, yes, of course; that's what you're here for, isn't it? But part of your duties, properly considered, consists in taking instructions and answering your employer's questions and so on, eh, doesn't it? Well, Miss Hilda Nora Kelly Melhuish, in the short time that you have been here among us have you discovered anything unusual or irregular in the conduct of this establishment?" Then as she stood irresolutely dumb at this the cripple unexpectedly swung one of his wooden props and brought it down with a terrifying crash on the bare table lying between them. "Answer me, girl; have you?"

"No, sir," she protested faintly.

"You haven't, eh? Then let me tell you that your eyesight is very little better than your Uncle Max's, Hilda Nora. You must have made very poor use of your opportunities here, for, you may as well know now, our business consists in imitating the paper currency of certain foreign countries—countries unfriendly to England and more or less actually at war with us if the truth was known. It's a political business but none the less it's technically illegal and so if it got about we should all get into trouble. You follow that?"

"Well, I suppose it's forgery in fact," she replied.

"Forgery! What do you know about forgery, girl? If I sign my own name on a telegram it may happen to be forgery in point of law. Think of that."

"But these are bank-notes you say."

"Well, what does it matter after all?" suggested Mrs Larch on a note of persuasion. "I mean to say, there's nothing really *wrong* about imitating things like that—it's only that they've made laws about it. It isn't as though you hurt anyone or did them out of something—which I certainly wouldn't hold with. It stands to reason that one bank-note's as good as another so long as people only think so; at least George's are, in fact they're better than the real ones if it comes to that. I often say it's the people who go kicking up a fuss when they find that they've been slipped a soft one who deserve to be put in the cart. Why can't they pass it on quietly to someone else and then no one would be a penny the worse off?"

"Well, it seems rather queer—" protested Nora, beginning to be a little reassured by the trend of the conversation.

"Never mind what it seems; I didn't have you up to listen to what you think but to tell you what to do," retorted Mr Joolby, taking over the conversation. "No doubt you thought you were very clever to get in here, didn't you? Well, we thought we were even cleverer to get you, so it wasn't very difficult you see. Now your Uncle Max Carrados has been interesting himself in our affairs much more than is good for him during the last few days. You say that you have noticed nothing going on wrong here. So why not tell him that and persuade him to drop it. Eh? Eh?"

It sounded too good to be true. All she would have to do would be to—

"Why certainly. I'll go at once and tell him that I've seen nothing at all wrong here."

"You will, eh? Very good. But you won't have the trouble of going. He may be here any minute now."

"Max Carrados here?" she exclaimed. "What is he coming here for?"

"It would appear that you wrote and begged him to come at once," deliberately replied Mr Joolby, and looking at his face—

which she had avoided doing to the extent of her power—the girl suddenly knew that the Thing before her was crudely and inhumanly evil. He was without pity, beyond restraint, and impervious to remorse; all the time he had been playing with her fears and enjoying the thought of the worse terrors he yet had in store for her. Oddly, the revelation helped her. "The message was rather ambiguously worded," he continued with meaning, "but it suggested a good excuse for him to call and it was sufficiently—shall I say disturbing—to make sure that he'd be a little anxious. Oh yes, he will come all right. In fact I can assure you that he is on his way now."

"So you forged my writing also—it's not only bank-notes it seems! And you think that Max Carrados will walk into a trap like that—or that I would do anything but tell him the whole truth the minute I see him?"

"The whole truth, so far as you are concerned, is that you have found nothing wrong going on here," he reminded her. "Convince him of that and all will be well for both of you... The little matter of our private activities that I mentioned just now was strictly confidential and you had much better dismiss it entirely from your mind."

"Yes; why should you have mentioned it at all?" she asked suspiciously. "Why need you?"

"I needn't. But I want you to understand that we really mean serious business, and that having very heavy risks to face we aren't going to stick at anything."

"You mean that I should league myself with you in trying to deceive Mr Carrados and the authorities? Is it likely?"

"I think it is quite likely when you have considered a little; so likely that you'll strain every nerve and try every artifice in your power to do it. You are very young to—to meet with an accident, Nora Kelly, and it would hardly be a pleasant thought that you had drawn Max Carrados into a trap with you. Ah; I fancy that must signify our myopic friend's arrival."

"That" had been the resounding clamour of an ancient bell somewhere below, for, side by side with its electric lights and telephone, the venerable mansion still retained the campanological features of its Victorian prime. Mrs Larch exchanged glances with her employer and significantly withdrew. These details were not lost on Nora (as, indeed, they were intended not to be) but surely her sagacious Uncle Max could be trusted not to be taken in by a ruse so transparent?

"It's no good, Mr Joolby," she challenged. "You think that you can frighten me with silly talk like that? You seem to forget that we are in London. Why, I have only to scream out to bring half a dozen policemen in. And I am quite sure that Max Carrados won't walk in here without making it certain that if he doesn't soon come out again the C.I.D. will smash down the door if need be to find out what has happened. I know him well enough for that."

"People don't scream out here, Hilda Nora," he replied, and his level assurance struck her coldly. "If they did nobody outside would hear them."

"It's no good talking like that," confirmed George Larch. "He won't be given the opportunity to arrange anything; he won't even know where he is coming. The person who gives him the note will deliver it when he's alone and he must come at once and be guided here if he is to come. No, Miss Melhuish, if Max Carrados does come here nothing but your doing exactly as we tell you will get either of you out again. And that's the best advice you'll have in this house."

"You hear what he says," directed Joolby. "That's the moderate view of the situation. Ah, here's Mrs Larch coming back. Now we shall know just how we stand."

"A Mr Carrados is below, sir," reported Mrs Larch, as indifferently as she might have announced the vicar calling.

"He says he would like to speak with the young person employed here if it's convenient."

"Ask him to wait a few minutes. And be sure to see that he has something to amuse himself with. Now, girl, you haven't much time to make up your mind. Which is it to be?"

"Just whatever I like," retorted Nora. "You can't bluff me into anything and I fancy that Max Carrados will be able to take care of himself if he's come here. That's all."

"All, is it?" snarled Joolby, beginning to display the familiar symptoms of his ire. "Oh no; not quite all yet, I think, Nora Hilda. Just open that door, George, and let's see if we can't find another argument why she should listen to reason."

The door thus indicated was the second one in the room—hitherto unused and not yet mentioned. It led into a small ante-chamber and so out again on to a passage and the stairs, this having been in the house's ampler days either a dressing-room or a service pantry as the conditions called for. This was the door George Larch now crossed over to and threw open and in the pause between the action and anything more happening a dreadful fear began to close in round Nora's heart while her knees grew as flimsy as stubble. *What* would emerge from that darkened room to confront her?

"Geoffrey!" was wrung from her lips as a figure, urged on by someone behind, stumbled into the light; "oh, my dear, how terrible you look. What are they doing to you?"

Geoffrey Tilehurst stood cowering and blinking in the unaccustomed glare but he seemed to make no effort to reply nor did he respond to her instinctive gesture of compassion. Then as he came further into the room—pushed forward by Won Chou—she understood. He was gagged and his hands tied behind him.

"What's this, Won Chou?" demanded Joolby, as though mildly surprised. "Who ordered like so fashion?"

"Make much noise," indifferently replied Won Chou. "Tellee shall do: do do."

"In that case it would appear to be his own fault," approved Joolby coolly. "Guests must conform to the rules of the house. Remove the gag now and let us hear what he has to say for himself—perhaps he has learned to know better."

"Nora! You are here to save me?" painfully mumbled Geoffrey, when Won Chou—none too gently as evidenced by a bleeding lip—had complied. "For God's sake don't believe anything they say. Only get me away from this dreadful place where I'm being—" A menacing gesture from another man who had silently appeared cut off the word and Geoffrey shrank back as though he knew only too well that the threat was no empty promise.

"Oh, Geoffrey, what can I do, only tell me," she begged—"We had no idea that anything like this—we thought that you were just being kept out of the way. Even now I don't understand—"

"Come, that will do," interrupted Joolby with an impatient growl; "talk, talk, talk—that's all it ever comes to with your kind of cattle. Do you still think that you are playing at charades, girl? Can't you see the sort of men you have to do with? You 'don't understand—!' No, I do not think you do, but we will very soon explain it... For the next three days we must be left undisturbed and to make sure of that there is nothing on earth that we are going to stick at. You and this man"—with a sweep of the minatory crutch—"must remain in our hands that long because you know too much. This Carrados has nosed into our affairs and so he must be reassured and headed off. We can't keep him as well—at least we'd rather not—because he's too influential it seems and he's set inquiry afoot, and before our time was up there might be the hell of a disturbance. Now you have it."

"But what have I—?"

"What you have to do is to convince him that he's been mistaken. If you do that you have nothing to be afraid of. At the end of three days you can both walk out—the best guarantee is that we have nothing to fear from you then and it would be inconvenient to have to leave someone to keep you. If you refuse—well, you see your friend there? A little more strain—a very little perhaps—and I'm afraid—I really am afraid, Miss Kelly—that his rather disturbed mind may be permanently unbalanced... As for yourself, I scarcely like to put into words what will probably happen to you before you get away. These crude Eastern races are so primitive in their ideas of the use they make of female captives."

"Oh, you fiend!" she flung back; "You unutterable brute! You would never dare—"

"Dare! I dare?" he retorted, dragging himself nearer to her and raising his form to the full on his props almost with a savage grandeur, "Look at me, brute that I am; look, look, girl, and then think! What is there that men can do to me now that nature hasn't done already!"

"Nora," besought the unfortunate Tilehurst, pitifully whining in his distress, "don't drive them to do worse than I've had already. Get me away on any terms for God's sake before I—I—Do anything they ask you."

"Oh, you poor, poor—" she cried out in her pain, immeasurably shocked at his pathetic deterioration, Then turning to Joolby again: "If I do as you want—"

"No harm will come to either of you meanwhile and at the end of three days you will be free."

"Tell me exactly what I have to do." At a sign the prisoner was led away again and the door of the ante-room closed on his humiliation. George Larch alone remained to lend Joolby whatever support the developments might entail and the moment was almost reached towards which so much preparation had been directed.

"When Carrados comes up you must receive him naturally and convince him that it's all been an unfortunate misunderstanding about us here," said the cripple, in reply to Nora's admission of surrender. "Don't try any half-and-half shillyshallying. Make no error about it, girl: you've got to succeed and to do it thoroughly."

"It isn't an easy thing to deceive Max Carrados. No matter what I say he may not— "

"Agggh!" he snarled impatiently, "It won't be an easy thing to watch your young man being put through a course or to find yourself strapped down, will it? You're clever enough in your way, I'll be bound, and the fellow's blind anyhow. You came to spy on us here, didn't you? You've—let us say—been in every corner of the house and gone through all the papers. Well, it's—what?—'a bloomer.' You have found simply an old fellow who has made a little something by years of hard work in his secondhand shop and is now retiring into private life and doesn't want to be troubled. Eh? Eh?"

"I must succeed," she whispered, more to herself than in assent. "God help me!"

13

NORA TELLS THE TALE AND CARRADOS SUPPLIES THE MUSIC

"Here you are, sir," announced Mrs Larch, piloting Mr Carrados solicitously into the room and then standing off to survey, as it were, her achievement in getting him safely there with some pride, "No more nasty stairs to climb up. And there is Hilda."

"Uncle Max!" exclaimed Nora, in her very brightest manner. "So you really have come then?"

Like many blind men of ingenious mind Mr Carrados prided himself on his ability to get about by himself and to tell the truth he was occasionally a little unceremonious in his rejection of sympathetic assistance.

"Let me find my own way; I'll manage to do it somehow," he would remark as he put these well-intentioned people aside. "If I do knock my shins it will teach me to remember the position of something for ever," and though none of his closest friends could recall the occasion when Mr Carrados had knocked his shins they all might have instanced rather odd little touches of clumsiness or unaccountable lapses in his form which had at the time seemed surprising. Inspector Beedel, whose Yard record was not unaffected by their acquaintanceship in the past, had his own views of these failings.

"When Mr Carrados makes a break," he had been known to say, "it's about time for some blighter to hop it."

On this occasion, however, there was nothing drastic to deplore. Smiling away Mrs Larch's proffered arm the blind man stretched out his hands right and left and—more than anything from a matter of habit one would judge—touched the door and wall here and there as though to learn thereby the points of his location. Certainly he narrowly escaped a minor disaster at the telephone table which lay in his path but with an exclamation of annoyance at the contact—a mere brush—he neatly verified its position and nature. And if this was a wily snare on the visitor's part to surprise a betraying sound from anyone who lurked, it failed signally in its object. Mrs Larch could not restrain a little gasp of dismay when she saw what nearly happened but Mr Joolby and George from their well-retired positions—the former seated, the more active man standing—were both too wide-awake to betray their presence.

"Well, my dear," admitted Mr Carrados in answer to his niece's greeting, "I gathered that you might not be altogether sorry to see me. So"—with a reassuring laugh—"here I am." A mild amusement at the possible humours of the situation characterised his manner.

"Now I'll leave you two quite alone, if you'll excuse me, Mr Carrados," tactfully remarked Mrs Larch, with an admonitory glance at the two figures in the background. "Being a gentleman, I can hardly expect you to understand, perhaps, but as it happens I'm rather busy."

"Oh, but I do understand," he gallantly assured her. "I get rather busy myself sometimes. You mustn't judge me merely from an idle visit."

All very pleasant, no doubt, but every one of the five people in the room had, in the vulgar phrase, "other fish to fry," and Mrs Larch's cue was to get out of the way without delay and give them the opportunity to be at it. This she accordingly now did closing the door with perhaps a little unnecessarily elaborate evidence of her departure, and uncle and niece were left "alone" together.

"What a very agreeable sort of person, Nora," he blandly observed, discovering for himself a suitably placed chair and occupying it. "Made me feel that I was giving no trouble at all in calling."

"Oh yes, she is," eagerly confirmed Nora. "And it's all the more because I feel so dreadfully ashamed of the trick I've played on them here. Uncle Max, you know we really *have* done it!"

"Ah?" he endorsed vaguely. "I guessed that there had been something of a fiasco from your hasty note, but—I could see that you wrote rather in a flurry—you know you left it all rather ambiguous. Indeed, from one thing or other you said I half thought that you might be in some sort of"—discreetly lowering his voice—"danger!"

"Danger!" she laughed, in great high spirits; "what a perfectly priceless notion! No, indeed, old dear; the only danger about here was the danger of making a great goose of myself, and so my first thoughts flew to you as the readiest means of getting me out of an awkward situation."

"Why of course," he agreed. "Always fall back on Uncle Max—if you remember I particularly put you up to that whenever you get yourself in any mischief. And in the present case I feel more or less responsible for I have half an idea that it's partly my fault your being here. Now as we are quite alone suppose you tell me exactly how you are situated?"

"Well, Uncle, it's really been a ghastly mistake from the very beginning. Of course I can't pretend to say what may have been going on anywhere else and certainly from one thing and another there seemed to be enough to make you suspicious. But these people at all events are as innocent of crime—it really makes me want to laugh—as district visitors, and I feel that we ought to do—well, to do anything we can to make up for perhaps getting them suspected."

"Um, yes; perhaps we ought, now that you've settled it," he admitted, with just a shade of lingering reluctance. "By the way, who are the people, Nora?"

"Well, there's Mr Joolby, of course. It's his house I believe and he is more or less—an invalid. He has a shop, an antique shop, somewhere else in London, I understand, but I think he's retiring now and that's why things are rather upset and haphazard yet as he isn't really settled. Then there's Mrs Larch, the housekeeper—you've seen her already."

"The agreeable lady?"

"Ye-es. Oh, but they are all quite pleasant and agreeable people really."

"All? There are others then?"

"I mean those who happen to call—visitors. They're quite ordinary, respectable people, you know. I think that they mostly have to do with Mr Joolby's business—I mean his shop of course."

"Not the sort of people who'd commit burglaries or plan elaborate forgeries?"

"The very idea! One or two of them may be rather foreign-looking perhaps but I suppose a good many people are what one would consider eccentric characters who have to do with the antique business."

"Yes, I imagine so: Bohemian and all that. And the providential gentleman whose name doesn't seem to figure on the medical register—Dr Olivant. He came here if you remember."

It was unfortunate that Mr Carrados should have recalled this. So far it had been quite plain sailing among airy generalities but Dr Olivant was a specific case and had to be dealt with concretely. For a moment Nora had to think; luckily the inspiration accorded her was on lines that admitted a certain amount of hesitancy when explaining the facts to an old-fashioned uncle.

"Why yes, to be sure he did, didn't he?" she admitted, with careful deliberation. "Well it's—it's rather mysterious about him until you know the circumstances. He really has been a doctor and a specialist and he is quite qualified to give advice, only Olivant isn't his proper name. He's—been—been struck off the register. He's a little queer they say, and at times forgets about what has happened."

"Tshk, tshk; sad, sad," commented Mr Carrados sympathetically. "And such an imposing presence."

"Yes, it does seem a pity, doesn't it? Illegal operations, you know. So of course it's rather a delicate subject with him."

"Naturally; naturally. How little we know after all, Nora, of the tragedy that may be going on about us under the quiet prosaic surface! And as he came here, I suppose that the doctor has turned his hand to the antique business also, has he?"

"Well, he had to do something for a living I imagine. Of course he can't be a doctor any longer, can he? I think he helps Mr Joolby with the shop in some way."

"Operates on the damaged articles of virtu doubtless. Well, Nora, you seem to have made pretty good use of your time here."

"Oh I have; I have. Of course no one suspected me of anything and I have watched them and listened at key-holes and looked at everything that I wasn't supposed to see in the most shameless manner. That's why I can be so positive that there's nothing at all wrong going on here."

"Then the only thing we can do would seem to be to get out of it as gracefully as possible. There's no point in your staying on any longer. After all, as a domestic help I have no doubt that—without being in any way critical of your abilities, my dear—Mr Joolby can replace you without much trouble."

Mr Carrados smiled a good-humoured tolerance of the imbroglio in which they had both landed, leaned back in his chair and dropped a careless right into his coat pocket.

"Look here, Nora," he suggested mischievously, "I have rather a bright idea. We shall cut pretty foolish figures when it comes to explaining, shan't we? What do you say to slipping quietly out and writing our apologies?"

For perhaps a couple of seconds the girl's mind poised, while her slanting eyes took in at a flash the essentials of the situation: the unguarded door, so near, George Larch away across the room and Joolby quite literally and negligibly "out of the running." So much had happened emotionally in the past short half-hour that, as the phrase goes, she scarcely knew which way up she was standing and for the time at least she had entirely lost touch with the vital crux of the situation. It remained for a rather uncanny happening to decide her. Apparently of its own accord the door of the anteroom noiselessly fell open and in the now well-lit space beyond her startled eyes took in the tableau of Geoffrey in his attitude of hopeless terror with the two custodians who had charge standing above him. Almost at once the door was closed again but the reminder had been sufficient.

"No, no; I really couldn't do that—not as things are," she protested rather wildly. "Don't ask me to, Uncle Max, because—well, I shouldn't like you to think that I can't stay and face it. And you do understand that everything's all right here, don't you?"

"Oh, bless you, yes," he replied. "All the same I think we could carry it off. It might be the simplest in the end. I'm almost inclined—"

"No, no!" she insisted. "I mustn't think of it. Don't, Uncle; please don't. We could never—I mean it wouldn't be *right* in the circumstances; it really wouldn't. Don't you see, I've bribed and persuaded their servant to let me take her place and if I run away like that they'll be left quite in the lurch—it isn't so easy to get anyone at a moment's notice as you may think and they'd perhaps have to go on for days and days servant-less. That's the only reason I have for staying; it really is. They're quite all right here in every way I do assure you."

"Oh yes; it isn't that. The boot's on the other foot in fact; I should like to think that we'd been clever enough to be on the right tack from the start but you've quite burst that bubble. Only I wish it had gone the other way for it's devilish awkward for me as it happens. Inspector Beedel of Scotland Yard is relying on my inquiries in this quarter and now I shall have to call it off and admit that I was mistaken... You seem rather pleased, my dear"—for Nora had given a sigh that unmistakably conveyed relief and satisfaction.

"Well, it is something of an event to find Max Carrados wrong for once," she retorted, turning it off into an assumption of skittishness. "You know, Uncle Max, it was dreadful to live up to your terrible omniscience."

"I'm afraid, young lady, you won't be the only one to enjoy a chuckle when I report to my professional friends," he confessed. "That's the worst of a reputation; but it has to be done. We haven't got a leg to stand on."

"And you will do that," she insisted, anxious to clinch the advantage; "you will stop Scotland Yard doing anything about them here for the next three days, won't you? I mean," she hastened to amend as she recognised the curious significance of a time limit, "it mightn't seem reasonable to ask anyone not to do anything, no matter what happened, for ever."

Possibly Mr Carrados was considering it from his own way round for he did not appear to notice anything in her stumble.

"Naturally I will," he replied. "I must, or I may land myself in rather serious trouble. You see, I'm not an official in any sense so I can't plead privilege and invoke the powers to back me. In the eyes of a jury I should be merely an interfering amateur—

and there's such a thing as defamation. Well, as you won't be persuaded to come now, when may we expect to see you back from this haunt of ancient peace?"

"Oh, by about Saturday I should think."

"Ah, Saturday?" he considered. "That will be three days from now, won't it?"

"Will it? I hadn't thought. It will be the end of the week, you see, and Mrs Larch fancied that by then she could find someone to take my place most likely."

"We must consider that as arranged then." He "looked" round the room in his usual deliberate way, turning his sightless eyes (as it might seem odd to say his nose and ears) to every point of the compass. "At any rate I'm glad to have seen you in an unusual setting, Nora. I hope your cap's becoming."

Nora had played her part—there could be no doubt of its success—but now she was uncertain of what next would be required of her. Her instructions had not gone beyond convincing Carrados—was she to let him go at this point on his assurance of putting things right with Scotland Yard or was some further guarantee required? She shot an inquiring glance in the direction of the two silent witnesses of the curious scene and Mr Joolby evidently decided that the moment had arrived for his own intervention. At a sign from him George Larch noisily threw open the door of the smaller room (they never fell into the mistake of making it too hard for the blind man to follow what was supposed to be going on) and to the accompaniment of a great business with his sticks Joolby "entered."

"Hilda, I want you to—" he began, failing for the moment to notice the visitor who was merely standing up in the middle of the room, "Eh, who have we here?"

"Oh, this is my uncle, Mr Carrados, sir," explained Nora. "He just called to see me for a few minutes. Now he's going."

"Ah, good evening, Mr Carrados," said the master of the house, his manner, so far, distant without being actually hostile. "I'm glad I happened to come up in time to see you. You doubtless know who I am, since I think you boast that you never forget a voice and we have met once already."

"What! Mr Joolby, the eminent authority on Greek numismatics? To be sure we've met. Let me see; the more primitive methods of disposing of one's enemies by obscure venoms, wasn't it?"

"Never mind that now," retorted Mr Joolby. "This isn't my shop. I am simply a private gentleman here. Let me tell you that I am not pleased with what has been going on, Mr Carrados. It seems that you have been making unfounded charges against my character and reputation. People are talking—I see them look after me and whisper as I go along. I don't know what isn't being said about me—what slanders aren't being spread. My intention in coming here was to give up my business altogether and lead a quiet but useful life. I might have put up for something—the Borough Council or what not—in time. Now that's all done for thanks to you and a lot of money wasted."

"Mr Carrados sees that he has been mistaken in what he thought," ventured Nora, anxious to keep this to the front. "He is willing—"

"Then there's another thing," went on Mr Joolby, impervious to soothing. "This young person who was got into my house on false pretences. There's no doubt that you sent her here to spy on me; the connection is quite obvious. That's a serious matter, Mr Carrados. People have had to pay very large compensation for that sort of thing before now. Not that she could do any harm, simply because there is nothing discreditable to find out, but the imputation is there all the same. In fact it's questionable if it doesn't amount legally to a conspiracy to blackmail and the penalty for blackmail doesn't stop at damages." With one of his terrifying changes of front he turned suddenly on Nora breathing menace: "Come now, girl, you've had the run of the house, you know; you may as well own up to it. What have you nosed out here that's wrong. Eh? Eh?"

"Oh nothing, nothing, Mr Joolby," she protested. "I've assured my uncle that we have been quite mistaken and that everything here is perfectly straightforward."

"And so it is. Everything O.K. and above the board. Well, well—"

"I'm quite willing to admit that a mistake has been made, Mr Joolby, and to shoulder all the blame," interposed Carrados. "I shall notify Scotland Yard through my friend Inspector Beedel that I have unfortunately been on a wrong tack and in consequence misled them. After that you will have no further trouble."

"You will, eh? Well, it's about the least you can do as things are, isn't it? Especially as I am considering bringing an action for very heavy damages if I don't get satisfaction. And how am I to know that you will do as you say after all? I haven't any guarantee."

"Well, really, I—I don't quite know what to say to that," admitted Mr Carrados. "What do you suggest for instance?"

Mr Joolby appeared to consider deeply.

"Suppose you write a letter now to Scotland Yard, admitting that you've been mistaken, and let me post it. Then there can't be any double shuffling. You say you are going to notify them, don't you? Well, if you are honest about it you may just as well write a letter here and now and tell them."

"Just as you like, Mr Joolby, if that will set your mind at rest. As you say, it's the same thing in the end. Have you a sheet of paper handy?"

"Ah!" pounced Mr Joolby with an unpleasant spit of laughter, "I thought as much! So that was to be the way, was it? On strange note-paper and written with my pen and ink—then it would not be a very hard matter to write a little differently and repudiate the whole business if it is more convenient afterwards, eh, eh? No, no, Mr Carrados; the special tablet that you always use and written with pencil if you please the same as usual."

Apparently not in any way disconcerted Mr Carrados produced one of the small writing-pads that he invariably carried.

"You seem to be a very well-informed, simple, private gentleman," he remarked good-naturedly as he began to comply with the injunction.

"You have to be, in the antique line," retorted the dealer.

"Paper is often the difficulty, I understand," was the dry thrust. "Well, how will this do, Mr Joolby? 'Dear Inspector Beedel, Not too late in the day to admit a mistake, I hope, I am hastening to let you know that I was entirely at fault in my suspicions of the Joolby *ménage*—"

"No, I don't like that," objected the gentleman concerned; "'Joolby *ménage*' is too familiar when you are supposed to be doing your best to get out of the pretty mess you're in; it doesn't sound natural. 'Mr Joolby's household,' or 'the establishment of J. Joolby, Esquire' is more what one would expect to be written."

"True; perhaps I was becoming a little too colloquial. 'The establishment of J. Joolby Esquire.' May I, by any chance, add 'O.B.E.', some little distinction of that sort? No? A pity but gross oversights were common. Well: 'From personal observation I am now satisfied that nothing in the nature of what I had suspected had been going on there.'"

Absorbed in the composition of this odd document Mr Carrados alternately spoke and wrote while Mr Joolby, offering frequent helpful comment, betrayed the excited state of his mind shuffling here and there about the room to accompaniment of the continual tapping of sticks and the slither of his crippled extremities, indeed to anyone less deeply engaged than the blind man appeared to be it might have occurred that the amount of noise which this performance raised was out of all proportion with the extent of ground covered. The move was not lost on Nora but she felt that it would be madness to intervene with an open warning that must inevitably precipitate a crisis. Even when Nickle and Won Chou casually but very quietly appeared on the scene she clung to a desperate hope that this did not necessarily mean a breach of faith, but as they began gradually to draw in significantly on each side of Mr Carrados it was no longer possible to doubt some crooked intention.

"Uncle—"

In three swift steps Nickle was by Nora's side. His attitude and action were an open challenge.

"Keep your mouth shut or—" they said as plainly as though it had been spoken.

"'Will you therefore please call off any attention—which might prove embarrassing to me—in that quarter,'" continued the writer, still blandly immersed in his task. "'Now that I am leaving London for a few days—'"

"Uncle! Don't—" The words half unconsciously sprang from her lips as she realised in a flash the possibilities that this opened up and the risk—the fatalness indeed—of the admission. There was no chance of more. Nickle's strong hand closed instantly over her mouth while his arms held her in a grip that smothered all resistance. Won Chou had already glided forward to add his weight and from his sleeve there appeared a stoppered bottle and a pad that had doubtless been intended for another. Neatly, expeditiously, and without a sound that would not pass for Mr Joolby's gasps and clatter, the work was done and the unconscious girl carried away through the open door of the ante-room. Joolby's twisted grin lengthened.

"But, my dear, I've already arranged it all," protested Carrados, at this point becoming aware of his niece's neglected interruption. "Thanks, nevertheless—it's very flattering to find that you are so appreciated on the spot, isn't it, Mr Joolby? And I wouldn't say that I'm not every bit as fond of her on my side. Between ourselves," he continued, writing a line that concluded the letter, "since our little misunderstanding is now satisfactorily cleared up, I don't mind admitting that I really came here with an absurd fancy that the child might be in some sort of danger." He chuckled quiet appreciation. "Sounds absurd now, doesn't it? Eh, Nora? Here we are, then"—running a confirming finger along the words he had last written—"'—Now that I am leaving London for a few days and shall not see you before I go I thought it better to put the matter straight at once by letter.' There, Mr Joolby, just see if that doesn't satisfy all your scruples."

Nickle had now returned, leaving Won Chou, aided doubtless by Mrs Larch's practical hand, to cope with any emotional outburst when Nora came round again. There remained Carrados to deal with but even if he should be armed, two useful men—Larch and himself; Joolby didn't count—could settle the issue of that without the possibility of mischance. He noiselessly closed and locked the door of the ante-room as he came back to secure the next few minutes from the chance of disturbing interruption.

In all good faith Joolby accepted the sheet and half turned away to get a better light so as to make sure that this shifty fellow Carrados had been playing no tricks with the composition... How it happened he never knew and the other two could not quite see as they were close upon the cripple, and behind, but in the second that his attention was directed to the paper something undoubtedly caused Mr Joolby to stumble back and he floundered into the arms—and incidentally upon the toes—of his fellow conspirators. That was the moment chosen for the room to be blacked completely out and Mr Carrados's dry chuckle from the neighbourhood of the door—the general door—made it comparatively obvious to connect him with the phenomenon. He had not attempted to escape; he had simply snapped the light off, locked the second door, and was now apparently enjoying the effect of his manoeuvre. Exactly what that move implied did not at first convey itself to any of the trio.

"What the hell's happened?" shouted Nickle—the first to find his voice because he was the least involved in the gymnastics. "Do either of you know—"

"Stop him, you fools—don't talk," rasped out the more discerning Joolby. "You know I can't get along. After him, can't you?"

"Blast that table!" was Larch's hearty contribution, and the sound of the impact that had immediately preceded the remark indicated his precise condition.

"That will do nicely," came Mr Carrados's unruffled voice across the darkness. "Please all remain exactly where you are or two of your heads may get in line and I don't want to shoot more of you than need be."

"Has he gone mad?" whispered George in genuine bewilderment. "He seemed all right up to now."

"He is still all right, thank you, Mr Larch." There was a smile yet in the voice but the tone was no longer that of the conciliatory Mr Carrados at the table. "Possibly it was the initial jockeying for position that may have misled you. You will surely recognise that it was necessary for me to finesse Miss Melhuish out of the room before we got on to the shooting?"

"Shoot and be damned, you skug!" exploded Nickle. "As soon as we can see, by God! you'll squeal for this pretty loudly."

"Doubtless," was the smooth reply "—as soon as you can see. But the point of the situation, Mr Nickle, is that you can't see, and as I am a trained dead shot by sound, it would almost seem as though it might be I who could enforce the squealing."

"He has us there," admitted George Larch. "By golly!"

"Has he!" The scraping of a match against its box-side followed.

Two spurts of light whipped into the black; one upwards from the match, the other across from the door. The match at once went out and Nickle only just saved himself from screaming.

"Damnation!" he yelled, spinning round. "He's shot the box out of my hand!"

"Quite a safe mark—it was such an explicit sound," said Mr Carrados reassuringly. "I was rather afraid that you might strike the match on your trouser seat. That would have been unfortunate, wouldn't it?"

It fell to Mr Joolby to break the silence that hung rather heavily over the room after this demonstration.

"Mr Carrados. I don't pretend to understand what grievance you think you have, but if you will kindly turn on the light again we can all discuss it amicably and no doubt afford you complete satisfaction."

"Mr Joolby," replied Carrados, determined to be no less civil, "whatever grievance I may think I have we can discuss equally well in the dark. And all my arguments are capable of being put even more forcibly in those conditions."

"But there must be some mistake—" pleaded George Larch, still hopeful.

"I think there really must—but it is yours... My dear sirs, did you actually imagine that one could not follow every clumsy move you made, with Joolby's low comedy tramp and the other two stealing in like a couple of hired assassins in a penny gaff melodrama?"

"All this is quite unknown to me—" protested the deeply hurt Joolby.

"But not quite to me. Why, our good friend Larch wears an old family watch that has a voice like an alarum clock to my ears. You, Nickle, use something for your hair that would serve a drag-hunt."

"You son of a bitch! We'll get you yet," snapped Nickle. Of the three he appeared to feel the reverse the most—to him, under Carrados's caustic tongue, it was a personal humiliation. Larch was ingenuously amazed, while Joolby—to Joolby, wrapped in an imperforable armour of fatalistic certitude, it could be nothing but a passing trial.

"Ah," replied Mr Carrados with his unquenchable aplomb, "I have often wondered where I got my nose from."

"Be quiet, Nickle," directed his chief. "What's the use of foolishness like calling a gentleman bad names when he can gun you in the dark and you're no good even at striking matches? But Mr Carrados will no doubt remember that whatever happens here, somewhere else we hold two hostages."

"Mr Carrados will," he assented. "And Mr Joolby will have no chance of forgetting that in this room I hold three."

"Short of shooting us all in cold blood how's that going to help you, Mr Carrados?" asked Larch, coming down to the commonplace of the situation. "It looks like stalemate to me and the sensible thing would be to make it a draw and all call off in good order. As things are what do you think you can *do*, sir?"

"To be quite candid, Mr Larch, so far I haven't given it a thought. But to a man of resource there's always something. If you happen to be a theatre- goer yourself no doubt you've seen a number of ingenious tricks brought off in what I believe are called 'crook plays'—the trouble is that one can seldom remember a suitable dodge just when it's wanted. Now there's wireless; any amount of plots turn on that, but how on earth am I to use wireless? If only you happened to have a telephone about the room I might manage to call up reinforcements."

"And do you think that we'd be mugs enough to let you?" contemptuously came from Nickle.

"Oh, I don't know. You might not—or on the other hand you might. You might be interested in hearing what I should send—at any rate I don't mind telling you in advance and you can say what you think about it. Something—let me see—like this: Yes, Exchange, quite right, but—one moment—this is special and urgent. I want to get through to Scotland Yard—Victoria 7000—but I can't wait for the connection, because it's a matter of life and death. Ask Inspector Beedel there to send Flying Squad to Max Carrados in immediate danger at source of this message. Yes, B-E-E-D-E-L and C-A-R-R-A-D-O-S. You've got that quite all right? Thank you."

"You bloody fools!" shrieked Nickle, stung by a sudden dreadful inspiration, "We've let him phone He *has* got through!" In a transport of infuriation his hand went to his hip and the telephone stand crashed to the floor under the impact of his erratic bullet. Another shot and Nickle's automatic followed his match box.

"It only needed that sensational touch to convince the young lady at the Exchange that she was in the thick of the Real Thing," remarked Mr Carrados. "Thank you, Nickle. I might have overlooked it. Now we can all close our eyes and open our mouths and see what the Yard will send us."

"Well, that about puts the lid on," summed up George Larch philosophically. "It's all U.P. this journey."

"Not quite I think," ventured a sad, unconcerned voice and before Carrados could move—the dramatic opening of the door barred all chance of interference indeed—the light blazed on again, and Won Chou was revealed standing apathetically before them. "I happen to have met Mr Carrados in the past and knowing how clever a gentleman he is I took the precaution of cutting the wires as soon as I guessed that he was likely to be busy. Always best with a gentleman so brainful. He got nothing through to anywhere."

"The hell! And how the blazes did you get here? He locked the door."

"Little tool," explained Won Chou, modestly displaying a delicate implement from his inexhaustible sleeve. "Turn keys from other side. Always carry. Very useful."

"This from the downtrodden brother!" bitterly exclaimed Mr Carrados, throwing away his pistol and folding his useless arms. "Trick and game to you, Mr Joolby!" True he might still have put up a hopeless fight, but it had been a battle of wits throughout and psychologically he was beaten.

"And this to remember *me* by, you swine!" The blind man went down at the blow—a vicious smashing right, delivered with all the pent-up spleen of a practised boxer, and remained down unstirring. Nickle, in one of his uglier moods, considered that he had settled that reckoning.

14

A SIGNAL OF DISTRESS INTO THE UNKNOWN

It was Saturday morning, the morning of the day when, according to sundry remarks, two things were going to happen, Vallett had promised that by that date he would be prepared to bring off their wholesale raid of the Tapsfield bank-note paper and Nora Melhuish had given Mr Carrados to understand that on Saturday she would be ready to quit Mr Joolby's house and service. Of the two contracts the first seemed immeasurably the more likely to be met for while Vallett was freely at large to mature his plans daybreak found—or would have done if it could have penetrated six feet of earth and several courses of brick and mortar—Nora asleep on a long stone slab which was the chief feature of a cellar that was unpleasantly suggestive of a prison cell or even at a pinch a dungeon. Mr Carrados himself was there also only he happened to be awake, the sleeping accommodation not being of the class to entice a man of slightly luxurious tastes to somnolence. Nora slept as a young animal will: without any particular regard to which way up she was or what she lay on.

No matter how much Mr Carrados might "look" around there was very little to see and he had long since investigated every loophole. Of these there was quite literally one: a grated opening, six inches square, above the door; possibly not without its use to ventilate the cellar but almost negligible as a source of light since it gave upon a scarcely less dark passage. The only real illuminant had been one candle at a time from the pair that they had found burning when they came to themselves and discovered their plight—the last of them carefully hoarded by Nora, she alone being concerned, but this had long since burned down to its last flicker.

The cellar itself was long and narrow, brick built and whitewashed, stone flagged, reasonably dry but intolerably fusty. Its smell was that of ancient lees, decaying mushrooms, bad earth, snails and just a dash of drain to spice it. The low stone bench, running all the length, had doubtless in its palmy days stored casks of wines and beer.

For the hundredth time the blind man paced the meagre limits of their cell and for the hundredth time he found that none of his senses brought the faintest ray of inspiration. The solid oak door—he fingered it again—was as though made to resist a ram, the walls built to withstand a siege, and every stone and brick in wall, bench, or floor was as immovable as the face of a rock. They built well in those days of leisure.

The fittings of the door were in keeping with its timber—massive and bolted through and doubly fixed by rust and long disusage. Under his hand a stubborn latch sprung noisily: on the bench Nora turned in her sleep, half rose with a sudden cry and at once began to pour out a wild string of protestation:

"I tell you it's all right! The people here are absolutely straightforward and honest. They are! They are! You mustn't think because the man is like a loathsome creature—Don't you hear, Uncle Max, I swear it's quite all right and Geoffrey isn't here only if you don't—Oh, that filthy dream again. Nightmares are bad enough but when it comes to night-toads—!"

Uncle Max walked unerringly to where she was, sat down and put a firm arm protectively about her.

"There, there," he said, as simply as though she had been a child of nine, "I'm here with you, little woman. This place certainly is enough to give anyone dreams about reptiles—not that there are any here as a matter of fact," he hastened to assure her. "But you're awake now and all right, my dear."

"I'm awake," she said, making some attempt to shake her hair straight, "but I don't know so much about the all right. Have they brought us any water yet? Gosh, but I know now what it feels like to be marooned in the Great Desert."

"Not yet," he replied, trying to make his voice sound cheerful without being too sanguine. "It must still be pretty early."

"It may be early for today but it's jolly late for yesterday and they didn't bring us any all day. Nor the night before—or the year before it may have been: I'm losing count of time here. Any food?"

His arm tightened on her shoulder in compassionate pressure. There was no need to say it.

"Oh well, I don't suppose that I could eat any now if there had been. My throat must be like a roll of emery paper." Suddenly she discovered by the feel that she had been covered with two rugs as she slept and she turned on him with a show of affectionate indignation. "Look here, Uncle Max, cheating again! It isn't fair spreading your rug over me when I'm asleep and I won't have it. You know you promised."

"I found that I didn't need one," protested Carrados. "I only had to think of that infernal Chink putting it across me and I went beautifully warm all over."

"You poor old dear! It does annoy you to be had, doesn't it?"

"It does indeed. And when it involves me in letting someone else be had as well, it's positively vexing."

"Don't worry, darling. It isn't you who've let me in, but me you. If I hadn't been so large-headed with that fantastic slavey idea of mine you wouldn't have been here."

"I don't know, Nora," he speculated. "I should probably have got myself in somehow simply for the fun of seeing if I couldn't get out again."

"Oh...the fun, is it?" she queried. "Had you been having many quiet chuckles to yourself before I woke up then? I could do with an occasional laugh myself to keep my throat from congealing."

"So far, I must admit, the humours of the situation haven't been conspicuous. For all practical purposes we are exactly where we were when we found ourselves here on Wednesday night. Except—"

"Except for being 'A day's march nearer home,' I suppose you mean? A day? Wednesday night? It seems years. What exact day is it as a matter of fact, if you happen to have been counting?"

"Saturday—Saturday morning early. About six o'clock I should reckon. It's easy enough to keep count of the time but I'd give something considerable to know just where we are in the matter of location. You're sure you don't recognise anything about this place? Long narrow cell—that thundering door—the grid over it?"

"They never let me explore, don't you fear. I hadn't an earthly. But why shouldn't it be just a cellar under Joolby's house? I should think that the most likely."

"It may be—very probably it is. It conforms to the period and the general feel of the place but so might thousands of others. You see, we were both unconscious for quite a time and we may have been carted anywhere. A cellar under the house is the most reasonable assumption but there's just the element of doubt. That's the rub: we can't be certain."

"Does it matter where we are? We're here right enough."

"It only matters if we can get a message out. Then, under some circumstances, depending on what form our medium took, it might be vital."

"Get a message out?" She fastened hopefully on the faint omen of the phrase. "Any chance of it?"

"Well, frankly, I don't see a glimmer. However much we may dislike this cellar one has to admit that with all its faults it certainly is not jerry built. It doesn't seem to have the semblance of a weak spot throughout and they haven't left us the faintest substitute for a tool in any shape or form."

"Did they take even your penknife?"

"Even my penknife! Good heavens, child, they took my braces and sock suspenders. What a pity young ladies don't wear corsets nowadays; I'm sure Mr Larch would have been too delicate to remove them. I suppose you don't happen to have metal parts about any of your fittings, Nora?"

"Nothing at all but artificial silk and elastic, I'm afraid. Not even a hairpin... Uncle Max, don't mind telling me now...does that mean...it's pretty hopeless?"

"Oh, lord bless you, no," he replied, with a jerk into cheerfulness that was rather too debonair to be convincing. "It's never hopeless in this life so long as—"

"So long as you keep on hoping?" suggested Nora tartly. "That's a very bright thought for the day, old dear, but somehow it would appeal to one more from the Wayside Pulpit than dwelt on in this putrid hole. And, oh my God, I am vilely thirsty! I know now what it feels like to be shipwrecked on a raft—two days after the last drop of water has been served out."

"Have you tried gnawing a bone button? I don't find it much good myself but I have known people who think there's something in it."

"I did that yesterday. I was wildly hungry then but there isn't much solid nourishment to be found in a bone button, Uncle. Nor illusion of a bubbling fountain. No, paradoxically enough, the button stunt is a wash-out. But I'm ready to sell my immortal soul for two gallons of ditch water at this moment."

"Child, child—"

"It's only my idea of fun, Uncle. I must do something to keep my spirits up—even to talk about a long drink may be slightly refreshing. It should at least make one's mouth water only I suppose the apparatus is out of order... If ever I get out of here I shall go to see the Niagara Falls. They ought to be well worth watching."

"This won't do," thought Max Carrados; "she will wear her resistance out. All this 'Water, water, everywhere' business is the very worst—"

It was not easy to find a subject strong enough to distract her from the other and he had to come down to one that was equally painful if less dangerous.

"What you told me about Geoffrey is very puzzling-"

"Puzzling!" The feeling in her tone left no doubt that he had found the subject.

"Appalling as well, of course, but I was only referring to one side of the queer proceedings. If you remember, I said that Geoffrey would no doubt be closely kept but hardly ill-used. There seems no point in systematic terrorism—apart from sheer cruelty, which isn't common, and certainly wouldn't be business."

"It was pretty effective in getting me to do all they wanted. I can't imagine acting like that if it hadn't been for poor Geoffrey's pitiable begging."

"It was effective in getting you to do what they wanted," he considered; "yes, Nora. But they must have been at Geoffrey for days to reduce him to a state like that and they could scarcely have foreseen what was going to develop until the Wednesday—"

"That knocking—you said you thought it might be him. Have you heard it again lately?"

"No, not since Thursday. It was two or three walls away... They may have moved him."

"Uncle Max...you don't think...they've killed Geoffrey?"

"I certainly do not, my dear. These people talk blood and thunder if it suits their book but they have no earthly object in killing anyone—intentionally."

"Intentionally. Intentionally? But—what is it, Uncle Max? You are keeping something back. You know more than you have told me."

For a few moments Mr Carrados did not reply. Then he ceased the rather aimless pacing of their prison that he had taken up again and sat down on the bench beside her.

"Listen quietly, my dear," he said, taking her hand, "and be the brave girl that I've always known you."

"I don't feel awfully heroic at the moment," she confessed. "But I *am* Captain of the Tapsfield Guides, aren't I? I must live up to that. What is it?"

"I said nothing about it yesterday, Nora, because it might have been premature, but I think the time has come... Since Thursday afternoon this place has been deserted. We are alone here."

"Alone?"

"Except for Tilehurst possibly, though even he has given no sign. But the others who were in the place—wherever it is—and were moving freely about up to Thursday afternoon, have gone. There isn't a step, there isn't a movement, above us."

"But why should they—what are you driving at?"

"Who can say why? Anything may have happened. With the exception of Joolby himself—and he's playing a desperate game—they are all birds of passage and must be prepared to fly at a moment's notice. Some of them may even have been arrested. But gone they have."

"He said they must have three days' grace. Today—Saturday—is the third. Can they have—?"

"Secured the stuff and cleared? That is quite possible."

"Then they would have no further interest in keeping us shut up here?"

"No further interest...but..."

"But? But what?"

"There may have been some misunderstanding among them. We—safely out of the way—are the least pressing factors in their plans. Someone who was to have released us when the rest were clear may have—oh, well, anything. But the fact remains. For more than a day and two nights no one has come near. We are abandoned; perhaps, among a wild scramble to get away, forgotten."

"Then if there's no one about they can't stop us trying to get out?"

"My child," he reminded her pityingly, "look at that door—those walls. Do you imagine that I haven't thought of escape every moment of the day and night almost? But they haven't left us a scrap of metal—not even a lump of stone. Nothing but our teeth and nails. Not in a year could we break out of here."

"Then shout, scream—anything to call attention. People must be passing somewhere near. They're bound to hear us in time—"

He shook his head sadly. "If there had been a footfall within reach of our shouts, Nora, you may be sure that my ears wouldn't have missed it. But we are muffled in the depths of the earth here; perhaps far from a road; not even on an outside wall. Five minutes of shouting and our poor dry throats would crack and madness begin to stare us in the face. No—"

"But what is to become of us?" she entreated wildly. "What are we to do?"

"Wait," he replied, trying by his own calmness to stem her rising agitation; "wait with all the patience we can muster and reserve every ounce of strength—we may need it. That is why I have told you now—to prepare you for the trial. Sooner or later the search must begin. In our absence suspicion will be raised—"

"Why should it? I had left a good excuse at home for being away and in that letter you said that you were going."

"I know I did. It was the final touch to make Joolby think he was safe, though the countermine misfired. But my secretary will realise that I had made no preparations of the sort—I had appointments fixed for every day—and Parkinson will not be satisfied. They will—"

"But it may be days—or weeks. Uncle, we can't stay here—I won't—we'd starve to death—we'd die of thirst—"

"Nora, Nora," he coaxed.

"I must have water," she insisted, growing more frantic as an understanding of the full horror of their situation sapped away her natural courage, "—I can't die here of thirst—it's terrible—it's getting worse and worse—"

"My dear," he pleaded. "I don't care if I do go mad—I mayn't know what it's like then—but I'm not going to wait here until I die of thirst—and I can feel that I am doing—my tongue's all thick and choky—and my throat feels closing up." She broke from him and sprang to her feet. "If you won't do anything I will! I'll make someone hear me."

Carrados had not the heart to restrain her by force, and no other form of argument would apparently have any chance of success. At all events, when she had worn herself out there might be some hope for the return of reason. Meanwhile she had flung herself against the impregnable door and was beating on it furiously with her bare hands, in turn commanding, threatening, pleading, until her poor frayed voice was past any further effort:

"Open the door! Open it, do you hear? I won't be smothered here. I won't die like a rat. Mrs Larch, Won Chou, Mr Nickle, Joolby—Joolby, you toad, you beast, you swine, come and let us out or you'll damned well hang for it. I'm going to—yes, I've written an account accusing you of murder and I've hid it where you can't find it but someone else will and they're sure to hang you."

There was no answer from the echoing space outside. She bent down, tore off a shoe and began to hammer furiously on and about the door with it.

"Damn and blast you all! Hiding round there and laughing at us, aren't you? When we do get out you'll pay for this; we'll kill the lot of you sooner or later, see if we don't, you yellow mongrels... No, I don't really mean that. If only you'll come now we'll give you a thousand pounds—two thousand—five thousand pounds—and get you all let off whatever you've done. Oh please, please, Mr Joolby—" The mood ran out, her voice trailed off and she turned away from the door baffled and broken.

"There, I've knocked the heel off my shoe and done no good at all. It's hopeless—I knew it all along—it was that that strung me out. Just hopeless."

But Max Carrados had risen from the bench as Nora sank down there in utter despair, and was running his hands up and down the wall against the door post, where some of her wild blows had fallen. He fixed on a spot and tried it several times with bare knuckles.

"I thought it sounded curiously," he speculated. "Not so hopeless perhaps, my girl, as it happens. Egad, there may have been a divinity that shaped your ends—your pedal end—when you went off in the tantrums. Anyhow you struck the one inch that may—well, it mayn't, after all, so don't think too much about it."

There was small need to tell her that. Huddled up in a corner on the bench Nora was taking no interest at all in what went on. Reaction, after the hysterical burst that had given her energy to lash out, was exacting the usual payment.

"Oh for a tool—a little bit of a thing of any sort," he continued desperately, as he again fell to tapping the spot time after time to confirm the blessed suspicion. And then the thought—the flash of inspiration: "Nora! that heel—they never reckoned on that. It should be like a rasp. Come, my dear, buck up and do your bit. What did you do with it?"

"Somewhere on the floor," she replied, just stirred enough by the vigour of his mood to understand but without energy to bear any share in whatever it was that was going. "What's the use of a heel—these walls—"

He found the heel readily enough without her help and, as he had expected, it was bristling with pointed ends of nails—in its way quite a useful file for working on a suitable material. Up the wall, where the door post stood, ran a couple of inches or so of plaster between the brick and wood. It was on this strip that Carrados now worked with patient skill, filing, crumbling, wrenching and tapping it out bit by bit until he had a sufficient space of the fabric underneath exposed to identify it. It was a lath as he had hoped and once he had bared an end it was an easy enough matter to break out a piece and reach what he had been seeking.

"Wake up, Nora my girl," he called across, trying to keep the exultation out of his voice until the thing was sure. "I think you've done the trick. It was a pipe you struck."

"I don't want a pipe," she muttered supinely. "I don't even want a cigarette. I'm just done and finished."

"Oh no, you're not," he assured her, going over and pulling her up; "not by several long chalks this journey. Come, you have a say in this. It's a lead pipe and with our little friend here I can be into that pipe within a few jiffies. But—"

"I thought there was a catch somewhere," she mumbled.

"I don't," he declared, "but there is just the possibility that there may be. A lead pipe ought to mean water but in these old places one can never be quite sure. They used all sorts of stuff for anything... So it may be the gas. What do you say?"

"Say? How?"

"If there's water in the pipe we get it. If there's gas it gets us."

"A good job too," she replied. "One way or the other."

"So be it. It's quite a level chance—in fact it's good odds in our favour." For the next few minutes there was nothing to be heard but the soft, regular abrasion of the metal; then he dropped the heel with an exclamation.

"Our trick this time, Mr Joolby, I think. *Water!* Nora, your hanky!"

That brought her up quickly enough and the next moment she was squeezing the saturated cambric into her mouth and fancying that the tepid, insipid stuff (it must have been in the pipe for days and nights) was the most delicious nectar she had ever tasted.

"More!"

"Nice stuff, water; eh, Nora?" he remarked, complying.

"Why don't you file it away a lot?" she demanded, pointing to the slight incision he had made. "I want to wallow in it galore."

"No need for us to drown ourselves out. This is direct from the main and we might have some trouble in stopping whatever we set going. If we make a big hole and the door fits tight you can calculate how soon in a little place like this—"

"Go on; what are you waiting for? I want more and more—gallons! buckets!"

He had been soaking his own handkerchief for the second time—alternating his turn with hers—when all at once he broke off and fell into an attitude of poignant attention. A finger of one hand closed the newly made leak, those of the other rested on the pipe lower down, as delicately-perceptive as the antennae of a butterfly—so significant of alertness that one might have said they were listening.

"Wait; wait," he cautioned, without relaxing his poise; "there's something going on here; some movement on the pipe. Somewhere, somebody else is in communication with it. Who? Where?"

"I know," exclaimed Nora with a sudden light. "It's because of the water famine. They did it at Tapsfield; they do it all over the shop. Someone goes round listening at those little trap-door affairs in the road to catch you wasting any." Just about a week before she had used the self-same words to warn Miss Tilehurst of the risk and now in all unconsciousness she repeated herself exactly.

"It is! It cannot be anything else—direct from the main at this hour. My God! Nora, *listening!* Think, child—I can get him; can he get me? Can he understand? Do you see: our message! Hope, hope, just a tiny flickering light—someone somewhere *listening!*"

He was not wasting the precious seconds now. Almost at Nora's first words he had searched for and found the heel and as he spoke he tapped the pipe sharply with the butt of it in a never varying sequence: short, short, short; long, long, long; short, short, short—time after time repeated.

"What is it you do?" she asked in a half-awed whisper. "What are you sending?"

"S O S; S O S; S O S," he explained, rather absently under the intense concentration of listening, touching, *feeling*for a movement in reply. "Can he hear me? Will he understand?" The seconds passed and nothing came: after all, was it likely?

"Has he gone—was it just the last movement that I heard; or was he only adjusting?" ran his thoughts as he never ceased the tapping. At any rate—"Nora, my dear,"—this time aloud—"the next minute will probably settle our business for good or bad. If you ever prayed in your life before, pray for an answer now, child."

15

THE MAN AT THE OTHER END

Whenever a house in Maplewood Avenue came on the market—a not infrequent occurrence in point of fact—the house agents were wont to dwell on the rural and secluded amenities of the neighbourhood, rather than draw attention to the architectural, domestic or social attractions of the "property:" wisely, no doubt, since the one could be convincingly adduced, whereas a tolerant if not absolutely apologetic course was desirable when skilfully leading a client on past a too detailed examination of the others. Certainly at six o'clock in the morning the Avenue wore as tranquil an air of detachment from a city's bustle as could be found within the ten miles radius. It was yet too early for dust-carts, milkmen, road sweepers and other kindred sleep-disturbers to be about while the intrusions of the official custodians of the law were, if leisurely in point of motion, in all other respects comparable to the proverbial angels' visits.

Such was the appearance Maplewood Avenue presented to the couple who turned into it, in pursuance of their rather mysterious ends, on the morning of the Saturday that was to be the climax of at least two adventurous enterprises. At that moment the only sign of life—other than vegetable—that the Avenue presented was a large Persian cat seated beneath a sycamore and a full-throated bird pouring out its string of melody from the precise apex of the tree, exactly above the spot where the cat was sitting.

"Now there ought to be a trap somewhere just about here," said the senior of the two intruders, when in due course their progress along the road had brought them to a part somewhere about midway along the thoroughfare. A substantially built, no-longer-young, level-headed-looking, workman of the capable if mildly pragmatic type, his status was sartorially proclaimed, for in addition to wearing the chaste blue uniform provided by the Metropolitan Water Board his official cap was embellished with the word INSPECTOR, clearly rather than aesthetically displayed within a neat oval. His underling, a mere youth who just escaped the category of "hobbledehoy" by virtue of a couple of months' mild discipline, did not appear to let his superior's rank and authority overawe him. On this not unattractive early morning round at least his usual title of respect was "uncle" or "dad" with an occasional lapse into an even freer style if the occasion seemed to permit it. The inspector received it all in the best of parts as became a man who was prepared to give and take, with the full assurance that if the need arose he could assert the dignity of his badge in a perfectly conclusive fashion. Both carried an implement of their craft, that of the inspector being a listening-rod—outwardly nothing more than a serviceable walking-stick with an overgrown head—while his underling had a sinister-looking tool that combined the unpleasanter qualities of a small harpoon and a native spear. Actually its industrial use was to impale and open trap doors but it bore little suggestion of this pacific function.

"It *must* be somewhere just about here," reiterated the inspector argumentatively. "See anything of it, 'Orace?"

"Not a trace," replied Horace, alternating his interest between the bird and the cat in a speculation as to which would afford the better cock-shy. "Reckon they must have tar-sprayed and gritted it over, same as we found that one in Badger Lane. Miaou! Miaou!"

"Well, dash my nob if the cat isn't sitting right atop it!" exclaimed his chief, now that his attention was turned in that direction. "Puss, puss. Come along, Thomas, we'll trouble you for that spot for a couple of minutes." Whereupon the Persian, rightly concluding that in the circumstances it was no use waiting any longer for the thrush to fall straight into its mouth, got up and walked away in a decidedly cutting manner.

"Keeping the place warm for us," grinned Horace.

"Picking it out to be cool for itself more likely. They're funny in their ways, you might perhaps think, but they have their own ideas," moralised the inspector. "Now I suppose you never take any particular notice of cats, 'Orace?"

"Can't say as I do. Except now and then to have a whang at one."

"Sometimes I wonder what you do take any notice of—except the whistle and short skirts," speculated his superior. "But no doubt ideas are germinating."

"I follow Chelsea," maintained Horace.

"Well, I should say that's harmless. But speaking of cats, there's a good deal to be learned about women from them, 'Orace. Not in a spiteful sense, mind you, but they're very alike in many ways—cats and women."

"You let some of them hear you say that and they'd scratch your eyes out."

"That being a case to wit," pointed out the inspector. "But it doesn't follow: it all depends—not on the woman as you might think but on the chap and his manner of putting it. Now if you made such an observation, 'Orace, no doubt, as you say, you'd carry away traces of it, but if it was done diplomatic—"

"Same as you would, for instance?"

"Approximately," admitted the inspector modestly. "At any rate I've known very few who wouldn't admit, between ourselves, that most others had a fair streak of the feline."

"I'm sure," sniggered Horace. "Regular old Don John you must have been in your time, I reckon, Uncle."

"It's not that at all," protested the inspector earnestly. "Don't go away with an erroneous impression of that sort, 'Orace, or I shall be sorry I allowed you to talk of your own affairs so freely. I regard the subject from a scientific, you might almost say Darwinian, standpoint. Now—there's no particular hurry, lad; it's no one's time between now and seven—now to give you an instance. When I was about your age we had a farm and one Michaelmas we left it and moved away to another, a dozen or fifteen miles off, that the old man had taken. Of course all the stock went by road and the house cat—a jenny it was—was put into a basket and driven in the trap along with one or two particular things and the women. No doubt its feet were buttered as soon as it was let out but the next morning it was gone and sure enough it turned up again—we heard this afterwards from a neighbour who was there—at the old place, pretty nearly dead beat but evidently come back with the intention of staying. Well—this is the point, 'Orace—that cat was seen to look into every room in the house and when it understood that they were all empty and no one living there, dash my nob if it didn't turn round and disappear again and the next day after that it was back at the new place and stayed on there quite content for ever... Do you get anything from that, 'Orace?"

"Everyone knows that cats can find their way back when they've never seen the road. An aunt of mine—"

"You've missed the point, my lad, but I didn't expect any better. Pigeons will do as much—for hundreds of miles if it comes to that—but there's nothing to be learnt—nothing that is to say on the human plane—from the behaviour of pigeons.

Well, what about getting on with it now? This is the last road of the round and then we may as well drop down into the High Street and get a snack to carry us on till breakfast. I know a place not so far off where they make coffee of coffee and not chicory and ground peas."

"Suit me all right," assented Horace. "As a matter of fact my internals have been complaining out loud for the past half hour. Reckon they thought that me throat must have got cut or something."

The inspector had taken up a position of ease, leaning against the sycamore from which the thrush had lately sung, while he proceeded to write up his report-book. At this avowal he looked across at his subordinate meditatively.

"It's symptomatic how most young fellows always seem to be thinking about their stomachs nowadays, if you come to notice it, 'Orace," he remarked confidentially. "They don't seem to have any what you might call reserve of endurance somehow. Did I ever happen to tell you how me and another signaller were cut off in a tower outside a little place called Binchey for the best part of a week and all the time we only had—"

"You did and that," replied the unimpressed Horace. "You told me at full length the first day I came on this job and you've referred to it now and then since at stated intervals. Don't gloat so much on that there war, Father William, and the deeds that saved the Empire. It's over and done with and we're never going to have another—not so long as it rests with me anyhow."

For a moment the inspector seemed to be in doubt whether the point had not been reached when it was desirable for him to explain to Horace the precise obligations of their respective positions. He put the temptation aside on the reflection that there is generally more than one way of attaining an objective. With the butt end of an admonitory pencil he indicated the unopened trap.

"Well, for the love of Moses get on with your job, boy," he directed severely. "I don't want to be kept messin' about round here all morning."

That was the chap all over, thought Horace bitterly, as he spiked open the lid and dropping the business end of his harpoon on to the connection inside applied his ear to the handle. Talk about his own blinking affairs for half an hour and then suddenly turn blinking well round and... Fat lot of good expecting anything to be worth while in a blinking shop where...

"Come, come, 'Orace," said the inspector, leisurely elastic-banding his book and putting it away, "you aren't supposed to be fishing down that hole, you know. Is it O.K. there?"

"Nowhere in sight of it, if you ask me," replied Horace, diffusing an atmosphere of gloomy satisfaction. "There's something going on somewhere here that's beyond me."

"H'm," said the inspector, either with or without a special meaning. "That's queer."

"Yes, it's—'ere, what d'ya mean—'queer?'"

"Well"—the inspector was satisfied now that he had restored correct relations and was mildly satirical—"I was only thinking that it must be queer, lad, if it's something past your comprehension. What's this miracle like?"

"Better have a squint yourself," suggested Horace, withdrawing his implement and resigning the position. "Listening posts are more in your line by all accounts, inspector."

Still smiling inwardly, the inspector stepped across and dropping the end of his rod into the cavity bent down and applied an ear to the bowl-shaped amplifier. Presently he twisted his head round a fraction so as to include Horace in his view and by a return to ordinary conversational terms indicated tactfully that so far as he was concerned their little difference might be regarded as settled.

"It's a rummy thing that we should have been speaking of signalling just now," he remarked tentatively. "If such a thing was credible I should have said that someone was talking morse along the pipe at this very moment."

"Oh," replied Horace, leaning against the tree in turn and languidly rolling a cigarette—doubtless equally prepared to let bygones go by but, as the aggrieved subordinate, inclined to be more guarded. "And wha' d'z 'e happen to be saying?"

"Nothing that you might call coherent—just the same word all the time: 'sos, sos, sos,' over and over again if I understand it right. Half a minute though; that 'sos' stands for something surely?"

"Yes it does—sossages. And very nice too for breakfast."

"Tchk! tchk! Can't you never leave off thinking of food even in your sleep, 'Orace?... Still going on: 'sos, sos, sos.' Why, of course—where are your wits, lad? It isn't 'sos' at all; it's 'S O S.' Signal of distress a sinking ship sends out. Now whatever—"

"Why, of course," contributed Horace, refusing to be impressed. "The *Clacton Belle* must have drifted in somehow and now she can't neither reverse nor turn round in the supply pipe. Why ever didn't you think of that at first, Uncle?"

But the inspector was not to be put off by the cheap witticism of irreverent youth. He had not lived for fifty years and gone all through the war without discovering that very queer things do occasionally turn up in real life. For a moment he thoughtfully balanced a spanner undecidedly in his free hand; then kneeling on the pavement he struck the metal connection below half a dozen times in measured succession.

"What's the game—what does that mean?" demanded Horace, intrigued into drawing nearer and looking on in spite of his blasé bearing.

"'R U'—code. 'Who are you?'" explained the other, returning to the listening attitude again. "Now we shall see where we're getting."

"Seems to me this isn't M.W.B. routine at all," suggested the flippant observer. "You must have got through to the picture house this time, Dad. 'Snatched from Death's Jaws' in seven snatches—" He stopped short at that for the inspector's right hand had suddenly shot out in a compelling gesture of warning and repression.

"Get this down, lad," he said, with a note of sharp authority that admitted no discussion. "You have a bit o' paper and a pencil, haven't you? 'C-a-r-r—'"

"Right-o," was the brisk assent, as the boy discovered a news-sheet and a stub of pencil in his pocket, and folded the paper to afford a white space of margin, "'C-a-r-r.' Carry on, sergeant."

"'-a-d-o-s.'"

"Carrados! Why, that's the name of the bloke—" He turned the page in an excited search for a heading. "There's something here about a mystery of his movements. You don't mean to say—"

"Shut it, you pup!" snapped the inspector fiercely. "Can't you attend two minutes? Here—take it: 'T-r-a-p-p-e-d p-h-o-n-e n-e-a-r-e-s-t p-o-l-i-c-e r-e-l-e-a-s-e u-r-g-e-n-t l-i-f-e d-e-a-t-h.'"

"My Gawd!" murmured Horace, experiencing a mental display of coloured lights. "That's the stuff to—"

"'A-m e-n-l-a-r-g-i-n-g l-e-a-k y-o-u l-o-c-a-t-e g-u-i-d-e p-o-l-i-c-e l-a-r-g-e r-e-w-a-r-d.'"

"Phew!" whistled Horace softly, drawing in his breath with an ecstatic foretaste of this shower of gain and glory. "Large reward!... Is that all, inspector?" he concluded meekly.

"'A-c-k-n-o-w-l-e-d-g-e i-f g-o-t'—you needn't put that last bit in the message. You know how to telephone, don't you, Horace?"

"'Course I do. I was in the yard office before I came on here. And you don't need a number for police; you—"

"That's all right, lad. Slip down into the High Street as quick as you can cut and put that through from the nearest kiosk. Here's a couple of pennies—"

"Don't need 'em for police."

"Take them all the same—you never know and we're running no risks; in fact you'd better have a few more to be on the safe side. Keep your mouth shut no matter who you meet and for the love of Moses don't stop to get your breakfast on the way, there's a good lad. This is going to mean a gold watch and a week's outing at Southend with full pay for both of us or I'm a Dutchman."

"Garn!" The prospect, added to the certainty of having a tale to tell that would thrill and fascinate young lady friends for many a bright month to come, was reducing Horace to a state of giggling bliss. "A silver lighter and a day on Hampstead Heath more likely!"

He set smartly off towards the shops while the inspector, humming a marching air as an emotional outlet to the suspense, proceeded to note the promised development in the volume of waste and to verify the direction. He was still testing the flow at intervals along the road when, some five minutes later, a closed motor car came along and slowing down as it went by turned in at one of the gardens. He did not fail to make a careful mental record of all its details.

The motorists must have been noticing on their side also for very soon—they certainly could not have been right up to the house—two men came out at the gate in question and stood admiring the day, as proprietorial gentlemen will when the rising sun, as seen from their own demesne, seems to be an individual asset produced for their especial service. Both were observable figures; one a personable individual of foreign cut, the other—obviously in spite of his well-wrapped-up form—a pronounced cripple. Presently they happened to notice the waterman trying the road at no great distance away and—what more natural?—strolled down to take a friendly interest in his doings.

"Morning, inspector," affably remarked the cripple—he had not failed to observe the badge—"rather early for your job, eh? Nothing wrong with our supply up here, I hope, eh?"

"Nothing at all, sir," said the inspector. "Just an ordinary routine round. We do them regularly."

"Ah, to be sure. I thought perhaps you might be calling here and there to see the taps and so on, eh? One likes to know—"

"No need for that, sir, when it's all O.K. We don't want to give any more trouble than we have to. Shouldn't be here myself only I'm waiting for my mate to knock off now for breakfast."

"Breakfast, eh? I'll see about mine since you remind me. And if I was in your place I don't know that I should be hanging about my job a minute longer than I had to. You get nothing extra for that, inspector, eh?"

With this pleasantry he swung off again and the pair disappeared into the gateway. The inspector slowly proceeded to fill and light his pipe and then, throwing the implement into the hollow of his arm, began to stroll casually up and down the roadway, never very far distant from that house—waiting for his mate. He had a particularly guileless face and mild speculative eyes that seemed to be quietly considering.

16

LAST LAUGHTER

When those two excellent, if not exactly good, companions, Messrs Joolby and Bronsky, approached the house after their interlude with the water-inspector they stood for a moment surveying its uncompromisingly reticent front before making up their minds to enter. To do the cripple justice all the reluctance was on his associate's part for, at the sight of a quietude which might equally be either ominous or reassuring, Mr Bronsky displayed a tendency to hang back and comb his impressive beard in characteristic discretion. Meanwhile the chauffeur who had driven them there—a subordinate member of the band—had garaged his car and was loitering about the drive in the expectation of further instructions.

"You are sure it would be quite all right?" questioned Mr Bronsky for the third time since they had left the vehicle. "I have grave misgivings."

"It's both quiet and all right." Joolby's whole frame, balanced on his props, was pulsing and throbbing with suppressed fires as he regarded the other askance. "Why shouldn't it be all right, eh? eh?"

"I did not like the affairs of yesterday to be plain-speaking between ourselves, Julian Joolby," recriminated Mr Bronsky. "There was air of something in the wind that did not mean nothing. You was not where you said you would and the others could not be found, did not know, or would not say anything. In short, it was dubious behaviour."

"That's soon explained," said Joolby, becoming comparatively amiable as he saw that there was nothing serious to rebut, "only I'm sorry that you should have been put out by it, Bronsky. As a matter of fact I had to go off at a moment's notice to arrange our connection at the coast. Fellow owning the bungalow wanted to crawfish. I left a message with Jake and I hear that one of his brats was run over and so he forgot everything."

"But however the others?"

"Same as with you. They found out that I had gone somewhere, couldn't get in touch, and that put the wind up and they began to imagine everything. The consequence was that you didn't find them either. That's all right, Bronsky; these little hitches are bound to crop up but a couple of hours more will see everything brought in and us well on our way with it."

"I hopes so. All same I begin to think it would have been more good to have met you at the other end; only I—"

"Only you wanted to see that we were really going your way when we'd got the boodle, didn't you?" supplied Joolby with rough good-humour. "Now it seems to me that we're the first here and, what's more, I don't mind laying a farthing bun to a penny tart as that slut Cora's skipped it. Well—" he instanced a crude proverb based on the assumption that in certain circumstances a riddance is no loss which, being obscene in the extreme, had the effect of somewhat raising Mr Bronsky's spirits.

Mr Joolby's surmise proved to be right. When they let themselves into the house it soon became evident that not only were they the first there, but everything pointed to the place having been left unattended for an appreciable period. Noticing one thing after another that showed neglect they climbed up to the dining-room on the first floor, where they had last sat, and there on the table were the uncleared remains of Thursday's lunch, plain evidence of someone's dereliction.

"There you are!" panted Joolby, waving a stick towards the table as if it had been a conjurer's wand and would cause everything to disappear by magic. "What did I tell you, eh? eh? The bitch never came here yesterday at all. Must have cleared off on Thursday soon after me and the others left. Anything might have happened. Fortunately," he added, with an eye towards the effect of this disclosure on Mr Bronsky's disquieted nerves, "fortunately it didn't."

"No, but it could have might," contended Mr Bronsky. "A woman can never be trusted to do the right until she understand that whatever she do it will be wrong."

"Everything pretty well as usual down below, boss," reported the third man, who had been sent to investigate the cellars meanwhile. "That's to say the three cullies is there sure 'nuf, but there's a goodish drop o' watt'r coming under the No. 4 door. Blind guy says he thinks a pipe must have burst or su'thing and he's kind of sore that he and the skirt haven't had nothin' since Thursday."

"Of course they haven't—with no one here how the hell could they? Well, they'll have to go without an hour or two more. But I won't have it any longer with George and his shirty bit—there's no room for a—madonna in the outfit. I don't half like the business of a water-pipe bursting and that inspector fellow nosing about outside. If I hadn't smoothed him over pleasant he might have wanted to come in and go right through the place and how'd we fix that up at a moment's notice? If it wasn't that we've only a few hours to go—"

"Someone coming round, boss," interrupted the third. "He gave the taps all right. Shall I go down and see to it?"

"Yes, yes," replied Joolby; "we're coming down as well. It's time they were all here. Which is this one—look over the stairs, Bronsky."

His progress, as usual, was slow and by the time they were on the landing the arrival had been admitted. The comrade leaned over the banisters and sent down a fraternal greeting.

"It's the little persecuted brother," he informed Mr Joolby. Ana to the victim himself: "God be with—No! no! I mean: To Hell with order, comrade!"

"Whichever you prefer, comrade," replied Won Chou politely.

"You came along the back street way, didn't you?" asked his master when they were all in the hall together. Won Chou nodded. "Any signs that side of Larch or Nickle?"

"Not see. By the way, when George does get here you may find that he has got a grunch about you."

"Oh, has he? Well, for that matter I happen to have a grunch about him to balance it and unless I'm mistaken mine will have bigger teeth than his will. He got a grunch!" The misshapen thing spat venomously.

"I have been hear of your outdoing that evil fellow Max Carrados just then," observed Mr Bronsky to the little brother as they stood about, waiting, with their various degrees of unconcern or the reverse, for the arrival of the others. "Freedom shake you with the hand for the occasion."

"I shake myself with the hand," was the modest assent, and he quite literally did so. "I have owed Mr Carrados one for several years."

"Is that what?" asked Bronsky.

"When I first met him—in Shanghai—I tried to do a small stroke of business between us. I offer to sell him my little sister Hwa for eighty trade dollars."

"Eh? Well?" Even at that distracting moment Mr Joolby found himself taking a passing interest in so human a theme. "What happened about it?"

"Knock me down," admitted Won Chou simply.

Mr Bronsky gave utterance to a "tsssk!" of disgust. "He had not the rightness," he pronounced with decision.

"No; all my people say it was too cheap; in fact I got a hundred and ten later. That was before I had education at the mission college, of course. Afterwards I learned that it was far better not to sell them—outright."

"Well, anyhow, it was time that Carrados was roped," summed up Joolby. "He was passing the ice too free; Bronsky here got the idea that he was a plaster-of-Paris almighty and could do anyone and knew everything... Did he talk Chinese to you, Won?"

"No." And then, without a flicker in his eye: "Did he talk Sudanese to you, Joolby?"

"Eh? What's that?" demanded Mr Joolby, beginning to glower ominously. Fortunately, perhaps, just then there was the sound of a car outside and the humbler member of the crew, who had small interest in these personal feelings, put his head inside to announce the arrival of "the others." These proved to be Nickle and George Larch who very soon appeared, both burdened with several packages which from their laboured movements had every appearance of being weighty.

"Ah, here we are at last," said Joolby with obvious satisfaction. "You've brought the lot, I suppose? Carry them through into the yellow room at the back for the time, you two. You had no trouble, Nickle?"

"Easy as toffee. We came Herriot Lane and there wasn't a soul to be seen. I've just run the car in loose. What about it?"

"Leave it there handy. We'll keep it in reserve and have it follow. Go now and see that both are filled up with enough spare juice for a double journey—we don't want to have to take in anywhere and leave our number. And make sure that everything's running smooth: there's got to be no tinkering this excursion."

"Say a matter of ten minutes."

"Eight o'clock's plenty of time. You take first car, cruise, and pick up Vallett and his load near the windmill on Keystone

Common not later than two. That gives you five hours to slip into Seabridge at dusk. We'll be there for you."

"All serene," undertook Nickle, hurrying out again. Joolby followed the stuff into the yellow room behind and waited for Larch to bring in the last package.

"Now look here, George, this won't do," he said roughly, when he was satisfied that all he had expected was there. "Orders are orders and what I say goes or you or any other man will find dam' quick that he's up against it. Your wife was to be here in charge all yesterday, seeing to those three below. Well, what happened?"

"I know all about that, Mr Joolby," replied George in his usual temperate, respectful way, "and I'm taking the responsibility for what did happen. You'll remember how I always told you that Cora must have the first chance to get away if anything went wrong—"

"Well, well," interrupted Joolby impatiently, "what's that got to do with your precious wife being kept on ice? Nothing went wrong anywhere."

"No, but you thought it would," said George, keeping his temper with admirable restraint. "I don't pretend to know what it was but something came through and on Thursday night you fancied anything might happen. When the rest of us were going about our jobs you and one or two others had quietly put on your roller skates and were lying doggo near the coast, waiting to get the tip and ready to do a bunk for safety."

"Does it sound likely?" The usual symptoms of resentment at being crossed began to suffuse the monstrous swelling body. "Haven't I got my shop and goods to consider—all I possess? How could I—as you say—skate off and leave everything I have behind? That's the way you talk, you foolish fellow."

"You sold your shop and stock a week ago, Mr Joolby," steadily replied George. "At least all the heavy stuff and I don't doubt that you have the valuables put away somewhere handy.

I tell you it won't do, it isn't the square thing—leaving Cora without a chance, to take the first concussion. If I'd known as much—"

"Oh, to hell with you and Cora!" Joolby exploded passionately. "You talk as if the piece was a bleeding Aphrodite in a tissue-paper chemise. I've had the sjambok put across the hams of better women than her for a dam' sight less than she's done. If you can't keep your Cora in line, Larch, you'd better clear and make way for men with more guts."

"Oh, so it's that, is it?" speculated George, regarding his employer gravely. "I thought you were beating up for a split as soon as I'd finished your job, Mr Joolby. Well, I'm quite ready to go—in fact after what you've just said you couldn't possibly keep me—"

"I've paid you up for all..."

"You have—at your price—and I hope it'll be the last money I shall ever earn in that way." He started to leave the room quietly enough, but as he reached the door a sudden impulse brought him in a couple of strides to Joolby's side and for a moment his placid eyes blazed as he stood with a fist drawn back and the cripple shrinking before it.

"No, you are quite safe after all," he said, turning away and dropping his hand. "Things like you burst if a man treads on you." Without a word to any there he marched from the house with head erect and—as it happened—left the grounds by the back gate; so that, all unknowingly, he passed out of the lane at the exact moment when a high-speed car, unusually well manned, whirled into it at the other end.

"Julian Joolby," said a disapproving voice, and sheering round—always an awkward move—Joolby saw that Mr Bronsky had looked in by another door and been a witness of the last stage of the quarrel; "Julian Joolby, when will you learn to snaffle your violent emotion?"

"Eh? Oh nonsense: that was all bunko," he replied, developing his malicious grin. "I put that across to work George up. Now he's clear out of it and a good job too, between us."

"Yes, yes, but is it safe?"

"Of course it's safe or d'y'a think I'd have done it? He's made the plates, hasn't he? He's done the actual work and if he tried to cross us now we could frame it for him to get the heaviest sentence. George knows that all right; besides he has his perishing Cora to think of. His sort never gets you shopped; and in the end they always go quietly. Now, don't you see, he's out of any shares? All in good time I shall work Nickle and Vallett out too. It's the sensible thing to do when it comes to cutting up big money."

"You have right, I believe. Yes, it's tamgod smart. I had not thought of that," admitted Mr Bronsky, shedding warm approval. It did not occur to him to speculate whether ultimately he also might not be involved in his fellow conspirator's squeezing-out process.

"All cars as right as rain," reported Nickle, discovering the two still in the back room. "Do I take these along?"—he indicated the stack of parcels. "By the way, what's the matter with old George? He went out looking as if he'd swallowed some hot thunder."

"Said he had to go to see a man about a rabbit. I think it was all an excuse to get a cooling drink," replied Mr Joolby in high good humour. "No, Nickle, the plates go in the second car. We decided to separate so you will only carry the paper."

"And Vallett? What about him?"

"He goes on with you and Jim. The two with him make their way back independent—they all know exactly what to do and how to do it. We're going to make use of those three passengers to cover the run if anyone tries to open on us. Carrados goes with you; Jim attends to him in the car and then you'll have Vallett later. Now bring up our distinguished myopic friend for a few minutes' conversation, will you? I'm not going down any more steps than I can help, so if you find the cellar unpleasantly damp you must take the change out of him."

"You bet I will!" undertook Nickle forcibly. "My infernal thumb pains yet like the very devil. Come along, Jim; you're detailed to it."

"But are you sure it is quite prudential, Joolby?" put in Mr Bronsky with an anxious flutter. "This fellow Carrados—"

"Oh, he's all over and washed out. These conjuring tricks don't come off more than once. It isn't that he's specially clever in the light, only our lot are so damned helpless in the dark. Besides, he hasn't so much as a toothpick on him now."

"But this taking him along when he could be lock up here—? No, I cannot relish the idea of that, Joolby."

"It's safer, take my word," said Joolby, lowering his voice. "The fact is, I like that water burst less and less and I've put things on an hour as it is so as to get away from here as soon as possible. It was just as it happened, of course, but for all we know it may mean someone being sent up along during the day, and that might be considerably sooner than we're timed for. This way we keep them under our eyes anyhow and I've got an idea for using them at the end that cuts the trail finely."

"Well, it may be as you think," admitted the dubious Bronsky, "but all the nevertheless I'd sooner rather—"

The return of Nickle and Jim cut short this interesting proposition. Mr Carrados seemed rather damp and his usually spruce attire certainly conveyed the impression of having been roughly used, but he did not appear to be inordinately depressed himself—not even when Nickle, to give point to his facetious: "Here's the goods!" propelled him unceremoniously forward.

"Ah, our principal guest," remarked Mr Joolby agreeably. "I trust you found the poor accommodation adequate, Mr Carrados? Owing to your unfortunate visual defect we knew that you'd forgive the meagre lighting provision of our best spare room. In other matters—well, as I daresay you've learned by now, we are rather rough and ready."

"Yes," supplemented Nickle threateningly, "infernally rough and ready for anything."

"Scarcely less ready than my companion and myself are—for breakfast," ventured Carrados. "Ideas of hospitality may vary, Mr Joolby, but I can't call to mind any civilized tribe where guests—since you call us that—are denied food and drink for forty hours."

"That's been a mistake—I apologise, I apologise," professed Mr Joolby, with the air of making amends very handsomely. "It was entirely without my knowledge—for say what you will when you are free again, Mr Carrados, none of you have been handled any rougher or used any worse than you brought on yourself or the necessity of keeping you safe required."

"Indeed? I wonder if you expect Geoffrey Tilehurst to subscribe to that?" he challenged.

"Tilehurst!" Eyes glanced from him to meet each other and a knowing smile went round. The blind man intercepted the atmosphere and it gave him a moment's pause but he was too alertly concerned in other signs just then to turn aside for what mattered very little.

"You ask him how he liked it when you next meet, and see," continued Mr Joolby dryly. "Now listen for we haven't much time to waste—least of all on passengers. I've said I'm sorry about the grub but we can't wait for that now. We'll take just what we find—most of us haven't had our own breakfasts yet—and you will get your share of what there is and can eat it as you travel."

"Travel?" interrogated Mr Carrados with some concern. "You surely can't think of taking me? Consider how a blind man would be in the way on a journey."

"Leave that to us," was the curt reply; "we're going to take you for a ride and—"

"Take me for a ride!" The victim seemed to grow even more apprehensive. "Not in the transatlantic—I might say the Chicago—sense surely, I hope, Mr Joolby?"

Mr Joolby snapped a raw laugh. "That depends on how you act," he replied, not sorry to have the opportunity to introduce the menace. "Do exactly as you're told and you'll come through all right; lack, and—" He did not resort to melodramatic signs but the hiatus was sufficiently expressive.

"You certainly hold all the cards this hand," admitted the blind man. "It's only for me to make the best terms I can as things have turned out."

This brought in Nickle who had been enduring his chief's derisive courtesy with rising impatience.

"Make terms, you hear!" he cried scornfully. "I like the beggar's cheek. Do you think it's a case of what you agree to or what you don't, damn your eyes, Max Carrados!"

"You can't do that, Nickle," replied Carrados with deadly quietness, "they are blasted already... Doesn't that inspire you with—I won't say pity or compunction in your case—but with a sort of vague misgiving? Superstition, if you like, but there has always been an uneasy dread of incurring the just resentment of the sightless. A blind man's curse—"

"Won't wash," interrupted Nickle. "Cut him short, for the Almighty's sake, Joolby. Can't you see he's only playing for time with all this day-of-judgment stuff patter?"

"Rather an ominous phrase in your position, Nickle—'Playing for time.' Suppose I get it for you?"

"This 'time'—I do not grasp quite what it imply," put in Mr Bronsky intelligently. "It is—"

"Just an idiom, Mr Bronsky," explained Carrados, becoming quietly amused in rather an inexplicable way considering his situation. "I almost think that you look like finding out what it means also."

"That's enough," announced Joolby with decision. "You've put up all the bluff you know, Carrados, and we've got you dog-beaten. Now listen to what you've got to do, and this time if you deviate a single hair or try any of your monkey tricks it's the deep end you'll go off at. We're going to take you in the car—"

"I don't think so now," broke in the prisoner, with so marked a change of front—so confident an air and smile—that they were paralysed into holding themselves up and letting him run on from sheer amazement. "You have waited too long; I've got to like it here. It's peaceful and almost rural. In the early morning—now for instance—one can scent the copse outside (another homonymous word, Mr Bronsky; it means woodland—among other things)—you can hear the song of birds: the early birds out to get their foolish worms. Really, they whistle more than they sing...surely you can hear them now?" and, account for it as they might, a series of low sharp whistles at various distances did reach their ears, as though a preconcerted signal was announcing, for instance, that a circle of men had taken up position.

"To hell!" suddenly exclaimed Nickle, making a dash. "The cops *are* here. They'll be on us next." An unnerving peal of the ancient bell and an insistent crash of the heavy door knocker gave point to this expression. Without waiting to think twice Nickle flung up a window and dropped down. A shout, a shot, and the sound of hard wood striking something slightly less solid followed in quick succession.

"Nickle will never make a reliable shot," confided Mr Carrados to the little band of paralysed listeners. "He always takes sight too low—fault of British army musketry training. Now, about the door? My friends are evidently waiting."

Won Chou slid his almond eyes to his master's face and getting no guidance from that rigid mask went off docilely on his own account to obey the summons. At this critical moment

Mr Bronsky, who from the first suggestion of alarm had been hovering between the expedience of following Nickle's lead, walking out by the front door in a dignified way, hiding under the table, or fainting, decided to be straightforward and honest. Although the detestable myrmidons of the law were not yet on the scene the good Mr Carrados would no doubt bear satisfactory witness.

"There would appear to be somethings going on but I do not gather what ensues," accordingly remarked Mr Bronsky with convincing detachment. "I understand that this was a peaceful place where a Mr Joolby merchandises antique wares. I have arrived here soon so as to make early bargains. Mr Joolby," he continued, raising his voice as steps approached, and cramming his silk hat more firmly on so as to demonstrate the casualness of his presence there, "if you have any particular articles of choice rarity I would address myself to your negotiations. I am in the desire for buying—"

"Number one man makee say must look-see and come-go every side," announced Won Chou, a little superfluously it might appear since the official referred to was following him in. There are occasions when members of the force do not trouble to stand on ceremony. But Mr Carrados, at all events, found it amusing.

"No, no, Mr Won," he protested, laughing appreciation; "I'm afraid it's really too late to get back to talkee talkee chop now. Not after giving us a taste of your college style, if you remember."

"Mr Joolby," insisted the honest customer, rising to a passionate intensity as he realised that Detective-Inspector Beedel was at the door and taking in the situation, "Mr Joolby, I am wholly a stranger to you, never having seen you formerly to this morning; but I am of the inclination to acquire works of ancient if you have of such for disposition at reasonable costages—"

Having surveyed the room and its inmates the inspector turned to speak over his shoulder.

"Come in, West," he said to a uniformed policeman behind. "You other two stay out there in the hall. See that no one passes on any pretext in either direction. Well, Mr Carrados, I'm glad to find that you're all right, sir. I made a dash for it when the district office passed your news on. You got us a bit anxious."

"No need, inspector," replied Mr Carrados—he had greeted Beedel's salute with a smile and a nod when he first appeared. "Children, drunkards, and the blind, you know—we have a special indulgence with providence."

"Providence—why yes," admitted his friend. "But this lot represent the other place, sir! Now let's have a look at them. I suppose," he spoke back as he strolled across to Won Chou, "I suppose we may take it that all are concerned, sir?"

"We can assume that much responsibility I think. I have been assaulted and forcibly detained and can identify all as actively or passively involved. Two others—Miss Melhuish and Mr Tilehurst—are still confined in the cellars. And then, of course, there is the original business."

"If they're in no immediate danger we'll go through the house when we've ticked off this lot, sir. Well, my lad, I think I've seen your face before. 'Snow,' wasn't it?"

"Very much no savvy," courteously replied Won Chou, evidently anxious to afford any information he could but unfortunately only imperfectly acquainted with the language.

"You wouldn't. Put them on and pass him out to wait in the hall, West," said the inspector. "Ah, Mr Joolby, I believe? I've often thought that I should like the opportunity of going through your little place. You should have some very interesting old stuff there—one sort and another."

"I am only a poor man," touchingly protested Mr Joolby, "but what little I have has been made by hard work and honest dealing. Still, there may be something you want—no matter how careful one is in buying, unscrupulous persons occasionally impose on one with stolen property. At any rate let us go there and you shall pick out whatever you consider doubtful." In his anxiety to attract the police away from that spot Mr Joolby seemed to have forgotten that he was no longer the proprietor of the East End business.

"All in good time, Mr Joolby," undertook the inspector. "But that doesn't come into the charge—so far."

"What is this charge?" inquired Mr Joolby faintly.

"Well, suppose we have a look at these now"—Inspector Beedel did not appear to have been taking any particular notice of the surroundings so far but doubtless he used his eyes and had his methods, for at the word he turned abruptly, penknife in hand, and a string was cut, the brown paper ripped, and the contents of one of the parcels exposed before Mr Joolby could do anything but give an involuntary cry of shattered hopes, and take a single feebly threatening step forward, or Mr Bronsky get off more than a faint "psssh" and "tsssh" of indignation.

"Books, eh?" observed the inspector picking up the topmost. "*Rise and Fall of the Dutch Republic* feels a trifle heavy for *my* taste." He shook it loosely open and a metal plate fell out and rang upon the floor—a copper sheet engraved, among other details of words and figures, with the name of the Bank of England. "Ah, I thought as much," commented Beedel as he recovered the plate and satisfied himself about its purpose. "George's work, I suppose? He's lucky—for the moment. Well, pass him out too, West."

"What about—?" The constable indicated Joolby's wrists. "He can't get along without using his hands, inspector."

"Search him and take everything away. Then let him keep his sticks," decided Beedel. "Be particular you miss nothing he may have got about him and tell them out there." He turned to give his attention to Mr Bronsky.

"I suppose we must call that the rubber, Mr Joolby," moralised Max Carrados, as the cripple was being put through this process. "It's been a very interesting game throughout with its surprising changes of fortune, but the break-up of a party is always a little sad though, isn't it? I'm afraid that it's no good to say that you can claim your revenge when we next meet on equal terms; we shall both be too aged to care about it."

For a second it looked as if the bankrupt plotter was attempting some reply; the muscles of his uncouth mouth were stirred and twisted, but if the impulse had carried to effect, not to retort by words but to spit venomously at his adversary's face would have been Julian Joolby's final gesture. As it happened, Constable West caught something of the baleful look and with even this meagre satisfaction just too late the prisoner was hustled away beyond the range of his recrimination.

"It is amusing if it should not be laughable," suddenly exclaimed Mr Bronsky, compelled to realise at last that his person was being regarded as no more sacrosanct than those of all the others. "Otherwise the injustice shall put back the day of freedom for a hundred year!"

"Oh, I don't think you'll get that long, Mr Bronsky," the inspector reassured him. "But it certainly looks like putting back the day of your freedom for about eighteen months or three years. Well, now that the lot's mopped up I'll go down and look into the matter of those two you spoke of, sir. Will you be all right here?"

"Perfectly," replied Mr Carrados, with a private smile at the ineradicable foible of even those who should know best to regard him as intrinsically helpless. "But if you happen to be too long I wouldn't say that you won't find me in the larder. By the way, we are not forgetting Tapsfield and that end of it though? Forgive my mentioning it but I take a kind of proprietary interest in that delightfully restful village."

"Quite all right, sir—just as well to speak. As a matter of fact I've sent a word. Of course after what you'd told me before, your SOS from here put two and two together. I've no doubt that at this moment the place looks just as peaceful as usual and it mayn't be hard to get into the works, but when it comes to getting out and away with it they'll find that they've trod on the live rail."

Actually Mr Carrados was neither in the larder nor in the room when the inspector was recalled, for as he was examining Mr Larch's consummate work with appreciative touch, a hasty call from the hall beyond brought everyone within hearing scurrying there to lend assistance at this new development. As it happened none was required—at least not what they had thought. Joolby—

"He must be in a sort of fit," the constable kneeling at his side explained. "Sitting quietly there and then without a word or sign he rolled clean off the chair and lay here. I can't make it out—you'd think he'd kick or twitch or make some sort of movement, wouldn't you?"

Carrados bent over his fallen antagonist, by the policeman's side, and brought his own face close to the upturned one which now made no motion to retort with venom. ("A damned sight closer than I'd ha' cared mine to go," was the frank pronouncement of the constable afterwards. "But then of course he couldn't see what I did—luckily.")

"Not now—he's given his last kick at this hated world," he said, rising from the contemplation. "I suppose you'll have to get in a doctor or call up your own man, but it makes no difference really."

"You mean that he's—gone?" Inspector Beedel was staring hard and inclined to be a shade incredulous in view of the suddenness of the unfortunate proceeding.

"Yes, inspector; he's managed to slip through your hands after all. Poison."

"He had no poison about him just now—that I will swear," warmly protested P.C. West, conscious of Beedel's rigorous eyes fixed accusingly on him. "I don't mind saying that I had that in mind and I went through the lining and every seam for the least screw of paper."

"Besides, he never made a move to reach anything while he was in here," loyally confirmed one of the other policemen. "Just sat with his hands resting on the top of one of his sticks and his face buried in them."

"Of course—his stick," exclaimed Mr Carrados, enlightened. "Please give me the one he had. Yes, there it is—that little cavity at the top. A tiny phial sunk in and undetectably covered over. An ideal place, you see, because he must always have it with him. Then as he sat, apparently sunk in thought, he worked out the little tube and crushed it up between his strong teeth and heroically swallowed the lot. You will find that his tongue is cut—just as it might very easily be in a fit, which makes it all quite convincing. Mr Joolby was a connoisseur of the subtler poisons, inspector, and I don't doubt that he had reserved something very choice indeed for his own consumption."

"Well I'll go to Hanover!" apostrophes Beedel, after exploring the stick. Despite a lifelong association with the conventional forms of crime, not even the contents bill of an evening newspaper were more liable to be "amazed" by the least variant of a ruse than was the worthy, and, let it be added, extremely capable inspector.

The net had been fully drawn; every member of the gang had been accounted for and now the outposts stationed in the garden were coming in to take over the work of guarding and escorting the haul of prisoners. Tapsfield was being spoken with over the wire; an antique shop in the East End would be inconspicuously watched by a perhaps rather too noticeably leisured stranger, and George Larch was in the process of being described (and surely we may hope unsuccessfully in his case this once) as "wanted." Mr Carrados, his work for the time being done, was following his usual rule of not getting in anyone's way and in conforming to this excellent precept had withdrawn to the deserted dining-room where in his rather famished state he found sufficient material to interest him. Beedel could be trusted to keep his word in the other directions.

"Uncle Max! Oh, my old darling, I *am* glad to find you here safe but please do leave me a spot of marmalade." Nora, of course, and the inspector had kept his word in that direction at least. "A policeman let me out but they sort of shuffed me through the hall. What's happening now?"

"Nothing, I imagine. It's all happened I should say. You've had your adventure, my dear, and no power below will ever induce me to put you in the way of another."

"But Geoffrey?" she interposed, paying no heed to that. "I thought I might find him up here before me. I wanted to look round down there but the policeman sent me on. Oh, Uncle Max, do you think—"

"No, I don't," anticipated Uncle Max cuttingly; "and I have more than half a doubt whether Geoffrey Tilehurst has ever been in any sort of—"

"I suppose I may come in since I think I heard my name," and Tilehurst himself appeared, looking of all three there considerably the most presentable.

"Geoffrey!" exclaimed Nora, running over with joy, and she had started across the room when—account for it how you will—she stopped, repressed by the sight of his remarkably sleek trim and a realisation of her own draggle-tailed appearance.

"I say—Nora, you, really you?" he cried, transported in turn, and to do him justice he did not seem to notice anything aversive in her disorder—or, indeed, to notice anything but her excited young face. "How on earth do you come to turn up here? I'm rather out of touch with what's been going on but it's like a twist of magic."

"But surely you could guess that I might still be here," she said; "after what happened—in this very room—on Wednesday?"

"Wednesday—in this room?" he repeated darkly. "But I haven't the ghost of an idea what did happen here. I've been shut up in a beast of a cellar for the past week."

"You didn't come up and see me here in this room?" she faltered. "You didn't beg me—to—to save you?"

"Not unless I was talking in my sleep," he declared, looking still more puzzled. "Or am now," he added.

"Geoffrey: let me introduce you to my uncle, Max Carrados. This is Geoffrey Tilehurst, Uncle Max. Now please go on and tell me all about it—I've given it up." She sat down, helped herself liberally to more bread and marmalade and her eyes ranged incessantly from one to the other in turn as she gorged steadily through the simple banquet.

"I don't imagine that we shall find that too hard," undertook Mr Carrados. "By the way, won't you join our modest picnic, Mr Tilehurst? I'm afraid that there's very little marmalade left by now but the cheese is there and the inner part of this loaf is reasonably edible. As you see, we aren't standing on ceremony."

"Thanks very much, but I'm not particularly hungry," he replied. "Of course I haven't had any breakfast yet but it must be pretty early still, I should say. If you don't mind I think I'll wait for something more—er, regular."

"You aren't particularly hungry!" For a moment Nora actually laid down her slice of bread and marmalade. "Geoffrey: when did you last have anything—er, regular?"

"Why, yesterday," he replied. "Though, as a matter of fact, it was a bit out of the routine. Something went different it seems, but old Chou looked in and foraged me a supply from somewhere. Very decent sort, that Chink; he often came down to bring me things and pass the time in one way or another. And that reminds me, by the by. I wonder if either of you would mind lending me a couple of pounds to settle with him until I get back home? You see, I taught him poker yesterday and somehow or other—"

"Uncle Max! You hear that? Why didn't we have—er, something regular?"

Mr Carrados looked slightly apologetic.

"I begin to suspect that Won Chou can't quite like me," he suggested. "You naturally come in too on the Chinese family principle."

"And he was here and about yesterday," she went on unsparingly, "and you can hear the slightest footfall! Oh, Uncle Max, after all I've been led to believe—"

"Human, my dear," he sought to plead, "human footsteps. That logically excludes panthers, Chinamen and fairies as they are constitutionally inaudible. Against that you may put how I have always maintained that Tilehurst would not be badly used—"

"Yes, you did," she admitted; "but now what about the dreadful state he was in on Wednesday?"

"That brings us to the point. Mr Tilehurst, one question please—hypothetical let us say. If a woman—Nora, we will suppose—could save you from a course of torture by submitting herself in your place, how would you decide if it rested with you?"

"Surely you can scarcely ask me that, sir? How could I—or any decent fellow for that matter—accept such a sacrifice from a woman? Especially, as you put it, from one whom he—"

Geoffrey broke off looking ingenuously embarrassed, finding it too emotional to explain the added restriction.

"You see, Nora," demonstrated Mr Carrados, "it wouldn't have worked. Our friend here would have hurled back the—er, dastardly proposal."

"Of course," added Geoffrey, anxious not to take too much credit for this heroic pose, "it's difficult to say what mightn't happen under harsh conditions. You have no idea what it feels like merely to be shut up in a mouldy cellar for days—"

"No, perhaps not," conceded Max Carrados tolerantly, "but I daresay we can faintly imagine the sensation."

"But Geoffrey," insisted Nora, not to be sidetracked from the main issue, "either you or I are certainly a bit dotty. On Wednesday night they brought you up here—"

"One moment, Nora," struck in Carrados with his suavest tone; "forgive me—but before you impugn the sanity of either. You say you saw *Geoffrey* here." He smiled significantly across at her as he underlined the point. "*Did you notice his finger nails then?*"

"Did I notice—?" Revelation came with a crash. "Oh, my gosh! Again! Do you mean he was—? But why—? How—?"

"Why not? It was essential to the plan that you should adopt a certain course and, as we have heard, Mr Tilehurst here was useless for persuasion. Tapsfield is not too far away. The double was free to come and go, and playing the part he could make just the points that would weigh with you."

"Look here,"—Geoffrey Tilehurst claimed his turn to speak and addressed himself solely to Mr Carrados's attention. "Most of this is pretty nearly Greek to me but there seems to be one thing that's really important. Did she—that is, was Nora—I mean to say, has your niece come to this infernal house because I—in order to be—well, with some intention of helping me if you understand what I'm driving at?"

"I think I may have a rough idea," was the genial admission. "But as to that, Mr Tilehurst, who can say what a young woman does anything for nowadays, if, indeed, most of them have any reason. I can only tell you this—it may help you. When I guessed something of the mad project my niece was embarking on, I said—for of course I felt it my duty to warn her—'You are risking your head inside a lion's mouth.' What was her reply? 'Uncle Max,' she said without turning a hair, 'what do I care about that? Isn't Geoffrey's there already?'"

"And if that doesn't do it," thought Mr Carrados, as he averted his face with the appearance of being moved, "all I can say is—curse you!"

"Uncle Max!" shrieked Nora at this romantic disclosure, "I am sure I never did—" but the time for such maidenly affectations was past. Geoffrey had taken the bit of irresolution firmly between his wisdom teeth and was bolting.

"Oh, you darling darling, did you really care so much?" he demanded hoarsely. "Why, my precious treasure, I'd gladly go through a dozen lions' mouths to hear that!"

"Why, naturally I cared, Geoffrey dear," she replied, with infinitely more composure. "I thought we'd settled all that long ago—but of course it's just as well to ask me."

"Isn't it simply wonderful, sweetheart"—by this time he has taken possession of her and was demonstrating his affection regardless of the bread and marmalade involved in the process—"isn't it simply wonderful that of all the people in the world just we two should be here—"

"Yes, dearest," she tactfully hastened to agree, "it is. Still you really must remember that there's Uncle Max over there as well and—"

"I beg your pardon, sir," apologised Geoffrey, "but you see—"

"No," amended Carrados sympathetically, "on this occasion I don't. Never mind us, children," he added benignly, "we are both, rest assured, quite blind."

"Both!" exclaimed two rather startled voices.

"Who—"

"I mean the somewhat sunderdressed little fellow over there with the bow and arrows," he explained, nodding vaguely. "I think he must have crept in after you two... My dears, try to keep him with you always."